"May I kiss you, Miranda?"

His words had already kissed her, his lips were so near hers. She wanted to kiss him, to clap her hand to the back of his head and bring his mouth down upon hers. But she knew she wouldn't be able to stop at one kiss, not from this man. One kiss would lead to another kiss, and another, and then senseless abandon right there on that big rock.

And then what? Her bags and her Bernie would probably be hastily packed and rushed to the airport for a red-eye back to Boston. In a moment of weakness, she had let herself be drawn into Lucas Fletcher's web. She wouldn't compound the mistake by kissing him. She sat up and returned his sweater to him. "I don't think that would be a good idea." She began climbing off the rock.

"Why not?" He jumped off the rock and landed next to her in the coarse sand.

"Because the last thing I need is a one-night stand with a rock star." She started back to the castle. "I'm sorry if I led you on. It was an accident. Honestly."

"I'm the one who should apologize. I didn't invite you here to take advantage of you in any way. You have my word on that as a gentleman."

She slowed her pace. "Why *did* you invite me here, Lucas?"

Because you are someone I could truly love, for always . . .

Indigo Love Spectrum

An imprint of Genesis Press, Inc.
Publishing Company

Genesis Press, Inc.
P.O. Box 101
Columbus, MS 39703

Copyright © 2007 by Crystal Hubbard

ISBN-13: 978-1-58571-243-4
ISBN-10: 1-58571-243-4
Manufactured in the United States of America

First Edition

Visit us at www.genesis-press.com
or call at 1-888-Indigo-1

CRUSH

CRYSTAL HUBBARD

Genesis Press, Inc.

DEDICATION

This book is dedicated to Val.
I wish I had a fraction of your strength,
temerity, heart, and courage.

ACKNOWLEDGMENTS

I would very much like to thank God and all His angels for giving me the gift of storytelling and allowing me to share it.

I would also like to thank my gang of superpals in Massachusetts. Every writer should be so fortunate as to have such good readers who are also such good friends.

To all of you readers who seek out and enjoy my books, I owe you the greatest debt of all. No story is complete until someone reads it, and without you, my work is left unfinished. Thank you for all of your encouragement and support, and please keep sending me your comments and questions at *crystalhubbardbooks@yahoo.com*.

PROLOGUE

Miranda had one dying thought. *I should have stayed home.*

The words formed within her head, but Miranda couldn't hear them over the ear-splitting music and deafening wall of noise from the crowd. That crowd, that single-minded, ignorant beast that Bernie had so wanted her to be a part of, surged forward, pressing Miranda farther into the unyielding apron of the concert stage and closer to death.

Above the stage in a specially constructed cage of chain link, Lucas Fletcher played the bass solo of "Snatched," his latest American and U.K. Number One hit. He was so involved in the moment, so attuned to his music; he didn't notice security guards rushing from the wings and onto the stage. It would have been a familiar sight. At every concert, security swarmed the stage at least once to remove girls driven temporarily mad by Lucas Fletcher and Karmic Echo's music. Female fans risked possible eviction from the venue and arrest just for the chance to let their fingertips glance off Lucas's denim-wrapped thigh or the scuffed steel toe of his fashionably working-class leather boots.

At the sold-out London opening of Karmic Velocity, the band's current tour, a fan from his hometown of Aberystwyth, Wales incredibly made it onto the stage and threw herself onto Lucas. She ripped off his T-shirt, along with a sizeable length of his chestnut hair. She might have pulled him bald if the Yellow Shirts, his personal security force, hadn't tackled the girl and whisked her into custody. She and the friends that had pitched her onto the stage were later featured on two English talkies, where the girl displayed her coveted prize: the eight-inch long tress of Lucas's hair.

The Boston concert was going well. "Snatched" was one of Lucas's favorite songs, and the fans always responded well to it. Its driving bass solo energized Lucas as much as it electrified the crowd. Only when

Arena security, in their heavy green jackets and black caps, joined the Yellow Shirts did Lucas glance down at the stage.

Dear God, it's a crush, he thought. Dread paralyzed him as he stopped playing mid-note. "Bloody hell!" he swore, dropping his bass and leaping out of the cage. He dropped eleven feet to a gigantic speaker, then jumped another eight feet to the stage. The crowd, still pressing forward, thought Lucas's acrobatics were a part of the show, and they cheered and screamed as he raced to the edge of the stage.

Crush, crowd crush, body slams, music mashes—however named, always resulted in tragedy. Everyone dreaded catastrophes like the 1979 Who concert in Cincinnati and Pearl Jam's 2000 concert in Denmark, where fans had been killed while the bands performed. No one had ever been killed at a Karmic Echo concert. Lucas prayed to keep it that way. As security guards lifted unconscious and injured concertgoers to the stage, dozens of other guards worked within the crowd itself, pushing back the frenetic mob. To facilitate the rescue of those being crushed, Len Feast, the lead guitarist, took to a microphone and pleaded with the audience to retreat.

Lucas, the muscles and cords of his well-defined arms and shoulders standing out, worked alongside the Yellow Shirts, pulling his fans to safety. The first five young ladies weren't so bad off that they couldn't find the presence of mind and strength to tear at his clothes and hair. He was shirtless by the time he grabbed his sixth victim. He kneeled, pulling her dead weight across his lap.

Under the bright wash of the stage lights, her terra cotta skin looked gray. Her full lips, which looked like they'd been built specially for kissing, were a shade of purplish-blue that Revlon hadn't created. Her hazel eyes were half opened and remarkably lovely, despite their glassy sheen. Lucas might have gotten lost in the pool of jade centered within the chocolate brown if he hadn't noticed the cold of her skin as he smoothed her long, molasses-dark hair from her brow.

"Miss?" He gently jostled her in his arms. She didn't respond and he splayed a hand over her chest. "Miss?" He felt no movement, and his panic reached a crescendo.

He curled over her, bringing his cheek to her nose and mouth. Feeling no breath, he laid her flat on her back. All around him, security guards were clearing the stage, his band mates were securing their instruments, and Feast was attempting to calm a somewhat impatient Beantown crowd. Lucas was searching his brain for the right combination of breaths and compressions to revive the cold figure at his knees.

He pinched her nose shut and clapped his mouth over hers, breathing as he'd been taught ages ago while filming a public service spot for the BBC. He tuned out the rhythmic chanting and clapping of a crowd denied a concert they'd paid upwards of $150 a ticket to see. He didn't hear the voices of the security guards restoring order to the venue. Lucas breathed for the fallen woman, compressed her chest, and he vowed to keep doing it until she fully opened her gorgeous eyes and drew breath on her own.

"Come on, lovely," he pleaded as he externally pumped blood through her heart. Fat beads of sweat rolled down the sides of his face. "Open your eyes and tell me to get my bloody paws off you."

"Lucas, the paramedics are here," Feast said, his blue eyes filled with worry. "They'll take care of her."

Lucas hunched over her, breathed into her.

"Lucas!" Feast clapped a hand on Lucas's shoulder. Lucas shrugged him off to continue his compressions. "Lucas, please, let the professionals at her," Feast begged. Lucas breathed for her, willing her to open her eyes, to move and to fill her lungs on her own.

His wish was granted when a choking gasp escaped her. She coughed, her whole body convulsing from its force. She tried to sit up, and she would have fallen back to the stage if Lucas hadn't caught her up in his arms. He took her chin and aimed her face at his.

Her eyes found his and remained there. With life now sparking within them, her eyes were even lovelier. Large and expressive, they were undoubtedly the most beautiful eyes he had ever fallen into.

She stared at him, too intent on breathing to speak. His collar-length hair, damp with perspiration, gleamed in the bright light as it fell forward to hood his face. He had striking features—a chiseled jaw, perfect cheekbones and a cleft in his chin—that were tense with worry, but his concern was most evident in his eyes, which were the color of a summer sky before a storm. Her breathing settled into a relaxed and comfortable pattern despite the pain in her chest, and she sighed. He shut his eyes in heartfelt relief and folded her into a close embrace. She didn't have the strength, or will, to withdraw from him. She drew comfort from his strong arms and the hard, steady beat of his heart. She had the sense to realize that any woman would be deliriously happy to be exactly where she was now, in the caring and protective embrace of Lucas Fletcher.

But Miranda wasn't any woman.

As paramedics moved in to take her, she drifted off, thinking, *I really should have stayed home . . .*

CHAPTER 1

Bernie's voice entered the hospital room before the rest of him caught up at Miranda's bedside. Armed with a final edition of Monday's Boston *Herald-Star*, a big foam cup of Metro Medical Center coffee and a gaudy bouquet of birds of paradise and gladioli, Bernie stood beside Miranda, his ebony face split in a smile that revealed two rows of bright white teeth.

His black eyes glittered beneath his freshly waxed eyebrows. "Did you enjoy the concert?"

A dry laugh caught in Miranda's throat. "Actually, I would have preferred watching the Red Sox give up twenty runs to Seattle's rookie pitcher. And why didn't you bring me coffee?"

Bernie set the *Herald-Star* across Miranda's knees. "I didn't want you to spit it all over me when you saw this."

Miranda picked up the newspaper, looked at the front page, and still didn't believe what she saw.

There, in living color, occupying the better part of the front page, she was. A *Herald-Star* photographer had captured the moment when Lucas had held her, tucking her body into his after breathing life back into her. His bare back glistened with perspiration. The overhead lights left blue and red patterns on his tanned skin. Miranda couldn't recall having hooked an arm over his shoulder, but there it was in the photo for the world to see. She couldn't remember having slipped her other arm around his waist, but that was there, too.

She took a measure of comfort in the fact that her legs didn't look fat in her black velvet jeans. That comfort was short-lived when she read the one-word headline: *SNATCHED!*

"Snatched?" Miranda said, aghast. "Who's responsible for this?"

"Well, it sort of wrote itself," Bernie smiled. "Lucas was playing that song when he—"

"'Snatched from the jaws of death by Lucas Fletcher at his Arena concert last night, *Herald-Star* sportswriter Miranda Penney is recovering at Boston's Metro Medical Center after almost losing her life to the phenomenon known as crowd crush,'" Miranda read aloud from the accompanying article. "I can't believe you let them do this to me, Bernie. I was getting squished to death last night while you were off somewhere interviewing Karmic Echo fans, and today I see that you let our managing editor slap me across the front page. I report news, I'm not supposed to *be* it!"

A wicked gleam sparkled in Bernie's eyes. "It gets better." He lightly blew on his coffee before he took a delicate sip of it.

Miranda read on, her eyes skimming over the highlights of each paragraph. "Kept overnight for observation, yes, that's true," she said. "Attended the concert in the company of Bernard Reilly, a *Herald-Star* music reviewer . . ."

"The chief *Herald-Star* music reviewer," Bernie corrected with an indignant toss of his snowy aviator scarf.

"Who are you supposed to be today, the Red Baron?'" Miranda scowled. "Halloween is two weeks away."

Bernie stuck his nose in the air and patted the back of his closely cropped afro. "This scarf is a gift from my little darling Pierre, the photographer I met this summer when I went to visit my parents on Montserrat. He's in Milan to shoot the debut show of an exciting new Ethiopian designer. This scarf is an Abu Ngatanze original made of virgin cashmere and—"

"Hold on . . ." Miranda interrupted, pulling her knees to her chest to bring the paper closer to her face. "'Fletcher contacted the *Herald-Star* in the hope of initiating further contact with Penney, who has agreed to meet the popular musician. Penney intends to thank Fletcher for saving her life, and she has agreed to allow a *Herald-Star* reporter to document the event.'"

Miranda read the sentences three times. As her ire grew, she curled the tabloid into a tight baton. "I've been in this hospital all night. I haven't agreed to anything. This is the first I've heard of any of it. Those harpies are behind this, aren't they?" She narrowed her eyes at Bernie, referring to the *Herald-Star* gossip columnists.

"You got it, kid, but save the evil eye for them, not me." Bernie took off his aviator's jacket and elegantly draped it over the chair at Miranda's bedside. "Meg LaParosa pitched the idea to King Rex, and Dee Fahey was there to second it. Lucas Fletcher is a big huge deal, way bigger than Jordan Duquette. Rex sold tons of papers when you were dating Jordan."

"Meg and Dee printed so much trash about us," Miranda sulked, her old resentment and anger surfacing.

"Actually, it was more like they printed a lot of things about Jordan and the women he was seeing behind your back."

"And they're just dying to do the same thing to me and Lucas Fletcher." Miranda curled up on her side. She jerked the thin blanket over her head. "I won't do it. I hope I never see Lucas Fletcher again. I'll send him a thank you note, or some cookies or something."

"The man saved your life." Bernie sat on the edge of the bed. "And you can't cook. He wants to see you. La and Dee didn't make that part up. Lucas's publicist contacted me about it first, since I covered the concert."

Miranda threw off the blanket and sat up to shout in Bernie's face. "You told those jackals that Lucas wanted to see me again?"

Bernie gave her a guilty shrug and wisely moved out of her reach. "I was so excited when he called, I just started screaming. I guess word spread around the newsroom."

Miranda easily pictured the scene. It had happened before. When Tina Turner's people called to thank him for the great job he'd done reviewing her last concert, Bernie had stood on his desk afterward, singing *"Proud Mary"* at top volume.

"I don't want to see him," Miranda said, knowing that she didn't sound very convincing.

"You may as well have dinner with the man. I would."

Miranda chuckled. "Be my guest."

Bernie gave her a playful swat on the knee. "He's my type, all right, but I'm positive that I'm not his."

"I assumed that this would be a private meeting." Miranda shot a cold glance at the two women already seated in Rex Wrentham's luxuriously appointed office early Monday morning.

"Miranda, dear, we're old friends here, aren't we?" Rex said, a toothy smile growing between his pale gaunt cheeks as he rose from his desk and crossed the room to greet her.

"No doubt she's a bit testy from her harrowing experience Saturday night," offered Meg LaParosa, the dominant half of *Psst!*, Boston's premier gossip duo.

Miranda felt fine. Well enough, in fact, to snatch the platinum highlights from Meg's overly frosted blonde hair and smack the smug, knowing grin from Dee Fahey's chinless face.

"Come, Miranda, have a seat." Rex eagerly took her elbow. While Meg and Dee occupied the comfortable, Italian-leather wing chairs facing Rex's massive teak desk, Miranda was escorted across the room to the decorative settee situated near a Chippendale highboy housing Rex's fine spirits.

The settee's cushions were so stiff and unyielding, they didn't give when Miranda set her weight upon them. She had a perfect view of the back of the leather chairs.

"Are you comfortable, Miranda?" Rex asked, starting away as if her answer didn't matter. Of course, to him, it probably didn't.

"Actually," she began, grabbing the tail of his tailored jacket, "my doctors have recommended that I avoid sitting on rigid surfaces for the next few days. My back was injured in the crush, and I'd hate to go on bed rest for who knows how long as a result of sitting uncomfortably."

To emphasize her point, she clutched at her lower back with both hands and mustered a pitiful, "Ouch!"

His bushy white eyebrows drawn together, Rex snapped his fingers at Meg and Dee. "A chair."

Meg studied her perfectly manicured fingernails. Dee, mumbling under her breath, grudgingly gave up her seat. She grumbled under her breath as she passed Miranda on her way to the settee. Miranda stuck her tongue out.

"We have very exciting things to discuss this morning," Rex said happily once Miranda had been properly seated.

"Yes, about this meeting with Lucas Fletcher . . ." Miranda started.

Rex clapped his liver-spotted hands with finality. "Everything's been settled. Quite frankly, I agreed with Meg when she told me that she saw no point in troubling you with the finer details while you were recovering from your terrible experience. We here at the *Herald-Star* do our very best to show our concern for our employees."

Miranda's left eyebrow rose. "I must have been sleeping when you called to show yours."

Rex cleared his throat. "Well, these things happen," he said quickly. "Now, Mr. Fletcher will send a car for you here on Friday, and—"

"Here?" Miranda said. "At the *Herald-Star*?"

"Certainly." Rex's steely blue eyes began to show his impatience. "You're an ambassador for the *Herald-Star* in this venture. You attended the concert as Bernard Reilly's guest and he was at the concert on assignment. None of this would have happened without the *Herald-Star*."

"You're damn right about that," Miranda snapped. "If Bernard hadn't dragged me to that concert, I wouldn't have nearly been squished to death at Lucas Fletcher's feet."

"You're only focusing on the negatives here, Miranda," Meg said, sounding every bit like the bossy older sibling Miranda never had. "We have a chance here to give the public something they don't ordinarily see. It's a real-life Cinderella story."

"Only because you're trying to turn it into something it isn't," Miranda charged, frustration strengthening her reluctance to cooperate. "I was being crushed and he saved me. He did what any normal, caring person would have done. I saw the television footage of the crush. Lucas pulled five other people out of that wild crowd." She took a deep breath and really launched into attack mode. "Do you know how hard it is for me to be taken seriously as a sports reporter in this town? This is Boston! It's an old-boy, *all*-boy town. This fairy tale princess crap will undermine my credibility. I take enough heat if I dare to wear a skirt on the job, and I can't have Lucas Fletcher hanging around my neck. Can't you find some other sucker to manipulate?"

Rex spent a moment tapping his tented fingertips on his desk. Behind him, a dizzying view of Boston Harbor featured the colorful yachts and boats enjoying a pretty October day on the dark blue water. There wasn't a cloud in the sky, but clouds aplenty formed in Rex's sixty-five-year-old face.

"Quite simply, Miranda, Mr. Fletcher wants you," Rex said. "I must say that I'm sorely disappointed in your unwillingness to be a team player for the *Herald-Star*. As the sole woman on my sports writing staff, I've always taken great pride in your ability to adapt to trying circumstances, both in-house and out in the field. I always thought you were made of tougher stuff than most."

Miranda's lips pulled into an icy smile. "Don't make this personal, Rex."

"Then let's keep it professional." He leaned forward, his palms flat on his desk. "Consider this engagement with Lucas Fletcher an assignment. If you don't take it, then you won't be fulfilling your end of your employment contract and I'll be well within my rights as publisher to demote you, or even terminate you." His ace in the hole played, Rex sat back in his leather swivel chair.

Miranda seethed. Seven years ago she had become the *Herald-Star*'s first full-time female sportswriter, and was still the only female member of the department. She had fought with managers and athletes in just about every sport, and waged full battles with an all-male editorial board that lived, ate and breathed all things sports . . . and therefore believed that they knew more than she did.

Ironically, the one person who had been her staunchest supporter was Jed "Hodge" Hodgekins, the head of the sports department. He had treated her the same as any of his other writers, perhaps even better in that he gave her a bit more leeway in pursuing stories. Miranda was a crackerjack writer and reporter, and she knew it. Fortunately, so did Jed. But even his support might not be enough to counter Rex's threat. No matter how capable she was, or how much Jed admired and valued her, Rex Wrentham had supreme power. As owner and publisher of the *Herald-Star*, he could fire her in a heartbeat and no one could do a thing to stop him.

Meg broke the uncomfortable silence. "Most women would die for a chance to have dinner with Lucas Fletcher."

"I almost did," Miranda reminded her.

"It's just one dinner, Miranda," Dee piped in from the far corner of the room.

Just one dinner, Miranda thought. *One dinner that I'm being forced into. One night of my life, which suddenly seems very much out of my control.*

"Do I absolutely have to have a *Herald-Star* reporter with me?" Miranda asked.

"Of course." Rex's expression brightened, his thin lips vanishing altogether in his satisfied smile. "That's the whole point of the arrangement. To share your experience with our readers."

"Could I pick the reporter?" Miranda peeped over her shoulder at Dee.

Rex exchanged a meaningful glance with Meg, who winked at him as if to say, "I can handle Dee."

"Okay," Rex agreed. "You choose your reporter." His knuckles tapped a merry beat on his desk blotter. "We have a deal, then? Dinner with Lucas Fletcher on Friday?"

"Sure," Miranda said dispassionately. "Dinner. Friday. And I choose my reporter."

"Hey, Penney, you're alive!" called Joe "Sully" Sullivan, the head of the sports copy desk. "I thought you were a gone goose. Told you not to go to that fruity concert."

"Yes, Sully, I was forewarned." Miranda walked past his cluttered desk to a wall of cubbyholes and retrieved her mail. She stood at a horseshoe-shaped configuration of desks that comprised the sports editorial department and sorted through her mail.

"Lookin' good, Penney." Oren "Krakow" Piekarski, one of the copy editors, sidled up to Miranda. At six-foot-seven and one hundred fifty five pounds, Krakow was built like a stilt. Almost a full foot taller than Miranda, he loomed over her shoulder to nose into her mail. "Any promotional freebies for your ol' pal, Krakie?"

Miranda handed him the wallet-sized Boston Bruins game schedule included in her press packet. Krakow looked like he'd been genetically engineered for basketball, but he loved hockey, and gifting him with the meager offering would save him the trouble of stealing it later. Pleased with his token, Krakow retreated to his desk.

"Hodge has been eyeing the halls for you," warned a voice over Miranda's right shoulder. The voice belonged to Paul O'Shea, the department's Methuselah. Paulie had been hired fresh out of Boston University to cover the baseball beat. Twenty-two years later, he was the senior member of the sports editorial staff, having given up the reporting gig—and the travel that came with it—upon the birth of his twins. With a mortgage and ten-year-old daughters in private school, Paulie was serving a life sentence at the *Herald-Star*.

"How are you, *chica?*" Paulie asked in the one moment of seriousness Miranda was likely to get from him.

"Good. Considering." She tucked her mail into her kidskin backpack, which she slung over her shoulder.

"There was a good story on the Brazilian national soccer team on the Associated Press newswire yesterday. I forwarded it to you by e-mail. Thought you'd like to catch up on the ol' home team once you finished your convalescence."

Miranda giggled in spite of her sour mood. "I was only in the hospital for half a day, Paulie. I'm back now, good as new, so Rex and Meg can get on with embarrassing me to death."

"Hang in there, kid." Paulie gave her shoulder a warm squeeze. "They can only kill you once."

Miranda smiled and started for her desk. Most of the copy editors in place along the rim paid her no mind, other than to glance at the front of her shirt as she approached or the back of her jeans once she had passed. She was accustomed to the crude behavior, but it bothered her no less now than it had on the first day she walked into the sports department.

Sports wasn't like the other departments in the newsroom. The entire building was a virtual shambles, with water-stained ceiling panels and decades-old newspapers piled shoulder high in just about every corner. The News, Sunday Features and Arts & Entertainment departments had a nice mix of male and female employees, but overall, the *Herald-Star* remained overwhelmingly white. The one black female news writer had left the paper two years ago, to marry some doctor in her hometown of St. Louis. There had been a black man in the Financial section, but he'd left after getting an offer to write for the *Wall Street Journal.*

The Sports department was the most homogeneous. Miranda was the only female employee and the only person of color. Sports had a long history of testosterone overload, and Miranda had volunteered to be the only woman in a world of Archie Bunkers and Peter Pans when she accepted the sports writing position Hodge had offered her. Her fellow reporters and editors had been brutal. Some of them had been convinced that she'd been hired because of her father's fame as a former major leaguer. Clayton Penney hadn't set any big records on any of the teams he'd played for, but he'd always been a reliable, all-purpose player whose skill thrilled male fans and whose dark good looks excited the women.

Others on the rim had arrived at another conclusion about Miranda's hiring as evidenced by the nickname "Double D," which had sprung up by her second day on the job. She'd first assumed that calling her Double D was a cruel reference to her extremely small bust size, like calling a chubby guy Slim. But then Bernie had emerged from Arts & Entertainment to introduce himself. He explained that Double D meant Double Duty. Miranda, being half African American and half Brazilian, gave Human Resources the opportunity to check off two boxes on its minority employee census with a single hiring.

The nickname eventually lost its luster, and the boys in sports resorted to schoolyard tactics, teasing her about her clothes ("What's with the bandannas, Double D? You ridin' with the gauchos today?"), her hairstyle ("Another ponytail, Double D? I thought you people liked big hair!"), her taste in sports ("Soccer is queer, Double D!"), her ethnic heritage ("If you're black and Hispanic, how come you don't have an ass? You should have twice as much!") and her writing ("You write like a girl, Double D.")

Once her three-month trial period had ended, she had spoken to Hodge about their flagrantly inappropriate comments and he had severely upbraided the entire rim. The guys had given her the cold shoulder from then on, and completely butchered her copy . . . that is, until she'd threatened to tell Hodge about their late-night video club.

Miranda, making an unexpected visit to the office after a Red Sox game that had run into extra innings, had caught the guys hooting and hollering at a videotape . . . *Forrest Hump*, *Shakespeare In Lust*, or something of that nature. The guys were so accustomed to ignoring her, Miranda witnessed their debauchery for a full ten minutes before Krakow had noticed her and rushed to eject the tape.

Sure that she would rat them out, the guys suddenly began treating her with a nauseating level of courtesy. Over the years, some of the guys—Paulie, Krakow and Sully—had come to genuinely like and respect her. The rest of them either quietly envied her position as a reporter or lived in fear that she would expose their down time good time.

Miranda kept her eyes forward as she passed her co-workers, friends and adversaries. The *Herald-Star* was just a job. It wasn't her life. The past two days had shown her that. She made a mental note to remind herself of it often as she dropped her backpack beside her cluttered desk.

"Penney!"

What now? Miranda sighed and turned toward the corner office, where Hodge stood in the doorway. Hodge, a former college baseball standout and major leaguer, still had the athletic build and cool demeanor that had made him one of the most intimidating switch hitters in the American League. Hodge could have been a great big league manager, but Miranda thanked her small and distant lucky star that he had chosen to manage the *Herald-Star* Bad News Bears instead of a major league club.

"What's up, Hodge?" she asked.

Unsmiling, he raised a hand and beckoned her into his office. His gruff expression melted the instant she entered. He closed his door, but a couple of the horse racing editors stared through the glass walls as if they could read lips.

Hodge didn't sit at his desk. Instead, he took one of the office chairs, his back to the door. His wide body blocked Miranda from the inquiring eyes that passed back and forth in front of the office. "If you need a few more days, you got 'em, Randy."

He was the only person who called her that. She had applied for the reporter's job under her University of Maryland byline of Randy Penney, to increase her odds of a callback. Hodge had called her back, hired her, and had insisted that she use her given name at the *Herald-Star.*

"I'm fine. Really." A strand of her dark hair had escaped her bandanna, and she tucked it behind her ear. Hodge had practically met her ambulance at the Metro Medical Center emergency room, and his concern for her still shone in his gentle brown eyes.

"I'm behind you," Hodge said firmly. "Two hundred percent. If you don't want to do this thing on Friday, I'll go to bat for you. Rex will have me *and* the communications workers union to go through if he tries to fire you."

"Thanks. That means a lot to me." She took a deep breath and sat up straighter, a tense weight suddenly lifted from her shoulders.

Hodge was a man of his word, and he'd always supported her, even when they both knew she was in the wrong or teetered on the edge of fine lines better left uncrossed to get a story. He was totally loyal to his family, his friends and his employees, and had become the father Miranda never had.

"I know you're perfectly capable of handling this yourself." Hodge's heavy black eyebrows met in a serious scowl. "But I'll speak to Rex, if you want to cancel this fraudulent date thing."

Miranda pensively scratched at the right knee of her jeans. It would be so easy to let Hodge handle everything and go on with her life as it had been before the concert. Of course, she probably wouldn't still have a life if Lucas hadn't saved her. The least he deserved was a thank you. In person.

"I can go through with it." She lifted her gaze to meet Hodge's. "Rex will sell his papers, Meg and Dee will get their big scoop and I'll get a free meal."

Hodge stood and patted Miranda's shoulder. "Watch yourself, Randy. I'm sure this rock star is used to getting what he wants, and you're a very pretty girl."

"I'm not a girl at all," Miranda said, Hodge's compliment so inconceivable that it didn't even register. "I'm a grown woman who can take care of herself. Besides, a *Herald-Star* reporter will be with me."

"Meg LaParosa." Hodge shuddered. "That's supposed to give me a sense of relief?"

"Sure." Miranda stood to leave. "Meg will hog every speck of his attention. Lucas Fletcher will forget that I'm even in the room."

Friday arrived before Miranda was ready for it. Even worse, it arrived before Bernie was ready. He took a sick day to help Miranda make the most important decision of all regarding her dinner with Lucas: what to wear.

Having awakened her at seven A.M. with a cell phone call from right outside her front door, he now stood at the sliding doors of her closet, his hands on the tiny brass knobs. Miranda tugged a pillow over her head, closing out Bernie's endless prattle and the bright light filtering through the giant circle of stained glass forming the east wall of her bedroom.

Bernie threw open the doors and shrieked in horror.

"What?" Miranda cried, bolting upright in her bed. "Did you see a spider?"

Bernie placed a palm over his pounding heart. "For what you pay for this place, there had better not be a bug within six blocks. But I would have preferred seeing ticks, fleas and bumblebees to *this*." He pinched the skirt of the one dressy dress she owned and lifted it. "Please, explain this to me."

She squinted against the blinding morning light. "Um . . . it's a dress, Bernie. I wore it to the Baseball Writers dinner last year, remember?"

Bernie harrumphed. "How could I forget? You were the only female writer there who looked like my Grandma Tillie."

"You don't have a Grandma Tillie." Miranda swung her long legs over the side of her bed. She stood and stretched while Bernie inspected and insulted the garments hanging in her closet.

"Miranda, this just won't work. T-shirts and jeans won't cut it tonight."

She glanced at the Starbucks cup on her bedside table. She lifted it, to find it empty. "Thanks for bringing me coffee."

Bernie inhaled deeply and gazed at the ceiling. "I just love the smell of sarcasm in the morning." He pulled out a long-sleeved dress made of black jersey. "This looks like something Morticia Addams would donate to Goodwill." He clucked his tongue. "This is pathetic. It's a shame, the way you dress that body of yours. You've got the best legs I've ever seen, and I'm the only one who's ever seen them."

"My knees are too knobby." She shuffled in her socks over to the closet.

"Your skin is prettier than Christina Milian's," Bernie said.

"Just yesterday you said I was ashy." She closed her closet and steered Bernie toward the stairs. "I have to pee."

"You might want to swig a little Listerine while you're in there." Bernie went back down to the main section of her apartment.

Her upstairs bathroom was separated from the bedroom by a dark green velvet curtain rather than a door, so she heard him clearly when he hollered up at her as he started breakfast in her kitchen. "Who's that Jamaican sprinter you interviewed last month? The one with the great abs?"

"They all have great abs," she answered.

"Your belly is just as nice. A few million more sit-ups, honey, and you'll have a six-pack, too."

"The only six-packs I want come in cans," Miranda called down as she placed a line of toothpaste on her toothbrush. "I can't help but notice that you've failed to comment on my upper deck."

"I've never been much of a breast man, which is probably why you and I get along so well."

"When God handed out the 'B's I opted for brains," Miranda said over a mouthful of toothpaste foam.

"And beauty," Bernie hollered up.

Even though she was alone in the bathroom, Miranda blushed. She spat out the toothpaste, rinsed her mouth, then splashed her face with cool water. She studied her reflection in the mirror above the basin. She had never thought of herself as beautiful. Or pretty. Or even cute. The best assessment she could give herself was that she wasn't ugly. Her legs were too gangly, her hair too straight and plainly brown, her eyes too tiny and close together, Seabiscuit's nostrils were smaller than hers, she barely had breasts, her feet were like ping pong paddles, and as she brought her face closer to the mirror and squinted, she could have sworn that she actually had a mustache.

Unlike her younger sister, Calista, she had inherited none of the distinctive and beautiful physical traits of her Brazilian mother and African-American father.

She gripped the edge of the basin and her head slumped between her shoulders. "What have I gotten myself into?" she whispered.

She wasn't into music, like Bernie, who had spent the past two days giving her a crash tutorial on Lucas Fletcher and Karmic Echo. She had heard of them, of course. Karmic Echo had been topping charts for almost two decades. The one Karmic Echo song Miranda knew word for word was "In My Heart," which had been the last dance at her senior prom. Miranda had never gone out of her way to listen to Karmic Echo's music, preferring the more layered, flavorful Afro-Caribbean beats of her mother's homeland and the old-school R&B her father taught her to love.

Bernie had told her that Lucas Fletcher was thirty-six years old, and that music was in his genes—his father had been a studio musician for Tom Jones. Lucas formed his first band at twelve and recorded his first Number One U.K. single, "In The Out," at sixteen. Praised as a precocious contender among the techno-heavy, synthesizer-laden British imports invading America's music scene at the time, Lucas's music was a throwback to classic rock.

He'd formed Karmic Echo at eighteen and received six Grammy nominations for the band's first album. They received no statues at the awards ceremony, but their live performance of "Beyond Dreams" stole the show and launched their American success.

Karmic Echo wasn't an older band that had made a successful comeback. On the contrary, its popularity had never wavered. Twenty years of gold records had made the band mates very rich and popular men, and they had managed to escape the sorrows and scandals of addiction and substance abuse associated with the industry.

As far as successful rock bands went, Karmic Echo was rather boring. Save for Lucas and his best friend and lead guitarist Len Feast, all the band members were married. As lead singer, Lucas was the focal point of the band and had acquired legions of female fans. Len Feast was a close second in popularity. He and Lucas, usually in the company of supermodels and actresses, regularly graced the gossip pages of major magazines.

"What could he possibly see in me?" Miranda murmured.

She pulled the curtain to the shower, started the water, and sat on the edge of the bathtub. The water warmed the plastic curtain at her back and the cool of the porcelain tub penetrated her thin boxer shorts as she thought harder on her situation. Karmic Echo was known for its blockbuster love songs, and when Lucas wrapped his honeyed tenor around the lyrics of tunes like "Pulse" and "Paradise Found," women lost control of their hearts and senses. Being a helpless woman's savior fit right into Lucas's image as a premier sex symbol.

Miranda stripped off her T-shirt and shorts and stepped into the stream of hot water. She came to the conclusion that Lucas Fletcher wanted to see her for the very same reason Rex wanted her to see him.

To sell more of his product.

"I can't believe you're wearing that." Bernie scrunched his nose at Miranda's outfit.

"I can't believe you wore *that*." Miranda glanced disdainfully at the tuxedo Bernie had custom tailored specifically for his dream encounter with Lucas Fletcher.

"I look good, and shut your mouth." Bernie brushed an imaginary speck of fluff from his lapel. "If you hadn't been so finicky at the boutiques . . ."

"Cut it out, Bernie. I'm nervous enough as it is."

Miranda hated to admit to weakness of any kind. She stood in front of the *Herald-Star*, waiting for her odyssey to begin. As staff photographers snapped her picture from all angles, she was happy to have Bernie standing there with her. If he hadn't helped her find something to wear, she probably would have shown up in her favorite faded jeans and her North Carolina Tar Heels sweatshirt.

Miranda glanced over her shoulder at Meg, who stood beside Dee just inside the lobby doors of the *Herald-Star*. Meg was always so well put together, and tonight was no exception. Every frosty tress was flawlessly in place; her lusty, matronly figure was impeccably clothed in a black silk pantsuit with just the right touch of shimmer for a cool fall evening.

Dee, her brown hair a perfectly serviceable shag, her broomstick figure wrapped in an understated black cocktail dress, self-consciously patted her hair and smoothed her hands over the front of her dress. She stared at her reflection in the smudged plate glass, her lips moving as she seemed to be practicing different smiles.

At least I'm not that *bad off,* Miranda thought.

Lucas Fletcher's car was supposed to arrive at six P.M., and by 5:50, the lobby was packed with the curious from the Newsroom, the Pressroom, Composing, Photography, Security, Maintenance, and every other department. The entire *Herald-Star* population gathered to witness Miranda's grand meeting with the superhero rock god. Outside the *Herald-Star,* corralled behind sawhorses manned by Boston Police officers, Karmic Echo fans seduced by *Psst!'s* teasers noisily waited for Lucas to arrive.

Miranda fought the urge to wipe her damp palms on her slacks.

"That Donna Karan sarong looked fantastic on you," Bernie said.

"I look fine," Miranda insisted. "It's a dinner, not a presidential inauguration." Two fans jumped the sawhorses and bolted toward Miranda, snapping pictures even as they were caught and dragged away by policemen. She grabbed Bernie's arm. "I want to go home."

"No, you don't." He wrapped an arm around her shoulders. "You want to have dinner with Lucas Fletcher. So do they." He tipped his head toward the fans. "You're living the fantasy most of us can only dream of, even if you do have to share it with one of Satan's baby sisters. So which gossip queen won the coin toss?"

Miranda found a reason to smile. "You."

Joy flooded his face. "Oh, sweetie, I take back everything I've said and thought about your dowdy church lady ensemble!"

Miranda didn't want to slug him in front of the entire *Herald-Star* and hundreds of Karmic Echo fans, but just as she drew back her fist, the fans started screaming. A black stretch limousine slunk down the street and came to an easy stop before the *Herald-Star.* "This is really happening," she anxiously whispered.

Bernie took her hand. "Stay calm, sweetie."

Meg and Dee swung open the doors and stepped forward, a tide of *Herald-Star* employees following in their wake. A stocky chauffeur in a dove-gray uniform rounded the vehicle. With a neat tip of his hat, he opened the rear door and the screams of the fans increased in volume. Miranda moved closer to Bernie. The screaming was so like the night of the concert, her chest tightened in remembrance.

"Miss Penney and guest?" the chauffeur said, a smile in his eyes.

Dee took a step forward. Meg loudly cleared her throat and pushed ahead of her. The two women moved forward as though they were playing a game of Mother May I. When they each dived for the interior of the limo, the chauffeur blocked their way.

"Miss Penney and guest," he repeated slowly, his smile a few degrees cooler.

"Well?" Meg demanded of Miranda, her fists on her hips.

Dee, half-hidden by Meg's width, waved at Miranda and pointed at herself.

"Miss Penney?" The chauffeur spurred Miranda into motion.

She forced her feet to move. Flashbulbs illuminated the dusky sky and the screaming grew louder as she neared the car, holding tightly to Bernie.

Meg grabbed Miranda's shoulder and spun her around. As if on cue, the fans quieted a bit. "What the hell is going on here, Miranda? Rex assigned *me* to this story."

Miranda shook free of Meg's grasp, earning a cheer from the crowds inside and outside the *Herald-Star.* "Rex and I agreed that I would pick my own reporter. I've chosen Bernard."

"The celebrity beat is *my* territory, Miranda." Meg delivered her declaration with an icy smile that did little to cloak her anger.

"Lucas Fletcher is a musician," Miranda countered. "Music is Bernie's beat."

The chauffeur waved Bernie forward. He leaped into the limo and began playing with every knob, dial and button within his reach. Windows opened and closed, lights flickered, the television and sound system blared and the minibar doors popped open.

"Rex is going to hear about this!" Meg promised through a grimace of fury.

As the chauffeur ushered her into the limo, Miranda looked up at the third floor of the *Herald-Star*, where Rex stood rigidly silhouetted in the big windows of the corner office. "He's already on to me, Meg."

Miranda couldn't take a breath until the limo had pointed itself into traffic and pulled away from the *Herald-Star*. Her anxiety lessened the farther she got from the noise and the newspaper.

Bernie tore himself from the extensive array of cordials and mixers to notice Miranda's pale face. "You're not fretting over Miss Thing back there, are you?"

"No," she said, which was half true. "I'm worried about where we're going and how long it'll take for Meg's contacts to phone in our location." *And how many people would already be there, swarming the joint, hoping to catch a glimpse of Lucas Fletcher and his manufactured fairy tale.*

She crawled down the length of the limo's long backseat. Still on her hands and knees, she tapped on the glass separating the driver's compartment from the passenger cabin. "Yes, Miss Penney," the driver said once he had lowered the glass.

"I've been kept in the dark regarding the fine details of this dinner thing," she said.

"Mr. Fletcher fiercely guards his privacy," the chauffeur explained.

"I don't suppose you could tell me where you're taking us?" Miranda asked testily. But realizing that she might need the chauffeur as a friend rather than adversary, she changed her tone and added, "I'm a big fan of privacy, too. I love the stuff, really, but this is practically kidnapping."

"Mr. Fletcher's instructions were quite precise, Miss Penney. I am to deliver you and Mr. Reilly to your respective homes to retrieve your passports and a change of clothing. Then I will deliver you to Logan Airport. Your flight departs in two hours."

Bernie asked one more time, and as promised, Miranda pinched him so hard he whimpered. "You're not dreaming, Bernie. We're in Wales." Even as their second limo in nine hours carried them from a small airstrip to a paved, two-lane highway traversing endless rolling hills, Miranda had trouble believing it herself. They really were in Lucas's homeland, transported there on the wind and across an ocean by Karmic Echo's private jet.

"Wales . . . Wales . . ." Bernie muttered as he noisily searched a tablecloth-sized map he had purchased at the tiny airstrip. "There's no Wales on this map."

Miranda spread the map between them on the seat. With her finger, she stabbed a small island in the North Sea. "This is the United Kingdom, and this part here is Wales," she said impatiently. "You were lost in western Europe."

"This little thing is the U.K.? There's hardly room here for even one queen."

Miranda didn't respond to Bernie's jest. Her nerves were getting the best of her.

"Mr. Fletcher values his privacy and wishes to have you join him for dinner at his residence in Wales," a flight attendant had told Miranda once she'd been seated on the plane. Before she could register an approval or protest, the attendant had gone on to recite the planned itinerary: a seven-hour flight through calm skies to the United Kingdom, then a limo ride to Lucas's estate. They would arrive at approximately eight A.M. local time, and had been given the options of settling in at the Fletcher residence for a rest or visiting a few tourist attractions. The same car taking them to Lucas's home would remain at their disposal.

Miranda sat in the limo as she'd sat in the plane, pensively staring past her reflection in the window.

"What's on your mind, dear?" Bernie asked as he mixed himself a mimosa. Two vodka martinis had put Bernie to sleep for the duration of the flight, and now he was as bright and chipper as a squirrel. "You've been too quiet, and too cranky, for far too long."

"I don't know what I'm doing," she said simply.

Bernie set his drink in a leather-lined cup holder before moving to sit beside Miranda. He took her hand and held it tight. They rode in silence for a mile or so before he said, "You know, you don't have to be so strong and sensible all the time. You should try to be more like me."

"Weak and foolish?"

"Exactly, and only when it comes to opening yourself up to possibilities. You keep yourself so guarded, yet at the same time you let people take advantage of you."

"People like who?" she demanded, crossing her arms over her chest.

"Everyone in that dreadful department of yours, save Jed Hodgekins."

"Krakow, Sully and Paulie are good to me," she countered.

"Jordan."

Miranda felt herself contract in some elemental way at the mention of that name. "This isn't the time or the place to discuss him."

"I agree. This is a time to think about kismet and love and—"

"Dinner," Miranda spoke over him, sighing nervously. "Even though we had to leave North America for it, this is still just a dinner date."

"So you've come to accept that this is a date," Bernie grinned.

"Two people make up a date, not three. This is a publicity and marketing stunt for the *Herald-Star* and Karmic Echo."

"Oh, yes, I'm quite certain that Lucas dived into a frenzied crowd, had his hair, clothes and skin torn, resuscitated you, shielded you from the photographers and held you until help arrived all because he wanted to have you over—to Wales, mind you—for stuffed peppers and a photo op."

"None of this makes any sense," she said, frustration and anxiety giving her voice a whiny quality that grated on her own ears. "And you're not helping by trying to turn it into something it isn't. *Cu de bêbado não tem dono!*" she fired.

"Oh Lord, she's bringing out *Avó* Marie Estrella's Portuguese commandments," Bernie exhaled, rolling his eyes at the roof of the limo. "Go on, tell me what that one means."

"A drunk's ass has no owner," Miranda responded defiantly.

"Your grandma was schizophrenic, wasn't she, because that's just crazy talk."

"It means you shouldn't put yourself in a situation where you're totally vulnerable," Miranda clarified.

Bernie leaned forward and peered into her eyes. "You're scared."

"Scared?" She choked out a fake laugh. "Of what?"

"Lucas Fletcher."

"Here's what's going to happen, Bernie." Miranda got angry all over again at the whole situation. "We're being driven to Lucas Fletcher's publicist's office or condo or whatever you call it in Wales, and we'll drink fancy bottled water until almighty Lucas himself bothers to show up. His handlers will pose and shoot us making chitchat, and those photos will be on all the wire services within minutes. Lucas Fletcher will be properly acknowledged as my hero, Rex will get his feel-good story and I'll get to go cover the World Series. The only thing I'm afraid of is that some photographer will take my picture while I'm blinking and that's the one that will end up on the cover of the *Herald-Star*.

"I am not afraid of Lucas Fletcher."

"I know you, baby doll." Bernie chuckled and patted Miranda's knee. "I know when you're frightened, and I know what scares you. Look me in the eye and tell me that Lucas Fletcher doesn't scare you."

Miranda stubbornly turned her gaze to the window. The Welsh countryside was an emerald blur as the limo cruised closer to its destination. She had never been to the United Kingdom, yet anxiety muted her excitement. Her career had been spent dealing with celebrities, and she had dated a professional athlete for over a year. Lucas Fletcher shouldn't have been any different. He was just a man, albeit one that had made a crucial yet still fleeting impact on her life. She searched her thoughts and her conflicted emotions, and still she couldn't bring herself to admit that Lucas had affected her in powerful, intangible ways. She was left with one troubling conclusion.

Bernie's right, she silently confessed. *I am afraid of Lucas Fletcher.*

CHAPTER 2

Feast squirmed in the leather seat opposite Lucas. "Two hours we've been sitting on this bloody jet," he complained. "I'm no expert, but even I know a plane can't take off when it's raining sideways."

Lucas peered over a thick pile of documents spread over the table separating him from Feast. He looked out of the window just as a blinding, jagged bolt of lightening electrified the sky above Rome. "The weather will clear." His brow furrowed, as if he could will the rain to stop through desire alone.

Thunder rattled the small luxury jet, and Feast would have leaped from his seat if not for his seatbelt.

"That's it, Fletch." Feast unbuckled himself. "I'm not getting blasted out of the sky all because you want to hook up with your señorita in distress."

Lucas didn't move, though his gaze shifted from his papers to his high-strung lead guitarist. In that moment Feast seemed to realize that the storm couldn't hurt him nearly as quickly or thoroughly as Lucas could. And that his twenty-year friendship with Lucas was the only thing protecting him from what typically followed one of Lucas's dark looks.

"You know, Fletch," Feast began carefully. "You don't *really* own a life you save. You're not obligated to keep tabs on that chippy."

Lucas shuffled through his array of papers. "She's not a chippy, and I'm not keeping tabs on her."

The storm lessened in intensity, and Feast relaxed enough to dart forth and steal a sheaf of Lucas's papers. Lucas grabbed at it, but Feast easily danced out of reach. Lucas sat back, his arms crossed over his chest, as Feast's devilish eyes danced over his pilfered treasure. "'Lou Holtz: Miracle Maker,'" Feast read. He turned to Lucas. "Who the dickens is Lou Holtz?"

"American college football coach." Lucas hunched over his the rest of his papers. "Known for his ability to transform problematic teams into winners."

"'Sox ace kills Yanks,'" Feast read from another page. "Ace? Like in cards?"

"Like in Pedro Martinez, a star pitcher formerly of the Red Sox of Boston."

"That's baseball?"

"That's baseball." Lucas reached forward to snatch his pages from Feast, who shuffled through them.

"Some of these stories go back years. Why the sudden interest in American sports?" Feast asked, unable to suppress the tease in his voice. The answer dawned on him as Lucas snatched back the articles and gathered them close. "Those are her stories," he said knowingly. "Miranda Penney's."

"The storm is clearing. We'll be taking off any minute now. You'd best strap yourself in."

Feast leisurely did so, a wry grin stuck between his nose and chin. "I don't quite know what's going on with you, Lucas, but you've not been yourself since we left Boston."

Lucas secured his documents in a pocket on the aisle side of his seat. "Your deductive powers rival those of the great Sherlock Holmes. Tell me, Feast, are all English as sharp as you?"

"Do all Welsh fall in love as easily as you?" Feast countered.

"Shut your head before you find yourself eating fist." Lucas leaned into the aisle to check for signs of activity in the cockpit of the small craft. "The storm has all but ended," he complained. "Why aren't we leaving? I could fly this bucket myself in this spray."

"I've never seen you this anxious to return home. You usually dread it. Of course, I'd hate going back to a big, empty, rambling—"

"Feast." Lucas made the name the equivalent to "Shut up."

Feast boldly continued. "This is the most trouble I've ever seen you go through for a date."

"It's not a date, and would you please, kindly, shut up?" Lucas rang for the flight attendant. She appeared before Feast could jab him with another pointed inquiry.

"Hello, Isabella," Lucas greeted. "Will we be taking off soon?"

"The captain just received clearance and a runway assignment," the beautiful Italian flight attendant said. "May I get anything for you?"

"No, thank you," Lucas said.

Isabella, hand-picked by the band's manager to serve aboard Karmic Echo's private Channel hopper, stepped behind Lucas's seat. She placed her hands on his shoulders and began massaging them. "Lucas, you are so hard," she sang in her heavily accented English. "Such tension in these wonderful muscles."

He reached back and took her hand to gently pull her back into the aisle. "Please tell the pilot that I'm in a bit of a rush. I'm already quite late for a very important engagement."

"I'm sure we can make up some time in the air." Isabella casually swept a fall of her dark blonde hair over her right shoulder. Her hands demurely on her knees, she bent over and spoke softly to Lucas. "The plane will be in Wales for the next three days. So will I. Perhaps we can meet for cocktails after your very important engagement?"

Isabella's tanned complexion was flawless, and her green eyes crackled with the raw sensuality she just barely managed to keep restrained in Lucas's presence. Lucas and Feast were the only riders on the ten-passenger plane, so there was no one to sneak peeks of what Isabella's short skirt surely revealed as she bent over Lucas's lap to offer a view of the contents of her ivory blouse.

For weeks, Lucas had engaged in a playful flirtation with Isabella, and with each flight, the game had become more provocative. A subtle caress here, a bold comment there . . . it seemed only a matter of time before the rising heat between them became all consuming. Isabella, understandably, was perplexed when Lucas responded to her invitation for cocktails with, "I'm sorry, but I just won't have the time."

She stood, blinking comically in disbelief. Color flamed in her cheeks at the unexpected rejection.

"Izzy, luv." Feast decided to strike her at a weak moment, worsening the blow through the use of a nickname she violently detested. "I'm free for the weekend. Let's say you and I have cocktails, ponytails, pigtails—any kind of tails you want, after the flight, and we'll think of ways to occupy our time."

"*Si*," Isabella said absently, her eyes still on Lucas. "*Grazie*, Len."

Feast, amazed at his freakishly good fortune, was too shocked to respond.

Isabella probably would have remained in her fugue if the captain hadn't directed all personnel to prepare for takeoff. The tension melted from Lucas's shoulders once the plane began its slow crawl toward a runway.

"All right, Lucas," Feast demanded. "Give it up."

Lucas stared at him curiously.

"One day you and Isabella are hotter than summer on the sun and the next, you're as cold as North Sea sturgeon. What gives?"

"Nothing. I'm just tired." Lucas settled into the plush, buttery leather of his seat and closed his eyes. *I am tired*, he admitted again, to himself. *I'm tired of waiting to go home. And I'm tired of Miranda Penney.*

He was exhausted from recalling the shiver in her lithe body as he had cradled her to his chest, and weary of picturing the moment when she first opened her eyes and dazzled him with their beauty. He had fallen into their depths and still hadn't climbed his way out. The vulnerability in her gaze had claimed a vital part of him, and he feared he could take it back only by hearing her voice, feeling her touch and gazing once more into her eyes.

He shifted in his seat, slightly turning from Feast. The plane picked up speed as it taxied down the rain-glossed runway. This was his favorite part of flying, his exhilaration building as the plane's speed increased, followed by its climax in that moment of weightlessness when the plane left the ground. His ears would pop, his heart pumped faster, he'd even go a bit lightheaded. It was a similar sensation to that he got every time he walked onstage to the cheers of thousands of fans.

It was the feeling he'd had since rescuing Miranda Penney from the crush.

And it was tiresome.

He reclined his seat, glad that he was finally on his way home. The sooner he saw Miranda, the sooner he could exorcise her from his thoughts. Over the past few days his imagination and affection-starved heart had crafted her into a most exquisite phantom.

The sensible part of his mind insisted that his emotional attachment to her was borne of the crisis that had thrown them together. As the plane climbed to its cruising altitude, Lucas found it easier to ignore logic. If all had gone as planned, Miranda would soon be comfortably settled in Conwy. His house staff had standing orders to see to her every request. If she asked to go home, Karmic Echo's jet was obliged to return her to Boston, but Lucas's neck and shoulders tightened at the thought of Miranda not being at Conwy when he arrived. He needed her to be there, to see her again. That was his only hope of ridding her from his heart and mind.

"Wake up, sweetie."

Miranda stirred and opened her eyes. She didn't remember falling asleep, or Bernie covering her with his tuxedo jacket. He leaned into the opened door of the limo and she handed his jacket to him.

"You're awake, Miranda." Bernie smiled with his whole head and offered his hand to help her from the car. "But you won't think so when you see this place."

Miranda exited the limo. The driver stood before her, his hat in his hand. "I trust you had a pleasant ride, Miss Penney. Welcome to Conwy."

The driver stepped aside. At the sight before her, Miranda staggered back a step.

Looming before her was an honest-to-goodness, genuine castle. Like something from a movie, the magnificent, earth-toned stone structure filled her entire view. Complete with a curtain wall that meandered beyond her line of sight in two directions, Conwy's keep and turrets rose splendidly toward the sky.

"Close your mouth, honey," Bernie whispered. "And work your walk."

Miranda finally noticed the wide red carpet that began at her feet and ended somewhere beyond the portcullis. Like sentries, dozens of uniformed people lined each side of the carpet. One of them, a stately gentleman in black and white livery, stepped out of place and bowed neatly before Miranda. "Mr. Fletcher regrets that he is unable to receive you personally," he said. "His flight home from Italy was delayed by weather. As you'll notice, the entire staff at Conwy is at your disposal. I am Kenneth Morgan, Conwy's Master Steward, and you need only ask, should you require anything."

I should have worn a dress, Miranda thought as she took her first hesitant step upon the red carpet.

"Afta'noon, Miss Penney," a woman on her left greeted warmly as Miranda took another step.

"Hello." Miranda was only mildly surprised that the stranger knew her name.

"G'day, Miss Penney," said a man on her right as he tipped his cap and gave her a friendly smile.

On and on it went, until Miranda, with Bernie on her heels, was safely inside the keep. The Great Hall was the biggest room Miranda had ever been in. She estimated that her entire condo complex, which had once been a working church, would fit within the space.

"This is what I call *living*." Bernie breathed deeply of the air of the keep. "I'd bet your life that those tapestries came with the place."

Miranda followed Bernie to a vast wall, where a gigantic tapestry in subdued shades of red, gold, black and umber vividly depicted a battle scene.

"This is indeed an authentic work by Auryn Fitzharrold," said Morgan, who appeared behind them. "He was a master weaver for the British court. Edward I's master builder, James of St. George, designed Conwy. It was completed in 1287. Mr. Fletcher has gone to great lengths to maintain the history and integrity of Conwy. You'll find that many of the items here are authentic, registered historical artifacts."

"Is he royalty?" Bernie asked, knowing that Miranda wouldn't.

"On the contrary. Mr. Fletcher is a commoner, despite his nobility."

Bernie narrowed his eyes at Morgan and scanned the shorter man from head to toe. "You're Irish, aren't you?"

"Yes," Morgan responded, raising his strawberry-blonde eyebrows. "How could you tell?"

"I'm Irish, too," Bernie winked. "I know a brother when I see one."

Miranda listened intently to the exchange between the two men. Morgan's accent was far different from Bernie's, whose had a distinct island twist.

"Begging your pardon, Mr. Reilly, but you're not exactly what one envisions when one speaks of Black Irish," Morgan said.

"I was born and raised on the island of Montserrat," Bernie explained. "Most of the people there are as black as me and as Irish as you."

Morgan finally cracked a big smile. "Then may I say welcome to Conwy, my brother. I'd love to spend some time talking with you about your home, and perhaps in the course of your visit, you'll find a moment to speak with Mr. Fletcher as well. He's made several visits to Montserrat and thoroughly enjoys the island. In fact, he recently sponsored a music program at several elementary schools there."

Miranda studied Morgan's face. He clearly respected and admired the man who paid his salary. The staff assembled outside to welcome her seemed quite happy to do so, which testified further to Lucas Fletcher as a boss. After coming this far, Miranda's reporting instincts kicked in. She wanted to know more about the "Mr. Fletcher" who would fly her to Wales on a moment's notice and have two hundred people waiting at a castle to treat her as though she were the Queen of the World. She wanted to know more about the man who had saved her life.

She took a step toward the wide stone staircase that accessed the upper regions of the keep. "Mr. Morgan, perhaps after you show Mr. Reilly to his suite, you and I could speak further about Mr. Fletcher?"

Morgan successfully diverted Miranda from her request for a sit-down by suggesting that she first settle into her own chamber, the Emberley Suite. She was so taken by the amenities Lucas had provided that she temporarily forgot about her plan to ferret into his private life. Lucas had arranged for in-house—rather, in-castle—spa treatments for her and her *Herald-Star* reporter. Bernie reveled in the hedonistic pleasure of kelp and avocado full-body wraps, and a manicure and pedicure. A hot stone massage eased much of Miranda's tension, but she couldn't help feeling as though she were being clipped, buffed, waxed and perfumed as an offering for the king of the castle.

She enjoyed another short nap, this time in the decadent comfort of a massive four-poster bed draped with ivory linen and silk. Soon after she awakened, stylists imported from London came to her suite to do her hair, makeup and wardrobe. She allowed them to wash and condition her hair but passed on a cut and style, opting to keep her hair subdued by a simple bandanna. The first hair plucked from her right eyebrow made her scream, so she passed on the makeover. And she insisted on wearing her own clothes: blue jeans and a formless sea-green sweater.

When Bernie came to her suite to escort her to dinner, his eager smile became a fright mask of disappointment. "This is the best you could do?" he squawked. He plucked at her sweater and flipped a hand through her hair. "They came to my room with a dozen or more designer gowns . . . all in Meg's size, of course, since they thought she would be the one coming here with you. I can't imagine that Fletcher's people didn't do the same for you." He turned to ring for Morgan.

Miranda grabbed him by his arm and stopped him. "I didn't want to wear any of those dresses. That runway stuff just isn't me. And I'm not some Barbie doll to be dressed up."

"Well, I am." Bernie clutched the satin lapel of his tux with one hand and passed the other over his recently styled hair. "'007 Ken,' Caribbean style. You likey likey?"

Miranda smiled in spite of herself. "You look great."

He took her hand and set it over his arm. "And you look like a farmhand," he said tenderly.

"I'm sorry if I'm ruining your fun, Bernie," she said as they left her suite and began the long, convoluted route to the Banquet Hall.

"It'll take more than your bandanna and blue jeans to ruin this trip for me. I just wish that you would loosen up and enjoy this."

Miranda looked up at the colorful banners hanging from the high ceiling of the corridor and she passed her hand along the huge stones that had been laid to form Conwy's walls centuries ago. "I do appreciate this. Parts of it. I didn't like being forced into it by Rex, and I don't like the pampered poodle aspect on this end. I don't know if Lucas Fletcher is trying to be nice, or if he's . . ."

"Preparing you for the slaughter," Bernie finished.

"Nothing like this has ever happened to me before."

"That's exactly why you should give the nerves and suspicion a rest and lap up every morsel of this experience. I'm being treated like a queen—no pun intended—and you know what? I deserve it. So do you."

"But you want it, Bernie. That's the difference."

He patted her hand and began leading her down a wide, steep stone staircase. Morgan was at the bottom of it, waiting for them. "You want this, Miranda," Bernie said. "You just don't know it yet."

Told to wait in the solar while Bernie was taken, presumably, to the Banquet Room in the Great Hall, Miranda's curiosity became impatience, then anger, as she wore a path in the floor. The solar was on the third level of the keep. The windows set in the rounded walls were modernized and as large and deep as the ones in her suite. They were polarized, most likely to cool the glare of the sunrise off the waters of the Irish Sea. The room was luxuriously furnished in subdued leathers and velvet, yet still maintained an inviting coziness. Thick carpeting in muted shades of rust and umber muffled her footsteps and warmed the stone floor. Under different circumstances, she might have taken a leather-bound volume from one of the ceiling-high oak bookcases and snuggled up for a quiet read.

But Miranda was too mad to read. She placed her palms flat against the wall, and the cool stone made a great sound barrier as she spat out a furious strand of Portuguese curse words.

"Who does Lucas Fletcher think he is?" she asked the empty room. *Just because he has money and celebrity and a frickin' kingdom, he thinks he can manipulate people!* she raged inwardly. She wanted to kick something, but she was afraid of breaking her toe—or worse, damaging Lucas's furniture, which looked plenty expensive.

She seethed. On both sides of the ocean, powerful men trapped her, and she resented it. Deeply.

And Bernie. Her friend, her confidante, her fellow Double D . . . he was already in the Banquet hall, socializing in the enemy camp. *It's my date,* she thought bitterly. *Why is Bernie having more fun than I am?*

The answer came to her quickly. He was having fun because no one had forced him to be there.

"That's it." She tossed up her hands. "I'm going home."

She marched to the wooden double doors. She would have dramatically thrown them open if they hadn't been fifteen feet tall and two hundred pounds apiece. She shoved the left door open just enough to slip into the wide stairwell. Careful to keep her feet on the wool runner to mute her footsteps, she made her way down a spiraling stone staircase. She walked for at least a mile it seemed, before she came to the Great Hall, where a few people hung about, talking. No one attempted to intercept her as she headed for Morgan's office. The Master Steward was supposed to be at her disposal at all times, and she was determined to turn him into her impromptu travel agent.

She wore sneakers, but her feet were killing her by the time she'd completed the hike from the solar to Morgan's office, a room just off the Banquet Hall where he managed the castle's daily business. Miranda stood in the low, narrow corridor leading to Morgan's office, her hands on her knees, catching her breath and steeling her nerves before confronting him.

The cheerful music of lively conversation drifted from the Banquet Hall. Bernie's distinctive voice and island dialect rose above all the others. "Tell me," he began, "how often does your lord and master entertain his paramours and their chaperones in such grand fashion?"

Miranda pasted herself to the stone wall and crept closer to the Banquet Hall for a better listen.

"Aye, he's never brought a lady friend to Conwy," said an anonymous female voice with a thick Irish brogue. "Lucas is a very private person."

"Then why, may I ask, has Mr. Fletcher gone to such extremes to please my darling Miranda?" Bernie asked.

Miranda peeped into the room. Bernie was the only person standing at the table, which was easily 25 yards long. Dark wood chairs with tall, intricately carved backs lined each side of the table, and bodies were seated in each. The diners, all of whom Miranda assumed were Conwy's staff, served themselves from lovely porcelain casseroles, platters and tureens situated amidst fresh bouquets of wild roses and ivy. Five chandeliers, four smaller ones surrounding a magnificent central one the size of her Toyota, hung from the ceiling, which was so high the rafters escaped the light cast by the sparkling crystal ornaments. Elegant tapers of ivory and ecru burned on the table and from brass sconces throughout the room. The flames danced when someone laughed or reached across the table. Miranda caught the scent of something warm and meaty, and her belly noisily growled.

"We don't question what Lucas does," said an older woman with silver hair and a Welsh accent. "Our instructions were to treat Miss Penney as though she was the bloomin' queen of England." The woman paused, and then said, "We took it upon ourselves to treat her better than that."

The table erupted in laughter. Miranda chewed her lip, desperate to join them. It spoke well of Lucas that his employees were so happy. But he was still the boss, and she was his queen . . . at least for the night. Since she was the one they were supposed to impress, they probably wouldn't be able to relax if she were to walk in on them and take a seat.

"Thanks, Lucas," she muttered sullenly as she turned and headed for Morgan's office.

"Ken, have you seen . . . Oh, my . . . Hello."

Miranda was sitting on a sofa, leafing through a golf magazine and she turned to face the man who had appeared in Morgan's doorway. It was in her mind to tell him that Morgan wasn't there, that she herself had been waiting for him for over twenty minutes, but the words fled her mind the instant the man walked into the room.

"Hello." Miranda stood on legs suddenly gone very weak and very shaky.

"Hello," he said again. "Miranda."

His melodic pronunciation of her name turned her belly to jelly. When he offered his hand, she didn't see it. Her eyes were fixed on his, marveling at their unusual shade of blue. Were his eyes really that blue, or was it the deep navy of his fisherman's sweater making them seem so? Her eyes dropped to his mouth. The delicious shape of it and how it formed her name thrilled her, and his accent gave her goose bumps. He spoke to her again and she heard nothing other than the tone and timbre of his sexy voice.

"Miranda?" he repeated. "Are you all right?"

This was the man who had saved her from the crush. This man with the broad, muscled chest, glossy hair and incredible smile, who looked at her as though he had found a treasure at the end of a rainbow was . . . "Fine." She shook herself out of her reverie. "I'm fine."

"You wanted to see Kenneth? Perhaps I can help you."

"No!" she said a bit too sharply. "Uh . . . no. I just . . . got a little bored waiting for you."

He smiled. "For a moment I was afraid that you were trying to duck out."

A loud, brittle laugh burst from her. She quickly turned it into a cough. "Don't be ridiculous."

"I'm sorry I'm so late. We had to reschedule some playing dates in Europe to accommodate a makeup performance for the concert last week in Boston," he explained. "Thunderstorms in Rome delayed my return. How was your flight over?"

Miranda still wasn't hearing him. She had interviewed hundreds of celebrities, both major and minor, and Lucas was one of the few who actually looked the same in photos as in real life. Actually, photos didn't do him justice. In real life, he was so gorgeous it was hard to breathe and look at him at the same time.

"I'm starving." Lucas took her hand. "I imagine you are, too. Shall we?"

Miranda gave herself a mental slap. All the man had done was walk into the room, and she had become a drooling, mindless slave to his exquisite male beauty. This wasn't like her, and it wasn't how she wanted to be. She cast her eyes to the floor. It was easier to remain in control when she wasn't swimming in his beautiful eyes.

"Yes." Miranda noticed that he wore jeans and athletic shoes. Heat surged through her as her gaze lingered on how well he filled out his jeans. "Do you need to dress or something?"

"No," he chuckled. "Do you?"

"No. Not if you don't."

He tucked her arm through his. "Then, my lady, we're off."

Lucas led her past the crowded Banquet Hall and up a long flight of stairs to a smaller, more intimate chamber. Smaller meaning that the room could seat only fifty people comfortably, where the Banquet Hall easily sat one hundred. A wooden table was set elegantly with an enormous floral display, and crystal and silver for a five-course meal. At one end of the table were a lit candelabra and one place setting. Twenty-five feet away, at the other end, was another candelabra and place setting.

Morgan posed staunchly near the center of the table, close to a standing bucket of ice from which jutted a bottle of champagne and at least three bottles of wine. He was dressed in a black cutaway coat and gleaming white gloves that matched his white silk cravat. Miranda wondered if he'd been waiting for her and Lucas all this time.

"Good evening, sir," Morgan began formally, "and lady. Tonight, a warm appetizer of escargot avec garlique will start your meal, followed by crab tartlets with leek puree accompanied by a lightly chilled Verdicchio from Conwy's award-winning wine collection. Next, we shall serve duck with kumquats, complemented by a well-rounded Brouilly. Blue cheese soufflés will follow, and the grand finale to your meal will be Belgian chocolate mousse and fresh raspberry sorbet presented with a sweet Gewürztraminer." Morgan bowed crisply before approaching them. With great ceremony he took Miranda from Lucas and escorted her to one end of the table.

Lucas went to the other end. He didn't sit until Miranda had been seated, but once he took his chair, she disappeared. His view of her was completely blocked by a three-tiered monument of roses, phlox, bear grass, philodendrons and Queen Anne's lace in the center of the table.

Lucas was glad that Miranda couldn't see him. It had taken every particle of will power he had to walk her to his private dining room when what he'd really wanted to do was pitch himself atop her right there on Morgan's sofa. He drank long, hard gulps of his ice water, hoping it would cool the fire burning through him. The woman wore jeans, a sweater that revealed only a bit of her collarbone, no makeup and no jewelry and she had done nothing to her hair other than restrain it with a rolled bandanna. Yet she was still the sexiest thing he had ever seen. *Maybe I've built this meeting up in my head for so long, I've made her something she isn't,* he considered.

To test himself, he cleared his mind completely, slowly stood, and peeped at Miranda over the top of the mountainous floral arrangement. She slumped against the tall back of her chair and appeared to be trying to hang the smallest of her three spoons from the end of her nose. She caught it deftly each time it dropped off. Her small frame looked even tinier in the massive chair. When she set the spoon back down, her sweater shifted, allowing him to steal a glimpse of the caramel glow of her right collarbone and the graceful place where her neck met her shoulder. Lucas winced in sweet pain at the sight of her smooth, ginger-brown skin, and the front of his pants began to feel more snug. Miranda tugged her sweater back in place, pulled off her bandanna and ran a hand through her hair. The spill of warm brown caught the candlelight, and Lucas was mesmerized by the crackle of natural red highlights in her hair. She looked forward, and her eyes pinned him in place.

"I-Is . . . uh . . . everything all right down your end?" he hedged, reaching for something to say now that he'd been caught staring.

Miranda slightly rose, to see him over the flowers. "Everything's fine. Thank you."

Her sweater slipped again, and Lucas dropped into his chair. "It's not me, damn it all," he cursed under his breath. "It's her."

Morgan and his nattily dressed assistants brought the first course and set it before them, and then retreated from the room. Lucas enjoyed escargot avec garlique. It was one of his favorite dishes, and he was starving. But as he stared at the arrangement of steaming, buttery delicacies on his plate, he realized that his hunger wasn't for food.

"Miranda?" he called.

"Yes?" She called back.

"Are you enjoying your escargot?"

"Yes. It's very . . . snaily."

"Very well, then." He set down his cutlery and began twiddling his thumbs. He listened to the sounds of Miranda's knife and fork moving against her plate.

"Miranda?" Lucas called again, this time startling the guilty Miranda in the middle of using her spoon to catapult snail bits into the gigantic floral arrangement.

"Yes?" she said.

"I've got Fenway Franks in the kitchen."

Miranda smiled. Whatever tension and unease she had felt vanished as she laughed out loud.

CHAPTER 3

The "kitchen" turned out to be a stadium-sized cooking arena. The wood-fired grill in the center of the space was large enough to accommodate a baby whale when all the pits were lit, and the stone hearth built into one wall was taller than Lucas and as wide as a bus. Conventional appliances lined the wall opposite the hearth; they, too, were of commercial, rather than residential, size. The kitchen was dark and empty when Lucas brought Miranda into it.

"Where's the chef?" Miranda asked as Lucas flipped a half dozen switches to illuminate the vast space.

"This is the old kitchen." He opened one of the stainless steel doors of the refrigerator and began searching various compartments. "Conwy has three kitchens. This one, one in the staff's lodge and one off the keep. This one is used only on special occasions. For holiday and record release parties, wedding receptions and the like."

"Will your chef be upset that we didn't eat his fancy dinner?" Miranda hopped onto a counter and watched Lucas. He finally found the Fenway Franks and displayed them for her with a tease of dimples that made her sweat.

"He'll recover." He turned the hotdogs over in his hands. "How does one prepare a Fenway Frank?"

Miranda scooted off the counter and took the package from him. "Usually, you boil them in a gallon of two-week old hotdog water. Do you have a small saucepan?"

"Probably." He set about looking for one. He opened a cabinet beneath a wide counter and began rummaging through the cookware.

"There's one." Miranda pointed to the rack above the butcher-block cutting table. "It's the perfect size, but I can't reach it."

Lucas, who was eight inches taller than she, reached up and easily unhooked the small pot. His movement hiked up his sweater, giving Miranda a glimpse of his taut lower abdomen and defined obliques. Miranda's hormones roared into overdrive. Nothing appealed to her more than nicely sculpted obliques, the muscles that created that delectable ridge of flesh right above a man's hips and anchored a tight and toned torso. "Do you have buns?" she asked.

Lucas, his eyes sparkling, handed her the saucepan. "Of course."

"I meant . . ." She waved a hand, floundering for words and hoping to fan the sudden heat rising in her face. "You know what I meant." She took the pot and the franks to the stove.

"You're very pretty when you blush."

Miranda felt a whoosh of heat, and it took her a beat to realize that it was coming from the stove. Lucas was standing beside her, and had turned on the burner. "How did you know that I liked hotdogs?"

"Your friend Bernard told us." He watched Miranda use a paring knife to split the wrapper on the franks. She pulled each one from the package and dropped it into the pot, and then filled the pot with water at the sink. "He was quite helpful. In fact, he provided more information about you than we actually needed."

Miranda set the pot over the gas flame. "Such as?"

"You were born on a Monday at Mercy Hospital in Silver Spring, Maryland."

"Anything else?" She faced him and set a hand on her hip. Her sweater slipped.

Lucas clutched at the insides of his pockets to stop himself from reaching for the inviting peek of skin. "He told us that you have a sister, Calista, who's marrying a baseball player in June."

"Who's this 'us' you keep referring to?"

"Me and my publicist, actually. He acquires things for me. What I want, it's his job to get."

Miranda turned away from him and stared at the simmering franks. "So am I just another acquisition?"

He stepped behind her and gently settled his hands on her shoulders. When he spoke, his words warmed her right ear. "Yes, in that you are something that I absolutely had to have. No, in that I'm not looking for a casual encounter."

She raised her head. Lucas didn't move. He spent a moment breathing her scent, infusing himself with the jasmine sweetness of her hair and skin.

Miranda closed her eyes and enjoyed his proximity. But for the movement of her chest and shoulders as she breathed, she kept perfectly still. She would practically be in his arms with the tiniest movement, and that was the last place she wanted to be. Lucas might belong only to her for this moment, here in his old kitchen, but he wasn't really hers, and never could be.

Lucas pulled away from her before he reached the point where he would never be able to do so. "I'll get those buns."

By the time he retrieved hotdog rolls and plates, Miranda had collected the condiments. The boiled franks steamed on a plate while Miranda and Lucas pulled stools up to the butcher-block table. Miranda was horrified when Lucas set his hotdog in a bun and then attempted to eat it with a knife and fork.

"That's got to be the strangest thing I've ever seen," she remarked. "It's a hotdog, not filet mignon. Get your hands dirty." She picked up her well-dressed frank and took a hearty bite.

"You've got mustard on the corner of your mouth," Lucas told her.

She used the heel of her hand to wipe away the mustard then licked her hand clean. She couldn't have charmed Lucas more if she had deliberately tried. He followed her example and chomped his frank in half in one bite.

"My God," he exclaimed. "This is the best hotdog I've ever had."

"Really?" Miranda was pleased.

"It's also the only hotdog I've ever had," he admitted around a second bite. "What's it made of? It's meat, yes?"

"Some say they're made of pork or beef, others say raccoon tails and possum lips." Miranda couldn't keep a straight face when Lucas stopped chewing and looked at her, his eyes wide. "I'm kidding," she giggled. "These are all beef."

"There's a relief. I once ate roasted spiders in South America, quite by accident, of course. The experience put me off my grub for a week."

"Ugh. Is that the worst thing you've ever had in the course of your travels?"

"Your American beer runs a near second. It's weak as spit, and your pubs serve it cold, as if it were lemonade."

"I can't have you insulting American beer. When he was giving you my life's story, did Bernie tell you that the one and only time I ever got drunk was on a single spit-weak American beer on my twenty-first birthday?"

"I apologize," Lucas said. "And please know that the quality of American women more than compensates for the deficient quality of the beer."

"I suppose you've sampled both quite extensively?"

"The beer, yes." He went to the refrigerator again and withdrew a bottle of sparkling white wine. "As for the women, don't believe everything you may have read about me in the gossip pages."

"I don't read gossip columns."

"Beautiful and smart, too," Lucas smiled.

Another irritating blush crept over Miranda's skin. Lucas busied himself with cutting the foil on the wine and easing out the cork. It shot into the air and landed on the other side of the room, near an ancient wooden door held shut with a thick wooden beam. Miranda jumped at the sound of howling, followed by loud, eager scratching and sniffing on the other side of the door.

"Those are my pups," Lucas said. "I haven't seen them in three weeks, not since we began the Karmic Velocity tour. Would you like to meet them?"

"Sure." She left her stool. Lucas took the wine and Miranda grabbed the two glasses and followed him across the kitchen.

"This is the Hound Room." He tucked the wine beneath his arm so he could use both hands to heave the sturdy beam off of its brackets.

He opened the door to the darkened room, and Miranda's first instinct was to climb up on his broad shoulders.

"What the hell is that?" She almost shrieked when a pair of silvery-green eyes at the level of her chest approached her.

Lucas turned a knob and brought up the lights. "These are my pups."

Miranda was pinned to the wall by a "pup" that was easily a foot taller than she, if it stood on its back legs. "P-P-Pups?" she gasped, eyeballing the dog and the rest of its pack. "They're going to get *bigger*?"

Lucas snapped his fingers and the dogs sat with military precision. Their tags chattered as they quivered with joy at seeing Lucas. "They're Irish wolfhounds. Reg here is leader of the pack." He scratched Reg's ears. The dog's soulful eyes closed in utter contentment, and the dog sniffing at Miranda left her to nose Lucas's free hand, placing her head under his palm. He kneeled to give her a good rub under her neck. "This is Sionne, Reg's wife. The other four, Emrys, Saeran, Owena and Spot, are their children." As he said the names, the "children" came to him, each of the gangly, long-legged beasts receiving a huge dose of their master's affection. "Walks?" Lucas said.

The full-throated howls of six Irish wolfhounds rattled the walls of the stone room. Miranda, a wine goblet in each hand, grabbed Lucas's arm. He grinned at her. Rather than making her shrink away in embarrassment, his smile encouraged her to hold him a bit tighter.

"Are you afraid of dogs, Miranda?"

"Dogs, no. Ponies with fangs take some getting used to."

Lucas steered her through a sea of tall dog. He removed the bar from a second heavy door and swung it open. Reg and his family bolted onto a gravelly stretch of moonlit beach and Lucas and Miranda followed slowly behind.

The view stole Miranda's heart. The dark, orange-pearl moon was partially shrouded by a thin layer of broken clouds and seemed to sit directly before them on the dark sand. The dogs ran at the moon, and Miranda had no doubt that they were capable of dragging it home for their adoring master.

"Did you plan this, too?" she asked.

"What? Walking the dogs?"

"This night. The way the moon scatters its light upon the black waves. The way the breeze holds just enough warmth to feel like a kiss on my skin."

Lucas gazed at her in awe.

"What . . . ," she said self-consciously. "Do I still have mustard on my face?"

"You have a poet's eye, Miranda," he said. She blushed yet again, and this one, by moonlight, made Lucas take one of her wine glasses so that he could hold her hand. "Your words paint beautiful pictures."

"It's easy, when beauty is right in front of you." And it was. It was in the ocean blue of his eyes and the sultry curves of his lips. It was in the shape and strength of his hand as he offered it to her, to help her over a particularly rocky part of the beach.

"How is it that you decided to become a sportswriter?" he asked.

"My dad used to play baseball, so I grew up with sports, and I like the newspaper business. Women are becoming so dominant in the sporting world, on the field and off. Women's gymnastics and figure skating have always been popular, and female tennis and softball players galvanized their sports. But now we have women's professional basketball, we had soccer and now we're dabbling with football. Of course, the *Herald-Star* doesn't give women's sports the space they deserve, but I'm working on changing that."

"What sports do you like most?" Lucas stopped at a large outcropping of rock overlooking the sea. He leaped onto it, and took Miranda's hand to help her up.

"To play or to cover?"

"Both," he said as they sat.

"I like covering baseball and women's college basketball. I like playing basketball and tennis, when I can make the time. I was pretty good at volleyball and softball when I was in school."

"I played football—soccer, to you—and rugby in school." He poured the wine and handed a glass to Miranda. "I was quite good, actually."

"Hey, soccer is football to me, too. To half of me, at least. My mother is from Brazil. We used to go there in the summers when my dad retired and started scouting for the major leagues. I follow the Brazilian national team—"

"*Canarinho*!" Lucas declared. "'Little canary.'"

"That's right," Miranda said. "Because of the yellow jerseys they wear for home games."

"There's a saying about football and Brazilians," Lucas started. "'The English invented it, and . . .'"

". . . the Brazilians perfected it," Miranda finished. "No truer words were ever spoken."

"So you're a staunch supporter of Team Brazil?"

Miranda took a sip of her wine and nodded. "I like a few of the African teams, too. Cameroon's been so innovative in the past few years, and Ghana's coming up, too. I love watching soccer matches. Soccer players have the best ass—" She caught herself mid-syllable and finished with, "accents."

Lucas took off his sweater and folded it. He invited Miranda to use it as a cushion, which she accepted, once she could think straight. *I must be drinking this wine too fast,* she thought after watching him take off his sweater had made her jaw drop. *It's not like he was topless,* she told herself. But just thinking of that image set her cheeks on fire. As he sat in his white T-shirt with the night breeze playing in his hair, Miranda knew that she had to get a hold of herself, and fast. "Did you always want to be a singer?"

"Actually, I tossed about the notion of being an architect. I was keen on building things when I was in school. Music was always a hobby I happened to do well at. Then came our first single, and the hobby became a career." He gazed out upon the waves and watched them break against the shore. "I have the best job in the world. I get paid an obscene amount of money to do what I like. Few people have that luxury."

"You seem as though you have regrets."

He was quiet for a long moment. Miranda studied his profile, and thought she saw a hint of sadness in his face. "I shouldn't," he said. "I've been incredibly lucky with my music for twenty-two years. My band mates are my best friends. I've got more money than I'll ever know what to do with. I've got nothing to complain about, but . . ."

"But?" she encouraged, sitting closer to him to offer what comfort she could.

He turned and looked at her, and his gaze sent a blazing current of longing directly to her heart. "It's a lonely life."

"Millions of people all over the world adore you. You live in a castle with a staff of what, about two hundred? All you have to do is snap your fingers and you'd have an instant party."

"Do you really think it's that easy for me?"

"Yep."

"You're right. It is. But do you think that's what I really want?"

She dropped her eyes to the tiny bubbles exploding to the surface in her wine glass. "I don't know you well enough to know what you want."

He hooked a finger under her chin and lifted her face to his. He held her gaze long enough for her to consider the possibility that what he wanted was the same thing she wanted: honest companionship. "I'd like to change that. I'd like to know you better as well."

She shrank away from him. "Mr. Fletcher—"

"Lucas. Please. Mr. Fletcher is my father."

Miranda clapped a hand to her forehead. "This is very strange."

He looked surprised. "I was enjoying the sheer normalcy of this. I'm sitting on a moon-drenched beach having a lovely conversation with a smart, fascinating woman. The only thing strange about the evening is that you actually accepted my invitation."

"I didn't really have a choice," she admitted. "My publisher made it clear that my job depended on going through with this date."

"I'm sorry, Miranda. That wasn't my intention."

"It isn't your fault. It's the way Rex Wrentham operates."

Lucas swirled his wine in his glass. "Is that the only reason you came here? Because of your boss?"

She took a breath and opened her mouth to answer, but she was distracted by laughter from farther along the beach. Miranda saw a couple playfully chasing each other along the shoreline. "I assumed this was a private beach," she said. "Or that your dogs would have eaten any other visitors."

"This *is* a private beach." Lucas grinned and shook his head as the couple neared. "Even so, the whole town is welcome to it."

"Do you know those people?"

"The tall one is my father. The short one in the skirt is my mum." He stood to greet his parents. Miranda followed suit.

"We didn't know you were out, Luke, or we'd 'ave carried about down coast a bit," said Mrs. Fletcher.

Miranda scarcely understood a word through the woman's heavy Welsh accent.

"It's all right, mum," Lucas said. "We were just enjoying the view. Mum, Da, I'd like to introduce you to Miss Miranda Penney."

"How do you do?" Miranda said.

Mrs. Fletcher reached up and took Miranda's hand in both of hers. "Aren't you the most darling thing? Very pleased to meet you. I hope you're enjoying your visit to Conwy."

Miranda nodded, having understood only the gist of what Mrs. Fletcher said.

"Me son tells me you're a writer, for sports," Mr. Fletcher said as he shook Miranda's hand.

"Yes, sir, I am," she said, relieved to understand him. Like Lucas's, his accent was softer and sounded more English than Welsh. He was heavier than his son and his hair was streaked with silver, but his resemblance to Lucas was uncanny. Miranda enjoyed the preview of what Lucas would look like in another few decades.

"What can you tell me about the Yankees pitching this season? Will it carry 'em to another World Series?"

"Ignore him, Miss Penney." Mrs. Fletcher took her husband's arm and dragged him back a step. "We spent a summer in New York City, and he's been addicted to American baseball since."

"The Yankees, my darling rib, not just American baseball," Mr. Fletcher clarified. "Year after year, the Yanks are far and above the best baseball organization the world has ever seen. From Joe DiMaggio on down to Derek Jeter, who by the way is the shortstop by which all others should be measured— "

"As a Boston sportswriter, I'm afraid I have to stick up for the Red Sox," Miranda said with a smile. "No team shows more heart than the Sox."

Mr. Fletcher's eyes twinkled so much like his son's. "Aye, that might be an argument worth having. But—"

"Miranda, it was a pleasure," Mrs. Fletcher broke in, "but it's time I got this crusty old codger home and to bed before he starts reciting Roger Maris's home run record."

"Home and to bed." Mr. Fletcher bounced his heavy eyebrows. "That's exactly the plan I had for you, love."

"Cheeky rascal!" Mrs. Fletcher swatted at her husband, who trotted out of her reach, luring her into a chase down the beach.

"Sorry about that." Chuckling, Lucas resumed his seat and guided Miranda down beside him. "They don't seem to know that they're not teenagers any more."

Miranda watched the Fletchers scurry along the shoreline. Mrs. Fletcher caught her husband, and they held hands, moving shoulder to shoulder before pausing for a long kiss. "How long have they been married?"

"Forever. That summer they spent in New York City was their honeymoon trip to the U.S."

"They seem very happy. And very much in love."

"They are."

"My parents have been married for thirty-two years." Miranda leaned back on her hands and crossed her legs at the ankle. "I don't think I've ever seen them look at each other the way your parents do. I've never even seen them hold hands."

"People have different ways of expressing their love for one another."

"My parents don't love each other."

He spun to face her. She stared unblinking at the sea with tendrils of her hair dancing on the breeze. "I'm very sorry to hear that," he said.

"Don't be." She folded her legs beneath her and struck sand from her hands. "They've learned to live with it. I guess I have, too. I know that they care for each other, in their own ways. My father plagues my mother with gifts. Flowers, jewelry, expensive vacations . . . It's generosity built on guilt. I give him credit for always working hard and providing well for us. My mother was a stay-at-home wife and mother, the ultimate Latina June Cleaver."

"What went wrong?"

She sighed. "I suppose things were never completely right, from the start. When I was first hired at the *Herald-Star*, I was sent to Baltimore to cover a Red Sox-Orioles game, and I was so excited. Camden Yards is a fantastic ballpark, the people in Baltimore are wonderful, and I was on an expense account on my first road assignment. I was the third man, so to speak, and the two other reporters decided that we should have dinner before the game. I got outvoted and we ended up at Hooters at the Inner Harbor, which is right near the ballpark."

Lucas spun a bit to face Miranda, who resolutely kept her gaze on the churning ocean as she recounted one of her most painful memories.

"We'd just been served our chicken wings when I saw this tall, handsome black man walk in with a red-headed woman. He was kissing and groping her and carrying on like a senior on prom night. The thing is, I probably wouldn't have given them a second glance if the man had not been my father. The woman was definitely not my mother," she laughed bitterly. "I went to him and he looked properly surprised, but then he acted like being with another woman wasn't anything out of the ordinary. Later, I found out that it wasn't."

She quieted, and she appreciated Lucas's silence. She spent a moment wondering if it was the soft music of the tumbling sea or Lucas's presence beside her that dulled the pain she usually endured whenever she recalled the moment she caught her father cheating on her mother.

She stared at her hands in her lap as she said, "I didn't know what to do. I thought maybe he was having some kind of late mid-life crisis thing. For two weeks I agonized over whether I should tell my mother. I didn't want to betray my father, but I also didn't want my mother to hear it from someone else, or to be surprised if my father told her that he wanted a divorce."

"Miranda, you're trembling." Lucas took his sweater and draped it around her, carefully moving her hair from the collar. He put an arm around her and hugged her into his side. A hard lump formed in her throat at his unexpected attempt to comfort her. "No one should ever be forced to chose loyalties between parents."

"I decided to tell her," Miranda croaked around the lump that refused to budge. "It was one of the hardest things I've ever had to do. I flew home, sat her down, and told her, but she already knew about the redhead in Baltimore. She knew about another woman in New York City and another one in Atlanta, and all the women that had come before them. By my mother's reckoning, my dad started cheating on her less than a year after they were married."

Miranda reluctantly pulled from Lucas's embrace to face him directly. "I never knew. Through vacations, Father-Daughter dances, charity events, family reunions and funerals, I never knew that my father wasn't faithful. He never forgot an anniversary or birthday. When I was sixteen, he bought me a used Honda and I thought he was the greatest dad in the world. The only complaint I had about my upbringing was the amount of traveling my father did for his job. I never knew that my family was held together with deceit and selective blindness."

"Perhaps, in their own ways, your mum and dad have found happiness," Lucas offered.

A tiny burst of rage flowered and died in Miranda's chest. "My mother isn't happy. How can she be, with her husband spreading himself thin with God knows how many other women? She makes me so angry! How can a smart woman be so dumb?"

Miranda's overly long shirtsleeves covered her hands as she gesticulated wildly before Lucas. "My mother is nothing like me, Lucas." She slapped a hand to her chest. "She's so beautiful and poised. When she met my father, she was a twenty-one-year-old college exchange student at the University of Southern California. She went to a baseball game in Anaheim and my dad was playing first base. He saw her in the stands and got the team's publicist to fix him up with her. They've been together ever since."

In a rush of words and emotion, Miranda further extolled her mother's virtues. "She speaks English, Spanish and Portuguese, and she has a degree in public health. And she's gorgeous, Lucas. She's *negro branca*, a Brazilian of African descent with very, very light skin. But she isn't enough for my father."

Miranda didn't realize she was clenching her fists until Lucas gently pried her fingers apart. "My mother thinks everything's okay as long as he always comes back to her, as long as he's a good provider and a good father. It wasn't okay." Her voice broke on a sob she managed to swallow back. "It's *not* okay."

Lucas embraced her and she hid her face in his shoulder. "This has been bottled in you for a long time, hasn't it?"

She laid her head on his shoulder, thankful for the solid, secure support. "I've never spoken to anyone about it, other than that one time with my mother."

"Why did you tell me?"

She looked at him, her face kissing distance from his. "Because of your parents. I want what they have."

"What's that?"

"Someone to love me truly, for always."

I'm halfway there, Lucas thought as he traced her jawline with the tip of his left index finger. Although she tried, Miranda couldn't suppress the thrilling shiver generated by his touch. "May I kiss you, Miranda?"

His words had already kissed her, his lips were so near hers. She wanted to kiss him, to clap her hand to the back of his head and bring his mouth down upon hers. But she knew she wouldn't be able to stop at one kiss, not from this man. One kiss would lead to another kiss, and another, and then senseless abandon right there on that big rock.

And then what? Her bags and her Bernie would probably be hastily packed and rushed to the airport for a red-eye back to Boston. In a moment of weakness she had let herself be drawn into Lucas Fletcher's web. She wouldn't compound the mistake by kissing him. She sat up and returned his sweater to him. "I don't think that would be a good idea." She began climbing off the rock.

"Why not?" He jumped off the rock and landed next to her in the coarse sand.

"Because the last thing I need is a one-night stand with a rock star." She started back to the castle. "I'm sorry if I led you on. It was an accident. Honestly."

"I'm the one who should apologize. I didn't invite you here to take advantage of you in any way. You have my word on that as a gentleman."

She slowed her pace. "Why *did* you invite me here, Lucas?"

Because you are someone I could truly love, for always, was the first response that sprang into his head. But he knew that voicing such an irrational thought would send her to Morgan, demanding to be returned to Boston immediately. "Your eyes. That night on the stage, when I looked into your eyes, I felt . . . right. All the way through."

She spent a thoughtful moment considering his words. "What the hell does that mean?"

He laughed. "I don't know. All I know is that I am glad that you're here, and that I don't want to end this night on a warped chord."

"Is that anything like a sour note?"

"Smart ass," he laughed softly.

"So how *do* you want to end this night?"

"I have Ben & Jerry's Heath Bar Crunch ice cream in the kitchen. It was specially ordered and shipped directly from Vermont. I believe it came over on the plane with you, from New England. Will that do?"

Miranda pinched back a smile. Bernie had truly given up all of her personal preferences. "You're spoiling me, Mr. Fletcher."

"That's the idea, Miss Penney." He walked her back to the castle, an easy peace made between them.

CHAPTER 4

On an afterthought, Miranda grabbed her jeans and sweater from where she'd carelessly tossed them over the back of a plush velvet and brass wing chair. She crossed the giant bedroom and opened the door to the dressing room, which alone was twice as big as her bedroom at home. She slipped her discarded clothing over a padded silk hanger. But for the simple garments she had put in the dressing room upon her arrival, the rest of the ivory hangers were empty.

After her walk on the beach and ice cream with Lucas, Miranda had returned to her room to see that her nightclothes had already been laid out for her. Candles had been lit and placed in ornate reflective sconces that cast an amber glow throughout the bedchamber. A fire crackled and popped in the hearth, adding its light and warmth to the room.

Miranda ran her hand over her flat belly and the pale, whispery pima cotton covering it. The short-sleeved, boat-necked top and its matching, wide-leg pants weren't hers. The pajamas had come courtesy of the castle, and had arrived in a perfumed box with her name on it in fancy gold lettering. Back in Boston, she had hastily packed an overnight bag when she'd been driven home for her passport. She had thrown in her favorite nightshirt, a XXXL Baltimore Ravens T-shirt.

That shirt hung in the dressing room with the rest of her clothes.

The pajamas that the castle—Lucas—had provided were girly, but not obnoxiously so. They were something she might have actually chosen for herself. And they were a far cry from the rubber and spikes ensemble she would have expected a rock star to provide for his overnight lady guests. Given the chance to be treated like royalty, Miranda was slightly embarrassed by how easily she was adapting to it.

Of course, across the corridor, Bernie shamelessly took advantage of his host's generosity. When Miranda had stopped by to say goodnight, a late-night "snack" of broiled scallops and lobster tails was being delivered to Bernie's suite as he bid farewell to a team of masseuses. Bernie had chastised her for not making the most of her stay as he was, and he had accused her of deliberately not enjoying herself.

"But I am enjoying myself," she admitted quietly. She went to the wall of giant windows and parted the drapes and sheers. The windows opened in, and she pulled them as wide as they would go. The breeze was cool, but not unpleasantly so, and she breathed deeply as it played in her hair. She had a postcard perfect view of the Irish Sea. The clean, salty scent of the water and its quiet song as it lapped at the shore infused her with a rare sense of tranquility. A long-suffering insomniac, she glanced at the magnificent bed. Pillows were stacked five deep at its head and the ivory coverings looked as soft as her pajamas felt. If all she got from the weekend was a good night's sleep, she'd have no complaints when she faced Rex on Monday.

The thought of Rex and his minions, La and Dee, made her stiffen with tension and drove off any hope she had for a peaceful night's sleep. Opposite the windows was a wall of bookshelves filled with leather-bound volumes. She usually spent her sleepless hours writing, but her laptop was at home in Boston. She gathered her hair and tied it into a loose knot as she scanned the titles on one of the shelves. She had decided on *Wuthering Heights* when a soft knock sounded on her door.

"What is it now, King Bernard?" she cracked as she opened it.

"As I said on the beach, I'd prefer Lucas."

"I'm sorry." She nervously gripped the doorknob in both hands. "I thought you were . . . never mind. Uh . . . I thought you had turned in for the night."

He leaned against the wide doorframe. "I was passing by and saw your light under the door. I thought I'd check to see if you needed anything."

"The suite actually has more than I need. It's beautiful." She self-consciously ran her fingers along her upper arm. Lucas's eyes followed the movement. "Thank you for the pajamas. They're very comfortable."

"Indeed." He lifted his eyes to hers.

"So you were just passing by?"

He nodded, unable to break his gaze from hers.

"Is your room close?"

"Oh, it's right down the corridor. Down the stairs. Across the Great Hall. And . . . up two more flights of stairs, down another corridor and at the end of the North Tower."

She grinned and took a slight step back. "So basically it's in the same general latitude and longitude."

"I'm something of a night owl. Most everyone else is asleep, except your friend Bernard. I believe he has half the waitstaff searching for chocolate chip cookie dough ice cream at this very moment. Are you sure you aren't in need of anything?"

Miranda had the strongest feeling that Lucas Fletcher would do anything she asked of him at that moment. "I'm good."

His smile faltered and his shoulders slumped a bit. "Then goodnight, fair Miranda." He took a step from her door.

"Would you like to come in?" She blurted the invitation before she could second-guess herself.

"Yes," Lucas said, perhaps too quickly. "Thank you."

She stood to one side, allowing him to enter.

"I won't stay too long," Lucas told her. "I have a full day planned tomorrow, and I want you well rested."

"If you're a night owl, then I'm a bat." She closed the door and led him deeper into the room. "I rarely fall asleep before dawn."

Lucas followed her to a pair of loveseats that flanked the wide fireplace. She was about to sit on one of them when Lucas took her hand and steered her toward the bed. "Lie down."

She took her hand back. "Say what?"

The left corner of his mouth rose in a mysterious, sexy smile. "Trust me, Miranda." He went to the bed and turned down the duvet.

"Lucas . . ."

"Indulge me." He began blowing out the candles.

It was late, well past midnight, and the moon's pale glow softly illuminated the suite. The sheers floated on the breeze, allowing teasing glimpses of the starry sky.

"Miranda," he prompted, his low, silky voice a melodic part of the night.

Well, she thought, *I am tired. It wouldn't hurt, to just lie down. He didn't save my life only to lure me here and kill me. I hope.*

She sat on the bed, and then stuck her legs beneath the covers. She almost purred in contentment when Lucas pulled the silk top sheet and goose-down duvet up to her shoulders. The bed had the right amount of firmness and the bed sheets whispered against her skin.

She was burying her cheek in a fluffy feather pillow when a weight eased beside her onto the bed. She turned her head to see Lucas. He rested on his left side, his hand supporting his head. "Turn on your side." Miranda did so, to face him. Again, his enigmatic smile appeared, to further bend her will to his. "The other side."

She rolled over, and as she did so, he lowered the covers. Her breath caught when he slid his hand beneath her top. She took slow, deep breaths in an attempt to still her racing heart as his hand warmed the cool skin between her shoulder-blades. Her skin goose-pimpled as his hand glided over the satiny expanse of her back.

"Why is this room called the Emberley Suite?" She hoped conversation would steer her mind from wondering what Lucas's touch would feel like on other parts of her body.

"This room has an interesting history, Miranda. Centuries ago, the mad daughter of Lord Sinclair Emberley leaped from those very windows."

"That's some bedtime story," Miranda chuckled.

"It has a happy ending. The girl didn't die. Some say a straw cart broke her fall, and she was carried off and found by the very man she had previously refused to marry. He nursed her injuries, they fell in love, and they lived happily ever after in the south of Wales."

"What do others say?"

"That she wasn't mad at all, that she feigned madness so that she would be rejected by the man her father had arranged for her to marry."

"Who was her intended?"

"One of two Moorish princes who traveled to Great Britain from Southern India. His name was Laith al Kadin, and he was knighted by

King Henry V for helping the English fight the French, who called him
Le Bête Noir de Brind'Amor."

The Black Beast of Brind'Amor, Miranda translated in her head.

"He was a fierce fighter who, legend has it, led his army in a
slaughter of a French village in one of the many skirmishes between the
French and English," Lucas went on. "Laith's nickname may have been
undeserved, as his twin brother Akil was more likely to have murdered
innocent women and children."

"Typical media, muddying up the facts," Miranda said in a sleepy
mumble.

Lucas's movements were gentle and carefully measured, his hand
never breaking its light contact with her skin as it covered every square
inch between her neck and waist. A moan welled in her throat, but she
held it in. He touched her back, and only her back, yet his touch resonated through her entire body. She rolled onto her stomach and
tugged at the back of her shirt, pulling it over her head then dropping
it to the floor. Hugging her pillow, she allowed him unrestricted access
to her bare back.

A noiseless whistle seeped from Lucas's puckered lips and his hand
trembled as it hummed over her skin. He moved closer, sharing her
pillow as he rested his head in the crook of his left arm. His fingers
brushed the hair at her nape and her toes curled in response. When his
fingertips trailed along her sides, barely grazing the outer curve of her
right breast, she stifled a sigh in her pillow.

She had never known that her back was so sensitive, that a man
could start her blood simmering through hypnotic touch alone.
Thoroughly contented, she concentrated only on the sensation of his
hand on her back and the warmth of his body as it molded itself to hers
through the bedclothes. She turned her head to face him.

He found himself again wallowing in the beauty of her sleepy eyes.
Her eyelids opened and closed slowly, as she fought to stay awake.
"Sleep, Miranda." His voice was as comforting to her ears as his hand
was to her back.

A lazy smile graced her lips as her eyes drowsed shut. He nestled closer, tucking her head beneath his chin, his touch the lullaby guiding her into a world of safe and beautiful dreams.

"I feel like an invalid." Miranda stared at the full breakfast tray that had been placed over her knees. A full pitcher of freshly squeezed orange juice captured the sunlight. Steam curled lyrically from a miniature thermal pot of fragrant coffee. She lifted the silver dome from a large plate to see a generous arrangement of plump sausages, broiled tomato halves, fried potatoes, two sunny-side up eggs, three thick strips of bacon, and four triangles of medium-dark toast. Little pots of butter, strawberry preserves, orange marmalade, sugar and cream and a bouquet of yellow daisies decorated the tray.

This was a radical change from Miranda's typical breakfast, a handful of heart-friendly Cheerios eaten directly from the three-month-old box in her desk drawer at the *Herald-Star*.

She was pouring herself a cup of coffee when Bernie, rivaling the sunrise in a quilted gold satin robe, burst into the room and took a running leap at her. She lifted the tray off the bed a split second before Bernie belly-flopped onto it. "Tell, tell, Andy-Baby!" he cried gleefully.

"Tell what?" She repositioned her tray and speared a sausage with her fork.

"Easy there, sugar." Bernie empathized with the defenseless sausage. "And you know what *what*. I saw his Royal Rockness leaving your *chambre à coucher* this morning."

"Why are you speaking French?"

"That was French?"

"Lucas tucked me in last night." She took a big bite of sausage and chased it with a healthy swig of coffee.

"You look like a princess," Bernie said, "of a Mexican mining camp. Slow down, Clementina, that sausage isn't going anywhere."

"This is really good." Miranda made an effort to chew before she swallowed. "I didn't realize how hungry I was."

Bernie rolled onto his back and rested his head on her knees. "Worked up an appetite last night, huh? You had sex, didn't you?"

"No."

"Red hot monkey sex, right?"

"No."

"You'd tell me if you did, wouldn't you?"

"No."

"Yes, you would."

"Not this time. You're a reporter on this trip, not my best friend. You're the enemy."

"Anything you say in this room is off the record," Bernie offered. "How's that?"

"Okay. That's fair."

"So did he make a man out of you?"

"We talked. He told me a bedtime story. And I fell asleep." She paused. "I had a really good sleep."

"Well, I saw your man leaving not more than twenty minutes ago."

Miranda set down her cutlery. "Shut up," she said, disbelieving him. "Honestly?"

Bernie laced his fingers over his belly. "Lucas looked like he'd had a pretty good night. He had that man glow."

"What the hell is that?'"

"It's that look a man gets when he knows what—or who, in this case— he wants." Bernie sat cross-legged, facing Miranda. "Whether it's a new power tool or a car or a person, men get a shine on when they really want something. That man wants you so much, I'll bet he glows in the dark."

"He didn't do anything to give me any indication that he wanted anything other than . . . friendship." She swirled a toast point in the yolk of an egg.

"Well, your *friend* looked awfully satisfied this morning." Bernie snagged a piece of toast. He took Miranda's knife from her hand so he could help himself to the strawberry preserves.

"Haven't you eaten?" she asked.

"Twice." He nibbled the crust of his toast. "Once in my room and once down with the kitchen staff. Those kids sure know how to have a good time, even at six in the morning. They served Bubble and Squeak. It's a skillet breakfast made from cabbage, bacon, ham, onions and last night's potatoes, but if I ever write my autobiography, that's what I'll call it."

"Did you go to bed at all last night?" Miranda ate her two remaining slices of bacon at once, to save Bernie the trouble of stealing them from her.

"Of course, but a good reporter gets up when the story does. I was coming back from the Banquet Hall this morning when Lucas left your room."

"Lucas has a full day planned for us." Miranda set her tray aside and climbed out of the bed. "I'm going to shower and dress."

"Come and get me when you're done, hon." He scurried off the bed after taking another piece of toast and a sausage. "I'll be in my rooms, recording my speculations about what went on in here last night."

Miranda nodded, preoccupied with her own thoughts as Bernie left. So Lucas had stayed the night. She didn't quite know what to make of that. The eight o'clock delivery of the breakfast tray had awakened her from a very pleasant, very sound sleep. She had remembered to put her top back on before inviting the butler in, but she almost hadn't remembered that Lucas had ever been there in bed beside her. She recalled his presence and his touch as one would recall a very happy, very pleasant dream. The kind of dream you tried to recapture every night thereafter, no matter how futile the pursuit. But by their very nature, dreams weren't meant to be reclaimed, or real.

Miranda tried to force herself to remember that very important point: that this whole experience with Lucas wasn't real, no matter how genuine it all felt. She paced the bedroom, telling herself that this weekend at Conwy would ultimately be no more than a modest sentence or two in the rich history of the Emberley Suite, and a nice memory for her to muse on when she was old and gray and covering cribbage tournaments for her convalescent home newsletter.

CRUSH

She went into the dressing room and grabbed a pair of jeans and a black V-neck sweater. She carried them into the bathroom and hung them over the clothes post. The shower distracted her from thoughts of Lucas. The thing was amazing. One of its walls was one-way glass and faced the ocean, giving the bather the impression of washing right there in Conwy Bay. There were four adjustable showerheads, each positioned at a different height. "Perfect for parties," Miranda chuckled.

She started the water and undressed. As she stepped into the spray, a devilish notion crept into her head. She wondered what it would be like to bathe in the ocean with Lucas's warm hands traveling over her skin . . .

Lucas blasted the cold water in all six heads of his shower. He was tempted to start running laps through them, hoping the brisk water would finally cool the heat that had been raging in him since he'd awakened in Miranda's bed. Bracing his hands on the slate tiles, he let the cold water batter him. He hadn't meant to stay the night in her room, and certainly not in her bed. He hadn't even meant to fall asleep. He'd closed his eyes just for a moment, to better focus his attention on the satiny texture of her skin, and the next thing he'd known, he was waking up with the bright sun in his eyes and Miranda's warm backside against his groin.

Not that he had minded. He could have stayed that way until Christmas, but the longer he stayed the bigger a liar he would have appeared to be. He had given her his word that he she would be safe from untoward advances, so he'd eased away from her, careful not to awaken her. But she had rolled over onto her back, partially into the space he had vacated.

In the morning sunlight, her beauty had drugged him. He knew that he should have gotten the hell out of her room, or at the very least he should have covered her. But he'd been transfixed by the sight of her.

The sheets were wrapped around her waist and her hair was a shining tangle of sienna on the pillow. Her golden brown skin was perfectly unblemished but for a tiny, heart-shaped birthmark low on her flat abdomen. One of her graceful arms was draped over her pillow, the other rested across her middle. Lucas's eyes had traced every lyrical inch of her neck and collarbones before coming to rest on her breasts. They were small but so exquisitely formed, Lucas yearned to touch them.

Under his gaze, the plumrose peaks of her breasts pebbled invitingly. Her nude torso was a thing of perfect female beauty—strong, healthy, soft, lovely. From stage light, to candlelight, to moonlight and sunlight, Miranda had grown only more beautiful, and the sight of her had violently aroused him. Even his toes had felt erect. His head had forced his feet to get him out of the room before his heart conspired with the rest of his body to crawl back into the bed and wake her with kisses.

"Fool!" He shook his hair beneath a swirling jet of water. Bringing her to Conwy had been a huge mistake. Her visit was supposed to make him forget her, not want her that much more. He exited the shower, and it had helped, although now he was so cold and numb that he couldn't feel his fingers or toes. But his fingers and toes weren't the problem. They weren't the parts that would betray him once he saw Miranda.

A whirlwind of activity and Bernie's boisterous presence managed to keep Lucas and Miranda from having to face each other one-on-one, a situation both dreaded given their convoluted feelings regarding the night they had spent together. As they browsed in Harrods, London's famous Knightsbridge luxury department store, Lucas wondered how he had gotten into so much trouble without having even slept with a woman with whom he'd spent the night.

Miranda barely noticed her surroundings. She was acutely aware of Lucas and the handsome figure he made in his long, dark wool coat. And the way he picked up things, such as a six-foot tall teddy bear and a diamond-studded choker, to ask her if she liked them. She was scared to say yes, for fear that he would buy them for her.

She showed a spark of interest in a Manchester United sweatshirt. She fingered the cuff and collar, looked at the price tag, then moved on to a display of men's underpants. In the tail of her eye she caught the slight nod Lucas aimed at one of the Harrods personal shoppers attending them along with the store's elite security team. But when she turned to get a better look, Lucas seemed inordinately interested in a mannequin modeling purple silk pajama pants.

By the time they were ready to leave the store, Bernie had filled six giant shopping bags with ties, shirts, shoes, belts, pants, and oddest of all, a tin of digestive biscuits. At a newsstand, Miranda bought a pack of Smarties, the English equivalent to M&Ms, and she had refused to let Lucas pay the starry-eyed cashier for her.

Weary from touring dozens of departments covering seven floors of everything from designer clothes to the Bagel Factory, Miranda was more than happy when Lucas asked her if she was ready to leave.

"I was ready to leave two hours ago, but I didn't want to spoil Bernie's fun."

Lucas stopped in the middle of the wide pathway. "Bernard told us that you loved to shop."

"He's the one who likes shopping. He should have his paycheck directly deposited at Abercrombie & Fitch."

Lucas glanced at Bernie, who was still grabbing at merchandise even as they were trying to leave the store. "He certainly seems to be in his element. I bloody hate shopping myself. The last time I came here, I was barred entry because of the dress code."

"No shoes, no shirt, no service?" Miranda guessed.

"This is the one and only Harrods," Lucas said. "The Harrods dress code, and I quote, 'Does not permit any person entering the store who is wearing ripped jeans, high cut Bermuda or beach shorts, swimwear, bare midriffs, athletic singlets, cycling shorts, bare feet, flip flops or thong sandals, dirty or unkempt clothing or any extremes of personal presentation.'"

Miranda laughed. "How very English. That last bit should have kept Bernie out."

"I'm somewhat more well known now than I was the last time I came here. These days, I could walk in bum naked on my hands and I'd still be permitted to shop."

"It's good to be the king," Miranda said.

Lucas asked one of the security guards to collect Bernie while another called for Lucas's car. At the Brompton Road entrance, Miranda couldn't see daylight through the glass doors. The scene before her was a hundred times worse than the one she'd suffered through at the *Herald-Star*. A full phalanx of English "Bobbies," standing with linked arms behind a barricade of portable steel fencing, held back a writhing mass of humanity that looked capable of swallowing Lucas's limousine. Autograph books flapped on the ends of arms jutting from the crowd. Though she was still safe in the quiet store, Miranda didn't resist when Lucas practically pulled her into the security of his coat.

"Perhaps we should utilize a more discreet exit, sir," offered the head of security in his very proper, very cool English. "We're well able to handle the safe arrival and departure of our more well known guests. Your shopping experience has been quite pleasant, up until now, may I presume?"

Miranda peeked out from Lucas's embrace. It was a Sunday afternoon, but the store was eerily deserted. She looked around more carefully and saw store guards at the doors and at various escalators. Now that she thought about it, each floor they had visited had been markedly empty, but for sales personnel who had been friendly, but not at all pushy. She had chalked that up to the nature of the English, rather than something she herself had been taught as a reporter: Don't go nuts over celebrities.

She now realized that the store had expected Lucas's visit and had prepared for it accordingly. The staff had probably been forewarned to be on its best behavior, and each floor had been cleared to allow Lucas to browse in peace.

All that trouble, Miranda thought, *and the only thing we bought was a bag of M&Ms with an English accent.*

"Sir," the security chief said, "I really must ask you to reconsider going out there."

"We have to," Lucas said pensively. He took Miranda by her shoulders. "Your newspaper and my label wanted photographs, and I refused to allow either party at Conwy. My publicist arranged to have some of our more friendly paparazzi here to shoot us, but apparently word of our presence has spread. Are you up to going out there? I leave it to you, Miranda."

She looked at the crowd, and the waiting limo that seemed small and vulnerable within it. The driver and two bodyguards stood ready to spring into action the instant she and Lucas hit the sidewalk. The limo was so close, really. And the photographs were a necessity. "I can do it."

"There you go, love." Lucas proudly kissed her forehead and turned to the security chief. "We're ready."

Reeling somewhat from his offhand kiss and his use of the word 'love,' Miranda tightly held his hand as the store security team closed in around them. They headed for the door.

"No!" Bernie protested as he was practically carried out ahead of them. "I never got to go to the music section!"

Bernie stilled when the doors flung open and the roar of the excited crowd washed over him. He shrank into a ball, clutching his bags for dear life, and let Harrods' security pitch him into the limo. Lucas hurried Miranda to the car, keeping his head bowed but pausing just long enough to allow a decent photograph.

"Sir Lucas!" his fans screamed. "Sir Lucas!"

Only when the crowd noise was a dull growl on the other side of the bulletproof vehicle did Miranda dare open her eyes.

Lucas poured her a glass of water. "I assumed that you would be used to crowds and the hoopla surrounding a celebrity. You are a reporter, after all."

"That's just it." Her hands shook, dripping water onto her lap. "I'm usually on the other side of the action. I don't think I'd like being famous."

Lucas helped steady her hands as the limo pulled into traffic and headed for a police heliport, where they would take a chopper back to Conwy. "I'm afraid you already are, love."

"That makes two." From the other side of the limo, Bernie rifled through his bags, making sure that he hadn't lost or forgotten anything.

"Two what?" Miranda asked.

"Two 'loves.'" Bernie withdrew one of his new ties and laid it over his hand. "This looked great on me in the store but now it looks sallow. Oh, well." He tossed the tie back in its slim box. "I'll give it to Rex. Sallow is his color. So what's up with the 'loves,' Lucas?"

"You reporters don't miss a thing, do you?" Lucas rarely blushed, but he felt one fighting from under the collar of his sweater. "I was wondering when you'd show your stripes."

"Answer the question," Bernie said. "If you don't mind."

"'Love' is just . . ." Lucas looked at Miranda as he pondered an answer. She had removed the black elastic ponytail holder from her hair and now wore it on her left wrist. She used her left hand to comb her hair from her face, and as it cascaded past her shoulders, she turned and looked at him. She wore no makeup. Her expression seemed troubled, yet her simple beauty was stunning. She was funny and smart, and touching him with nothing but her trust and intellect, she had made him feel like more of a man than any woman ever had. All at once, he knew that the woman sitting beside him was someone he could . . . "'Love,'" Lucas began again, "is just an expression. Like 'duck' or 'egg.'"

"It's an expression of affection, though, right?" Bernie persisted.

"Yes."

Bernie sat back, letting Lucas off the hook. "I like 'love'. I'm more of a 'duck' man, truth be told, but love is nice, too."

CRUSH

Love wasn't just an expression of affection. For Miranda, it was also a curse, and the very thing she wanted to avoid. As a reporter, she had learned to read people, particularly those who didn't wish to have their true feelings or thoughts known. Lucas had explained his use of the word love, but Miranda had sensed more meaning behind it.

The chopper ride back to Conwy had seemed too quick. Miranda had focused on the scenery beneath them, and listened as Lucas had pointed out key landmarks and sites. But every time she had looked up at him, he had been looking at her, not at what he was describing.

The helicopter had delivered her and Bernie to the Welsh airstrip where their bags awaited them on the jet that would take them back to Boston. As much as she had dreaded the big date, Miranda scarcely believed that in eight hours or so, she would be right back at the *Herald-Star*. And Lucas Fletcher would be out of her life forever.

He accompanied them to the plane. "I'd fly back with you, but I have to meet the band in Tokyo for the second leg of our tour. Our schedule is fairly tight, and I'm afraid I can't deviate from it." He rested his hands on her shoulders. "I'm not ready to say goodbye to you, Miranda."

She stared at the asphalt. If she looked into his eyes for one second longer, she would never be able to get on the plane. Most men had a way of cloaking their feelings, either by avoiding eye contact or by lying outright. Lucas's eyes hid nothing. His emotions were naked and honest and, for Miranda, overwhelming.

"Did you have a good visit?" he asked.

She finally lifted her face. "I had the best sleep of my life."

"I hope that wasn't the highlight," Lucas remarked. The sky was overcast, as it often was in the north of Wales, and the absence of sun left the air chilled. Lucas didn't mind the grey sky or the cold, not with the bright shine of Miranda's magical eyes on him.

She smiled, unwittingly giving herself a firmer hold on Lucas's heart. "It wasn't." Having Fenway Franks in a seven-hundred-year-old kitchen had been nice. Knowing that he'd slept with her—without *sleeping* with her—had been really nice. But the best had been sitting in his arms beneath the full moon and having him genuinely listen to the secret contents of her heart. "I had a very nice weekend," she said. "The commute stinks, but other than that . . . it was perfect."

"Do you think Mr. Reilly had a good time?"

Miranda nodded toward the limo. The driver and one of the flight attendants were trying to pry Bernie's fingers from the frame of the door. "I think he wants to stay."

"Conwy could use a good music reviewer. And a sports writer."

"The perfect gifts for the man who has everyone," Miranda joked somberly. "*Thing!*" she blurted. "I meant—"

The backs of his fingers tickled over her temple as he brushed a windblown tress from her face. "I know what you meant."

She wanted to kick herself for ruining their farewell with a lousy Freudian slip, and there was nothing she could do now but to end it quickly. She held out her hand. "I had a great time. Thank you. And thank you for helping me at the concert. For saving my life."

He took her hand in both of his and gave it a warm squeeze. "It was my pleasure, Mir—" was all he got out before she tossed an arm around his neck and drew him in for a kiss. He jumped on her lead, deepening the kiss as he wrapped his arms around her and brought her into his coat. Her hands moved through his hair, luxuriating in its softness while she savored the heat and taste of his mouth. Her fingertips played over the lean planes of his face, memorizing the feel of him, and she let herself go lightheaded rather than break their kiss to breathe.

Go, the sensible part of her brain told her, but her heart was too busy with its gymnastics routine to listen.

Go, girl! her brain insisted, even as her hips pressed more firmly into Lucas.

Jordan, her brain sang matter-of-factly. The name was like a bucket of ice water, and Miranda abruptly backed away from Lucas, leaving him bewildered and panting.

"You changed your mind about kissing me," he gasped. Her kisses had stolen all but the obvious.

"What harm can it do?" She touched her lips, which were ripe from his kisses. "I'll never see you again. Goodbye, Lucas." She turned and fled up the portable staircase that had been parked alongside the plane.

"You're wrong about that, love," he whispered as she vanished inside the plane.

CHAPTER 5

Miranda stared at her sister from across the table. Calista Penney lived up to the meaning of her name, "most beautiful." Like their mother, she was *negro branca*, and her long, thick hair was more curly than wavy. Her black eyes, another gift from their mother, crackled with vitality. Calista had a lush bosom, full, rounded hips and a small waist; basically the body of Salma Hayek and the brain of a financial planner, which she was.

She tried not to, but Miranda envied the way her younger sister moved even while performing the mundane task of laying out refreshments. Calista had all the fire and feistiness of their mother's roots in Bahia, Brazil. She oozed passion and vitality, everything intoxicating about being Latina. From her soft, floral perfume to the way her hair floated on the slightest breeze, Calista always seemed to be dancing to some secret rhythm only she could hear. Unlike Miranda, who'd inherited her father's eyes, mouth and lanky, angular build. There was no inner music when Miranda moved. She was more like a broken marionette than the Queen of Carnivale.

Miranda turned her attention to her sister's labors. Calista had layered the white, wrought-iron table with all the tabloids, newspapers and magazines that had run cover stories on Lucas Fletcher and his "crush," Miranda Penney. The papers and periodicals covered the five-week span since Miranda's weekend in Wales, but each story had basically the same photos, the shots of her and Lucas in London exiting Harrods, in varying degrees of clarity.

"Lucas was very cool about the photographs," Miranda said. "His people did a good job of keeping our plans private. The only paparazzi we ran into were at Harrods."

"I read Bernie's article about the date online." Calista set out a plate of freshly baked *biscoitos de maizenas,* the Brazilian cornstarch butter cookies Miranda loved. "He did a really good job of conveying the romance of the date without over sentimentalizing it."

"I didn't realize that he'd noticed so much." Miranda stuffed a cookie into her mouth, her jaw jutting out as she tried to chew and talk at the same time. Calista daintily handed her big sister a paper napkin with lacy embossing on the edges. "Bernie was all about Bernie over there. He's a crackerjack writer, though. I'll give him that."

Calista wore beige cotton twill Capri pants, a burnt-orange twin set and a pair of jute-colored espadrilles. The garden boxes in her enclosed back deck overflowed with mums in russet, butterscotch, goldenrod and rust. Against the riot of rich fall colors, Calista looked like a junior version of their mother. "So tell me what really happened in Wales," she said.

Miranda didn't answer right away, although she stopped chewing her second cookie. Her eyes fixed on one of the magazine covers, and she could almost feel Lucas's arm around her, steeling her to face a crazed mob of Karmic Echo fans.

"You're thinking about him, aren't you?" Calista said.

"Who?"

"Lucas Fletcher."

Miranda snorted and finished her cookie. Calista patiently leafed through a magazine. "How could you tell?" Miranda finally said, rolling her eyes.

"You get a gooey look on your face when you hear his name."

"I do not."

"Lucas Fletcher." Calista abruptly leaned forward and pointed at her sister's face. "That's it. That's the look."

"I came all the way down to Silver Springs to help you choose the menu for your big Penney-Henderson engagement dinner, not to talk about Lucas What's-His-Butt." Miranda wiped her hands on the leg of her jeans before she gathered the publications from the table and set them in Calista's recycling bin. She went into the spotless kitchen, retrieved a pile of menus from the counter beneath the wall phone, and thumped them down in the middle of the deck table.

"Okay," Calista said matter-of-factly. "I can keep this up as long as you can."

"Keep what up?" Miranda groaned.

"Not talking about your date with Lucas." Calista opened a bridal magazine that was as thick as the Baltimore phone directory. "According to *Psst!*, you and Lucas were secretly married on a private beach in a moonlit ceremony in Northern Wales. The bride wore overalls, I assume?"

"Shows how unreliable their informants are." Miranda flipped through the pages of a magazine. She was halfway through it before she noticed that it was one of Alec's baseball weeklies, and not a bridal magazine. "I'm still very single."

"But there was moonlight?"

"There was a moon."

"And there was a private beach?"

"Yeah. So?"

Calista marked her place with a pink Post-It and clapped the magazine shut. "Moonlight. Private beach. Lucas Fletcher. You! That sounds like a recipe for romance to me."

"I suppose."

"You kept him at a distance, didn't you?" Calista asked knowingly.

"He was a perfect gentleman. I didn't have to hold him off."

"I don't mean physically."

Miranda feigned interest in a story about the latest Japanese pitching sensation. She knew what her sister meant. "Don't you ever have doubts? That maybe getting married is the worst thing you can do?"

"I love Alec," Calista said, her expression, to use her word, gooey. "He loves me. When he proposed to me, I felt complete. I knew he was the one for me the first time we met."

Miranda pushed her magazine aside. She had been covering the baseball game that night eighteen months ago in New York, when star right-fielder Alec Henderson had proposed to Calista. Right there on the mound during the seventh-inning stretch, he had asked Calista to be his wife. Jordan Duquette, Alec's teammate and best friend, had handed him the ring and had lead the audience in the applause once Calista had accepted. Jordan had never been more of a phony than in that moment—applauding his friend's commitment knowing that he himself was a devout two-timer.

Miranda rested her elbow on the table and played with her gold stud earring. "Didn't that scare you, knowing from the start that Alec was someone you could fall in love with?"

"Now I know for sure that you really like Lucas."

"Who?" Miranda raised her guard just as quickly as she had lowered it.

"You know who. The man you seem to have fallen for."

"It's not worth talking about. It would never work out between us."

"Because he's famous, like Jordan, or because you think he's *like* Jordan?"

Miranda avoided looking her sister in the face. "This has nothing to do with Jordan."

"You're right, it doesn't. It has to do with you and your inability to trust."

"I trust you," Miranda fired. "I trust Bernie."

"Not every guy you meet is like Jordan. Just because Lucas is famous, it doesn't mean that—"

"Fame just gives men more opportunities to be cockasses."

Calista gave her sister a glassy smile. "Of all the foul words you've picked up in that sports department, that one has to be the blue-ribbon prizewinner."

"Sorry," Miranda sulked.

"Every man you meet isn't like Dad, Miranda."

Calista's soft, measured tone didn't soften the impact of her words. "Wh-What do you mean?" Miranda stammered.

Calista smiled sadly. "I think you know, Andy. You grew up in that house, too."

"You know about dad's affairs?"

Calista nodded and opened her magazine again. "I caught him in the equipment shed with our softball coach when I was fifteen. It was the day you hit that three-run homer and won us the state championship. Up until then, I thought Dad had gone to all of our games because he liked seeing us play."

"He did." Miranda's stomach turned. "He was proud of us. He called you Rocket, because of your pitching, and he called me Slugger, because I could hit. Damn it, Callie, he was cheating with Coach Kiley, and you knew about it? You've known all this time that Dad was an adulterer? I only found out a few years ago."

"I'm sorry, Andy." Calista went to her sister's side of the table and hugged her. "I thought you knew, too."

Bile bubbled to the back of Miranda's throat. "How could I have known? I was too busy thinking that I had the perfect father. He sure made an idiot of me. How could he love us, and take such pride in us, yet regularly betray Mom?"

Calista stepped into the kitchen to get Miranda a cup of coffee. "Is that why you stopped coming home for holidays?"

"I work on holidays. Usually. Thanksgiving is a big day for high school football in Massachusetts. I always volunteer to work so one of the guys with a wife and kids can spend the holiday with his family."

"You have family, too, Miranda. You could have come home for Thanksgiving last week. You haven't been home for Christmas in seven years. Mom said you stopped coming home because you two had a fight."

"It wasn't a fight." *At least I don't remember it that way,* Miranda thought. "I told Mom that she should think about leaving Dad."

"She won't. She's . . . stuck, or something." Calista set a steaming mug before Miranda, then sat back down. "She misses you. She says she misses us being a family."

Miranda laughed bitterly. "Like we were ever a real family."

"Come on, Andy, be fair."

"It was a lie, Callie. On the surface, it was flawless, but underneath it was totally rotten and fake."

"I don't remember it as being bad. Dad's cheating didn't affect us."

"It affected me!" Miranda slapped her hands flat on the table and vaulted to her feet. "He does it over and over again, and Mom *allows* it. She goes on as if what he does is acceptable."

"I found out about Dad when I was a kid, so maybe I've had enough time to come to terms with it. You were an adult, so maybe that's why it's so hard for you take. Did you really think that Dad was perfect?"

"Infidelity is one hell of a flaw, Callie! I never thought that anyone I loved so much could hurt and humiliate me so deeply."

"Is this about Dad or Jordan?"

"It's about me," Miranda said. "And how stupid I am to trust men who claim to love me."

"Not every man will hurt you, Andy. There are some good ones out there."

"Oh really?" Miranda challenged. "Bernie can't find a good man, and he works at it full time."

"Speaking of Bernie, I thought he wanted to come down and help us pick out wedding favors."

"He's still reaping the rewards of his big cover story on my weekend in Wales. He got sent to the European Music Awards in Madrid. I've been assigned to high school wrestling for the foreseeable future as punishment for taking Bernie instead of Meg with me. It seems that every man involved in that date got something out of it. Me, I get the short end. I'm a carpet, just like Mom."

A fine furrow appeared between Calista's elegant eyebrows. "She wanted to keep her family together. She handles her life the only way she can."

"What about you? How will you handle it when Alec cheats on you four months into your marriage? Why don't the two of you just live together for a while before Alec pushes you over the broom?"

"I want to marry Alec," Calista said. "I want to be his wife."

"Se o casamento fosse bom, não precisava de testemunhas," Miranda muttered. *And I agree*, she thought to herself: *if marriage were a good thing, it wouldn't need witnesses.*

"*Avó* Marie Estrella was married five times and she never got it right," Calista fired back. "Of course she would think that. And quit quoting *Avó* Marie Estrella like she wrote one of the gospels."

"From April to September, Alec is in a different city every week," Miranda persisted. "You don't know what he's doing or who he's doing it to. He's just like—"

"Dad?" Calista cut in. "Jordan? Alec isn't like them, Andy. I look like Mom, but I'm no more like her than you are. Stop trying to scare me just because you're scared."

Miranda tucked her fists under her arms and retreated to a corner of the screened deck. "Why does everyone keep accusing me of being scared?"

"Because you are. You're scared to fall in love, especially with Lucas Fletcher."

Miranda listened to the whisper of Calista's turning pages and the random twitters of a family of sparrows living in the yews in the backyard. Miranda had always thought herself the bumbling Oscar Madison to her sister's well-appointed Felix Unger. Despite their differences in personality, appearance, style and temperament, they had always understood each other. Miranda returned to the table, surprised that Calista knew her better than she had realized. "It's been a month and he hasn't tried to get in touch with me," she said after a pensive silence.

"He's on the road," Calista said. "According those magazines, when he left Wales he had to play thirty-five shows in twenty-one cities in forty-two days. That's got to be exhausting."

Miranda drummed her fingertips on the tabletop. "He had his publicist call the paper when he wanted to reach me before."

"He's coming back to Boston to make up the show they had to postpone because of the crush," Calista said. "He'll get in touch."

Calista had voiced Miranda's fondest hope. "You sound so sure that he will," Miranda said.

"I know he will."

"How can you be sure?"

"Because he'd be a total cockass not to."

Miranda chuckled. Her sister's faith was formidable, and the right medicine to soothe her anxious soul. Miranda sat down beside her and shared her magazine. "That's a nice dress." She pointed to a straight, floor-length gown made of ivory silk with white embroidering on the skirt.

"I don't have the figure for that one," Calista said. "I have too much bust and hips. This dress would look good on you, though."

Miranda mustered a weak smile. "Me getting married . . . I can't even picture it."

"I can." Calista touched her forehead to her sister's as she hugged her. "The bride will wear Patriots blue and Bernie will be your maniac-of-honor."

"What's up, baby?"

Miranda, who had been poised to unlock the door to her apartment, whirled around. Startled by the deep voice issuing from the dark recesses of the corridor, she struck a fight pose, her right fist drawn and ready to fracture the windpipe of the tall, broad and shadowy figure approaching her.

"I'm unarmed," the figure said with a snicker as he raised his hands halfway in surrender.

Miranda, still poised to attack, dropped her guard only slightly when her night visitor's face came into view. "What do you want, Jordan?"

Jordan Duquette had an excellent mouth, and it pulled into the devilish smile that most women found irresistible. The smile that had won Miranda over on their first meeting now reminded her of Sylvester the Cat's smug expression in the brief moments when he had a live Tweety Bird in his chops.

"I wanted to see you." Jordan stuck his hands in the pockets of his team bomber jacket. "It's been a long time. Too long."

"Six months isn't a long time." Miranda unlocked her door and shouldered her way into her apartment. "In fact, I don't think it's long enough."

Jordan tried to follow her but Miranda blocked his way. "Come on, Andy. You can't still be mad."

He flashed the smile again, this time with a tilt of his head to showcase his dimples. Miranda swung her knapsack at him. The blow bounced off his thickly muscled chest. "I haven't heard from you since I found out that you were 'done' with me by having Meg's trashy column shoved under my nose at work! Do you have any idea how humiliating it was to walk into the newsroom after that? Especially after every move *you* ever made was chronicled in that damn column?"

Miranda could almost hear the rusty cogs of Jordan's brain working beneath his salon-coiffed Afro. "So you're still mad," he finally said.

She tried to slam the door. When he shoved his foot in the gap, she slammed it even harder. "Stop being so theatrical, Miranda. You're acting like we were married or something."

"Go away, Jordan, before my neighbors call the police."

"I'll comp the cops to a few home games and they'll let me camp out here all night, if I want to. I just want to talk to you. You don't have five minutes for an old squeeze?"

She scowled in annoyance and anger. Even knowing how stupid it was for her to do so, she opened her door. "Three minutes."

He moved through her apartment with familiar comfort after taking off his jacket and carelessly slinging it onto her small dining table. He went straight to the fridge, which had been his habit, and grabbed a beer before zeroing in on her worn slouch sofa and grabbing the television remote. He turned on the television, and like a big lazy dog, he paced in front of his spot before he sat down. The television was already tuned to ESPN, so Jordan set down the remote, propped his beer upon his belly, and put his feet up on the cocktail table.

The sight was as familiar and welcome as a scene from a recurring nightmare. Jordan's big, muscular body, dressed in its usual off-field costume of khakis and white button-down shirt, dominated the living room section of her apartment. It had been months since his last visit, but he easily settled into his favorite spot with her favorite beer and her favorite television program. Six months ago, she would have been in the comfy depression beside him. But that was in another time, when ignorance had granted her what passed for happiness.

"Don't get too comfortable," she said. "Tick, tock."

"I came all the way over here from the ballpark after my exhibition game for a reason, Miranda." He switched stations to watch scrambled porn.

"You mean a reason other than to annoy me?" She set her knapsack on the counter that divided the kitchen from the living and dining room areas. "Spit it out."

He tipped his head sideways and squinted as he tried to make out the pornographic images. "How was your date with the rock star?"

"Pick up a *Herald-Star* on your way home and find out. They re-ran Bernie's article in today's paper, to correspond with Karmic Echo's return engagement in Boston tomorrow night."

"I want to hear the story from you. Alec says you didn't give anything up to Calista." When she didn't answer, Jordan pressed further. "Did you give anything up to Lucas Fletcher?"

"That's none of your business."

He turned off the television and joined her in her tiny kitchen. "It's my business because I care about you."

"Then why didn't you call me or come see me when I was in the hospital?" she snapped. "The only reason you're here is because you saw my name in all those newspapers and magazines and yours wasn't attached to it!" She stormed out of the kitchen, kicking off her sneakers and untucking her white shirt as she went. "You can't stand the fact that my involvement with Lucas Fletcher scores bigger headlines than your name ever did."

"Look, I wanted to see you because, honestly, I've missed you."

She wanted to hit him with something, but she had nothing large enough within reach. His ego would have to do. "You're here because someone who's more famous, more rich, and more popular than you showed a slight interest in me."

Jordan stayed close on her heels. "I know I made some mistakes while we were together, but I'm willing to make it all up to you, if you'll give me a chance."

She sank into her sofa, tired in body and mind, and she just wanted to go to bed. "It is so predictably and so typically you to think that you can say all the right things and I'll just let you back into my life as though you hadn't hurt me so badly that I couldn't breathe without pain for two weeks. You never even apologized! If you didn't want to see me anymore, Jordan, I could've dealt with that, but you let a gossip column do your dirty work for you. I've already given you all the chances I have in me."

"Alec said that he saw you at Calista's last weekend." He sat on the end of the sofa. "He said you never looked better. I couldn't wait to see you. That's why I hit two homers tonight, to make sure the game didn't go into extra innings. I waited outside this building for you for two hours. I had to promise the building manager tickets to a game next season just so he'd let me in."

Miranda made a mental note to have a word with her building manager.

"You're the perfect girl for me, Miranda. You've got legs from here to Canada, a really nice face and you know everything about sports, even the dumb ones."

She was not moved. "Well, with all that going for me, why'd I bother with four years of college?" She picked up the remote and changed the station to *Lifetime*, just for spite.

"You have a good sense of humor, too," Jordan added.

"So do you, if you think I'm interested in seeing you again."

"Things wouldn't be the same, Miranda."

She was sure that this was his way of saying that he'd be more discreet about his dalliances. He met her skeptical gaze, and for a fleeting moment, she saw him as she had when they first started dating. He was handsome, there was no denying that. The amber eyes dancing against his velvety brown skin could be so kind, when he wanted them to be. His nose had been broken once, but it added a manly ruggedness to features that might have otherwise been a bit too pretty. Jordan commanded attention when he entered a room with his easy grace and charm. He was as powerful and handsome as a mythical god. Too bad he was as monogamous as a Boston tomcat.

"Was it all bad?" he asked.

"That's not fair." She rested her elbows on her knees and buried her face in her hands. "You know it wasn't. You had your moments."

"*We* had our moments. You haven't forgotten the weekend we spent in St. Kitts, have you?"

She had, actually, until he'd mentioned it. "That was fun. It was nice." She deliberately understated how much fun that weekend had been. They had been dating for five months when Jordan surprised her with the trip. He had been attentive and caring, and just when she'd thought things couldn't get better, he'd arranged to have a hot air balloon ride over the island. On the day they had returned to Boston, Jordan's road exploits began appearing in *Psst!* Miranda hadn't believed the stories at first. A true journalist never put too much stock in unattributed reports.

It was Jordan himself who had given credence to the gossip.

Miranda had been in St. Louis covering one of Jordan's interleague games against the Cardinals. She had gone to the team's hotel to surprise him with a piping hot deep-dish pizza and a cold six-pack of beer. Jordan always registered under a false name to avoid the hordes of "baseball Bambis" that hunted him down in every city. When "Oliver Closhoff" tossed open his door and stood there, wearing skin-tight sports briefs, a smile, and acres of rippling chocolate muscles, Miranda had thought his sexy outfit was meant for her.

He had grunted her name in surprise as she moved past him and into the suite . . . where a pair of blonde baseball Bambis in various degrees of undress lounged on his emperor-sized bed.

"You've got the wrong room, lady," the green-eyed blonde with the dramatic overbite had said. "We ordered us up some lobster and champagne, not a pie and suds."

"You're right," Miranda had said, glaring coldly at Jordan. "I definitely have the wrong room."

"Give her a nice tip anyway, Jordan," a blue-eyed blonde with gigantic breasts had generously advised.

"Quiet, Kit," Jordan had growled.

"I'm Linda," the blue-eyed blonde had corrected as the green-eyed one whined, "*I'm* Kit."

Jordan had glanced over his shoulder and said, "Whoever you are, shut up."

Miranda had sped from the room, and she'd thrown the hot pizza at Jordan when he attempted to stop her at the door. He had bellowed her name as she hurried down the corridor and toward the elevators, but Jordan hadn't bothered to pursue her. Before her flight had landed back in Boston, Meg and Dee had broken the story in *Psst!*—complete with a quote from Jordan stating that he "was pretty much done with Miranda anyway."

As she sat in her living room, listening to Jordan plead for another chance, she wished she had another hot pizza to throw at him.

"'I'm so excited!'" Bernie sang. "'And I just can't hide it!'" He grabbed Miranda and shook her. She sluggishly wobbled back and forth. "Tonight's the night, butterbean! Our Lucas is coming for us tonight!"

Miranda stood in the men's room off the second-floor corridor, where Bernie had dragged her to enlist her help in choosing the perfect outfit for Karmic Echo's make-up concert. She found it impossible to work up any enthusiasm. The concert was in less than four hours, and Lucas was surely in Boston already, yet he still hadn't contacted her.

She had regretted her last words to him more and more as his return to Boston had drawn nearer. She'd made it perfectly clear that she hadn't intended to ever see him again. Perhaps that's why he'd kept his distance.

"Miranda!"

"Huh?" She snapped to attention. "What did you say?"

"I've been calling you for five minutes. What's the matter with— you're not dwelling on your midnight visit from Jordan, are you?"

"Goodness no. I was thinking about . . . well . . ."

Bernie stood in front of the mirror. He took off his blue silk tie and put on a debonair, black-on-black paisley, both of which he'd purchased at Harrods. "Use your words, honey, I can't read that perplexing little mind of yours."

"I was hoping that Lucas would have called me. Or sent a postcard. Or something."

Bernie slowly turned to face her. "You're acting like a girl. This is scaring me."

"Forget I said anything. It's stupid. It's pointless. He's probably already forgotten about me."

Bernie turned and leaned heavily on the edge of one of the basins lining the wall. "Good grief, Peppermint Patty. How long has this been going on?"

"Since we left Wales." She covered her face in shame with the overlong sleeves of her Boston Breakers shirt.

Bernie went to her and put an arm around her. Sort of. He didn't get too close for fear of wrinkling his black shirt. "Baby didn't stand a chance. Sir Lucas fought the dragon and won your damaged little heart."

Miranda flung her arms into the air. "Will you please explain to me why people call him *Sir* Lucas? Is it some kind of nickname?"

"Lucas was knighted a few years ago for his work with the International Children's Rescue Fund and the Cancer Research Society of Great Britain." Bernie started a stream of water and wet his hands before patting down his neat afro. "I told you that he was a knight when I prepped you for your date."

Miranda slumped against the dingy mustard tile of the wall. "I thought you were feeding me another fairy tale metaphor. Man, I thought Jordan was a mistake, but this . . . I've outdone myself. How can I be so stupid?"

"I don't like this ride, chile, and I'm getting off. Let me know when you want to talk sense instead of self pity."

"He's a knight, Bernie." Miranda grew more dejected with each passing second. "He lives in a castle. *Meu Deus,* he even shops in a building that looks like one!"

"Harrods," Bernie said in a mock English accent as he spritzed his hair with a citrus conditioning spray. "You gotta love a mall with turrets."

Miranda slid to the floor. "For six weeks, all I've been able to think about is a man with whom I have absolutely zero chance of a future. All this time, I've been nursing the secret hope that he'll ride in and sweep me off my feet. I bought into the fairy tale when I, of all people, should know that there are no happy endings. There are just endings."

Bernie tore himself from the mirror to see her sitting on the floor in a miserable heap of knees and oversized sweatshirt. "Honey, you have reached a whole new level of nastiness. I won't pee in here, let alone sit on the floor." Using the very tips of his fingers, he helped her stand.

"I'm serious, Bernie. I'm really unhappy."

"I don't know what to tell you," he said. "Yes, I do. First of all, you're always unhappy." He held up a finger when she started to protest. "Yes, Miranda, you are. I didn't notice it until we were in Wales. Happiness made you beautiful. That was the first time I'd ever seen you truly happy, and now I finally have a basis for comparison. Second of all, I think you should go home. Right now. And don't give Lucas Fletcher another thought."

He may as well have told her to go home and practice biting the back of her own neck.

"Do as I say," he commanded. "If you love something, set it free. If it comes back to you, it was always yours."

"I swear, Bernie, if I had any other friends, I'd cut you loose so fast. Was that supposed to be at all helpful?"

He gave her a genuine hug. "It's written on the wall over there. I was just reading it out loud." He gripped her shoulders and spoke directly to her. "Go home. If you need me, you can always page me at the concert."

"Could I go to the concert with you?"

"Either you're beginning to stink of desperation, peanut, or someone forgot to flush one of these toilets."

"I know!" she grimaced. "And it's so embarrassing."

"Go home," Bernie said very precisely. "Take a shower. Read a book. Count the number of angels that can dance on the head of a pin. It's Saturday night and I can't babysit you any longer because I have to get to the Arena. *Your* knight awaits!"

Even though Miranda lived only two miles from the *Herald-Star*, it had taken her almost an hour to get home. She had spent most of the time sitting behind the wheel of her car, stuck on Massachusetts Avenue in Boston's evening rush-hour congestion. Ordinarily, her horn would have joined the broken symphony coming from the other cars, but she couldn't work up the heart to honk at anyone, not even the pierced and tattooed teenaged skateboarder that had darted into the street from between two parked cars.

Two blocks from her apartment, she had stopped at Mama Brown's Sandwich Shop on Columbus Avenue to get a cubano for dinner, and she had forgotten to put a quarter in her parking meter. She hadn't batted an eye when she'd left the shop to find a neon-orange ticket under the wiper blade of her Toyota. Boston's meter people were the human equivalent to the Ebola virus: they struck fast and hard and there was nothing you could do once you were tagged.

A stranger's car illegally occupied her assigned spot behind her apartment building, leaving her to park a bit too close to a fire hydrant four blocks away, but she didn't cuss or complain. Her sandwich tucked under her arm like a rugby ball, she had stepped in gum as she had walked home, telling herself that she would feel better after the concert, once Lucas had performed and left town again. She wouldn't miss him any less, but she wouldn't feel quite so neglected once he was in a different time zone.

She took a shower, which didn't help her mood, and then dimmed her lights and put on some music. It only reminded her of Lucas, even though she was listening to Al Green and not the type of music Karmic Echo played. She lay on the sofa, her forearm covering her face. "I can't go on like this," she said. "I'm acting like an infatuated seventh-grader. And I never acted this way even when I *was* a seventh-grader."

What am I gonna do?

The answer that came to her was as obvious as it was simple. "I could call *him*, damn it."

She sat up. That was it. All she had to do was call the Arena and ask for Lucas's manager. The man might give her a song and dance about Lucas being too busy to talk to her, but at least she'd know once and for all where she stood.

Her door buzzer sounded just as she started for the wall phone in the kitchen. Bernie had his own key and no one else ever visited, so that meant her uninvited guest was probably the very person she didn't want to see.

"Jordan!" she hissed through gritted teeth, wondering what part of "Don't ever bother me again" he'd failed to comprehend during their short goodbye the previous night. She ignored the buzzer and went for the phone. She searched through her work address book, looking for the business card Kenneth Morgan had given her at Conwy. It was as good a place as any to start and might actually have a useful phone number on it.

Her visitor leaned on the buzzer. The noise was maddening, but at least the building manager had heeded her warning to never let anyone into the building on her behalf. The persistent buzz eventually stopped and Miranda assumed Jordan had finally given up, until she heard footsteps tromping up the fire escape outside her open living room window. She ran to the front closet and grabbed her emergency defense system—a Louisville slugger. Pressing herself to the wall by the window, she was ready to knock her intruder out of the ballpark.

"Miranda?"

Her whole body went weak at the sound of the voice she had heard only in her dreams for the past month and a half. "Lucas?" She dropped the bat and opened the window wider, and Lucas climbed into her living room with the easy grace of a shadow. For a moment he stood there, looking at her. She wore a silky black shirt that was two sizes too big and unbuttoned to the middle of her chest. Black, man's-style sports briefs revealed the sensuous lengths of her elegantly muscled legs and the supple rounds of her backside. She looked more delicious than she had in any of the memories he'd conjured during their time apart.

Miranda smiled for what felt like the first time in years.

"I called your paper but I was told that you'd gone for the day." He framed her face in his hands. "Your home number is unlisted, or I would have called first. I had to come by. I had to see you."

"I can't believe you're here." She clasped his wrists, squeezing them warmly.

He took her hands and pressed his lips to their backs. He was touched by the tremble in them. "Are you disappointed?"

Smiling, she shook her head. "Surprised. Not disappointed."

"I have missed you so, Miranda," he said, grossly understating his feelings. Her parting kiss in Wales had bewitched and bedeviled him, and had replayed so many times in his mind, he had worn holes in the memory. Throwing himself fully into the Asian leg of the tour was the only way he'd been able to give himself any peace.

"You could have called me." She cringed. That was the thing she'd least wanted to say to him.

"If I'd heard your voice, I would have dropped everything and come to you on the Concorde," he said. "Karmic Echo would have been sued for millions, my mates would have strung me up with my own guitar strings and the world would have known that I'd gone ziggy for a woman I'd only just met." The backs of his fingers tickled over her cheeks, and the innocent gesture sparked a meltdown deep within Miranda's lower abdomen. "I could wait for you because I knew you were worth waiting for. You missed me?" Lucas dared to hope.

Never one to easily share her feelings in words, Miranda jumped into his arms, wrapped her legs about his waist, and kissed him, burying her fingers in his hair and tasting the night air on his lips. He supported her weight with one arm, and cradled the back of her head with his free hand. Her lips parted and coaxed him into deepening the kiss, and she felt him rise between her legs.

"Good," he said in a husky voice between kissing her throat and suckling her earlobe. "I was hoping we could pick up where we left off."

"I was just worried," she said on a heavy breath as she set her feet back on the floor.

"About what?"

"About not seeing you again. And about seeing you again. How did you get here without causing a riot?"

"I rode a bike over from the Arena." He pointed to the Harley-Davidson motorcycle parked below her window. "I hid in plain sight, as it were. Just another guy in a helmet on a hog."

The motorcycle explained his scuffed leather pants and jacket. She appreciatively eyed the big bike. "That looks like way more fun than Bernie's Vespa."

"I've been crazy the past several weeks." He cradled her to him, kissing her fingers one by one. "Right here, right now, I finally feel sane. I want you to come to the show tonight, as my guest. I brought an extra helmet."

"Give me a minute to change."

"I like what you have on." He toyed with the plunging neck opening of her shirt.

She slowly withdrew from his embrace. "I think I'll wear my athletic singlet. Or maybe my high-cut Bermuda shorts and thong sandals."

He laughed as she trotted off. Miranda bounded up the open stairwell to her bedroom. When she caught her reflection in the mirror above her dresser, she did a double take. She didn't recognize the wide, shining kaleidoscope eyes, or the fresh, relaxed features. For the first time, she looked as though she were dancing to the joyous music of her own heart. *Bernie's right,* she mused silently. *Happiness makes me beautiful.*

CHAPTER 6

It had taken Miranda exactly two minutes to pull on a pair of slim black jeans and black penny loafers. But once she was dressed, she had spent another ten minutes trying to decide what book to take to the concert. "It's just something to keep me busy backstage," she had explained as she'd tucked the paperback into her coat pocket. Lucas had laughed all the way down to the street.

Once they had reached the Arena, Miranda was certain that the ride on the Harley would remain the best part of the evening. Lucas had moved in and out of Boston's awful traffic with the ease of a life-long resident. Sitting behind him, framing him between her legs with her arms tightly around his torso, had been as enjoyable to her as it had been to him, perhaps more. Lucas had liked the feel of her against him so much that he had driven around the block twice before roaring into the restricted section of the underground parking garage.

Lucas, and by extension Miranda, began receiving the VIP treatment the instant he took off his helmet and shook out his hair. While waiting crewmen nattered like howler monkeys at Lucas, he helped Miranda from the bike as though they had merely stopped for burgers and fries on any Main Street in America.

A Karmic Echo crewman took the bike and helmets while Lucas maintained charge of Miranda, holding her hand tightly to keep her from being separated from him once they entered the Arena's congested underbelly. Miranda was no stranger to this part of the building. She had often been one of the media sheep forced to flock around hockey or basketball players to gather quotes or finish interviews as they went to their limos and chartered buses. Security was much tighter now because of Karmic Echo's presence. Lucas led Miranda through four security checkpoints and still had yet to reach the dressing rooms. People were everywhere, some in the green uniforms of Arena security while others were part of Karmic Echo's huge road and stage crew. Most of the people milling about were female Karmic Echo fans who had scored limited access backstage passes from radio shows, the tour's sponsors, Karmic Echo crewmembers or the Arena.

Miranda almost jogged to keep up with Lucas's brisk pace. She held his hand in both of hers, sure that if she let him go she'd never find him again. She half wished she were out on the concert floor with Bernie, but when Lucas smiled at her, she decided that she was perfectly happy where she was.

After what felt like a mile of twists and turns through half the population of Eastern Massachusetts, they were ushered into a large, quiet odd-shaped room that looked like a typical hotel room—at a very expensive hotel. A white leather sectional sofa lined the wall opposite a giant, flat-screen plasma television. A fully stocked bar, on which sat a gigantic fruit basket filled with Cristal champagne and Godiva chocolates, rested against the wall facing the door. Another wall was completely mirrored and framed by theatre lights. A wide white shelf bisected the mirrored wall, forming a table upon which sat a guitar case.

Lucas took the case to the sofa. He opened it, and with great care withdrew an onyx Fender electric bass, his favorite. He sat on the sofa and braced his right foot on the low white table before him, then settled the instrument across his lap. He picked out a few soft notes while Miranda sat on a tall stool at the bar, watching him. His head bowed over his instrument, his expression was serious, as though he were working on calculus problems rather than music. Her gaze was drawn to the movement of his lips as he softly sang part of a song. When he lifted his face and fixed his heavenly eyes on her, Miranda came the closest she ever had to an actual swoon.

He smiled softly. "You're looking at me strangely."

"It's always amazed me how English people speak in perfectly incomprehensible accents, but then when you sing, you sound like you're from Nebraska."

"First off, I'm Welsh, not English, woman, and second," he set aside his bass, "get over here."

She joined him on the sofa, sitting thigh to thigh with him. "I shudder to think how many rock guys like you have spread their booty cooties all over this thing."

"Booty cooties?" He put an arm around her. "I was told that this dressing room is new. Everything, even the insulation in the walls, had to be replaced after Blind Rage played here last week."

"I heard about that," Miranda said. "Bernie refused to cover their concert because of their lyrics bashing women, homosexuals, blacks, Hispanics, Asians, Jews, Catholics, Muslims—"

"Blind Rage is about stirring up controversy, not making fit music. Good bands, authentic bands, are rare these days."

"You have to look outside the mainstream Top 40 charts to find good music," Miranda observed. "My mother comes from Bahia, 'The Land of the Drum.' I grew up on samba. It's rich and colorful music that makes you want to move. It makes you feel alive. You can't beat Tito Puente, Chavela Vargas, Luiz Carlos da Vila . . . I can't dance, but those guys make me wish I could."

"Perhaps you can't dance because you haven't found the right partner," Lucas suggested.

To avoid pursing that debate, Miranda asked, "Whose music do you like?"

"U2, of course, and Outkast from your side of the pond." He mentioned their names with reverence. "I really like Missy Elliot. She's a visionary, a true artist."

"I would never have pegged you as an Outkast or Missy Elliot fan," Miranda said.

"You can't see an old white guy like me down with Andre 3000 and Miss E., is that it?"

"No . . . well . . . yes," she confessed.

"When I was a kid, I'd sit up listening to my dad play with some of the Motown studio musicians who'd come to London to record with English artists. My dad would be in heaven. You should have heard them.

Until then, I never knew that my dad had soul, that he had rhythm! Up 'til then, Tom Jones was the only Welshman allowed to have rhythm."

Miranda laughed. "I'm glad that he passed some of it on to you."

"That's not all he passed on. My dad taught me that music doesn't know race. It's something you feel, something you share. It comes from under your skin." He stroked his fingers along Miranda's jaw. "You have such lovely skin."

"*Branca-suja*," Miranda sighed.

"What's that?"

"It means dirty white. My *avó*, my mother's mother, used to call me that. She didn't like how I was so much darker than my mother and my sister. I don't know what she expected, seeing as how she used to call my father *bailano*."

"Ebony," Lucas translated aloud.

Miranda gave him an appreciative smile. "Impressive."

"Brazil is one of my favorite countries to visit," Lucas said. "The people are so diverse."

"There's been so much intermarriage over the centuries between the Spanish, French, the native Indians and Africans that people literally come in every color," Miranda said. "When we used to go to Bahia, to visit my *Avó* Marie Estrella, no one ever asked me if I was mixed or if I was black or Hispanic. It didn't matter, not with just about everybody being mixed with something else."

"What's it like here?"

"You generally have two colors in good ol' Boston: white and not white. Co-existence is possible, but rarely seen."

"It's been difficult for you?"

Miranda dropped her eyes. "When I was a kid in Silver Springs, we lived in a predominantly black neighborhood. People thought my mother was white because she's so fair-skinned. The kids used to think I was mixed. I suppose I am when you boil it down, because obviously there are some European genes in my family tree. But I consider myself African American and Afro-Hispanic. My father is black, my mother is Brazilian *negro branca*."

"There were only two black students in my school when I was young," Lucas said. "One was from London and the other had come from Jamaica. Most of the black people I came into contact with were American musicians and singers who worked with my dad. My dad was the minority in those situations, but he never had any problems."

"I didn't have any problems until I hit the *Herald-Star* newsroom," Miranda remarked. "Most of the guys I work with were born and bred in Massachusetts. This tiny little state is their whole world, and sports is their religion. I flew into their world like some lost exotic bird. I think they resent that I'm a woman more than they resent my race. I don't know . . . I guess some guys are threatened by a woman who knows the difference between Lou Holtz and Lou Piniella."

"Lou Holtz turned the University of South Carolina Gamecocks into a winning football program," Lucas mentioned smoothly. "Lou Piniella was the coach of the Tampa Bay Devil Rays baseball team."

Miranda's eyebrows arched in surprise. "You know your Lous?"

"I've picked up a few things here and there." Lucas brought his face closer to hers.

He might have shown her a few more things he'd learned if someone hadn't knocked on the door and announced, "You're on in five, Mr. Fletcher."

"He must be new," Lucas said. "Else he wouldn't be calling me 'Mr. Fletcher.'" He stood, taking Miranda's hand and bringing her with him.

"I could stay here," she said, "and read until you're done. If that's okay."

He picked up his bass. "If you'd rather, sure. But if my preference means anything, I'd like you to come up with me. We musicians like showing off onstage for our girls."

"That's just it. I'm not sure I'm up to being one of the girls."

"What are you talking about, Miranda?"

"You didn't see all those women out there? Each one of them had lots more hair, lots more makeup, tons more boobs and way less clothes than I do. You can't tell me that you didn't notice them."

"I can because I didn't." He took her shoulders firmly. "You would laugh your beautiful head off if you knew how long it's been since I enjoyed the intimate company of a woman. For twenty years, women have been throwing themselves at me. I confess, there was a time when I caught as many as I could. For a long time, I've wanted more than what the women out there want to give me." His body brushed against hers and she took the flaps of his motorcycle jacket. "I want a woman who will throw her mind and soul at me, not just her body. When I least expected it, our paths crossed. And since then, I haven't been able to think of anything but you."

She didn't smile, but dimples appeared at the corners of her mouth. "I'll bet you say that to all the girls."

"We need you onstage, Lucas," came a hurried voice from the other side of the door.

"You'd better go," Miranda said, though neither of them made a move to separate.

"I only knew what I didn't want before I met you, Miranda. Now I know exactly what I want."

Her heart thumped hard, echoing in her ears when she said, "I'm afraid to ask what that is."

"I want you," he volunteered.

"Fletch!" Feast's shriek was accompanied by a furious pounding on the door. "Get your arse out here! There are paying customers waiting to watch you beat your bass!"

Lucas ignored his lead guitarist. "What makes you smile, Miranda? What's your favorite book? What's your worst fear? Do you like Thai food? When you kissed me on that airstrip in Wales, I knew that I wanted to know so much more about you."

Nothing he said was foreign to her, for she had wanted the exact same thing—to know him. Voicing the desire seemed to give it more power, and words meant to draw her in instead made her pull away. "Home runs, *To Kill A Mockingbird*, spiders, and yes. Don't expect fireworks and shooting stars from me, Lucas. I'm just a regular person."

"If you were merely regular I wouldn't be in this dressing room keeping my mates and thirty thousand fans waiting."

"Then you'd better go. I'll wait for you here."

He reached into her coat pocket and took out her book. He read the title as he settled onto the sofa. *"Rapturous Revenge."* With raised eyebrows, he opened it to Miranda's page marker, leaned back, crossed his long legs at the ankle and began to read aloud. "'Her lips parted in an expression of sheer bliss as his velvet tumescence artfully breached the moist petals of her throbbing womanhood.'" He chuckled. "Velvet tumescence?"

Miranda lunged for the book. Lucas caught her around the waist and held her atop him. She grabbed at the paperback, which he easily held out of reach. "I never would have known you for a romance fan," he said.

"I'm still in the closet," she grunted, snatching at the book.

Lucas pitched the book across the room so he could use both arms to subdue her. "Don't be embarrassed, Miranda."

"I'm not." A raging blush belied her words.

"Kitty Kincaid isn't half bad, actually," he said.

To Lucas's regret, she stopped writhing upon him. "You know her work?"

"Her publisher once asked me to pose for one of her book covers." He gently smoothed strands of Miranda's tousled hair from her face. "It was called *The Virgin Whore* or *The Sergeant's Staff,* or some such thing."

Miranda giggled. Lucas kissed the end of her nose, which made her giggle more.

"Did you pose for it?" she asked.

"No. I had a scheduling conflict. But I read the samples of her books they sent."

"Sure, you did," she said skeptically.

"I've been known to read ingredient lists on candy wrappers if that's all that's available to me," he said. "The road can be dead boring."

"No one, not even Bernie, knows that I like to read romance novels," Miranda said. "Promise me that you won't tell anyone. Not your friend Feast, not your parents, not your pups, not anyone ever."

"Kiss me, and forever seal the Pact of the Velvet Tumescence."

Miranda happily obliged. She gently touched his lips, the chaste contact lighting fires beneath their skin. His hands went into her hair and under her coat. One of her legs slid between his and she pressed her hips into the hard ridge that had grown along his thigh. Her blood pulsated through her body, generating a heat that ignited every cell of her body. Her coat was in a pile on the carpeted floor and Lucas was kissing the bit of shoulder bared by her oversized shirt when she realized that the pulsating was coming from around her as well as within.

"What's that noise?" she asked, mildly alarmed.

"I expect it's the stomping of thirty-thousand fans." Lucas ran his hands along her back and discovered that she wasn't wearing a bra. "They do that, when the band is late taking the stage."

"You have to get up there." She pulled her shirt back into place and tried to get off of him.

Lucas held her tight. "Only if you come with me. You can come on stage and sing backup."

"I have a voice like a wooden bell. Lucas, I'd rather stay here with Kitty Kincaid."

"As would I, given the state you've worked me into. But I can't disappoint the people who've been disappointed once already."

A muffled roar reached them in the dressing room. "The band must be taking the stage," Lucas said.

"Go!" Miranda urged. "There might be a riot if you don't show."

"Boston Police are out there in force," he told her. "The crowd will behave. Come up with me."

"What if the audience gets so excited, they create another crush?"

"My security team reconfigured the first twenty rows of the Arena," he said. "The first row is thirty feet from the stage. No one is getting crushed tonight."

A muted rift from an electric guitar reached their ears. "That's 'Snatched,'" Miranda said. "Is that Feast?"

Lucas nodded. "There's about forty-five seconds of his posturing and playing before I'm to come in on bass with vocals. Bloody shame Feast will have to take over. The poor git couldn't carry a tune even if it were tattooed on the palm of his hand."

Miranda slithered out of his grasp and grabbed his hand. She dragged him onto his feet. "Come on!" She took his bass by the neck. The thing was heavier than it looked and she had to hold it with both hands to keep from banging it onto the tabletop.

"Are you coming up with me?"

"Yes," she grumbled. She opened the door and pushed him through it, handing him his bass as he went. She dove into the corner, got her book, grabbed her coat and stuck the book in one of the pockets. "Just in case," she said sheepishly.

Every time Lucas took the microphone, frenzied screaming drowned out the first few bars of his song. From her perch just inside the backstage area, Miranda plainly saw that every woman in the Arena wanted Lucas, and every man wanted to be him.

Handsome athletes peopled Miranda's everyday world, but she'd never seen a man as beautiful as Lucas. His beauty was ancient, borne of his Celtic ancestry, wild but not uncivilized. The warmth of his voice and the passion in his eyes tempered the intensity of his features. His was a face capable of brutal honesty, yet incapable of cruelty. His sort of beauty had only existed in the overblown romance novels she secretly read, yet there it was, singing and playing before her.

She was surprised at how thrilling it was to watch him perform. It wasn't overtly exciting, like watching a sudden death overtime in the Super Bowl. Lucas's performance was . . . stimulating. His music was a sensuous, consuming accompaniment to the sight of him in his black leather pants and tight white T-shirt. The muscles of his arms and chest flexed and his long hair flew as his fingertips danced over the strings of his instrument. Miranda dared to imagine how it would feel to have those strong, agile fingers artfully dancing over her.

She glanced at the audience and saw that she wasn't the only woman with thoughts of artful dancing. Women pushed at sawhorses and security guards, hoping to get close enough to the stage to pitch bras and panties at Lucas. Most of the undergarments fell short and gathered at the base of the stage, but one inspired fan, a young black woman with a shaved head, managed to slingshot a red G-string high above security. To the cheers of the overexcited crowd, the thing landed on Lucas's microphone stand and dangled there. He laughed mid-lyric, but didn't miss a beat of his song.

Miranda wondered what he would do with the G-string. Would he ignore it? Or would he use it to further play up a crowd that he already had in the palm of his hand?

Lucas didn't have to do anything with it. Len Feast sidled up to him and snagged the lacy undergarment with the end of his guitar. He took it to the other side of the stage, where he put it on over his tattered khaki cargo pants. The crowd went crazy as Feast, his twig and berries bulging from the tight confines of the ill-fitting G-string, strutted back over to Lucas. Not to be outdone, Lucas broke out of the song to say, "And this is why you should always put your name in your knickers. Glad to get those back, Feast?"

Laughing, Feast curled two fingers toward Lucas in what Americans interpreted as the "V" for victory sign.

"Lucas is so cool," Miranda overheard one of her fellow backstage guests say.

Miranda wasn't a part of the core group of Karmic Echo wives and girlfriends who stood right inside the wings, bobbing and weaving to songs they must have heard ten million times. They all looked alike, as if they'd been engineered in the same genetics lab. They were all tall, thanks to five-inch-and-higher heels, and had massive volumes of hair crispy with styling spray. Their mouths were shellacked in lip gloss, and one woman had on so much eye makeup, her eyes looked like cigarette burns. The women were all built like pencils with marbles—*big* marbles—attached, and even though they wore clothes, they still managed to look naked. Their backstage credentials hung around their necks just as Miranda's did, but Miranda was the only one who was repeatedly asked to show her pass.

She didn't care. How could she, when Lucas sought her gaze every time he looked into the wings? The other women might have been sexy and desirable with their shirts opened low and their skirts hiked high, but it was Miranda who caught Lucas's notice each time he peeped into the wings.

The band and their significant, and insignificant, others gathered in Lucas's dressing room after the concert. Some of the band had already opened the champagne and were lounging about the dressing room by the time Lucas and Miranda joined them. Lucas proudly introduced Miranda.

"That's Garrison Coe, the best drummer since Keith Moon," he said. A tall, blue-eyed man with a goatee tipped his knit cap at Miranda. "And that lot is 'Wet' Willie Weingart, who plays second guitar and keyboards."

Wet Willie, a native of Glasgow, Scotland, said something that to Miranda sounded like, "Goona funna gow meedya."

"You, too," Miranda said with pleasant uncertainty as she laid her coat on the stool beside Wet Willie.

"And last, I give you lead guitarist Len Feast," Lucas said.

Feast stared at her for a long, silent moment. "Have you hired a new housekeeper on, Fletch?" he finally asked.

If the rest of the band thought Feast's comment was funny, they didn't show it. If anything, they became too quiet. Lucas gave Feast a stiff smile as he went to the bar and took up one of the fluffy white towels stacked there. Miranda tried to remain close to him, but he made a beeline for the bathroom. "A quick shower is in order for me, love," he told her. "The boys will keep you amused."

Lucas left Miranda to fend for herself, as much as he hated doing it. If she couldn't hold her own against Feast, then she wasn't the woman he thought she was.

Miranda bit the inside of her lower lip to stop herself from calling after him. After a two and a half hour set followed by a forty-five minute encore, Lucas was drenched with sweat and in dire need of a wash and rinse. The whole band could use it, from what Miranda saw. Feast, whose saturated T-shirt lay in a wet heap on the floor, lounged on the sofa in only his pants and his recently acquired G-string. A very pretty woman with green eyes, blonde hair and the shortest miniskirt Miranda had ever seen lay half sprawled over him.

"So," Feast started. "Lucas says you're a writer."

"I'm a reporter." Miranda wanted to put her coat on, to better facilitate a fast getaway, but Wet Willie was now wearing it and rifling through her pockets.

"What do you report on?" Feast grabbed a bottle of Cristal by the neck and took a noisy swig of it.

"Sports." Miranda narrowed her eyes. She didn't care for the demanding tone of his questions.

He snickered. "What does a bird like you know about sports?"

He'd struck her most sensitive spot, and Miranda returned fire. "I know that the English aren't particularly good at too many of them."

Feast didn't respond immediately. When he did, he got personal. "I've always found Americans to be rude and insulting and too bloody stupid to know that they're being so."

"I find the English to be pretentious, overbearing, self-righteous, supercilious blowhards," Miranda responded prettily.

Feast sat upright, rolling the woman off of him. "Americans are frivolous and gaudy."

Miranda took a step toward him. "Your accent is prissy."

"Your accent is obscene."

"English football is a sport for bloodthirsty hooligans," Miranda said.

"American football is for head-banging morons."

"The monarchy is obsolete," Miranda spat.

Feast shot to his feet. "Your president is a fool."

Miranda's path cleared as she made her way toward Feast. "America, for better or for worse, gives the world the promise of possibility."

"You gave the world Happy Meals and Levis!"

With stealthy calm, Miranda went in for the kill. "You gave the world the Spice Girls."

An audible wince resounded through the room. Feast stomped toward the bar and was pouring himself a short whiskey when he noticed the book poking from Wet Willie's pocket. He took it, read the front cover, and laughed.

"That's mine," Miranda told him.

Feast leaped out of her reach. "Finders keepers."

"Give it back," she demanded.

"You didn't say the magic word." He held the book behind his back.

Miranda held out her hand. "Give it back *now*."

"Make me."

Those two words had gotten Miranda into countless scrapes during her grade school years, and the words had the same effect on her as an adult. Taking a page from Blind Rage's book, she lunged at Feast when he rounded the bar. She grappled with him for the paperback while the band egged them on. Feast's woman ran to the bathroom door and pounded on it with both fists. "Your new maid is killing Len!" she wailed through a thick Italian accent.

"I'm all right, Izzy!" Feast yelled. He impishly transferred the book from hand to hand, holding it well out of Miranda's reach as she tugged on his arms. She hooked her heel behind his ankle and tripped him to the carpet, and he brought Miranda down with him. His hand slipped as he tried to brace her fall, and he struck her across the cheek with the book. Miranda, who was only mad before, got pissed.

Lucas heard Feast's shouts and Izzy's banging on the door the instant he turned off the shower. After hastily swathing a towel about his hips, he sprinted from the bathroom and parted the circle of fight fans to see Miranda and Feast on the floor. Miranda had him in an iron headlock, and Feast's face was the color of an overripe raspberry.

"I leave the room for five minutes and a Wrestle Royale breaks out between my girl and my best friend?" Lucas railed as he separated them. "Honestly, Feast."

Feast's normal color was slow to return. "She started it!"

"No, I didn't." Miranda panted for breath and used the back of her hand to touch her nose to make sure it wasn't bleeding. "*He* started it."

"Anyone but you two, tell me what happened," Lucas ordered.

Feast's blonde stepped forward. "Your servant—"

"You're hardly an impartial witness, Isabella," Lucas said. "And Miranda is not my housekeeper, maid or servant." He shook his head, amazed that he'd never noticed Isabella's intellectual shortcomings.

"Feast took her book," Garrison said from his corner far out of the fray. "Then he hit her with it."

A storm brewed on Lucas's face. He tugged Feast to his feet and slammed him against the nearest wall, to Isabella's screams.

"It was an accident," Feast insisted as his band mates scattered.

Miranda grabbed Lucas's arm. "It really was an accident. He was teasing me. I overreacted. We were just playing around, right Feast? Mr. Feast?"

Lucas held him a moment longer before releasing him with a little push. "You'll go too far one of these days, mate." He cupped Miranda's face. She seemed none the worse for the experience. Unlike Feast, she actually looked like she had enjoyed the scrape. "I'll dress and then I'll take you home."

"Izzy's got a friend in, Fletch," Feast said. Miranda followed his line of sight toward the bar, where a buxom redhead sucked on a maraschino cherry. "Come back to the hotel with us. You're well overdue for a some good fun."

Miranda, convinced that her spine was telescoping, made an effort to stand taller.

"I have other plans, Feast," Lucas said sharply.

"What?" Feast said, shrugging a shoulder. "You and Yoko have tickets for a midnight mumblety-peg tournament?"

"Give Miranda her coat, Wet." Lucas fixed his dark gaze on Feast. "We'll be leaving soon."

"Look at yourself, Fletch," Feast demanded. "You're a love-struck poof! You're supposed to be our dark, brooding god of sex, not bloody Hugh Grant pining after Divine Brown!"

Lucas's knuckles cracked as his hands fisted at his sides. He fixed a cold stare on his oldest friend. "Don't make any plans for tomorrow. You and I need to talk."

"Agreed." Feast shot a withering look at Miranda.

Lucas left her alone again, to get dressed. Miranda half hoped for another round with Feast, but he disappointed her by collecting Isabella and her redheaded friend and leaving. Garrison tugged Miranda's coat from Wet Willie, and helped her into it. The coat was damp and warm, evidence as to the origin of Wet's nickname.

"I didn't mean to cause a fight," Miranda said. "I'm sorry I disrupted your band."

Garrison returned her book to her. "Lucas has to smash Feast's face in a' least once every couple 'a years. Feast needs it. 'E never got his arse kicked in enough at Oxford, the spoiled wanker."

"Feast went to Oxford?" Miranda was surprised.

"Aye," Garrison said. "'E's got himself papers in applied chemistry. 'E's a bloody brain. 'E just doesn't got a full servin' 'a common sense."

"It's been a hard tour, but I shouldn't be this worn out," Lucas said. He set his motorcycle helmet on the small circle of Miranda's dining room table. His heavy black boots clomped noisily over her bare hardwood floors as he joined her in the confined space of her kitchen. "Perhaps I'm getting too old for all this travel."

"You're not old. Mick Jagger was still putting on a good show into his fifties." Miranda's voice came from deep within her refrigerator. She was starving, and all she'd done was sit on a stool in the darkened wings of the Arena stage, unlike Lucas, who'd spent over three hours on full throttle. She wanted to feed him, and she was embarrassed that she had little more than condiments and leftovers to serve.

"Jagger hasn't toured in decades," Lucas said. "He's a national treasure that must be preserved. In fact, for the past twenty years he's been kept under glass in a museum basement in London. An animatronic replica is sent out when the band tours."

"That would explain his dancing." Miranda withdrew from the fridge clutching a small bowl of day-old rice, a grilled chicken breast, half a Vidalia onion, a green net bag holding a few grape tomatoes and a tiny tin of sliced black olives. She set the items on the countertop next to the stove. "I could order in Chinese. There's a place near here that stays open until three on the weekends, or I could throw something together. I think."

"Bernard said you didn't cook," Lucas smiled.

"Chopping and re-heating is not cooking."

"What can I do to help?"

The kitchen seemed to shrink with him in there with her, and she was keenly aware of his every move. He reached around her for a paring knife, and she felt the warmth of his body. She turned to grab something from the fridge, and she caught a whiff of his freshly showered scent. He worked beside her, chopping garlic gloves, and Miranda was alarmed by her comfort with him.

He leaned in close to her to scrape his garlic into a skillet where Miranda had started the rice dancing in hot vegetable oil with a dash of *dendi*, the bright orange oil extracted from the African palm of northern Brazil.

"My *Avó* Marie Estrella used *dendi* the way Italian cooks use olive oil," Miranda told Lucas, who had begun slicing the chicken breast into long strips. "She was a very good cook. That gene bypassed me and went to my sister, Calista. I got my other grandmother's cooking ability. Grandma Ilene's food was just awful. She thought she was the best cook in the world, though."

Lucas laughed lightly. "I think every family has one of those. For me, it's my Aunt Kerry. Every year at Christmas she makes rum cakes for everyone. My dad's still using his as a doorstop."

"My Grandma Ilene made macaroni and cheese for a potluck dinner my softball team in high school was having to raise money for new uniforms," Miranda started while she sautéed her garlic and rice. "She used to cook pasta the way normal people cook rice, you know, until all the water is absorbed. She put the gloopy, watery macaroni in a baking dish with about six bricks of Velveeta and cream cheese, baked it for twenty minutes, threw some crushed saltines on top, and then presented it at the potluck. She was so mad because everyone thought it was a dip."

"Well, it seems her heart was in the right place," Lucas said, laughing along with Miranda as she added his chicken strips to the skillet. The tomatoes, sliced onion and black olives followed, and once satisfied that everything had warmed through, Miranda scraped the contents of the skillet into a big glass bowl. With the steaming bowl propped in the crook of one arm, she grabbed two forks from her cutlery drawer and led Lucas into her living room.

"I'm sorry," she said when he took a fork and sat on the sofa. "Do you want a plate?"

"This is fine. I'd do it like this myself, if I were at home."

Miranda sat on the floor on the opposite side of her low cocktail table. "If you were at home, your chef would've had a seven-course meal waiting for you. My place is much more humble."

"It's charming." Lucas liked the simplicity of Miranda's apartment. Since it was the third floor of a deconsecrated church, it had fascinating architectural details: wide, deep windows, exposed brick walls and polished bird's eye maple floors. The lower level was an open atrium sparsely furnished with light-colored, natural woods and upholsteries, and the upper level was accessed by a set of wide, bare maple stairs. Lucas assumed that her bedroom was somewhere atop them.

Miranda took a bite of the rice. It wasn't her best, but it would do. "Your guitarist doesn't like me."

"It's not you." Lucas ate heartily. This was truly the best meal he'd ever had, and it was only leftovers. "It's any woman. Most of them couldn't survive Feast's baptism by sarcasm."

Most? Miranda wondered how many there had been.

"Feast was particularly virulent with you because he feels especially threatened. We've been together from the beginning. It's always been hard for him when someone comes between us."

Miranda blanched as she set down her fork. "I'm the Other Woman?"

"You're *the* woman. Feast knew that I'd fall in love someday, and that I'd belong to someone else."

"You say things that make me doubt my sanity." Miranda went to the kitchen for something to drink.

"He'll adjust, in time," Lucas called after her.

"I didn't mean Feast. I meant that word. You use it so easily."

"Which word?" Lucas asked.

"Love."

"On the contrary, Miranda, I use it only when I mean it. I don't even use the word in my songs."

Miranda returned with two bottles of beer. She gave one to Lucas.

"I've got another Corona in there, too," she said, holding up the beer she'd chosen for herself. "I've got some *cachaça* and a couple of limes. I could make a couple of *caipirinhas*, if you're more in the mood for a cocktail. If you like *mojitos*, you'll love *caipirinhas*."

"As much as I like *cachaça*, this Guinness suits me perfectly, you wonderful girl," he chuckled, saluting her with the dark brown bottle.

"Bernie loves Guinness." Miranda resumed her seat at the cocktail table.

"The man has excellent taste," Lucas proclaimed. "And now who's guilty of the liberal use of the word 'love?'"

"I used it in this case because Bernie genuinely loves Guinness. He says it tastes like soy sauce, but he loves it because it's Irish, and he's very proud of his heritage. But you write love songs. How can you say that you don't use the word love?"

"Love is a feeling that can be conveyed far more effectively using other words." He moved the rice bowl and their beers aside, and leaned closer to Miranda, overwhelming her with his proximity. "For example, I died of old age every day I spent waiting to see you again. I lost my heart the first time I looked into your eyes, and I lost my soul the first time you kissed me."

"Are those lyrics from a song?" she asked softly, his gaze making it impossible for her to move or even look elsewhere. "Because if they are, they're really cheesy."

He leaned over the table until his mouth was an inch from hers. "Those are lyrics from my heart, inspired by you." His words had turned her to honey and when his lips met hers, his touch set that honey boiling. Her desire for him mounted within her with the force of a geyser.

In a show of monumental restraint, Lucas didn't strike the bowl and the beers onto the floor and spread her over the cocktail table. He'd been hungry after the show, yes, but he could have done without food. He could have done without air. All he wanted was Miranda. Every time he had looked offstage, he'd seen her there in the wings, and at no point had she taken out her book. He'd sung some of his favorite songs not to the thousands of fans who had paid to see him, but to the one woman who was the answer to his unspoken prayers.

As she rose on her knees to deepen the kiss between them, he knew that he had to end it before it got out of his control.

"I should have asked before I did that." He licked his lower lip, tasting her sweetness on it. "I guess I'm not the gentleman I thought I was."

She took a deep breath, and her billowy shirt seemed to flutter against the rapid beat of her heart. "I'm sure you've got a great room at the Ritz-Carlton or the Harborfront Regency, but you're welcome to stay here tonight. It's no castle, but it's cozy. And I have a really big bed."

He threw back his head and laughed out loud. "How can I resist an invitation like that?"

She sat back on her heels. "I'm no seductress, Lucas. I'm twenty-nine in two days and I've had exactly three lovers in my life."

"Only three? Did you grow up in a convent?"

"I was a late bloomer." She grabbed the rice bowl and took it into the kitchen.

"How late?"

"Not until the night of my college graduation." She returned to the living room, this time sharing the sofa with him. "I was twenty-one years old. My best friend Tracey and I decided that we were tired of being virgins, so—"

"Tracey?" Lucas interrupted with a titillated twitch of an eyebrow.

"Tracey is a he, not a she," Miranda clarified. "He was a computer information systems major with this big, crazy Afro and the nicest smile. He had this really attractive self-conscious quality. He was a high school nerd who blossomed in college, but never realized that he'd blossomed. On graduation night, we just did it. We got some books—"

"How studious." Lucas sat to face her.

"*The Joy of Sex, Kama Sutra* . . . you know. We spent the night at his place."

"Was it satisfactory?"

"Some parts of it were better than others." She lowered her face to study her thumbnail.

"It didn't end well with this man?"

She shook her head. "He was more serious about me than I was about him. I went into the whole thing as a reconnaissance mission. It was a learning experience, and I never pretended otherwise."

"Did you care for him?"

"Of course. He was my best friend for four years. He showed me how to computerize my football betting pools, and I taught him how to fill out a baseball scorecard. We couldn't have done what we did if we hadn't respected and cared for each other. I just didn't love him the way he loved me."

Lucas stretched an arm invitingly over the back of the sofa. Miranda moved into it and allowed him to hug her to his chest. "I'll wager you've broken a number of hearts over the years," he sighed into her hair.

"Look who's talking. Women probably hug their pillows in bed at night, pretending that the pillows are you. How much fan mail do you get?"

He gently combed his fingers through her hair. "The last figure I recall hearing is a half-million pieces annually. It wasn't always like that, even after my first American single hit number one. I was something of a late bloomer myself. I had a man's voice at thirteen, but physically, I was a skinny bobolink until I turned seventeen. In the course of a year I went from eleven and a half stone, five-foot-ten to six-foot-four, fifteen and a half stone of solid muscle. Women began taking notice of me in ways they hadn't before."

Using her reporter's tact, Miranda asked, "How many lovers have you had?"

"It's unseemly for a man to talk about his sex life."

"So it was always just sex?"

"And it was always safe. My father was a musician, so he drummed into me from the beginning how important it was to keep the cannon capped until I was ready to bring children into the world."

"You want children someday?" She looked up at him, and Lucas lost his heart all over again.

"Absolutely. You?"

"I never thought about it." She laid her hand flat over his lower abdomen. He almost groaned as his cannon strained against his blue jeans. "Kiki Langlois seemed pretty set on getting you to the altar."

"Don't tell me you actually believe those tabloid reports, Miranda."

"This one came firsthand, from the Bernie's mouth. He saw you with her at a party after the Grammy awards. He said that she was stuck to you like a spray-on tan."

"Kiki and I met on the set of one of my videos," Lucas said. "Our relationship lasted as long as the three days of filming."

"Rock stars and supermodels." Miranda sat up off of him and swung her feet to the floor. "They're like chocolate and peanut butter. Kiki Langlois isn't just a regular supermodel, Lucas. She's an *American Swimsuit Magazine* supermodel. I see her face and her skinny arms and knobby knees on every magazine—including *The Great Outdoorsman* and *Fitness For Seniors*—every time I go to 7-Eleven for Slim Jims after a game."

"What are Slim Jims?"

"Don't change the subject. What are you doing here with me when you can have your pick of the Kiki Langloises of the world?"

He sat up, bracketing her between his legs. "Because I want you. I want a one-of-a-kind, exotic Miranda Penney, not a run-of-the-mill Kiki Langlois."

"I guess I am a nice change from the long-legged, plucked, waxed and exfoliated beauties you're accustomed to."

"Miranda, you're beginning to exhaust my patience." He took her by her shoulders and turned her to face him. "Hear well what I'm about to say to you, love. When I pulled you from that crush, and you opened your eyes and looked at me, I thought you were the most exquisite creature God ever dared set before me. In your eyes I saw the inspiration for every love song I've ever sung."

She opened her mouth to argue, but the words stalled in her throat. No matter how much she wanted to believe he was just feeding her a line, she couldn't, not while he was holding her gaze and giving her an unobstructed view of the contents of his heart.

"I'm more of a Looney Tune than a love song," she said. "Who knew your idea of beautiful is a mouth that looks like a fist."

"Picasso couldn't have created a lovelier face."

"My fingers are fat."

"Like Portuguese sausages."

"I have flat feet." She crossed the bare toes of one foot over the other. "My sister used to call me Slappy."

Lucas eased her back on the sofa and lifted her right foot from the floor. His thumbs glided over her sensitive instep while the rest of his fingers moved over the smooth top of her foot. He kissed her instep, then the spot just beneath her ankle, and her toes curled as an erotic shiver traveled through her.

"My legs are too long and skinny." She arched her back a bit and spread her arms over her head in response to the way his fingers worked the sensitive places between her toes.

"Like twin telephone poles." He set her left leg over his shoulder and moved forward, using his teeth to tease along the inseam of her jeans.

"My thighs are too big." A choppy breath escaped her as his hot breath penetrated the fabric over her inner thigh.

"Postively ponderous." He clutched her hips and softly mouthed the "V" at the apex of her jeans.

Miranda pushed her hands into his hair. "I have no waist," she moaned.

"Nor much of a neck to speak of." He parted the flaps of her shirt to expose her midriff and flick the tip of his tongue across the shallow indentation of her navel before trailing kisses up to her chest, unbuttoning her shirt as he went.

Just as he would have exposed her completely, Miranda regained her senses and grabbed the flaps of her shirt, holding them closed until Lucas softened her grasp with kisses and a gentle touch. She watched his face as he lowered her hands and then opened her shirt. Her heart, and several other parts of her, throbbed under his gaze. "My boobs are way too small," she said.

"Small, agreed." He dipped his head to them. "Humble in their perfection." Her toes curled at the brush of his breath over her skin, but when his lips closed around the dark bud tipping her right breast, she groaned, clasping his head to her.

He hunched over her, tasting and tantalizing with his teeth, lips and tongue. She took his hand and guided his longest finger to her mouth to suckle it, matching her rhythm to his. Her hips rose against him, grinding into the hot coil of want between his legs. When his mouth left her breast to claim her lips, she sat up, kissing him even as she grabbed his shirt and worked it over his head.

Lucas broke away to look at her tousled hair, kiss-swollen lips and flushed skin. The tip of her tongue licked the right corner of her upper lip, and Lucas thought he would explode. He pushed his fingers into her hair and cupped her head. "Are there any more complaints, love? Any other faults I should seek out?"

Faults? How could she admit to any, with him looking at her as though she were a goddess. "I have this one weird hair that—"

"We'll tie a jingle bell to it come Christmas," he chuckled.

She hooked her fingers into the front of his waistband and tugged him closer, as if to kiss him. "We may not be together at Christmastime."

The left side of his mouth rose in a grin though the sparkle in his eyes dimmed. "We're together now." He slipped his hand inside the back of her jeans and cupped her bottom. "What should we do about that, Miranda?"

Moonlight shone brightly through the stained glass window in her bedroom, tinting Lucas's bare torso in deep reds, blues and golds, as he kneeled before her, unfastening and then lowering her jeans. Miranda struggled to breathe evenly as she ran her fingers through his soft, thick hair, but a sharp gasp escaped her when she felt the heat of his breath on the damp cotton between her legs.

As he stood, his body grazed along hers. He held her hips, steadying her while she stepped out of the pool of denim and cotton at her feet. His hands fisted as he fought for control. If her wetness was a fair indication, she wanted him as badly as he wanted her. He wanted nothing more than to flatten her body beneath his and plunge into her, but at the same time he wanted to take the time to cherish every part of her.

"Are you sure?" he asked her. He lowered his head to take her nipple through the fabric of her shirt. She pressed her hips into him and pitched her head back, allowing his strong hands to keep her upright.

"I want this," she said in a breathy sigh. "I want you."

He slipped the shirt from her body and moved her to the bed, forcing his thoughts to cool as he gazed upon her. Miranda sat up on her elbows, the lower right corner of her lip caught in her teeth as she watched him strip off his pants. His was a notch above the ornamental beauty of a male model, and his physique rivaled that of the fittest athletes. He was perfectly proportioned without being bulky, and Miranda loved the way his broad chest and shoulders tapered to a trim waist with chiseled abdominals. His legs were long and well muscled and there, where his legs met, strained a part of him that would have made him the envy of every man in locker rooms across America.

"It's so big," Lucas said.

"I'll say." Miranda's eyes zeroed in on what she thought he was talking about.

He appreciated her agreement, but had to clarify his comment. "Your bed. You weren't exaggerating when you said it was really big."

"It's a queen-size king, according to Bernie." Miranda said. "It sleeps six. Bernie has one, too, only his has a built-in 8-track tape player. He dated a furniture designer who spoiled us silly."

A shuddering breath left Miranda's parted lips as Lucas joined her on the bed. She usually didn't care for nudity, her own or anyone else's. Too many athletes had used nudity to try to intimidate, shock or distract her in the course of her career. She had to reconsider her preference when Lucas covered her with his body, warming her skin with his.

"I didn't expect this, Miranda," he said. "I didn't bring any caps for the cannon."

It was hard for her to think with his soft touch at her temples stealing rational thought from her brain. "I have some," she managed. She rolled onto her hands and knees and crawled to the edge of the bed. Lucas almost drooled as he watched the movement of her shapely backside. She hung over the bed and retrieved a shoebox from under the edge. Lucas didn't know whether to laugh or run when he saw that the box overflowed with dozens of condoms of all sizes, colors, textures and flavors.

"I know what you're thinking," Miranda said after meeting his questioning gaze. "And it's not what you're thinking." With one hand she sifted through the dusty box, which she had set between them. She ran her other hand through her hair, absently guiding it over one shoulder to cloak her breast.

Watching her, Lucas felt his heart beat out of rhythm.

"These are freebies from a lot of the stories I've covered," Miranda explained. "They come in a lot of the press goodie bags. You'd be amazed at how many sports-related functions are sponsored by condom manufacturers." She picked out a single gold packet and peered at the expiration date. "Wow. This one's three years old." With a perfect flip of her wrist, she used a hook shot to pitch it into the waste can across the room. "It's been awhile since I've had to use anything from this box."

Lucas pushed the shoebox aside. He pressed her onto her back, spreading himself over her, and ran a gentle hand over the length of her hip. "It's been awhile for me, too." Miranda focused on his caress, which moved to her thigh.

"How long of awhile?" Her eyes slowly closed now that his hand settled between her legs.

"You tell and I'll tell." One of his fingers slowly traced the sensitive cleft hidden by her damp curls. "On the count of three. One . . ." Her lower belly jumped when his finger breached her silky folds. "Two . . ." Her thighs fell apart as his finger slid into the welcoming heat of her body. "Three."

"Six months," she groaned breathily over his "Fifteen months." Her hips thrust upward to meet his finger as it withdrew and slid into her again, and he watched her face as he stroked deeper, slightly curling his finger each time he withdrew it. He added another finger, and used the heel of his palm to apply gentle but firm friction to the hard kernel tipping her sex. She moaned, her back arching, her elbows and heels pressing into the giant mattress.

Lucas bent over her to take a pouty breast into his mouth. He drew on it, first hard and sudden then slowly, tenderly, sending bursts of pure pleasure through her. With maddening expertise he nipped and licked, teasing her nipple into a hard pebble. Miranda cradled the back of his head, losing her fingers in the softness of his hair. Her body writhed under his hand and his mouth, and he knew that she was close. He grabbed a condom from the shoebox, tore it open with his teeth and quickly sheathed himself before she pulled him atop her.

He kissed her, his tongue probing her mouth, imitating what a more needy part of his body was poised to do. She took him in her hand and guided him, forcing her head into the mattress as he angled into her, filling her. A long, satisfied groan climbed from her throat and she hugged him to her, wrapping her legs around him. His body quaked from the strain of trying to hold back, to bring her with him to the summit of pleasure. He gritted his teeth and forced himself to find a slow, languid rhythm, to prolong the most exquisite agony he had ever known.

She matched his movements, her body gripping him with each thrust of his lean hips. Her eyes closed, her cheeks flushed and her pearly teeth caught the corner of her lower lip as her passion climbed.

"Miranda," he grimaced as if in pain. "Look at me."

Her eyes met his for a fleeting instant before she closed them again. The glimpse of naked heat shimmering in them sent him straight to the pinnacle of his climax, and with a feral grunt, he exploded within her. He slightly changed his movement, shortening his strokes and tilting his pelvis more toward hers to create delicious pressure on the quivering epicenter of her passion. The effect was immediate. He brought Miranda to a howling, body-shattering climax that violently pulsed from the place where they were joined. She constricted around him as though the tight glove of her body contained a strong, determined fist. Lucas gritted his teeth and cried out his seemingly endless release, her flesh ruthlessly milking him as he went rigid atop her.

Her body held him prisoner even after he was spent, and he slipped a hand between them to seek out the slippery pellet of heat between them. He kneaded it, sending wave after wave of toe-knotting pleasure coursing through her. Lucas was amazed by her voracious response to him, and how rapidly his own body recovered to start anew.

He glanced at the full shoebox, thankful for it as he dipped his head to claim her mouth in a tender yet penetrating kiss. His immediate hunger for her satisfied, he took the time to love her as he had meant to all along.

Miranda was lost. Her eyes closed tight, she surrendered to pure sensation. Lucas's lips and hands and limbs against hers were heaven, and she delighted in her fierce response to him. This was the first time sex had made her want to scream, rather than yawn, or stop to draw a diagram for her partner. Lucas didn't just know her anatomy; he was learning her body. He discovered he could make her purr by kissing the backs of her knees, that he could make her beg by whispering his songs against the moist petals of her womanhood.

She was so comfortable with him that she called upon skills and techniques she hadn't used since the night of her college graduation. They had meaning this time rather than textbook applications, as she gave and received pleasure with glorious abandon. Using every square inch of her gigantic bed as though this first night together would be their last, Lucas gave himself entirely to her. In the course of his life, he'd had enough sex for ten men. Usually it was a matter of satisfying a base, physical urge, but his need for Miranda went well beyond the physical. He wanted her with his whole self, and that feeling was new. He had shared his body before, but never his soul. On this night, he gave it freely to Miranda, hoping she would reciprocate each time he asked her to look into his eyes as their bodies fused.

"Are you there, God? It's me, Margaret."

Miranda rolled onto her belly, tangling herself further in her bed sheet, and picked up the phone before Bernie began another rant into her answering machine. "Good morning. What's up?"

"You, finally," he said. "It's almost two o'clock. I called you three times. Where were you?"

"I was here." Miranda buried her face in a pillow to smother a smile.

"Was Lucas there, too?"

She pulled her face from the pillow and ran a hand through her hair to smooth it from her face. "Are you friend or reporter right now?"

"Friend. Tell."

"Lucas left a little while ago."

Bernie let loose with a joyous whoop that Miranda practically heard in stereo—over the phone and through her bedroom window, which was four blocks from Bernie's. "How was it, baby girl?"

"It's unseemly for a lady to talk about her sex life."

"It wasn't unseemly before Sir Lucas rode into your life. Or did *you* do the riding? You ain't no damn lady, so spill it."

Miranda slid onto her back. Her big bed seemed as vast and empty as the Mojave Desert without Lucas there sharing it with her. She sighed, running her hand over the space he had recently occupied.

"That good, huh?" Bernie said. "Well, let us discuss this in terms you understand. Stamina?"

"Boston Marathon."

"Execution?"

"Sixes all across the board, both in technical merit and artistic presentation."

"What about his equipment? Standard issue?"

She was tempted to make a Kentucky Derby analogy. "You know that pitcher I told you about, the one who stuffs tube socks in his cup when he dresses for games?"

"Yes . . ."

"Lucas's tube sock is one-hundred percent natural."

"Overall performance?"

"Olympic caliber."

"The morning after?"

"It was the best I've ever had," she laughed, kicking her heels against the mattress. "It stretched into the afternoon. And guess what else?"

"What?" Bernie responded greedily.

She paused dramatically before saying, "He brought me coffee. He made it himself."

"Oh honey, I'm so happy for you!"

Miranda smiled into the back of her hand. "I'm happy for me, too."

"Does he want to see us again?"

"He's taking me to dinner tomorrow night, for my birthday."

"What about tonight?"

"He wants to spend some down time with his band. Garrison Coe brought his whole family to Boston, and Lucas promised the kids that he'd take them to The Rainforest Café for dinner. I think things might get ugly between him and his lead guitarist."

"Lucas has carried Len Feast for the past twenty years, and the guy knows it," Bernie said. "He's been working on a solo album called *Feast or Famine* for the past three years. He talks about it in every interview, but no one has ever heard any of it. It's the modern rock equivalent to the Loch Ness Monster."

"He could always take up professional wrestling if the solo act doesn't work out," Miranda said. "We got into a scuffle last night."

"Roughneck. Did you scratch his eyes out?"

"No. Lucas separated us. I thought he was gonna knock Feast's lights out."

"Way to go, Yoko! Break up the most popular rock duo since Lennon and McCartney."

Miranda's happy mood diminished a bit. "Don't be ridiculous, Bernie. Last night was just one night. It's not a lifetime." *Although it was certainly life changing,* she allowed.

"You're completely deluded. You had a better view of him at the concert than I did and I was in the front row. He stared backstage practically the whole time. The venue was sold out, but Lucas Fletcher played for *you*. And you're fooling yourself if you think you haven't fallen for him, too."

Miranda sat up and rested her bare back against her headboard. She brought her knees to her chest. "I enjoy his company. That's all."

"Have it your way," Bernie said. "I won't press. Why don't you shower and dress and meet me at Mama Brown's? I wanna hear more about Lucas's gold-medal winning tube sock."

"I'm surprised to find you alone," Lucas said, accepting the Foster's Lager Feast offered him as they seated themselves in the living room of his hotel suite. "I expected to find you me-deep in conversation, surrounded by Isabella and her entourage of flight attendants."

Feast, not amused, turned his beer in his hands. "Let's get this out and over with, Fletch."

"Right." Lucas's brow wrinkled in concern. He and Feast had worked through plenty of disagreements over the years, and most of them had been far more difficult and distressing than what had happened the night before.

Feast slumped deeper into the suede sofa. His baggy cargo pants blended in with the taupe color of the sofa. "You called this meeting. You start." Before Lucas could speak, Feast erupted with, "You behave as though you're in love with that reporter woman."

Lucas sat back in a deep, buttery-soft suede recliner. He tapped a finger on his fat beer can. "Perhaps I am."

Feast sat forward, his pale eyes beseeching. "How would you even know, Fletch? There've been so many women through the years, some a damn sight more interested in you than your Boston brawler seems to be."

"I've never felt for any other woman what I feel for Miranda. Feast, I was in hell while we were in Asia. I have two weeks with her before we have to go to Australia, and I'm already dreading having to say goodbye to her again."

Feast stubbornly shook his head. "I just don't see it, mate."

"You don't have to," Lucas said simply. "Perhaps our paths are diverging. Maybe we want different things from life now."

"You've gone insane, Fletch. And over a bird!"

"Don't you ever feel the urge to settle down? To plant roots?"

A shrill laugh escaped Feast. "You want to marry that skinny woman and fill your castle with the pitter-patter of little brown Fletches, don't you?"

"Would that be so bad?" Lucas said through a slow grin.

Feast covered his face with his hands. "No." His hands dropped into his lap. Lucas noticed how tired he looked. "In all fairness, I've fancied being an uncle. Are you sure you're willing to pack it all in for Miranda Penney?"

"I've never been more sure about anything. Without Miranda, none of this means anything to me any more, and it all means nothing compared to her."

Feast held his tongue. Lucas thought he was working on an obnoxious response. "I guess it's time the boys in the band grew up. Myself included."

Lucas chuckled and took a swig of his beer. "That'll be the day."

"It's coming sooner than you think," Feast laughed somberly. He stared at the beer grasped in his hand just long enough to concern Lucas.

"Len, what's wrong?" Lucas suddenly realized that something else had been behind his tangle with Miranda.

"Izzy's pregnant."

"Shut up," Lucas said, adopting one of Miranda's expressions of shocked disbelief. He joined Feast on the sofa.

"It's mine."

"Who else's would it be? You two have been glued at the hip—and every place else, apparently—since Rome. What do you plan to do?"

"Are you daft? I'm gonna marry her, if she'll have me."

Lucas laughed softly. "Look at us. Last night, we were the carefree loverboys of Karmic Echo, the very poster children of rock and roll and hedonistic excess. This morning, we're ready to trade it all in for nappies and minivans."

"Better to burn out than fade away," Feast said, offering his beer can in salute.

"Better to make little brown babies and live forever," Lucas said wistfully as his Foster's clunked dully against Feast's.

CHAPTER 7

Miranda sat on her big bed staring at a black dress. Her right hand picked at a cluster of hives on her neck. Her left hand clutched her cordless phone to her ear. She listened to the incessant ringing on the other end of the line, willing her sister to come to the phone. No one combined sex appeal and sophistication as well as Calista, and Miranda desperately needed her sister's help in deciding what to wear to dinner with Lucas. The more times the phone rang, the higher Miranda's anxiety climbed and the bigger her hives became.

"Hello?" came the voice of her salvation. With a grunt of relief, Miranda balled up Grandma Tillie's shroud and pitched it into the closet.

"Callie, I need something to wear tonight." Miranda frantically paced the room. "Lucas is taking me out."

After a short beat of silence, Calista hollered, "You had sex with Lucas Fletcher!"

Miranda snatched the phone from her ear and stopped pacing. "I didn't say that."

"That's the only reason you want to look sexy for your birthday dinner."

"How did you know it was a birthday dinner?"

"Don't you read your own newspaper?"

Miranda's hands went cold. "Only the sports section. Why?"

"No reason," Calista said quickly. "About tonight, your fairy god-brother already gave me a call. We put our heads together and came up with something we think you can live with. Bernie will bring everything by."

"Should I be worried?"

"You're already worried," Calista said. "Have you broken out in hives yet?"

"No." Miranda stopped scratching a hive.

"So are you and Lucas official?"

Miranda stood at her stained glass window. She peered through a gold section of an angel's wing. Elongated cars and squatty people moved along the street and sidewalks below. She didn't care for the distorted perspective. She had always put more trust in what she could see clearly.

"Miranda, are you and Lucas a couple now?" Calista asked.

"He's here for two weeks." Miranda turned away from the window. "I don't know what will happen after that."

"What do you want to happen?"

"I don't know, Callie." Miranda started scratching again. "I just want to get through tonight."

"Think of it as an adventure . . . a safari, where the prey has all the weapons of destruction."

"*Ó Deus*, Callie, what have you and Bernie done?"

"Let's just say that tonight, Lucas will get a present, too."

Miranda felt naked even though she was fully clothed. The "little black dress" Bernie had brought for her whispered against her skin as she studied her reflection in the full-length mirror attached to her bedroom door. The straight neckline of the sleeveless silk dress rested against her collarbones. The straight skirt flared just a little at the hem, which grazed her legs at mid-thigh. The back of the dress, or absence of it, compensated for the modesty of the front. Miranda twisted to see the smooth expanse of her back, which was bared from her nape to just below her waist. She had styled her hair in a simple, sleek ponytail secured with an elasticized band the same dark hue as her hair.

Her second and last pair of sheer black hose—she had put her thumb through the delicate silk of the first pair—highlighted the elegant, sinuous lines of her legs. She spun carefully in her four-inch black heels. She bent over to adjust the suede strap circling her left ankle, and she wondered how she would make it through the night without tripping. When she stood and looked at her reflection anew, she actually liked the total picture. She hoped the man waiting for her downstairs would like it, too.

Miranda was extra cautious as she picked her way down the open staircase. She paused at the bottom step, hoping that her ensemble met with approval. She grew increasingly nervous as she waited for her guest to say something. Anything.

"Well?" She shifted her hip as she hooked a finger under the back of the skirt to adjust her silk G-string.

"Oh for Heaven's sake, Miranda!" Bernie chastised. "We're going for Halle Berry meets Victoria's Secret, not Moms Mabley at a Fanny-Picking Picnic. Promise me you won't do that in front of Sir Lucas."

"I can't help it," she pleaded. "My ass has been chewing on this thing since I put it on."

"Get used to it." Bernie took her hand and helped her to the sofa. "You can't wear your tidy white boy-cut panties because they'll ruin the line of the dress."

Miranda wriggled in her seat.

"You can always go au naturel," Bernie suggested.

"I'll get used to the butt floss," Miranda decided.

"You really look stunning, doll."

"Thanks, Bernie."

"Good choice in going natural with the makeup. I can barely tell that you have any on."

"I don't."

Bernie touched her cheek then examined his fingertip. "My, my. You're a natural beauty."

"Shut up," Miranda said, a blush tinting her face.

"The whole city knows what I've been trying to tell you all along," Bernie said. "My friends at the Herald-Star switchboard told me that they've gotten hundreds of calls about your photos."

"What photos?"

Bernie's eyes widened in disbelief. "You haven't seen it?"

"Seen what?"

He went to the dining table, where he'd placed his jacket and his tote bag, and retrieved a *Herald-Star*. Miranda, almost tripping over her right foot, went to him and took it. She set it on the table and flipped the pages, looking for *Psst!*

"It's a nice spread," Bernie offered, hoping to diffuse the anger he saw blooming on Miranda's face. "It's nothing bad."

Miranda stopped at the middle of the paper. She covered her mouth with her hands when she saw herself in a big, half-page black-and-white photograph. She was standing on the top of the fire escape, right outside her living room window. A corner of her giant cotton bed sheet was wrapped around her, covering her from her bosom to mid-thigh. The bulk of the sheet formed a train that remained in her living room. Her hair was a wild, kittenish tumble about her head and bare shoulders as she smiled and waved down at Lucas, who looked up at her from the street level.

Beneath the large photo was a series of jumbo wallet-sized pictures forming a perfect storyboard of their Sunday afternoon good-bye. The first photo showed Lucas climbing out of her living room window and onto the fire escape, with Miranda close behind. The second photo illustrated the wonder of the telephoto lens. It had captured Lucas's hand on Miranda's face and wisps of her hair tickling about his head as they had warmed the December afternoon with a steamy goodbye kiss. The third photo depicted Lucas going down the fire escape, and the fourth showed him running back for another kiss, which was depicted in the fifth photo. The next two photos showed Lucas going back down the fire escape and leaping over the railing to drop to the street. In the last shot, Lucas roared away on his Harley in the foreground while Miranda stood at the top of the fire escape looking after him in the background.

"*Psst!* trackers caught Welsh Romeo Lucas Fletcher leaving the oh-so-chic South End crash pad of our very own junior varsity Juliette, Miranda Penney," read the accompanying article. "A little Bernie—er, *birdie*—told us that the love bug has bitten Sir Lucas. (And so did our leggy Juliette, according to noise reports from her downstairs neighbor and building manager!) Stay tuned for Act II, when Sir Lucas helps our lucky Penney celebrate her big 2-9!"

"I'm never going to live this down," Miranda said. "I can't ever show my face in the newsroom again."

"I'm just wondering, honey," Bernie said, "but why didn't Lucas use the front door?"

Miranda chuckled dryly. "I didn't want any of my neighbors to see him."

The first car picked up Miranda at home. The driver, who was built like a New England Patriots linebacker, carefully whisked Miranda through a sea of people, half of whom cheered her when she left her building while the other half—mostly female—heartily booed her. Karmic Echo T-shirts were waved at her and cameras blinded her with their flashes, but not before she caught a glimpse of the blood-red lettering on a piece of black poster board: Back Off Lucas Is Mine!

The driver handled her with the utmost care while bulldozing his way through the unruly crowd. When he helped her into the Rolls Royce, Miranda was disappointed to see that she was the only passenger.

"Mr. Fletcher has arranged to meet you elsewhere this evening," the driver told her once he had taken the wheel. "He sends his regrets regarding the roundabout way of meeting you. I'm afraid paparazzi have been dogging him relentlessly."

Miranda turned in her seat to look out of the rear window as the Rolls pulled away. The crowd in front of her building had settled, but showed no signs of dispersing. *They're going to wait for me*, she thought. *This is serious crazy.*

Her thoughts scattered wildly in every direction as the limo eased through surprisingly light Boston traffic. It was past rush hour on a

Tuesday night, which accounted for the ease of movement. It also made it easier for the Rolls to be followed, although Miranda didn't realize that they were being tailed until she noticed that they had driven past Trinity Church three times.

"Are you lost?" she asked the driver.

"No, miss," he responded, glancing at her in the rear view mirror. "We have company."

Miranda turned again and saw two cars vying for positions behind the Rolls. Photographers hung out of the front passenger windows of each. They couldn't shoot her through the tinted windows, but she nonetheless shrank deeper into the backseat. "I'm not Lady Di, for crying out loud," she muttered. "Why are they chasing me?"

The driver thought she was talking to him. "You're a very beautiful woman who's caught the eye of a very famous man. The press assumes ownership of stories like that."

Great, Miranda thought dismally. *I've got Joe Philosophy for a driver when I need Mario Andretti.* "Are we there yet?" she asked.

"Almost."

Two minutes later, they pulled in front of Guiglio's Trattoria on Newbury Street. The vans that had been pursuing them skidded to a stop as the driver was helping Miranda from the car. He quickly hustled her into the restaurant, where a nattily dressed maitre d' took her arm. "Good luck, Miss Penney," the Rolls driver said. He smiled, tipped his hat, and backed away from her.

The maitre d' briskly walked Miranda through the restaurant, giving her no time to appreciate the luxe décor or the famous faces dining at candlelit tables. Guiglio's was one of Boston's ritziest restaurants, and this was Miranda's first time in it. She had no genuine interest in dining there, but she would have liked seeing what all the fuss over the place was about.

"Forgive me for being so brusque," her escort said. "But it won't be long before the vultures see through our ruse. Your driver is waiting for you."

"But . . . I thought . . ." She gave up trying to figure out what was going on. She kept stride with the maitre d'. He took her to the rear of the restaurant, through the bustling kitchen, and out to the alley in back of the building. A Mercedes and its driver awaited her.

"Thank you," the driver said to the maitre d' as Miranda was literally handed over to him. She was quickly deposited into the back seat of the Mercedes, and the driver took off with a start.

"How many more times am I going to have to switch cars before I get to see Lucas?" Miranda asked. The car pulled out of the alley, and she saw the photo vans idling outside Guiglio's. The paparazzi, some of them with lenses as long as their arms, had their cameras trained on the interior of the restaurant.

"One more stop, ma'am," the driver said. "Mr. Fletcher—"

"I know," Miranda interrupted wearily. "He sends his apologies."

Lucas entered the bar on a rush of cold air. The place was crowded, with most of the male patrons gathered at the far end of the long bar. The men were in business suits, for the most part, but they hooted and whistled as though they were watching a Red Sox game in their own living rooms. Lucas scanned the room for Miranda. When he didn't see her, he bellied up to the bar and ordered a club soda.

"Quiet guys, here's the next question," said one of the men at the end of the bar. "This lady beat the boys in the Yonkers Trot and the World Trotting Derby and went on to be named Horse of the Year in 1995."

"I've never heard of any of these nags," one of the men complained as he read the multiple-choice answers. "Who the hell knows this stuff?"

"CR Kay Suzie," came a soft, female voice that brought a smile to Lucas's face. He took his drink and moved to stand on the fringe of the gathering at the end of the bar. Miranda was in the middle of a dense sea of corporate manhood. She sat on her coat, which had been laid over one of the high bar stools. In front of her was a large computer monitor with ALL-STAR SPORTS TRIVIA in bright blue letters across the top of the screen. Miranda touched the ENTER button on the screen, and a second later, the men erupted in cheers when CORRECT! flashed on the screen.

"Unbelievable!" exclaimed a man near Lucas. "She's a friggin' savant or something."

"Definitely something," Lucas agreed with a proud smile. He moved deeper into the crowd and saw six drinks of various heights and colors standing next to the computer monitor. Judging by the way none of the men claimed them and how the ice melted in them, Lucas rightly assumed that the drinks had been purchased for Miranda.

"I've never seen anyone play five games on one quarter," the bartender said, approaching Miranda. "If you get this next round of five questions right, the next round for the bar is on the house."

"Are you sure?" Miranda asked calmly. "There are a lot of thirsty guys here." One of them laughed as he placed his hand on Miranda's bare back. She turned and gave him a shove that would have landed him on his backside if two other men hadn't caught him up. Lucas inwardly cheered.

"I'm sure," the bartender said. "Only I get to pick the category."

"Then let's up the ante," Miranda said. "If I answer all my questions right, then the house gets the free drinks and I get that Boston Celtics snow globe over there." She pointed to a dust-covered plastic orb sitting atop the cash register.

"You're an easy lady to please." After wiping his hand on a bar towel, the bartender offered it to Miranda. "Deal."

They shook on it, and Miranda pressed START on her free game. The bartender reached over and pressed HODGEPODGE in the category column. His finger darted to the neighboring button and pressed DIFFICULT under the skill level column. The men booed.

"What do I get if I earn the time bonus, for answering quickly?" Miranda's calm settled the crowd.

The bartender grinned confidently. "Angel Face, I will give you everything in my tip cup if you outrun the timer."

"Then let's go." Miranda pressed BEGIN. The first question popped up, along with the black bar that counted down the time.

"It's tennis, guys," a man announced. "Who is the only player to defeat Steffi Graf and Monica Seles at Wimbledon in the same year?"

Miranda answered Zina Garrison before he finished reading the question.

"In 1990 in Australia, he was the first player to be disqualified from a Grand Slam tournament."

Miranda banked John McEnroe. Her audience opened their wallets and began stuffing tens and twenties into the bartender's tip cup.

"It's golf now. What tournament did Tiger Woods win in 1996 for his first tour victory?"

"Las Vegas Invitational," Miranda mumbled as she selected that choice.

"Everybody knows that," scoffed one of the spectators.

The bartender angrily slapped his bar towel against the top of the monitor.

"Okay, hockey. Who was the first NHL player to score at least twenty-five goals for two different teams in the same season?"

Miranda picked Dave Andreychuk.

"Last question . . . Oh jeez, it's World Cup soccer," the question reader said. The other men quieted and the bartender pumped his fist in triumph. "Which English player received Pele's praise after his performance against Argentina in the 2002 World Cup?"

"She can't know this," someone said as Miranda logged in her answer.

"That was an unfair question," said another man.

"Holy cow," said the man who had read the questions aloud. "Nicky Butt? She did it. She got them all right!"

"What about the time bonus?" the bartender asked anxiously. He spun the monitor and read the information on the screen. "'New record, forty-seven seconds. Free game.'"

The drink orders started flying at him, but the bartender took a moment to grab the snow globe and his tip cup. He presented both to Miranda with a wink. "Way to go, Killer. Stop in again soon."

"Thank you." Miranda stood. A man took her coat and shook it out for her. He helped her into the leather trench, and then whispered something in her ear that made her lip curl. She whispered something back, something that made him back off as the blood drained from his face. Miranda saw Lucas as she pushed her way through the men, who thanked her for the drinks.

Lucas was wearing a black Chesterfield over a tuxedo. He was so handsome that Miranda knew right then that her best birthday present was there before her, wrapped in custom-tailored wools and satins.

"I've never seen anyone hustle sports trivia before." He took her hand to kiss it, but met the snow globe she had clasped in it. "Why on earth did you want this thing?"

She displayed it, moving closer to him. "See that little '11' in there? This is a special issue that came out after Bill Russell won his eleventh NBA championship. This thing is in great condition." She shook it. Lucas watched her watch the swirl of the snowy glitter, and his heart swelled as he gazed at her. "This is worth a fortune," she whispered.

"Speaking of fortunes, perhaps you should pay for dinner tonight." Lucas raised the hand holding the bartender's tip cup. It was stuffed with bills, and Miranda looked upon them proudly.

"The first rule of sports wagering is to know your opponent," she said. "Men never think women know anything about sports."

"Then he bloody well got what he deserved. Are we off?"

"We're not staying here for dinner?"

"It's your birthday, love. I've something far better planned than hot wings and mozzarella sticks at an upscale sports bar."

"But I like this sports bar."

"Which is why I wanted to meet you here. Unlike you, I tend not to stick out so much in places like this. What did you say to that bloke that just tried to pick you up?"

"He told me I was making him 'so tight,'" Miranda said. "I said I appreciated the compliment because this was my first night out as a woman following my sex-reassignment surgery in Argentina."

"Miranda, you're wicked," he laughed.

She took his arm and they started for the door. "Where are we going?"

"Dancing," he said.

"Um . . . do we have to?"

"Of course not." He stopped just inside the entrance. "We can do whatever you'd like."

"I'm not in the mood for crowded places." She opened the door and spied a shadowy-grey limousine double-parked in front of the bar. "Yours?"

"None too subtle, is it?"

The limo driver opened the door and Miranda hurried inside. "I think we're safe, Miranda," Lucas said, settling in beside her. "You lost the photographers at Guiglio's."

"Meg and Dee have snitches everywhere." She wriggled out of her coat and laid it over her knees. "Her network of waiters, bartenders, valets and maitre d's is tighter and harder to detect than members of al-Qaeda."

"That limits our options this evening, love. Are you sure you don't want to go dancing?"

She turned slightly, to face him. "The last time I danced was eleven years ago with my dad's uncle Harvey at my father's retirement party. I tripped over his feet about ten times. I went and hid in the bathroom when he wanted to do the Macarena." She lowered her eyes, knowing that dancing with Lucas would be a far different thing than doing the Macarena with her late uncle. "Genetics somehow denied me both a sense of rhythm and basic body mechanics."

Lucas stretched his arm over the back of the seat. He used the end of her long ponytail to draw a heart on the back of her neck and the pleasing feathery sensation made her breath catch. "I know a very quiet, very private place. No one will bother us or spy on us."

"Where?" She hoped it was nearby.

Lucas turned toward the driver and said, "Home, Jeeves."

"His name is Jeeves?" Miranda asked.

"No," Lucas grinned. "I've just always wanted to say that."

Miranda probably would have enjoyed the view of Boston's skyline from Lucas's penthouse if she had been able to see it. A mountainous heap of boxes and gift bags festooned with ribbons and bows blocked the living room windows. It didn't take her long to figure out what was going on, especially after the name on one of the ribbons tipped her off.

"Harrods," she said, whirling on Lucas. He was on the phone, placing an order with room service. "This isn't . . . you didn't . . . Lucas!"

He covered the phone's mouthpiece with one hand. "Happy birthday?" he offered with a slight shrug.

She stepped deeper into the penthouse, dragging her leather coat behind her. "This is obscene. Are all of these gifts for me?"

He finished his order, hung up the phone, and scratched his head as he approached her. "It depends. Are you going to get angry at me and storm out if I say yes?"

"No."

"Then yes."

Miranda clutched at her throat. A six-foot teddy bear wearing a plaid ribbon about its neck sagged against the tempered glass of the living room window. A leather chair in the shape of a baseball glove, a giant bow slapped onto its back, looked ridiculously out of place amid a sea of smaller bags and boxes. Lucas retrieved a small box wrapped in blue foil from the pile. He stood behind her and watched as she opened it and drew a blue velvet pouch from it. She unfastened the drawstring, and the pouch flattened to reveal a choker comprised of emeralds and white and yellow diamonds. Like a disco ball, the rocks glittered, casting stars of light in every direction.

"I don't know anything about jewelry," Miranda choked, her mouth gone dry, "but I think this necklace is probably worth more than my whole entire life."

Lucas chuckled as he pulled the choker from her hands and set it around her neck. "It matches your eyes." He fastened it on. "I knew it would." He walked her a step to her right, so she could see her reflection in the mirror behind the bar. "I had it designed especially for you. Do you like it?"

She stroked a finger over it. It was pretty, in a shiny, playing-dress-up kind of way. "It's not really my style, Lucas." She reached to unclasp it. "I'm not a jewelry person." She took his hand and set the choker in his palm. "I can't keep this. I'd never wear it. I'd be too scared of losing it. Or being decapitated by someone determined to steal it right off me."

He dropped the choker onto the flattened pouch. "You are the first woman I've ever met who didn't enjoy diamonds. I'm sorry if I've offended you. I suppose I was a bit overzealous on my shopping spree. You aren't a very easy person to shop for."

"I have simple tastes, Lucas." She slipped her arms inside his jacket and hugged him close. "I don't need a lot of expensive gifts, and I especially don't need diamonds. Every time one of the women in the newsroom gets engaged, she prances around the newsroom showing off her diamond ring, like it means something important. All it means is that her fiancé has too much money and not enough sense to get her something practical."

"The ring is a symbol of a man's willingness to commit."

"Rings don't stop men from cheating, and they certainly don't stop other women from helping men to cheat. A big ol' rock is just a big ol' rock. It doesn't mean a thing."

Lucas threaded his fingers through hers. "I'm afraid to ask what you would consider a practical engagement offering."

"A grill."

"A what?"

"A grill. A Weber grill. Preferably black or burgundy, with a twenty-seven-inch diameter cooking surface. And charcoal. Never gas. Marriages fail, but good barbeque is forever."

"I see you've given this considerable thought." He shook his head, marveling again at her ability to shock and surprise him.

"A grill is something useful. It has meaning."

"I'll keep that in mind." He kissed her forehead.

"I can't keep these gifts, Lucas."

"Of course you can. They're for you."

"I don't want them." She eased out of his embrace. "I would prefer that you didn't buy things for me."

His dimples faded away along with his smile. "I'm not trying to buy you, Miranda, if that's what you're thinking."

"I know." She chewed her thumbnail. The night had taken an awkward turn, and she couldn't figure out how to get it back on track.

Lucas lowered her hand from her mouth. *I'm bloody stupid,* he thought. *I've tried to impress her with gifts, just as her father uses gifts to placate her mother.* "I'm sure I can find a charity or two here in Boston that could sell these things at auction." He curled her hands over his and kissed them. "I'd like you to keep at least one of the gifts, though."

"It depends on which one," she said warily.

He left her to sort through the stack of boxes and found a long one wrapped in gold paper. "Now this," he said, beckoning her to the sofa, "is a birthday present you'll like."

She sat beside him on the chintz-covered sofa and opened the box. Inside it, underneath layers of gold tissue paper, was a Manchester United sweatshirt. She looked at the label. It was a Triple Extra Large. She smiled and hugged the sweatshirt to her chest. "I wanted this," she admitted. "When we were at Harrods, this was the only thing I almost bought."

"Why didn't you?" Lucas asked.

"I didn't want any souvenirs of the trip. At the time, I thought it would be best not to bring any reminders home with me."

"And what do you think now?"

"I think I owe you a big thank you for this wonderful birthday present." She draped the sweatshirt over the back of the sofa.

"And I think you owe me some dancing." Lucas left the sofa to go behind the bar. Ten seconds later, the soft notes of a song Miranda knew well drifted to her ears and turned her knees to jelly. "That's Al Green," she whispered to herself. "That's 'God Blessed Our Love.'"

It was one of her favorite songs. She stood and held Lucas's gaze as he returned and took her hand. He led her clear of the glass cocktail table and the heaps of presents and spun her into his arms. Clasping her right hand to his heart, he laced his fingers through hers as he swayed to the beat of the song.

"Sorry," Miranda said, her cheeks aflame with embarrassment when she stepped on his foot. Lucas pressed his cheek to her temple and wrapped an arm around her waist. He hummed along with the song, his voice a perfect harmony to Al Green's. "Oops!" Miranda said after stepping on Lucas's foot again. She pulled free of him. "I'm sorry. I'm ruining this whole night. I'm a crappy dancer. I'm used to Uncle Harvey letting me lead."

Lucas took her by her waist and pulled her against him. "This is a wonderful song, you know."

"I know."

"It's about a man who finds heaven in the arms of the woman he wakes up with, after spending the night making love to her."

Miranda watched his lips as he spoke. The movement of his gorgeous mouth, his accent and the words he shaped with it was a three-pronged attack that left her weak and willing to do anything he would ask of her.

"Could we try it this way?" he asked after she tramped his feet once more. He draped her arms over his shoulders, his fingertips leaving goose bumps in their wake as they traced her bare arms and went down to her sides. The warmth of his palms between her shoulder blades and at the small of her back made her tingle. His chin brushed her hair, and he felt her relax in his arms. In perfect concert, they moved to the music. As the song ended, Lucas drew away just enough to ask, "Was that satisfactory?"

Miranda nodded, having decided to use her lips for something far more interesting. She cupped Lucas's face and lowered it to hers, until his warm and eager lips touched hers. He didn't know which thrilled him more, the sweetness of her chaste kiss or the semblance of nudity offered by the scandalously low-cut back of her dress. Both combined to ignite a blaze behind the zipper of his tailored trousers.

He broke the kiss, hoping to quell the rising heat in his loins. "You drove the men in that bar crazy tonight. Is that what it's like when you're on assignment? Are you swarmed by handsome, athletic superstars clamoring for your attention?"

The light dance of his hands over her back made her itch for more intimate contact. "For every athlete that's hit on me, there are a thousand women willing to give their souls to be with you. What's it like, being adored by every woman you see?"

His fingertip lovingly glanced off the tip of her nose. "Not a fraction so good as being adored by the one woman I adore."

She locked her fingers at his nape. "You adore me?"

"Yes. Well . . . most of you, anyway."

Miranda blinked, her eyes wide. She was no swimsuit model, but still . . .

Lucas chuckled lightly. "I adore your eyes," he said, softly kissing each of them. "And your chin." Her head tilted back as he placed a nibbling kiss on her chin. "And your freckles." The innocent kisses he planted on her cheeks sent a wicked heat straight to her center. "I'm rather partial to your ears, and this sweetly scented place just beneath them." She hugged his head to her and pressed her body even closer to his as he suckled her earlobe and teased it with his teeth.

"Anything else?" she sighed dreamily.

"Yes," he whispered in her ear. "Everything."

He would have gone on singling out his favorite parts of her, tasting and taunting them each in turn if room service hadn't arrived with the meal he had ordered. Miranda scurried out of sight while Lucas opened the door for the waiter. The shorter man wheeled the food in and took the time to arrange the silver-domed plates on the linen-draped dining table.

"Thank you, Mr. Fletcher," the man said exuberantly, his long, needle-thin braids bouncing after Lucas pressed a large folded bill into his hand.

"Thank *you*, sir," Lucas said. He was turning to call Miranda out of hiding when the waiter doubled back.

"Mr. Fletcher, I'm not supposed to do this, and I could lose my job, but would you mind giving me your autograph?" the waiter asked, a hot blush heating his bronze cheeks. "It's for my wife. She's your biggest fan."

Miranda peeped around the corner to see Lucas graciously accepting the pen and hotel notepad the waiter offered.

"What's your wife's name?" Lucas asked.

"Johnetta," the waiter said. Lucas hastily scribbled the autograph and handed it to the waiter. "Thank you, Mr. Fletcher. This is so good! My wife will be so happy when she sees this."

"No problem," Lucas said. "Goodnight."

The waiter headed for the door and Lucas turned to retrieve Miranda. "Mr. Fletcher?" the waiter called. Lucas froze in his tracks, smiling around his gritted teeth. Miranda pinched back a laugh.

"Yes?" Lucas said. "Is there something wrong?"

"Well," the waiter began nervously, "it's just that my daughter really likes your music, too. Her walls are covered with posters and pictures of you and your band."

Then she likes more than just Lucas's music, Miranda thought, surprised at her sudden flash of jealousy.

"Could I get your autograph for my daughter?" the waiter asked. "She's seventeen and she just loves you."

"Certainly," Lucas said. "What's her name?"

"De'Nosha," the waiter said. "It's spelled like it sounds. And, Mr. Fletcher, while you're at it, could I get one for Kesse, Alison—with one "l"—Martika, Cassie, Rachel, Jessica and Dimitri?"

"Dimitri?" Lucas questioned.

"Those are students in my daughter's dance class," the waiter explained. "They all love you. Dimitri, he's . . . you know."

"No, I don't know," Lucas chuckled.

"He's a fan, too," the waiter said innocently.

Momentarily, Lucas handed the waiter the notepad, which was now filled with autographs for the varied and sundry women—and men—in the waiter's life.

"Thank you so much, Mr. Fletcher," he gushed, bowing as he backed toward the door. "You don't know how good it's been meeting you. We get a lot of stars here, but you are by far the coolest one I've ever had the pleasure to serve."

"Thank you," Lucas said.

The waiter kissed the pile of autographs. "This autograph just bought me a thousand soft kisses from my Johnetta!"

"Wonderful," Lucas muttered through an impatient smile.

"Mr. Fletcher, one last thing—"

"Sir," Lucas said, "please forgive me for being so abrupt, but I'd like to have dinner before it gets cold. You see, I need to be well-nourished so that I have the energy to make love all night to the beautiful woman currently hiding in the nether regions of this penthouse."

Miranda's eyes grew as wide as those of the stunned waiter, who began to laugh. "I can't wait to tell my wife about this, Mr. Fletcher," the waiter said. "Good night, sir, and thank you!"

After a dinner of lobster with roasted figs and a sumptuous chocolate tart, Lucas directed Miranda to the view while he went to the bar to pour two brandies. A glass in each hand, he turned to see Miranda awkwardly using her right hand to tug at the right underarm seam of her dress.

"This thing has been pinching my armpit all night," she complained. "Bernie picked it out because he said it highlights my best features."

"Indeed," Lucas agreed.

"Highlight, schmighlight," Miranda fussed, accepting the dark beverage Lucas offered as he joined her at the sofa facing the one-way glass. "I can't wait to take this thing off."

Lucas's eyes seemed to darken to the color of a midnight sky as he swirled the liquid in his brandy snifter. "Why wait?"

Two perfectly ordinary words became a thrilling invitation that Miranda readily accepted. She set down her glass and stood framed in the sprawling window. She kept her eyes on his face as she crossed her arms over her chest and slipped the straps from the caps of her shoulders. Lucas seemed to hold his breath as she held the dress in place for a brief instant before letting it slide to the floor.

Lucas's breath left his body in a low groan that sounded almost painful. His eyes tried to take in her features individually and all at once. He said nothing, but his expression and the deep heaving of his chest told Miranda that he wanted her perhaps more than she wanted him.

His hungry gaze moved over her, making her burn from the inside out. Standing before him in nothing but her G-string, stockings and high heels, she felt brazen and truly sexy for the first time in her life. She liked it. When she freed her ponytail and tossed her head back to shake out her hair, Lucas vaulted to his feet to cover her exposed throat with kisses.

Her hands went inside his jacket, removing it from his shoulders. She blindly worked at the buttons of his shirt, driven to feel his bare skin against hers. An animal surge of want took control of Lucas, and with one hand, he ripped his shirt open and shrugged out of it. With the other he cupped Miranda's breast. He used his thumb to tease the dusky-rose tip of it into hardness before he took it in his mouth and drew long on it.

Miranda raised her right knee, resting it against his hip. Lucas clasped her right thigh and drew her closer to him, grinding the damp triangle of silk between her legs against the hardness tenting the front of his pants.

"I can't wait to get you into that bedroom, Miranda," he said into her breast.

"Why wait?" She turned and took a step toward the bedroom. As much as he liked the sight of her backside, Lucas liked the feel of it even more. He took her arm in a firm but gentle grasp and pulled her to him, hugging her back to his chest. He lowered his head to nuzzle her neck, his hands roaming down her sides, over her garter belt and to the tops of her stockings. His fingertips, calloused from years of plucking bass strings, could barely distinguish the silk margins of her stockings from the silk of her skin. He pushed his fingers under the top edge of her stockings before bringing his hands together between her legs.

Miranda curled an arm around his head, guiding his mouth to hers. Her right hand covered one of his, urging him to continue his exploration of the sensitive territory between her thighs. She pressed her backside into his hips, grinding her flesh against the hot knot burning through his pants. One of his hands moved over her abdomen and up to her breast to tease its tender tip. His luxuriant kisses moved from her mouth to her neck and shoulders. Miranda turned, clapping her body to his as she kissed him. Lucas spun them, sending a surge of adrenalin washing through Miranda. She half expected to hear a sizzle when the hot skin of her back touched the cold one-way glass. When she reached down to free her stockings from her garter belt, Lucas closed his hand over hers.

"Leave them on," he murmured into her mouth. "Please."

As if rewarding her acquiescence, he kneeled before her. His hands glided over the whispery soft lengths of her legs as he parted them, and nestled himself between them. He shifted the silk concealing her glistening curls and her breath quickened. His expert touch parted the slick curtain hiding the swollen seed of her passion. His thick, soft hair brushed her lower abdomen and her thighs as he took that supersensitive pellet between his lips and nursed it as he'd nursed her breasts. She melted into the glass at the first leisured rasp of his tongue, her breath leaving her in a guttural hum of utter pleasure. He held it between his lips and flicked his tongue over it. Her legs went weak and her body seemed to float, as if the glass had vanished and she was freefalling the twenty-five stories between the penthouse and the ground.

Lucas's strong hands and arms supported her, holding her to his busy and talented mouth. His tongue slipped inside her, and a desperate whimper of tortured bliss escaped Miranda. He hummed his approval, his voice creating a vibration that added another layer of unbearable pleasure. His lips, tongue, teeth and voice worked in concert to bring her to sparkling, soul-shattering life. Her hands tightened in his hair as her hips bucked, an aching emptiness within her yearning for deeper fulfillment.

Lucas's want of her turned savage as he heeded her body's unspoken call. He wondered how it was possible to want a woman so much, to be enslaved by animal cravings for her tastes and scents. Each coupling had only made him want her more.

He stood, opening his trousers as he went. He seemed to spring from them, his heat drawn magnetically to hers. He clasped the firm, supple rounds of her buttocks and lifted her. She assisted by wrapping her arms around his neck and fastening her legs around him. Awkwardly, he used one hand to tug aside her G-string just enough to lunge into her, his muscles taut from the strength it took to hold off the eruption building within him.

Her strong, lean thighs gripped him, flexing minutely as she moved to meet each of his thrusts with unrestrained anticipation. She hugged his head to her breasts, glorying in the scrape of his teeth and the texture of his tongue against her straining nipples. He braced her against the glass so he could gain more leverage as he forged a primitive pact between them with each thrust into the dark furnace of her body. Her thighs pulsed around his hips; her flat abdomen kissed his over and over with each stroke.

Miranda panted for breath as she felt him grow larger within her. She raised and lowered herself, displaying a selfish nature she never knew she possessed. Every cell of her body cried out for Lucas and the wonderful release only he could give. His hands moved into her hair, to brush it from her face. He murmured her name, gasping it at turns when the sweet torture of her movements threatened to rob him of his resolve to make this interlude last. With one arm he supported her weight while he used his other hand to frame her face and guide it toward his. He fought for her gaze, but she kept her eyes closed as she kissed his forehead and his temples. Lucas lapped at the mist of perspiration coating her collarbones. He dipped his head farther and kissed her breasts, exuberantly laving their pebbled peaks before taking the tempting buds full into his mouth.

Miranda grew noisy as she climbed closer and closer to the pinnacle of her bliss. When he wrapped his arms around her waist and lifted her away from him, setting her on her feet, she almost cried out in frustrated surprise.

"The cap for the cannon," Lucas breathed heavily, tucking himself back into his trousers as he backed away from her. "I forgot."

She slumped against the glass, panting to catch her breath as Lucas fell heavily to the sofa. She went to him on legs quivery with unspent desire. Lucas's shoulders heaved with his deep breathing. His hands trembled as he swiped them over his sweaty face.

"Lucas?" She set a hand on his shoulder. "I'm fairly certain that you stopped in time." She did a quick calculation in her head, then said, "If my math is correct, this isn't one of my fertile days. I'm as regular as Big Ben in that department."

"It's not that." He rose and headed for the bedroom. Miranda grabbed his discarded shirt and slipped it on before following him. He was coming out of the master bathroom, a boxed hotel courtesy kit in hand, by the time Miranda caught him.

She stood in the doorway and watched him dump the contents of the kit on the bed. From amidst the tiny toothpaste and toothbrush, mouthwash, shampoo, conditioner, hand lotion, face and body soap, shower cap, breath mints and lip balm, Lucas selected a strand of three condoms. His apprehension made him clumsy as he sat on the foot of the bed, his head bowed. He turned the condoms over and over between his fingers.

"Lucas, you don't think that I . . ." Her mind fed her a rapid replay of the various ways their bodies had combined in the past forty-eight hours. ". . . have something," she finished.

"Of course not. As I said, it's not you." He braced his elbows on his thighs and sank his face in his hands.

"You mean *you* have something?" She nervously pulled the flaps of the shirt closer about her body.

He looked up at her and he couldn't blame her for the worry he saw in her eyes. "No, love. Well, yes, but not in the way you must be thinking."

Her ardor reduced from a roiling boil to a simmer, she sat on the bed and leaned over to unfasten the velvety straps circling her ankles. Her shoes gone, she peeled off her stockings. The sight only reminded Lucas of the cold ache between his legs. Her oversized shirt gaped open as she crawled over to him and straddled him, keeping the turgid flesh between them in plain sight. "What's the matter?"

His fingertips traced her spine as he met her confused gaze. "I've never forgotten to put on a condom before. Never."

Strangely humbled by his admission, she took the condoms from his hand and tore one of them open. She carefully dressed him, further stimulating him in the bargain. "All better?"

"Not yet." He cupped her face in his hands and kissed her, his mouth drawing hers into a dance their bodies would soon emulate.

Eager to pick up where they had left off, Miranda raised herself on her knees. Lucas captured her left nipple in his mouth and hungrily drank from it as his fingers pulled aside the wet satin gliding against his hardness. Miranda steered him inside her, a moan of unabashed delight oozing from her throat as she lowered herself upon him. Without breaking contact with her, Lucas lay on his back. Miranda reached back and gripped his thighs, her body undulating upon him and clenching around him.

"Look at me," he begged between gritted teeth. "Miranda, love, please . . . look at me."

Her hair fell in a shining curtain as she bowed her face, but she didn't meet his eyes. Her gaze fell upon his lips and his chin, and the space between his eyes, but she wouldn't lock her eyes with his. When he brought his thumbs to the slick valley crowning the place where they joined, and he used them to massage her into a wild, mewling creature of passion, she shut her eyes tightly and surrendered her body to his loving.

Passion stole Lucas's fight for her soul as his body shuddered beneath her. His spine curved and his climax burst from him, leaving his skin humming and his ears ringing. Miranda folded herself upon him, kissing his lips, his earlobes and his throat as waves of sweet sensation churned through her. He smoothed her hair and returned her delicate kisses, all the while wondering how she could share all but her eyes with him.

CHAPTER 8

Miranda woke up tangled in Lucas's sheets. The bed was otherwise empty, but she heard voices—one familiar, one foreign—in the living room.

"Her name is Tabitha," the stranger's voice said. "That's T-A-B-I-T-H-A."

"Like the daughter on *Bewitched*," she heard Lucas say.

"Yeah, man, that's right!" the stranger crowed. "You know that show? I love that show! Boy, it sure must take a long time for American shows to make it over to England."

Miranda smothered a laugh in her hand, and wrapped the sheet around her as she left the bed to go to the bathroom. When she came out, the stranger was thanking Lucas for an autograph. Although she was eager to get her hands on the coffee she smelled, she lingered in the bedroom, waiting for the coast to clear.

One of the bedroom walls was made of one-way glass. Miranda stood before it and stretched, staring down at the congestion on Boston's busy downtown streets. The city was so much prettier and peaceful from twenty-five stories up. Miranda wished that she could wake up to such a view every morning, instead of the garbage cans and the brick sides of neighboring buildings.

She left the window and drifted to the gigantic console housing the television. She figured she'd watch *SportsCenter* while Lucas tried to politely extract himself from a conversation about the merits of Prince versus Stevie Wonder. Miranda forgot about *SportsCenter* when she opened the console and saw a photograph propped in the space between the television and the inside of the console.

She had picked it up and looked at it before it occurred to her that it was none of her business. Her stomach dropped. The glossy 8x10 pictured her on the top of her fire escape. She was dressed much as she was now, in a bed sheet, with her hair a sleep-tousled tumble about her face and shoulders. In the photo, she smiled and waved down at Lucas. Now, as she gripped the photo in her hand and stormed out of the bedroom, vinegar began to brew in her veins.

Lucas, having successfully gotten rid of the latest star-struck room service waiter, was pouring coffee into two cups when Miranda stomped up behind him. "Where did you get this?" she demanded, whapping his bare back with the photo she wielded. "Did your people call Meg and arrange for photographers to be outside my window when you left the other day?"

Lucas calmly turned and took the photo from her. "The hotel provides complimentary daily papers," he began. "Coe's daughter saw the fire escape photos of us, and she brought them to my attention. I liked this one, so my manager called the photographer at the *Herald-Star* and asked him for a print of it." He set his hands on her shoulders, close to her neck. "That's all, Miranda. I wanted a picture of you, and you have to admit, those photos of you are beautiful."

Miranda's wrath vanished, to be replaced by a brilliant flash of embarrassment. "I'm sorry," she started. "I'm so sorry I reacted that way, Lucas. I just . . . I don't like being in the paper and I thought . . . it's stupid. Forget it. Forgive me. Please?"

Lucas handed her a cup of steaming coffee. Miranda held it in both hands and allowed Lucas to seat her at the table, where a lavish breakfast had been spread out for them.

"You thought I tipped off the press, to gain publicity," Lucas supposed as he sat in the chair opposite her.

Miranda stared into her coffee, too ashamed to admit that his guess was exactly what she'd thought.

"Is that what Jordan Duquette used to do?"

She lifted her eyes. "He always denied it, but there was no other way the *Herald-Star* could have found us at some of the places we went to. Sometimes the photographers would beat us to the location."

"I would never use you to sell records, Miranda."

"How do you know about Jordan? Bernie?"

Lucas gripped the knees of his white cotton pajama pants. He thought carefully about his next words before he spoke them. "Bernard certainly gave us a full dossier on you. But prior to our meeting in Conwy, my publicist did an Internet search and a background check on you."

He braced himself for her reaction. The morning sunlight illuminated the annoyance and frustration that took turns shaping her features, but she said nothing.

"Please, don't be insulted," he said. He set his elbows on the table and balanced his chin upon his thumbs. "I wanted to know more about you, of course, but I also had to consider the well-being of the residents of Conwy. I couldn't very well invite you to my home if you turned out to be a serial killer out on parole."

"I still might become a homicidal maniac." She nodded toward the *Herald-Star* that had come tucked under their breakfast tray. "I know where I'd start."

He reached around a carafe of pomegranate juice and a platter of Belgian waffles to take one of her hands. "Background searches are a necessary part of my personal relationships. I've had death threats from everyone from radical religious groups, irate husbands whose wives played a particular Karmic Echo song too much, and women convinced that they're my secret lover or long-lost wife or daughter."

"How can you really trust anyone?"

He held her gaze, and yet again the beauty of her clear, bright eyes threatened to overwhelm him. "I've found that a look in the eyes tells quite a bit about a person's true character."

Miranda agreed. Lucas's deep, ink-blue gaze held nothing back. She wallowed in its warmth. Even if she refused to believe the honesty and love she saw in them, she couldn't deny their existence.

"You may as well know that I plan to hire a bodyguard for you," he said.

"I don't need a bodyguard. Are you serious?"

"That room service waiter last night could have gone for my throat with a steak knife because of his wife's interest in me just as easily as he'd asked for an autograph," Lucas explained. "We can't be too careful, particularly given the e-mails I've received in the past two days."

"What did they say?"

"The basic 'I hate you and want you dead for being with Miranda Penney instead of me' sort of missives from the deluded and jealous segment of Karmic Echo's fan base," Lucas said. "It will pass."

"I guess most of your fans would rather see you with a nice blonde with blue eyes," Miranda supposed.

"My true fans want only for me to be happy," Lucas assured her. "I can do without the ones who think I shouldn't be with a black woman."

She picked at a slice of cantaloupe on her plate. "I've gotten e-mails, too," she confessed quietly. "At work. My *Herald-Star* e-mail address runs at the bottom of all my stories, so readers can write me to tell me how wrong I am about a team or an athlete. Since I came back from Wales, I've gotten hundreds of e-mails, most of them from your fans. Some of them think I've stolen you away from them, others think you're too good for me, others think that you'll get sick of me and move on soon."

"What do you think?"

"I think that it's hard to think with you sitting there, looking like a Greek god come to life."

"I leave for Australia in eleven days," he began. "I'll be there until the end of the month, and I would love it if you joined me there for Christmas. But before we go one minute further, I need to know something, Miranda." Holding her hand over the small table, he stood and urged her to his side of it. He sat her on his right knee and locked his arms around her. "I don't want this to end."

"What to end?"

"This." He kissed her bare upper arm. "I want to know that I can go on the road and that it will always lead back to you. Or that you can come to me. I want to make a serious go of this. Do you?"

She opened her mouth to scream that she wanted nothing more than a serious go, but she caught herself. He would be in Boston for eleven more days. If they were as good as the past two days had been, then she could easily contemplate something more permanent. The logical part of her liked that plan, but the wounded, irrational part of her dealt reason upon reason to get out while she had only pleasant memories.

Jordan had never made her feel the way Lucas did. Lucas made her feel as though he were the luckiest man alive, all because she was with him. Just sitting on his lap stirred hot and reaching sensations that made her willing to agree to anything. Lucas, quite simply, was an easy man to love.

And there lay the problem.

"I have a job, Lucas," she said, glad that her hair hid her face from him. "I start a ten-day work week tonight. I'm on high school wrestling. I don't think I'll have much time to spend with you before you leave for Australia. Maybe . . . maybe it would just be best if we . . ."

He brushed her hair from her face. "If we what?"

The words sat in her head, waiting to be spoken, but she couldn't make her mouth say them. Lucas stole them, and they sounded even worse from him than she imagined they would have tasted in her own mouth. "If we didn't see each other again?"

"No!" She almost screamed, twisting to face him directly. "No," she repeated calmly. "I don't know what I want. I wasn't expecting you to bring this up."

"I suppose I should have left well enough alone, then."

She cupped his face with her right hand. "I don't want you to feel obligated to me while you're here, that's all."

"Is that what you think you are to me? An obligation?"

"I didn't mean it like that." She wrapped her arms around his shoulders. "I don't know what I mean about any of this."

"Have you ever dated anyone like me before?" he asked.

"You're my first musician," she answered, deliberately misunderstanding him.

"That's not what I meant. Have you ever dated anyone outside your race?"

"Of course. My job makes it easy. Sports is like an international dating pool."

"So my race isn't an obstacle to you?"

"No. I hope mine isn't the only reason you're attracted to me. Interracial pairings seem to be fashionable among the rich and famous these days. I'm just a regular person, Lucas. I don't want to be some sort of accessory."

"Don't be scared, Miranda." His understanding, strength and warmth as he returned her embrace helped ease her niggling doubts and distrust. "Perhaps I've made a wrong assumption or two about us," he said into her hair.

"You haven't." She drew away and touched his lips with a fingertip. "You're right. Bernie and Calista were right, too. I'm scared out of my head about what's happening between us, Lucas. I felt something, too, on the night of the crush. When I opened my eyes and saw you, I was sure that I'd died and was looking into the face of one of God's highest angels." She caressed the side of his face, seeing him as she had at their first meeting. "I didn't feel pain, or hear the noise of the crowd. I didn't even remember how I'd gotten there. I just wanted to spend the rest of time right there, in your arms, looking into your eyes."

"We belong together, Miranda," he said before catching her mouth in a kiss that made them forget about breakfast, crazed fans and what the next eleven days would hold. The present was all that mattered, and how quickly they could bare themselves physically as they had emotionally. Lucas made love to her right there on the plush, triple-padded carpeting, this time verbally proclaiming his love for her as eloquently as he had shown her through touch. While Miranda wouldn't say the words aloud, her kisses, caresses and responses left no doubt in Lucas's mind that she shared his feelings.

"Can we make this work?" he asked her soon after their interlude. He had drawn a crystal dish of sliced tropical fruit to the floor, and he fed her chilled slices of sweet blood oranges there on the carpet.

"I suppose so," Miranda said, unsure if the decision had been made by her head, her heart or her hormones, or all three acting in concert against her better judgment.

Lucas opened the door to the Walker S. Hill Athletic Building, and then followed Miranda inside. He took a deep breath, and chuckled as he exhaled. "All school gymnasiums smell the same," he said. "Like feet and floor polish."

"If I could bottle it, I'd wear it as cologne," Miranda said. "I'd call it Eau de Past Glory. Some of my best high school memories took place on the basketball courts."

"My road crew likes a good pick-up game of basketball," Lucas said. He glanced at the trophy cases and championship banners lining the walls of the lobby as he followed Miranda deeper into the building. "I've got a pretty fair jump shot, for a bloke who grew up on football—sorry, soccer—and rugby."

Miranda gave him an indulgent smile. "I'll believe it when I see it."

Lucas stopped her. He took her by her waist and pulled her against him. "Are you challenging me to a game of one on one?"

She stared at his sensuous mouth as she said, "Is that really how you want to spend your last night in Boston?"

"Absolutely."

Miranda lifted her face to taste the word on his lips. She stopped and abruptly drew away from him when a scream began to echo through the otherwise empty corridor.

"Oh my God, it's Lucas Fletcher!"

The scream could have been adolescent or adult, male or female—Miranda couldn't tell. Regardless, it triggered a rush of bodies through the double doors leading to the gym floor. Miranda let the wave of people carry her away from Lucas, and she watched as a familiar scene once more repeated itself before her.

Until tonight, she had gone on her stories, unnoticed and unrecognized until she had to gather post-match quotes. She had written and filed her stories via e-mail from Lucas's penthouse or her apartment—when she and Lucas could sneak past his fans.

Being in public with Lucas was a lot different than being in public with Jordan, Miranda had realized in the past week and a half. Sports fans recognized Jordan, and all but the most overexcited baseball fanatics had typically kept a respectful distance, happy with just a nod and a whisper in Jordan's direction, or a quick handshake and a compliment on his latest game performance.

Everyone recognized Lucas. Even the fifty-year-old wrestling coaches had shamelessly crowded around him, clamoring for autographs the moment Lucas entered the gymnasium. The grandfatherly J.D. Campbell, Haverford High's varsity coach, had asked for an autograph supposedly for his wife . . . Jerome David.

Lucas was patient and oddly beautiful in his humility at being asked for his name on the strips and scraps of paper waved at him. He treated each person as though he or she were a friendly neighbor. Miranda recalled how Jordan would inflate like an African puff frog when someone, especially an attractive woman, asked for his autograph. He would strut around for hours afterward, referring back to the incident as if he had just bestowed the Holy Grail upon a tortured and desperate soul.

Miranda cringed when she thought of how Jordan had always expected her to stand in the shadows of his limelight when fans approached him. He'd once left her sitting alone at the end of a bar for two hours while he regaled a half-dozen Boston University coeds with his on-field exploits, and then had yelled at her in the parking lot for talking baseball for ten minutes with a man old enough to be her father. Back then, she had confused his possessiveness with genuine affection. With Lucas standing amidst a sea of adoring fans, his eyes searching her out and softening each time he found her, Miranda now knew what true affection was.

One of the boys slated to wrestle in the match Miranda had been sent to cover seemed to speak without breathing as he told Lucas all about his own musical pursuits, and then brought up Karmic Echo's ill-fated opening night show in Boston.

"Me and the guys from my band, Black-Eyed Dog, camped out to get tickets," the young grappler said, his dropped r's and ing's revealing his South Boston roots. "My brother saw you in Boston in October and he said the show was wicked good. The cancellation was a pisser, but the makeup show was too good, dude."

"Speaking of performances," Lucas said as he furiously scribbled his name on the back of a sweatshirt worn by a quivering young girl, "I hope to see some good wrestling here tonight. I'm told you're quite talented."

The boy's blush of excitement swallowed his ruddy freckles as he passed a hand over the scruff of his fiery buzz cut. "Are you shi—" He caught himself. "Messin' with me? You heard about *me*?"

"You're Thomas Winsor, aren't you?" Lucas said.

The kid put his hands on his head in disbelief. "What, are you psychic?"

Lucas gazed at Miranda. "See that woman over there by the water fountain? The woman in the white shirt and jeans?"

"The hottie?" the wrestler said casually.

Lucas fought back a laugh. "Yes. The hottie. Her name is Miranda Penney, and she's here to report on your match."

"From the *Herald-Star*? That's Miranda Penney?" The champion wrestler's words trailed after him as he zipped over to Miranda. Three of his teammates joined him, and a sea of maroon and gold warm-up suits soon surrounded Miranda.

"I read your column every day," a larger teen said.

"I don't have a column." Miranda scarcely heard her own voice over the hard pounding of her heart.

"I have your picture on my wall," a man-sized sophomore said, grinning through a mouthful of clear braces. "It was in the paper."

"I got mine outta the *Herald-Star*, too," stated another boy, who bore such a strong resemblance to Jordan that Miranda's stomach jumped a little. "You're much prettier in person, ma'am."

Ma'am? Miranda thought, horrified. *I'm not old enough to be a ma'am.*

Miranda was ready to climb the water fountain to get away from her hormonally-challenged audience when a gaggle of petite young girls descended upon her en masse. The multicolored jewels of their eyes, bright with the shine of having first met Lucas, pinned her in place.

"Oh my God, you are so pretty!" one of the girls gushed. "I seen you in the papers and I was like, 'Oh my God, she's so pretty! She's like, ten times prettier'n Penelope Cruz and Jennifer Lopez put together.'"

"Lucas is a wicked good kisser, I bet," another girl said, the words 'paypuhs,' 'wicket' and 'kissuh' striking Lucas's funny bone.

"No comment," Miranda said, glaring at him. Lucas's crowd had thinned while the one around her steadily deepened. He gave her an unassuming smile that made the overlapping chatter bearable.

Almost.

"Are you gonna marry Lucas Fletcher?" a gum-popping, Meg-in-training asked.

"If he won't, I will," said a suave senior who sidled up close to Miranda.

"Miss Penney?" Lucas called. "Will you be entertaining your fans much longer?"

The group of high schoolers, the girls in particular, pushed in closer to Miranda. "Can I have your autograph?" they each asked.

"You're kidding, right?" Miranda asked, dumbfounded.

A wave of high-pitched "Please's" pierced Miranda's eardrums. She scrawled her name beneath Lucas's on the papers forced on her. She silently thanked God when the wrestlers were called into the gymnasium, and the students tore themselves away from her.

Lucas went to her and threaded his fingers through hers. "I shouldn't have forced you to drag me along tonight. I didn't mean to interfere with your job."

"My work doesn't start until those kids hit the mat. I'm worried that you'll be bored. Although with you in the bleachers, those boys are going to wrestle their unitards off."

Lucas cringed. "There's a graphic I could do without."

"How did you know that the red-headed kid was Thomas Winsor?"

"You told me about him this afternoon, when you were trying to talk me out of coming to this meet with you. You said that Winsor was an honor student, that he played in a band called Black-Eyed Dog and that he was having an undefeated season." Lucas gave her a playful shove. "I listen, Miranda."

Hiding a delighted smile, she said, "C'mon," and took his hand to lead him to the gym doors. "We won't get seats if we don't get in there."

He opened the door for her. "Is high school wrestling so very popular?"

"Only since you got here," Miranda said, entering the gym. "Look." She gave a subtle nod toward the bleachers, which seemed to writhe with overexcited wrestling fans clutching cell phones to their ears. "Even the teachers are calling their friends and family to tell them that Lucas Fletcher is at a Haverford-Parkington wrestling meet."

"Perhaps I should leave," Lucas said. "I don't want to steal the attention from the athletes who came here to wrestle tonight."

Miranda pulled him along to a bench on the gym floor. "You being here is the best thing that could happen to both of these teams. I just hope that when Meg's photo rats show up, they have as much respect for these kids as you do."

Miranda was glad that the walls of Hodge's office were glass as she approached. He hadn't told her why he'd summoned her to his office, but she saw a moment or two in advance that Meg and Rex had something to do with it, since they, too, were waiting in Hodge's office.

"You wanted to see me?" Miranda said to Hodge as she closed the door behind her. She cast a guarded eye at Meg, who stood behind Rex's chair like a demonic First Lady and looked as out of place in Hodge's distinctively masculine office as a pickle in a pumpkin patch. Meg's alien presence raised the fine hairs on the back of Miranda's neck. "You know, Hodge, if you're busy, I can come back later."

"Miranda, please sit down." Hodge's use of her name made her shoulders tense. The last time he'd called her Miranda, it was because he'd gotten a complaint from a team owner who had been offended by a reference Miranda had made to his pitcher's creative use of tube socks.

"Whatever it is, I probably did it, and I'm sorry," Miranda said as she sank heavily into a swivel chair.

"Miranda," Rex said, leaning toward her from the one cushioned wing chair in Hodge's office. "I can't allow you to cover high school sports any longer." He took a *Herald-Star* off of Hodge's desk. "It's these photographs." Rex handed her the issue. It had been folded open to her infamous "Bed Spread," as the guys in sports had come to call it. "We got some complaints today, from Haverford and Parkington High parents who don't think a woman of your character should have access to impressionable young people."

Miranda spat a furious epithet. "I didn't authorize or support these photos in any way," she ranted. "You put my private life on display, without my permission or knowledge, and now—"

"You became a limited access public figure when you appeared on our cover and with every byline that appears in the paper," Meg said coolly. "You're fair game, Miranda."

Miranda's knuckles cracked as her hands clenched into fists and she faced down Rex. "You can't punish me because a few uptight parents have the wrong idea about what I do in private."

"So you aren't engaging in premarital sex with Lucas Fletcher?" Meg said, her voice a slithery hiss.

"That's uncalled for!" Hodge shouted, nearly startling Meg out of her chic Ann Taylor pumps.

"Rex," Miranda started, straining to keep her tone calm, "Karmic Echo fans have been camping out in front of my building. The crowd shrank dramatically today, now that Lucas is on his way to Australia, but there are still enough fanatics out there to fill out an NFL roster. I can't make a move without someone asking me for my autograph or a photo, or asking about Lucas. Your cover story, and your intrusion in my life, are the reasons why all these parents have burrs up their—"

Rex stopped her words with a wrinkled hand. "You're not being punished for these photos, Miranda. You're being promoted."

Miranda's head whipped around to look at Hodge. "What is he talking about?"

Hodge sat back in his chair, his distaste for what he was about to say plain on his face. He tossed a pencil onto his desk the way a trainer would toss a towel into the ring to stop a fight. "No more wrestling for you, Miranda," Hodge said on a frustrated sigh. "As of today, you're on baseball and basketball." He shot a dirty look at Meg.

Rex delivered the deathblow. "You're interviewing Jordan Duquette at one tomorrow afternoon. His contract is being renegotiated, and things could get pretty tense. We haven't featured him in the paper since the season ended, and it's time we changed that."

The wide-eyed shock Miranda showed Hodge became blind fury by the time she turned to face Meg and Rex. Their motives couldn't have been any plainer. *Lucas left for Australia this morning,* she thought, *and they know it. That's the only reason they want me to meet with Jordan.* "Shouldn't I be interviewing Alec Henderson, too? He's the team captain, and I'm sure he'll have an opinion on what the team should do."

Meg's shifty gaze lit on Miranda. "Is there a problem with the Duquette interview, Miranda?"

Miranda shot to her feet, jabbing a finger at Meg. "Since when do you sit in on sports assignment meetings?" She took an angry step toward Rex. "Why are you letting this obnoxious gossip hound dictate the content of the sports section?"

"Because our focus groups say that they're buying my papers because they want to know what happens next with Lucas Fletcher and Miranda Penney," Rex said.

"It's not everyday that a world renowned tomcat settles for a saucy little tomboy," Meg piped in.

"I like that," Rex said, turning to look up at Meg. "The Tomcat and The Tomboy. What can you do with that? You're brilliant, Meg."

"Oh, get a room for God's sake!" Hodge shouted. He stood and, at six-foot-five, he had the immediate attention of everyone in the room.

"I've had enough of this, Rex. This is my department, and I say who does what." He left his desk and set a gentle hand on Miranda's shoulder. "If you don't want to sit with Duquette, you sure as hell don't have to. It's your call, Miranda."

"The only thing sadder than an old jock throwing his weight around is an old jock standing in an unemployment line," Rex said as he slowly stood.

"Mr. Wrentham, is that a threat?" Hodge's half step in their direction made Rex and Meg recoil. "How would you like to see this old jock on a witness stand, testifying to your harassment of my reporter?"

"Harrassment?" Rex tittered, the chalky sound making Miranda's skin crawl. "I'm merely expecting *my* reporter to do her job."

Hodge's forearm muscles flexed as he crossed his arms over his chest. "You're pimping Miranda's past association with Jordan Duquette and her present one with Lucas Fletcher to sell this rag. Your motives are as transparent as the walls of this office. I'm sure the union's lawyers will see it just as clearly."

"I can't help but notice how vigorously you've come to Miranda's defense," Meg said. "It makes me wonder just how close you two have become over the years, especially in light of the fact that Miranda is the only woman in your department."

"Don't be sordid, Meg," Hodge said.

"Don't stand in my way, Jed," Rex warned. "Or have you forgotten that your contract is up for renewal in two months?"

Miranda moved with the lethal grace of a truly pissed off cobra as she put herself between Hodge and Rex. "I'll meet with Jordan," she said. "At the ballpark."

Meg started to speak, but Rex stopped her with a firm touch. "The photographer is expecting you and Jordan at Le Fin," he said.

Miranda bit her tongue to hold back the chain of swear words in English and Portuguese she wanted to spit at Rex. Le Fin was one of Boston's coziest and most romantic restaurants. It specialized in seductive, gourmet desserts that tantalized the senses. It was the sort of place where couples went on first dates and returned to, months or years later, to stage proposals. "My interviews have never included photographs of me and my subjects," Miranda said. "And I've never conducted one at a place like Le Fin. I won't start now." *Not with Lucas half a world away*, she thought with a pinch of anguish. "If you want me to interview Jordan, he and your photographer had better be in the press room at the ballpark."

Miranda knew that she had the upper hand after Meg and Rex exchanged a shady look before agreeing to her terms. *They need me way more than I need them*, Miranda realized. The thought gave her a small measure of security, even as she saw that it didn't do a thing to protect Hodge.

"You're on administrative leave for two weeks," Rex glowered at Hodge as he started for the door. "Effective immediately."

Miranda waited for Rex and Meg to disappear before she turned to Hodge. "Krakow's our union rep," she said urgently. "I'll go get him, and I'm sure you can get that leave stricken."

Hodge laughed, shocking Miranda. Hodge rarely smiled, let alone chuckled, and this turn of events hardly warranted laughter. Miranda reconsidered her position when Hodge explained why he wouldn't fight the leave.

"This is a prime example of how stupid Rex is," he said. "As of tomorrow, I'm on personal leave anyway. I'm finally taking my kids to Disney World, before they get too old to enjoy it. I put in for leave three months ago."

"But what about your record? Rex can still put the leave in your personnel file."

"Randy, you should know by now that there only three reasons people leave the *Herald-Star*," Hodge said.

"They quit, they retire, or they die on the newsroom floor," Miranda said.

"You got it, kiddo."

"Thanks for sticking up for me. I really do appreciate it."

"I just want you to be happy, kid," Hodge said. "If I can piss Rex and Meg off in the bargain, then I'll just consider that a bonus."

Hodge winked, sending Miranda on her way with the knowledge that she had at least one powerful ally at the *Herald-Star*.

Miranda rubbed her mittened hands together, trying to keep her fingers warm in the freezing ballpark as she paced before the first row of seats near the gangway leading to the home team's locker room. Fenway Park had been her second home at one point. It was there she had first met Jordan, and where she had lived out her humiliation at his betrayal. Hodge had offered to put her on the professional hockey beat, but she had insisted on going about her usual routine. Hockey would have been a nice change of pace, but the last thing she had wanted was for Jordan to think that he had gotten the best of her.

Even though she hated the reason behind it, she was glad to be back on baseball. It was one of her favorite sports, truth be told, and she had missed it.

Miranda was recalling some of the best games she'd seen in Fenway Park when Jordan appeared and climbed up to her row of seats.

"You're twenty minutes late," she said by way of greeting.

"I hit some traffic." His brown cheeks were ruddy with the chill December air. "I didn't know that our meeting spot had been changed until I was already at Le Fin checking my messages."

"Great," she said absently. She lifted her backpack from one of the seats and led the way to the press room inside the stadium. Once there, Jordan took a seat opposite her at a small white table. Miranda took a pen, a reporter's notebook and a microcassette recorder from her bag. She set the recorder in the middle of the table while Jordan took off his wool coat. Instead of his usual white shirt and khakis, he wore pleated wool slacks and an understated cashmere sweater.

"Why are you all gussied up?" Miranda asked suspiciously.

"Where's the photographer? I was told that I'd be shot today."

"I wish," Miranda mumbled.

"Don't be mad, Andy. This will be a lot better for both of us if we just keep it friendly."

"My thoughts exactly." She hit the start button on her recorder and uncapped her pen. "Jordan, you had the best batting average and the highest slugging percentage on the team last season, and you've asked to be compensated for your achievement. What makes you think you deserve more than what your original contract entitles you to?"

"I deserve more because I've shown that I'm worth more." His charming smile was designed to blunt his conceit, but Miranda knew him well enough to know that he meant what he said. "If you looked at all of my numbers, you'd see that I had a career season."

"I'm aware of your stats. What I'd like to know is how much of your success you can attribute to the new coaching staff, and whether you think the team is stronger since Marty Grobin, whom you described as 'disagreeable, flaky and a whiny cry-baby,' was traded."

"Wow." Jordan stroked his chin. "I said all that about Marty?"

"Yes. Right before you attacked him in the locker room last season after that New York game."

"I punched him because he made a pass at you," Jordan argued.

"I was handling it just fine before you pulled your dramatic He-Man crap," she snapped. "We weren't together anymore at that point anyway, so what did you care if Marty Grobin wanted to take me to dinner?"

Jordan stared at her. "Seeing Marty with you like that made me crazy. Almost as crazy as seeing you with Lucas Fletcher."

Miranda stopped the tape. "Do you hear yourself? You're the one who threw *me* away, remember? You're the one who shacked up in a hotel room with not one but *two* naked women." The memory no longer had the power to hurt her it once had, but Jordan's next words stung her all the way through to her heart.

"You acted like you didn't care if I strayed or stayed," he said. "There's so much temptation out on the road. Even guys with wills of iron give in once in awhile. What was I supposed to do? You never acted like you cared what I did while we were apart."

Her throat felt like it was closing. "That's your excuse for what you did? That it was *my* fault because I wasn't a clinging vine who needed to call you every minute of every day just to make sure that you weren't sleeping with some woman you picked up at a game? I trusted you, Jordan, and you knew perfectly well how I felt about you."

"Actually, I didn't," he insisted. "You never said it. Not one single time. You never gave me your heart, Miranda."

"Funny how it got broken, just the same."

He rubbed his knuckles along the creases in his pants. "You never looked at me the way you look at Lucas Fletcher."

"I didn't come here to rehash the past." She steered the conversation back to safer waters. "I need fifty-five lines by six o'clock, so could you please just answer my questions?"

He took her hand, startling her with his quickness. "I'm sorry, Andy. I humiliated you and showed a really nasty part of myself that night in St. Louis. There have been so many times that I've wanted to take that night back and do right by you. But I can't go back in time. All I can do is look forward, and hope that there might be room for me in your future."

His earnest delivery touched her, but she wanted to get the interview back on track. "Let go of my hand," she said softly.

"I know you don't want to hear this, and I'm not trying to interfere with your thing with Lucas," he went on. "I just want you to know that I'm sorry. And that I really, really miss you." His reluctance showed as he released her hand and pressed the start button on the recorder. "Now, about the Marty Grobin trade . . ."

Miranda sat alone at a wide, circular table at Chikakó, the Brazilian restaurant Calista and Alec had chosen for the Christmas Eve Penney-Henderson engagement dinner party. She watched her sister, who was breathtaking in a tight, ice-blue cashmere dress that made her look like

Miss Universe. She set her right elbow on the table and half-heartedly picked at the pork cracklings on a plate of *mandioca*. She had spent her childhood and most of her adolescent years envying Calista's incredible beauty. Now, seeing her on the down slope to thirty, she envied her sister all over again.

Calista looked so happy as she worked the room with Alec, chatting and laughing with various members of the Penney and Henderson families and flirting in Portuguese with Roberto Rosada, Chickakó's owner. Alec fawned over his bride-to-be as though she were his fondest dream made real. He was the rare combination of a great athlete and a great man. He was never the most dazzling player on the field—that was Jordan's specialty, the flashy combination of luck and aggression that made the highlight reels. But Alec was a strong, solid player. Where Jordan would tally three homers in one game after a two-week scoring drought, Alec would consistently score runners with solid singles and doubles. Alec had gone pro straight out of the University of Georgia, but he had planned for life after the pros with a double major in business and finance. With his ebony skin, tall, muscular build and dazzling black eyes, Miranda had no doubt that Alec and Calista would make beautiful children. Alec would be a wonderful husband and father, and Calista deserved nothing less.

Miranda stared vacantly at the centerpiece, an ice bowl with slices of fresh lemons, limes, coconut and sweet pea suspended in it. "*I* deserve nothing less," she muttered, startling herself out of her reverie with a desire that she'd never meant to acknowledge. She glanced around self-consciously, hoping that no one heard her. Thankfully, the Penneys and Hendersons were having too much fun to notice her talking to herself.

Calista and Alec had invited their respective families to Boston for this big dinner party to give them a chance to meet. Miranda's parents were only children and her grandparents were deceased, so the Penney clan consisted of four. Since Alec's family lived in Dorchester and was ten times the size of Calista's, Boston had won out over Silver Spring as the site for both the dinner party and the June wedding. And, as Calista had pointedly told Miranda, "If we have the dinner party in Boston, you won't have any excuse to get out of spending Christmas with your family."

Miranda sighed, missing Lucas all over again. The party would have been so much more fun with him there, and she would have loved introducing him to the family recipes Roberto had prepared at Calista's request. Aña Penney hailed from Bahia, a region known for its neo-African cuisine, and Roberto had done an excellent job turning out dishes such as *frango a passarinho*, the fried, sliced chicken that had been a Sunday night staple in the Penney household. Lucas liked bananas, and Miranda was sure that he would have enjoyed *banana frita*, the fried plantains.

Miranda's favorite dishes were *lombo à mineira*, grilled pork loin with sautéed collard greens, and *tutu de feijão*, a mix of thick, sticky cassava paste flavored with smoked sausage, beans, scallions and egg. Not terribly impressive on their own, they made Miranda's taste buds dance when served over rice flavored with *dendi* oil. She was sure that Lucas would have savored the meal as well as the chance to meet her mother and sister.

She had wanted to visit him in Australia, but when she'd told him about Calista's dinner party, he'd convinced her to stay in Boston by telling her that it was the "sisterly" thing to do. And she was doing it very well, if being sisterly meant sitting alone at the table while the plates were being cleared away to make room for the cornmeal pudding and caramel custard.

Miranda caught sight of Alec's parents, who smiled and talked as they danced to music dominated by a six-piece percussion ensemble that specialized in *batacuda*, the African influenced rhythms of Brazilian samba. Alec's parents were natives of Jamaica. They had been married for thirty years, and as they danced, Mr. Henderson looked at his wife as though she were still the fresh-faced teenager who'd been his first girlfriend.

Miranda found her own parents sitting near the open bar. Aña wore a red cocktail dress that complemented her petite figure. Her smile didn't quite reach her eyes as she looked at her husband, Clayton, who had his high voltage smile aimed at one of the pretty waitresses. If she looked at her father with an objective eye, Miranda knew that she would have seen a well-built, handsome man who was aging remarkably well. Silver threaded the black hair at his temples, and deep laugh lines creased the nut-brown skin at the corners of his hazel eyes, but Clayton Penney still had the star quality that had made him such a popular baseball player.

Beyond that, Miranda couldn't view her father objectively. She knew too well what he was.

She knocked back the remaining drops of the mango martini she had ordered earlier. By the time she was slamming the glass back down on the table, she wasn't alone anymore.

"Hey," Calista said, taking a chair near Miranda.

"Hey what?" she grumbled.

"I haven't had a chance to talk to you since I hit Boston." Calista gave her a crooked smile. "It's a good thing the tabloids keep up with you, or I might never have known that Lucas Fletcher is practically my brother-in-law."

"I've been busy with work and stuff," Miranda said glumly.

"By 'stuff' you mean Lucas?" Calista persisted.

"Why do Alec's brothers keep staring at me like that?"

Calista looked over her shoulder. "Like what?"

The Henderson brothers stood in a huddle at the bar. Chas was the tallest and youngest, and, like Alec, he had their father's merry black eyes and mahogany skin. Chas kept peering over his shoulder in Miranda's direction. Tucker, the oldest, repeatedly glanced at her over the tops of his glasses. Tucker had a slightly slimmer build, square jaw, and his mother's dark cocoa complexion. The looks the handsome Henderson brothers gave Miranda didn't bother her as much as the enigmatic little grins they kept flashing at her.

"Maybe they want you to get them tickets to Lucas's next concert," Calista joked, earning a scowl from Miranda. "What's the matter? I was only kidding."

"Is that all people see when they look at me?" Miranda whispered, leaning in toward her sister. "Lucas Fletcher's girlfriend?"

"They see a smart, beautiful woman who's been hiding out at this table all night. Is there something on your mind? Do you want to talk?"

"This is your big family powwow," Miranda said. "You should be mingling with your future mother-, father-, sister-, brothers-, aunts-, uncles- and cousins-in-law."

"Unlike you, the Hendersons aren't family. Yet." Calista scooted her chair closer to Miranda's and elegantly crossed one knee over the other. "How are things with Lucas?"

A surge of unfamiliar emotion calmed Miranda. "Good," she smiled. "Surprisingly good. We're spending New Year's in Barnsley Gardens."

"Is that in Wales?"

A blush darkened Miranda's cheeks. "It's in the Blue Ridge Mountains in Georgia. It's sort of a resort. Julia Barnsley, the daughter of the man who built the place, supposedly originated the 'With God as my witness, I will never go hungry again' line that Margaret Mitchell used in *Gone With The Wind.*"

Calista rolled her eyes. "I don't know why you're so enamored of that stupid book. I'm guessing it was your idea to go there?"

Miranda didn't answer. "He wanted to come here with me tonight."

"Why didn't he?"

"At the time, I didn't want to have him spend Christmas with our family." Miranda looked at her father. He was standing at his table, holding a waitress's hand in both of his. "It would have been too depressing. Plus, Jordan's here."

"Well, he is Alec's best friend."

"I just think it's best to keep Lucas and Jordan as far apart as possible. Lucas would be cool about the whole thing, but Jordan would make a scene. He'd do anything to get his picture in the paper."

"You're going to have to introduce Lucas to us eventually."

"I haven't been seeing him for that long. I'd rather not bring him into my personal life."

"Andy, you're sleeping with him. How much more personal can it get between you?"

"I can't explain it, Callie. I can't just bring him down to Silver Springs for Mama's *bobó de camarão* and to meet the family."

"Is that because he's allergic to shellfish or because you're sure that he's not going to be in your life long enough to make meeting us worthwhile?"

Miranda wanted to deny her sister's speculation, but it happened to be the truth. "I just want things to stay the way they are. It's perfect the way it is, when it's just the two of us. I don't want to tamper with it."

Calista nudged her sister with the toe of her shoe. "You mean you don't want to move forward."

"I think I need another drink." Miranda signaled for the waiter.

"What you need is to get over your extreme mistrust of the men you—"

Clayton Penney's loud appearance drowned out Calista's words. "What are the two most beautiful girls in the world talking about over here?" He rested a hand on the backs of their chairs and bent over between them to give them each a kiss on the cheek. Calista, ever the sophisticate, took up a linen napkin and delicately dabbed at the bourbon-scented spot of moisture Clayton's kiss had left on her face. Miranda used the sleeve of Grandma Tillie's dress to give her cheek an angry rub. "It's a party, girls," he went on. "You look like you're over here discussing nuclear disarmament. Let's drop the intensity from a ten to a two."

"I have to go check my college basketball scores," Miranda said, rising from her chair.

"Or maybe you just want to sneak off with Jordan," Clayton loudly guffawed. "I saw the picture the *Herald-Star* ran of you and Jordan at the ballpark. Great interview, honey. Are you and Jordan getting back together? I thought you dumped him for that musician."

Calista quickly stood between Miranda and Clayton. "Dad, why don't you go get Miranda and me a couple of cocktails?" Calista took her father by the shoulders and gave him a gentle nudge toward the bar.

"The *Herald-Star* would love to have people thinking that Jordan and I are an item, but nothing could be more ridiculous," Miranda hissed. "And just so you know, Daddy, Jordan tossed *me* aside. I wasn't enough for him." Miranda saw herself reflected in eyes that were exactly like her own. "One woman doesn't seem to be enough for certain men."

Clayton couldn't have looked at her with more distaste if she had spit on him. His smile froze as he took a step closer to her. "You just can't stand to see other people happy, can you? Why are you trying to ruin your sister's dinner by bringing up something that just doesn't matter?"

"You're the one who brought this up," Miranda said.

"Don't you have any respect for your mother?"

Miranda shook with anger as she pushed her chair in and readied herself to leave. A soft but firm voice held her in place.

"Hypocrite."

Miranda and her father turned toward the tiny figure of Aña Penney. "How dare you, of all people, question Miranda's respect for me?" she said quietly, her words carrying the lilt of her native land.

Clayton's hazel-green eyes searched his wife's knowing black ones, then narrowed at Miranda. "It's been years, and you just had to tell her, didn't you?" he accused.

"She didn't tell me anything I didn't already know, Clayton," Aña said. "I've known about every one of them." She fingered the diamond and pearl necklace he had given her seven years ago following that particular "business" overnight in Baltimore. "The wife is the last to know, but only if she isn't the one doing her husband's laundry. You were smart to pay for gifts and hotels with cash, but you shouldn't have left so many restaurant receipts in your pockets."

A burst of laughter came from the dance floor as Alec and Jordan danced with each other. The dinner guests seemed to have no idea that while they were celebrating the building of one family, another one was breaking down.

Clayton's broad shoulders sank as he eased himself into a chair. "Why didn't you say anything, Aña?"

Her mother's bitter smile chilled Miranda's heart. When Calista moved to her side, Miranda put an arm around her waist. "I thought that you would leave me if I said anything," Aña admitted. "You see, Clayton, I loved you more than I loved myself for a long time." She sought Miranda's gaze, and found it. "For too long."

Miranda wasn't the only one who heard the finality in her mother's tone. "We need to talk about this, Aña, please, before you do anything rash," Clayton pleaded.

"Sure." Aña nodded thoughtfully. "But I'm not sure how much good it will do."

"Mama," Miranda intervened. "Please . . . don't do anything hasty. I'm sorry about bringing any of this up tonight."

Aña took her daughter's hands. Miranda was surprised by the strength in their delicacy. "Don't apologize. I owe you an apology. My lie," she shifted her gaze to Clayton, "*our* lie, has affected you in the very way I'd hoped to avoid by keeping up this masquerade of a marriage. I'm sorry, for deceiving you."

"You're not the one who should be apologizing, Mom," Miranda said.

"I don't owe either of you anything!" Clayton snarled, his face darkening with fury. He calmed enough to take Calista's arm and draw her to his side. "Can't you see that your sister is trying to ruin my marriage?"

"Dad," Calista said evenly, disengaging herself from her father's grasp, "you beat her to it."

CHAPTER 9

Lucas surveyed the suite, making sure that everything was just right. For the past month, he and Miranda had been meeting in various hotel rooms in North America, rarely spending more than a night together before one or the other was forced to jet to another city or time zone for a game or a concert. The travel was little more than a necessary inconvenience when compared to the ongoing nightmare of the paparazzi.

The *Herald-Star* had placed a premium bounty on photographs of them together, and stories about them had been appearing regularly in Meg LaParosa's egregious column. Some were clearly made-up, mean-spirited musings—such as one accusing Miranda of sleeping with every man in the sports department—and others were just plain ludicrous.

One item had given Lucas momentary pause. His manager had secured an issue of the *Herald-Star* in Sydney. The paper, dated two days after his arrival in Australia, had carried a photograph in *Psst!* of Miranda leaving Fenway Park with Jordan Duquette. Miranda hadn't seemed aware of the camera as she exited the ballpark, pulling her collar up against a blustery winter wind. Jordan, on the other hand, looked directly at the camera. He had a million-dollar smile befitting a multi-million-dollar baseball star.

The picture was wholly innocuous at first glance, but had become irritating at second glance. Upon closer inspection, Lucas had noticed four big brown knuckles peeking around Miranda's right hip. The picture—the knuckles—wouldn't have bothered him if not for the blurb beneath it:

When the Tomcat's away the Tomboy will play. Luscious Lucas Fletcher was still in the air bound for the Land Of Aussies when our eagle-eyed photog captured this cozy couple leaving Fenway Park . . .

In finer print at the end of the column was a tease referring the reader to Page 89 and Miranda's interview with Jordan.

Common sense told Lucas that Miranda's meeting with Jordan had been strictly work related. Still, he had suffered a piercing flash of jealousy at seeing her with another man. Particularly the one who had dealt some of the emotional bruises she still bore.

Lucas paced the suite, repositioning a vase of four-dozen scarlet roses, and wondering why Miranda hadn't told him of the interview. But then she never spoke of her work, unless he prodded her into it. She hadn't mentioned the paper at all during their three-day New Year's retreat to Barnsley Gardens two weeks ago. As he brushed an imagined speck of lint from the heavy white drapes, Lucas recalled that she had gone oddly quiet when, on the same holiday, he had asked about her family's visit to Boston.

He'd had the best New Year's of his life in their cozy mountain resort. Every morning he'd awakened to mist-shrouded mountains and his body wrapped around Miranda's as though they were a pair of linked question marks. It was the offseason, so the resort was in hibernation, for the most part. The quiet was a nice change from the hustle and hassle of sneaking in and out of big-city hotel rooms.

Lucas stood at the windows and stared out at his perfect view of Capitol Hill. Washington, D.C. was a beautiful and energetic international city. As such, reporters and photographers from all over the world lined the street ten stories below his windows, and they were probably waiting on the same thing he was: Miranda.

Her flight had landed an hour ago, and Lucas had arranged for a car to bring her to the hotel. The driver would take her directly through the underground garage and she'd enter the hotel through the service doors. If all went as planned, Miranda would be spared yet another run through a gauntlet of media.

The media had been a part of Lucas's life for twenty years. He was used to it, and now it bothered him only as much as it bothered Miranda. In London, he'd assumed that she was as voracious and intrusive as all the other reporters he'd ever encountered. But having seen her in action, he knew that her style was far less aggressive and much more comfortable for both her and her subjects.

It was also more fruitful. Miranda was an excellent researcher, and she knew her sports and stats thoroughly. She managed to be warm yet professional, and she had a knack for drawing out that ephemeral something that gained an interviewee's trust. Lucas had accompanied her on one of her interviews in Dallas. He remembered staring wide-eyed in amazement when a strapping star basketball player spilled his past as an abused child after Miranda asked him about his volunteer work with foster children. And true to her word, she didn't print any of his pained memories in her story. Miranda was that rarest of creatures—a gifted reporter who could be trusted.

The more time he spent with her, the more he came to know her. And to love her.

Lucas stepped away from the windows. His bare feet moved soundlessly across the white shag carpeting. The room was an opulent study in white and chrome. It was very nice; then again, all of his hotel rooms were nice. But Lucas was tired of meeting her in hotels, no matter how luxurious. Nothing compared to the nights they had spent at Miranda's, in the gigantic bed in her rented apartment. He wanted more nights like that. He suddenly wanted a place of permanence to share with her, a sanctuary. Like Conwy.

He looked at his watch. "Where is she?" He was like a schoolboy anxious for the afternoon bell to ring. He started for the phone, to call her on her cell, when a soft knock sounded on the door. Lucas couldn't answer it fast enough. He flung it open, expecting Miranda to be standing there. She was, and still his heart seemed to fill his entire chest cavity as he gazed at her.

She was coming off a three-day stretch of games in Miami and a four-day road stretch in Cleveland. An overstuffed backpack and duffel bag weighed down her shoulders, and her ponytail was a little off-center. The corners of her lips rose in a watery smile, and when Lucas took her in his arms, she seemed to melt against him.

"Tired, love?" he asked. He kissed her cheek and the side of her neck before nuzzling her ear.

She nodded into his chest and let him walk her into the suite. "How were your shows?"

He took her bags and set them on a white marble table. "Annapolis is always good. All three shows were sold out. Midshipmen always turn out for the show and give it that extra charge. Baltimore was a bit better only in that I like playing the smaller venues. I can relate to the fans more intimately."

Her face stiffened as she unbuttoned her coat. "Exactly how intimately?"

Lucas shrugged and helped her out of her coat. "I dunno. The venue held about fifteen hundred."

Her forehead relaxed, but her mouth remained in a severe line.

"We do a shorter set, but it's more intense," Lucas said, hanging up her coat. "I like being able to pick individual faces out of the crowd."

"I'll bet," Miranda said under her breath as she went to the bar area and inspected the contents of the fridge at the minibar, which in Lucas's luxury suite, was actually more of a maxibar. She pulled out a small carton of orange juice and poured it into a crystal tumbler. Lucas quietly watched her gulp it down.

"What?" she snapped.

He approached her, tapping his fingertips together. "I haven't seen you in person in two weeks. Ordinarily, you would have fallen victim to my irresistible charms and covered me with your delectable kisses by now." He braced his hands on his side of the bar. "You've been distracted and somber since New Year's," he said gently. "Have you gone off me?"

She set down her empty glass, hooked her thumbs in the back pockets of her jeans and stared at her feet. "I'm just feeling a little run down. I haven't had a break since New Year's. Rex is trotting me around like a prized pet, I haven't slept since we left Barnsley Gardens, my stomach's been bothering me, and . . ." She finally looked at him. His attentive and concerned gaze made her feel guilty about her lukewarm reception at the door. He had gotten his hair cut since the last time she'd seen him, and as usual, the handsome planes of his face were clean-shaven. The first three buttons of his black shirt were undone, he wore his favorite pair of faded jeans, and his feet were bare. He looked fresh and relaxed, and Miranda envied him for it. "It's been a rough stretch," she finished.

He cupped her cheek. She turned her face into his palm and pressed the heel of it to her lips. "I'm not off you," she said. "Looking forward to seeing you today is the only thing that kept me going for the past two weeks."

Lucas leaned over the bar and framed her face in his hands. He pressed kisses to her forehead and her cheek, and he was embarrassed at how relieved he was to know that she still wanted him.

"I need a shower." Her eyes closed as she savored his touch. "I'm covered in grime from airplanes and cheap hotels."

"You take your shower and I'll order up a hot dinner."

"I won't be long." She gave him a peck on the lips, teasing him with a soft nip at his lower lip before she left him panting after her at the bar.

As befitted a suite in a five-star hotel that catered to royalty and rock superstars, the bathroom was fit for a king. Stars of light twinkled off the 18-karat gold fixtures and faucets. The white marble tile had been polished to a mirror shine. Thick white towels had been rolled and stacked in a pyramid upon a glass table, with the exception of two large towels, which toasted on a wall-mounted warmer between the glassed-in shower stall and the deep, four-person whirlpool bath.

Miranda stared at the bidet while she used the toilet. Once she started giggling, she couldn't stop. *I'll have to ask Lucas to show me how it works later,* she thought.

She stripped off her traveling clothes and opened the door to the shower stall, which by itself was bigger than the motel rooms the

Herald-Star usually reserved for her. The shower was so big, she had to go down three stairs and walk six paces just to get to the controls to start the water. There was a fixed head and a flexible head, and she turned both away from her before she started the hot water. She stood under the wide, fixed showerhead, her hands braced on the wall, and let the water strip away layers of grit, grime, stress and pure weariness.

From the corner of her left eye she noticed the change in the glass surrounding her on three sides. Temperature sensitive, the glass grew opaque as the steam hit it. The steam also activated the aromatherapy chamber recessed high in the tile wall, well above a long grab bar.

Miranda recognized the delicate scents of orange and lavender, but the underlying aromas were a mystery as she breathed deeply, allowing the steam to revitalize her from the inside out. Each inhalation brought her closer to the peace and contentment she always found with Lucas.

I'm a junkie, she thought with a chuckle, *and I'm addicted to Lucas Fletcher.* The shower was so wonderfully relaxing she was convinced that she could curl up and sleep in it, if she could pillow her head on the one thing she most wanted. Lucas was the only piece missing now, the only thing she needed to free herself completely from the grip of her broken family and her increasingly toxic job.

"Lucas," she whispered, his name a balm to her overworked spirit and food for her undernourished heart.

"Yes, love?"

She wiped water from her eyes as she turned and saw him step up to her through the billowing puffs of steam. She smiled, and it was exactly what Lucas had been waiting for. "I've missed this." He touched a fingertip to the corner of her smile. "You looked so unhappy at the door."

"It wasn't because of you." She wrapped her arms around him, putting as much of him in contact with her as possible. "The only time I feel good is when I'm with you. Thank you for being here."

His soft laughter resonated against her ear, which was pressed to his chest. "I couldn't get here quickly enough after last night's concert. I had some business to attend to today, and every five minutes I'd look at the clock thinking that at least two hours had passed, and I was that much closer to seeing you." He shifted a bit, so that the hot water washed over both of them without gathering in the tight spaces between them. "Time plays hateful tricks on me. Today was endless, but now that you're here, tomorrow will come in a few heartbeats. It's a shame we won't have the time to really enjoy the amenities this hotel offers. The spa is excellent."

"I'm so tired of hotels," she said, luxuriating in the easy movement of Lucas's muscles as he took up a bottle of shampoo and squirted a glob of it onto his palm. "I just want to go home and stay there. Bernie says that people are still hanging out in front of my building, even though I've been gone for the past nine days."

Lucas massaged the shampoo into Miranda's hair. The scent of apples soon mingled with the orange and lavender. "You're off to Toronto tomorrow, aren't you?" he asked.

She nodded. "Six baseball interviews in Toronto, then a ten-game basketball stretch in Boston. I'm going to ask Hodge to let me spend some of my vacation days after that. I need a serious break from sports."

"I thought you liked basketball." He tried to translate her expression before he unhooked the flexible showerhead and used it to rinse her hair. She tipped her head back to keep the soapy water out of her eyes. Lucas gave her pleasant goosebumps as he moved his fingers across her scalp and through the length of her hair.

"Basketball's fine." She raised her head and met his gaze. "I'm more sick of Jordan Duquette than anything else. The paper has been trying to manufacture a love triangle between the three of us. Rex forced me to interview Jordan the day you left for Australia." She used a loosely curled fist to gently grind water from her eye. "That's the only reason I agreed to do it."

"You know I don't put stock in tabloid reports." He kissed the top of her wet head. "But thank you for telling me about the interview."

"When you were in Australia, Meg ran an item she called 'Beach Blunder from Down Under,'" she said. Lucas used a citrus-scented bar of soap to lather his hands, then ran them over her shoulders and back.

His hands glided over her skin as he massaged her knotted muscles, giving special attention to the big one across her shoulders. "It was a picture of you, Len and his wife, and that redhead I saw on the night of your makeup concert in Boston."

Lucas pursed his lips in annoyance. "That damned photo hit the wire services two minutes after it was shot, and of course, it was taken wildly out of context."

"It looked like you'd pulled off her—"

"Ariadne," Lucas said. "Her name is Ariadne. She's Isabella's cousin."

"Okay. It looked like you'd pulled Ariadne's bikini top off when you were reaching out to hit the volleyball. You both were laughing your heads off."

"Ari's string snapped on its own."

Ari, is it? Miranda sniped inwardly. *And no wonder the string broke, given the hefty masses the two Dorito-sized bits of pink spandex had been expected to support.*

"Her bikini was made of cellophane and dental floss," Lucas said. He cupped Miranda's chin and made her look at him, rather than at his chest. "Garrison and his family were there on the beach, too. So was Ari's new boyfriend, Eugenio."

Miranda tapped her inner right knee against his outer thigh. "You don't have to explain."

"I want to. I want no worries or secrets between us."

"I only had a flash of worry," Miranda admitted. "It was like St. Elmo's fire. It flared and died and I didn't dwell on it. You'd already told me that Feast and Isabella had eloped down there, and that Ariadne was the maid of honor."

"And I was best man," he pointed out.

"It was just strange seeing you frolicking on a beach with another woman. You looked really good in those swim trunks, though."

"Did I?" he said knowingly, raising an eyebrow.

"You look better out of them."

A tiny groan left Lucas's parted lips. With one sultry, sparkling glance, Miranda had full command of his body. She took the soap from him, worked up a thick lather, and ran a soapy hand over his chest, across his lower abdomen, and along his inner right thigh. She used the tip of her tongue to lift a drop of water from his chin. When he inclined his head to kiss her, she stepped back out of reach. She stood deeper under the shower spray, and let it rinse the soap from her body.

Lucas watched her twist and turn, torn between enjoying the vision of the water tracing the supple hollows and curves of her body, or giving in to the primal urges the sight invoked. When she raised her arms and tilted her head back to smooth her hair from her face, Lucas stepped up to her and traced a rivulet of water with his tongue. Starting at her neck, he followed the droplet over her collarbone and down to her breast. He spent a long moment drinking from her nipple, his lips pinching and pulling at the tight peak until Miranda went loose and limp. His hands at her waist and hips supported her as he went lower and lower still, until he sank beneath the cover of the steam. He hung her right leg over his shoulder, and she sucked in a sharp, chattering breath when his tongue burrowed through the silky darkness between her thighs. She leaned heavily against the tile wall. His mouth temporarily cooled the searing kernel of desire cloistered behind her slick folds before stoking her internal fires even higher. She pushed her fingers into his hair, gasping for breath as the water coursed over her hypersensitive skin. Her head pressed into the wall and her eyes rolled back as the rasp of Lucas's tongue and the delicate scrape of his teeth turned her insides to molten heat. Her left leg began to shake and Lucas supported her by propping up her buttocks. The water beat upon his back as he held her to his mouth, voraciously drinking from the chalice of her body.

A senseless, guttural language of carnal satisfaction left her as pulsating circles of pleasure radiated from the place where Lucas's expert lips loved her. He kissed his way back up her water-encased body. Her renewed vigor more than compensated for her passionless greeting earlier, and she claimed his mouth with her own, kissing him deeply, mimicking the rhythm of what she wanted next. If he had any doubt as to what that was, she removed it by wrapping her hand around the hard baton of flesh between them. Her touch was light but firm, easy but forceful as she stroked him, her speed increasing but never losing contact.

He tore away from her just before she breached a point from which he couldn't return. On a whoosh of steam he quickly left the shower to retrieve a small square packet from the courtesy box on the edge of the sink. He sheathed himself as he returned and in the next smooth motion he scooped Miranda up by her backside. She took hold of the grab bar affixed to the wall and wrapped her legs around his middle. He filled her in one easy stroke that stole her breath and made her heart jump. He held her by her waist as she met each of his thrusts with a downward movement and a flex of her thighs, shattering their mutual determination to prolong the moment. They generated their own slippery heat as the warm water drummed upon them, adding their unique and spicy aromas to the puffs of steams.

Their coupling was as wild and enthusiastic as that of a pair of rainforest animals. Lucas kissed her breasts, her throat, her lips. Miranda responded violently, arching her chest into him as the depths of her silken tunnel clamped around him again and again. Touch and smell became one as their bodies fused in the hot and humid atmosphere.

Lucas's whole body went rigid for an instant and then shook as his release came powerfully and seemingly without end. Breathless, he slumped against Miranda, still holding her, still kissing her throat and her earlobes as he regained his strength. Her thigh muscles quivered weakly as tiny spasms of pleasure still moved through her with each of his touches to her overly sensitive skin. She released the grab bar to smooth his wet hair from his face. When her fingers moved lower and began to play with the tawny buttons of flesh capping his hard pectorals, she felt him rising once more within her.

She wrapped one arm around his neck as she moved herself upon him. He clasped her bottom, helping her find a deep, quick rhythm. She used one hand to gently pinch and tease his nipple while she suckled and nibbled his earlobe until he reached his climax with a jaw-locking groan. He brought her with him by tilting her hips forward a bit and creating a wondrous friction against her. She locked her arms about his neck and her sweet gasps and sighs bathed the cup of his ear as her feminine darkness locked about him, drawing every twinge and hitch of passion from him.

They remained huddled together, shivering, in the aftermath of their vigorous acts. "The water's gone colder," Lucas said, kissing her.

"I hadn't noticed," Miranda laughed.

"I've taken dozens of cold showers because of you. This is the first I've taken *with* you."

She kissed his puckered fingertips. "You sound as though I'm some kind of succubus who reaches across time and space to leave you blind with raging lust and desire."

"I couldn't have said it better." He kissed her lips, raising the heat in the shower by at least twenty degrees.

Less than twelve hours after Miranda arrived in D.C., she was in a limousine with Lucas, headed back to the airport. They held hands like seniors after prom, and Miranda was happy that they were caught in traffic. With any luck, she would miss her flight altogether and get fired from her job.

"Where are you off to next?" Miranda asked Lucas. She put her feet up on the seat and rested her head in his lap. "Conwy?"

Lucas, his right elbow braced on the window frame, thoughtfully tapped his chin with his thumb. "Not exactly."

Miranda laid her hand along his jaw and aimed his face at hers. "What aren't you telling me?"

"That business I spoke of yesterday involves my work with the International Food Relief Service," he said. "A U.S. team based here in D.C. is accompanying an aid package to Central America. I've donated money to the effort and my name for fundraising purposes." He paused, considering how much he should tell her.

"No secrets," Miranda said. "You said so yourself."

"Indeed, I did." He stroked her hair, as though it would soften what he had to tell her. "They've invited me to accompany them. And I've accepted. My flight leaves at noon."

Miranda sat up, her hair spilling about her face and shoulders. "Is that really a good idea? Is it even safe? If this is a publicity thing cooked up by your label . . ."

"You and the other envoys are the only ones who know that I'm going. I want to go, Miranda. I want to see firsthand how these people are living and how the money and aid gets dispersed. I'll be gone less than three weeks."

Miranda knelt on the seat. "Regular people get kidnapped and killed down there, Lucas. You would be an especially valuable target."

He embraced her, pulling her partially onto his lap. "You're genuinely frightened for me."

She tightened her hold on him. *I can't lose you,* she thought earnestly. *I just can't.*

"I love you, Miranda." He held her close. "I'd never do anything to jeopardize what we have, and getting kidnapped or killed tops that list."

"You've been doing that a lot lately." She drew back to look at him. "Using love as a verb."

"I think it best to say it direct. To leave no doubt in your mind how I feel about you."

Miranda bit the inside of her lip. The unfamiliar pressure of tears built up behind her eyes. "I want to say it back, but . . ."

"You don't have to." He gave her a smile that was nothing short of rapturous. "I already know."

"Why are you so understanding?"

"I just told you why."

"Love is some magic thing to you, isn't it?"

"Because it is," he said simply. "If you're willing to give it a fair, honest chance."

"Amor con amor se paga," Miranda said. "Love is paid with love."

"Is that one of your Grandmother Marie Estrella's sayings?"

Miranda shook her head. "It's one of my mother's." She lounged against Lucas, enjoying the ride of the rise and fall of his chest. "Maybe that's why my parents are getting divorced," she said quietly. "My mother finally realized that she wasn't being paid enough."

"Shouldn't that make you happy?"

"I thought it would."

"You can't let their failure decide your fate, Miranda. You know that, don't you?"

She nodded. "My mom said the same thing, in her own way. We were supposed to be there for Callie and Alec on Christmas Eve, to celebrate the building of a new life and a new family. And right there in the background, my own family crumbled. Mom apologized to me. She thinks that she's the reason that I . . ."

"Can't tell me that you love me?"

"It's more complicated than that."

"Your mother is giving herself a new start," Lucas said. "It sounds like she's trying to give you one, too. If my vote means anything, I think you should take it."

"Me, too." She turned and began giving him the kisses he would miss while he was in Central America.

He stopped her, holding her by her upper arms so he could look into her eyes. "Will you?"

"I'll try."

Knowing that was the best he would get from her, he picked up where he had interrupted.

The ten-game basketball homestretch was a much-needed vacation from traveling for Miranda. She loved being able to go home after a game and sleep in her own bed. On the night of the third game, a 72–68 Saturday afternoon victory over Philadelphia, Bernie came over to

Miranda's. She had just filed her story and was checking her e-mail, and Bernie spied over her shoulder.

"'Testicular nectar?'" he read, glimpsing a phrase in an e-mail from Lucas.

Miranda closed her laptop and took it into the kitchen. "Lucas can't always call me so he sends me e-mail. Every day." She smothered a grin. Lucas's description of the things she could do to "force the surrender of" his "testicular nectar" probably violated dozens of international communication laws in addition to a few moral ones. But as a co-founding member of the Pact of the Velvet Tumescence, Miranda was flattered and impressed by his efforts. She looked forward to being alone, so she could reply to his message.

"I have an early edition of tomorrow's *Herald-Star*," Bernie said once she returned to the living room. "But I want you to promise me that you won't go insane when you see it."

Miranda's stomach sank. *Psst!* had been mercifully quiet since Lucas left for Central America. With his whereabouts unknown to most of the world, it had been impossible for Meg to cull misleading photos or erroneous tips. The best Meg had been able to do was to run an old locker room photo of Miranda trying to get quotes from Alec while Jordan stood a yard away in his sports briefs, his eyes fixed on Miranda.

Bernie opened the paper on Miranda's cocktail table, and she saw that the dragon had only been sleeping.

The Top 25 Loves Of Lucas Fletcher stared up at her from a headline spanning the tops of both center pages. "We've gathered the top 25 'loves' of Lucas Fletcher's life," read the accompanying text. "We only had room for 25. We would have needed the Encyclopedia Britannica to catalog the full list of Luscious Lucas's lusts and lady friends!"

Five rows of five glamorous mug shots covered the two pages. Names, occupations and dates were printed beneath each photo, as if each past love was a lost life. "Rex let her run this in full color," Miranda chuckled miserably. "He wouldn't even run the Super Bowl pictorial in full color."

"I interviewed her about a thousand years ago," Bernie said, pointing to the first photo.

Her name was Mikela Moore, and she had been one of Lucas's backup singers on Karmic Echo's second album. Miranda's insides clenched as, against her better judgment and sincere desires, she looked at each face and caption. The women had names like Pasquelina and Princess Marianna, and they were doctors, choreographers, graphic artists and pet groomers. Box #24 was a photo of Kiki Langlois. She was on her knees in the sand. A triangle of fine chain mail barely covered her crotch while her hands hid the parts of her breasts left exposed by her leonine mane of sun-bleached blonde hair. The photo credit stated that the picture was used with the permission of *American Swimsuit* magazine. The date beneath "Kiki Langlois, Supermodel" read simply, "February."

Miranda's own face stared back at her from Box #25. Meg had used a cropped shot of Miranda's notorious fire escape farewell photo. "Miranda Penney, Sportswriter, October–Present" ran beneath the photo.

Box #26 injected a tumult of sickening emotions into Miranda's bloodstream. The box had a white silhouette of a head and shoulders against a black background. A big, fat gray question mark was centered over the face. "Who's next in line?" was beneath it.

"*Psst!* has learned that 18-year-old songwriter/chanteuse Tess Cullor is the most likely candidate for the Number-26 spot," Miranda read to herself. "Lucas's label, Bilious Records, is trying to broker a deal with the precocious newcomer who hails from West 'O The Mississippi. Our sources tell us that Miss Cullor has the voice of an angel and a face to match. We're working on acquiring a photo of Lucas's (maybe!) next flame, so keep your eyes on *Psst!* With Lucas being incommunicado, we haven't been able to ask the man himself."

Miranda leaned back onto her sofa and covered her eyes with her hands. "Eighteen," she muttered. "That girl is half his age."

Bernie clapped a hand on her knee. "I didn't bring this over here to upset you, baby love, you know that. I didn't want you to be surprised when you went into the newsroom tomorrow. Sully has already changed your mailbox nameplate from Penney to 25."

"Mark McGwire was number 25, too," Miranda said. "It's a good number."

"Only if you're a baseball player," Bernie joked. He sobered under Miranda's pained expression. "You can't let Meg and Dee get the best of you with this." He tapped the Top 25 layout. "These women don't matter. Lucas is with you."

"Right," Miranda said, standing up to go to the kitchen. *But for how much longer?* she wondered to herself. She opened her laptop. She looked at Lucas's e-mail for a second before deleting it and snapping the laptop shut.

Lucas, in a plane high above the clouds, tried to speak softly to keep his fellow relief aid workers from overhearing his heated phone call with Miranda. He hadn't heard her voice in over a week, nor had she returned any of his e-mails. He had been keeping up with her stories via the *Herald-Star Online*, and he, too, had seen *Psst!*'s Top 25 piece. It hadn't bothered him, and he hadn't expected it to bother Miranda as much as it clearly did.

"Have you really been with all of those women?" Miranda asked. It was eight in the morning on an overcast day in Boston. She was still in bed, curled up in a ball in one corner of it. The darkened hues of her stained glass wall bathed the room in somber light.

"I've been seen with hundreds of women, Miranda," Lucas said. He hunched over the phone, shielding his head and voice from his flying companions. "That doesn't mean that I've shagged them all."

"What about Number 26?" Miranda was making herself nauseous just by talking about the feature. "Does Meg know more about your love life than you do? She certainly knows more than me. She says that you're supposed to be at some club in St. Louis tomorrow night, to see Tess Cullor sing."

"I hear young artists all the time." He stroked a hand over the stubble covering the lower half of his face. "As for St. Louis, the details were only e-mailed to me yesterday. Meg LaPirahna has obviously got a connection at Bilious who relays information to her faster than my manager relays it to me."

"What's the band called?"

"Vera Chipmunk 5-Zappa."

Miranda grudgingly admired the name. "That's a character in a Kurt Vonnegut book."

"*Slapstick*," Lucas said. "I know."

"She must be a very smart girl."

"She reminds me of myself at that age. Totally driven."

"How did you find out about her?" Miranda's jealousies were slowly ebbing the more she learned about potential Number 26.

"When we were in St. Louis last year, one of my roadies heard Tess perform at a riverfront club called Under The Bridge. He passed one of her demos on to my label, and I've been asked to consider recording a duet with her, to help launch her career. The girl is very talented, Miranda, much more so than I was at her age. She's not prefabricated. She writes and sings her own stuff, plays seven instruments and fronts the band.

"Talk to me, Miranda," he pleaded softly. "Obviously something has happened to make you speak to me as though I were a steaming heap of donkey sh—"

"I don't want to talk about this anymore," she insisted sharply. "Go to St. Louis. Do whoever you want."

"Whatever."

"Excuse me?"

"You said, 'Do *who*ever you want.' Don't you mean 'whatever?'"

Miranda didn't answer. She picked at a fraying spot on the bed sheet.

"Do you actually believe that I'm going to St. Louis to hook up with an 18-year-old girl?" he whispered.

"It's a possibility. We both know that."

"I had a life before I met you, Miranda," he said patiently, "but I never knew how empty it was. I breathed life into you that night on stage, but you breathed it right back into me. I have not been the same man since you came into my life. I'm a much happier man."

Miranda spent a thoughtful silence contemplating his words. They did little to steer her thoughts away from what most troubled her. "Is she pretty?"

Lucas hesitated. "The label says she'll sell a million records with her looks alone."

Miranda was surprised, and ashamed, of the strength of her jealousy.

"Would you like to come to St. Louis with me?" he asked. "If I arrange for a ticket at Logan, can you meet me in St. Louis?"

"Why?" Miranda bit. "So I can sit alone in the penthouse at some hotel while you meet with your singer? You'll come back at dawn full of apologies, you'll kiss me, and tell me how you just couldn't get away."

"Miranda," Lucas said carefully, "I think you have me confused with someone else."

She slapped a hand over her eyes and choked back the envy clogging her throat. "I'm sorry. Lucas, I'm . . . that was uncalled for. It was unfair and mean, and I'm sorry."

"Clearly, I've been away too long."

Miranda wanted to weep at the compassion in his voice. She knew she didn't deserve it.

"After St. Louis, I'm off to Conwy to record some tracks for my next album," he said. "Will you have any time to join me?"

"I don't have any days off until Valentine's Day weekend," she said. "I took two vacation days this week."

"Then I'll meet you in Boston on Valentine's Day," he vowed. "That's ten days off. And wear something red, or else I'll have to pinch you."

"Lucas?"

"Yes?"

"I miss you."

"Then spend the next ten days replying to my e-mails," he suggested. "This half of the Pact of the Velvet Tumescence has been sorely neglected." When he heard her laugh, he was finally able to hope that everything would work out for the best.

Lucas had flown back to Washington, D.C., and he'd returned to the same hotel suite that he'd last shared with Miranda. He had showered and shaved and had handled all of his necessary correspondence and communications. Wearing a thick, warm hotel bathrobe, and nothing else, he lounged on the sofa and stared at the starry sky over America's capitol.

Beneath a distant part of this same lovely sky was a woman whose eyes rivaled the jewels that twinkled at him from above. He mused on her fears and insecurities, and realized that she'd come by them honestly. Her father had disappointed her. Her last boyfriend, Jordan, had devastated her.

The fragile pieces of Miranda's broken heart rattled within an exterior toughened by her will to hide the true depths of her pain. Her lingering wounds were never more obvious than when they made love. She never surrendered completely to him as he couldn't help but surrender to her. She kept her soul tethered, as though it were the one part of herself she refused to share.

Miranda deserves no less than a man who will be one-hundred percent faithful, and who will love her with his whole heart, truly and for always, Lucas thought. "I'm that man," he said aloud. Thoughtfully stroking his chin, he sat up and set his bare feet on the floor. "Now to think of a way to convince Miranda . . ."

CHAPTER 10

Miranda tried to use two glasses filled with water to weigh down the pages of the cookbook opened in the middle of her stovetop. The glass on the right tipped over, spilling some of its contents into her cashew nut gravy and the rest onto the bright red rear burner. The resultant cloud of angry steam blinded Miranda to the chicken breasts spitting and squeaking in *dendi* on the front burner. In her effort to dissipate the steam by waving a scarcely used oven mitt, Miranda noticed flames leaping from a corner of the cookbook, which had come into contact with the red-hot eye. Conceding defeat, she used the glass of water on the left side of the book to extinguish the flames.

She turned her back to the steaming, smoldering, spitting and singed affair that was supposed to have been *vatapá de frango*, a romantic and home-cooked Valentine's Day dinner meant to make up for the grief she'd caused Lucas on his return trip from Central America. He hadn't mentioned her behavior again, and she was grateful for it, but she couldn't forgive herself for having behaved like a jealous adolescent.

She took up her glass of red wine and pressed it to her sweating forehead. Cooking, no matter what anyone said, was damn hard work. Chasing down a Heisman Trophy winner was easier than stuffing a chicken breast with mortadella and wrestling it shut with a series of knots and strings that would have given Houdini a bleeding ulcer.

When the phone rang, she hurried to answer it, grateful for the excuse to leave her culinary disaster behind. She pressed the speakerphone button on her wall-mounted telephone. Bernie's voice came through loud and clear, singing an Air Supply song.

"Why do you sing 'I'm All Out Of Love' every time I put you on speakerphone?" Miranda demanded as she returned to the stove, suspicious of the sudden quiet of the chicken breasts. "I really hate that song."

"Why do you put me on speakerphone when you know all I'm going to do is sing 'I'm All Out Of Love?'" Bernie countered. "How's my little Honey Julia Child this afternoon? I haven't seen any fire engines yet. That's a good sign."

"The *feijoada* came out well," Miranda said.

"Yes, well, you've always had a way with black beans and collard greens."

"I went all the way this time," Miranda proudly stated. "I used farofa yucca flour, orange slices, and made the vinaigrette."

"How did the entrée turn out?"

"Too well done."

"Café Brasil begins delivering at five," Bernie said. "Sir Lucas doesn't have to know that you didn't do it all yourself."

Miranda wrapped a kitchen towel around the handle of the skillet. The plump, seasoned bundles of chicken breast she had first set in the hot skillet were now charcoal corpses. She put the skillet under cold water, and jumped back when the first droplets ricocheted at her within a cloud of thick, smoky steam.

"Are you okay over there, Miranda?" Bernie asked. "It sounds like you're deep-frying a baby elephant."

"I don't suppose you have a Café Brasil menu you could fax to me?"

"Get it online. What time are you expecting Lucas?"

"Around seven."

"Do you need any help getting dressed?"

"No, but thanks for the offer. I'm wearing red."

"Tell, tell!"

"I'm wearing those disgraceful red boots you gave me Halloween before last." She pressed her wine glass to her lips and smiled, waiting for Bernie to ask the next logical question.

"The Emma Peel boots!" He clapped. "What else?"

"Never you mind," Miranda said casually.

"That's my girl." Bernie pretended to weep with joy. "There's hope for you yet."

She turned off all the burners and removed the sodden cookbook to her trashcan. "My street was closed off this morning. Only residents are allowed in. Did you hear anything at the paper today, about what might be going on?"

"I didn't go anywhere near News today," Bernie said. "All that murder and rape and politics gives me irritable bowel syndrome."

"What are you doing for Valentine's tonight?" Miranda asked.

"Well, darling," Bernie began, "while you were off fiddle-de-deeing with Lucas Fletcher on New Year's Eve, I was making the acquaintance of a very interesting antiques seller. We're going to Olives. An antiques dealer and Todd English all in one night . . . I couldn't have scripted a better Valentine's Day."

"I hope you have a good time," Miranda said.

"Likewise, I'm sure," Bernie responded. With that, he started singing again, and Miranda hung up the phone.

"Lost in love," she repeated as she sat down at her laptop to call up the menu for Café Brasil. She hummed the song, her anticipation of Lucas's arrival mounting as she selected a feast fit for a god.

Miranda, dressed in red, was lighting the candles on her dining table when her buzzer rang. It sounded in one long irritating note rather than the code of two short, one long and two short notes that she had worked out with Lucas. She blew out her match and grabbed her Manchester United sweatshirt from the coat tree before she depressed the first button on the recently installed security panel next to her front door.

The security panels were equipped with video and audio monitors and had been installed in every unit in the building to protect residents from overzealous Karmic Echo fanatics who had been inadvertently buzzed in by unsuspecting residents. Miranda's mail had been stolen numerous times, as had the nameplate on her mailbox. All of it had eventually shown up for sale online. The nameplates had fetched a game fifty dollars each, but a postcard of a kangaroo eating a hotdog—addressed to 'M.' from 'L.' with a Sydney postmark—had sold for two thousand dollars. Coincidentally, that was the amount of bail the seller had to post after being charged with mail theft.

Miranda, keeping her own security in mind along with that of her neighbors, didn't buzz her visitor up straightaway. "Who is it?" she asked into the intercom.

"Delivery, ma'am," a young man in a white shirt and navy trousers said.

"Could I see your service badge?" A fake delivery was one of the oldest and simplest cons to pull off. Miranda was sure that the world's first reporter had invented it.

The young man held a card before the camera. QWIX, Inc. was printed on it in big, blue block letters. The *Herald-Star* used QWIX, but it was easy to fake a business card. Miranda recited the phone number on the card over and over so that she wouldn't forget it as she hurried to the phone and dialed the number. "Hi, my name is Miranda Penney," she said before the QWIX operator could finish his recitation of the company's long motto. "Can you tell me if you have a delivery scheduled for me tonight?"

"Ma'am?" the courier at the door said, the intercom feeding his voice throughout her living room.

"Penney, Miranda," the dispatcher said. Miranda heard the tap dance of his fingers on a keyboard. "Yes. QWIX has you down for a hand delivery at seven. Our courier should have been there by now."

"He's here," Miranda said. She brought the phone with her to the security panel and buzzed up the courier. "I wanted to make sure he was the real thing. Thank you."

Before she unlocked, unlatched and unchained her door, she looked through the peephole to make sure the courier was alone and unarmed—that he wasn't packing Polaroid. Satisfied that he was clean, she opened her door.

"That's some outfit, Miss Penney," the courier said, scanning her from sweatshirt to boot heel. "Are you expecting someone tonight?"

Miranda's cheeks turned as red as the knee-high, kidskin boots she wore with her formless, oversized sweatshirt. "You have a package for me?"

The young man handed her a box wrapped in brown paper. It fit in her palm. She signed for it, and bid the nosy courier goodbye. She closed the door and sealed it tight before studying the little box, which had no markings. Miranda was equally excited and frightened. What if the box had come from one of Lucas's more disturbed fans? What if there was an explosive device in it? Or a poison dart frog? It was just the right size for that.

"I'll call Bernie," Miranda decided. "I'll get him to come over and open it."

She remembered the phone in her hand, and as she raised it to dial Bernie's number, it rang.

"Have you opened the box?"

Miranda's skin pleasantly prickled at the sound of Lucas's voice. "I was just about to call someone to come over and open it for me. I'm worried that it's a black widow spider, the perfect Valentine's gift from one of your more unhinged fans."

"Open the box," Lucas said.

Miranda circled her dining table. It was set simply for two, and the flames of three candles danced merrily in anticipation of Lucas's arrival. The box sat on the edge of the table. "Where are you?" Miranda asked.

"Open the box," Lucas repeated, a faint tremble in his voice.

"Why do you sound so funny?" Miranda picked up the box and shook it. It seemed empty.

"Because it's winter in New England and open the bloody box, woman!" he laughed.

"Okay, okay," Miranda said. She pressed the phone to her ear with her shoulder while she peeled away the brown paper to reveal a black velvet ring box. She released a long exhalation with, "Lucas," on the tail of it.

"Open the box, love," he said tenderly.

She held her breath and snapped open the tiny lid. A nervous giggle escaped her when she saw a folded piece of paper tucked into the slot that typically accommodated a ring. She set down the box and unfolded the paper. Lucas's bold, neat lettering was on it:

Sometimes a big rock does mean something.

"Lucas?" she said curiously.

"Hmm?"

"Where are you?"

"Right outside your living room."

She hurried to the window and tossed open her curtains as she skidded to a stop. Her jaw dropped, and the phone fell from her hand to bounce on the hardwood floor. Lucas was right outside the window, indeed. He was across the street and twenty feet off the ground, on a giant hunk of black rock that had no earthly right being on a flatbed truck blocking the street. The rock, and the man waving his cell phone on top of it, belonged on a beach in Wales under the light of an orange-pearl moon.

He pointed to his phone and she scurried to pick up hers.

"Happy Valentine's Day," he said.

Her smile was so big, it hurt. "Now I know why my street was closed off today, and why there are no campers in front of the building."

"I do my best," Lucas said.

"Are you coming up?" She glanced at the brownstones lining the opposite side of the street. "The neighbors are starting to stare. And take pictures."

"I have to ask you something first," he said. "It's very important."

Her smile wavered. Her heart slipped into her throat. *Everything's perfect,* she thought anxiously. *Don't ruin it, please . . .*

"Miranda?"

"Yes?" she croaked.

"Will you . . . buzz me in?"

A goofy belly laugh of relief burst from her. "Run!" she ordered before disconnecting the call. She raced to the buzzer and leaned on it until she heard his footsteps bounding up the stairs. She cracked the door open as she yanked off her sweatshirt and threw it at the coat rack, where it landed in a pool of blue at the base. She took her place by the dining table and was wrapping her hand around the neck of a chilled bottle of wine when Lucas tossed the door open.

Miranda turned with a flip of her shining hair. Lucas watched it fall softly in place around her shoulders. After kicking the door shut, he stood there, drinking in the mouth-watering vision of her. He had sprinted up four steep flights of stairs, but by no means was he out of breath. That didn't happen until his gaze took in the full picture of Miranda.

From the top of her head to her knees she was as bare and beautiful as Eve before the fall. From the knees to the tips of her stiletto heels, she was something else entirely. Her skin seemed to glow from the fire of an all-over blush, and her hair was loose and voluminous. Her breasts were like dollops of caramel cream sprinkled with cinnamon, and they seemed fuller and jauntier than he had remembered. And her legs . . . her legs were twin towers of sensual elegance that beckoned him to discover the fleece-covered treasure at their convergence. The sight of her ignited him from the waist down, but her smile sent one of Cupid's holiday arrows directly through his heart.

"You told me to wear something red." She would have run to him if she hadn't been sure that she would trip in her kidskin stilts and break her ankles. "I didn't have anything to go with the boots, so . . ." She cast her eyes in a lingering gaze downward before meeting his once more.

Lucas quickly closed the distance between them. His hands were cold and seemed to sizzle when they touched the warm skin at her waist and her back. Underneath his long, black wool coat he wore jeans and a blue sweater, the same clothes he'd worn on their first date at Conwy, and she could almost smell the North sea air on him. His eyes searched hers, mutely conveying how much he had missed her.

He meant to speak to her, to tell her how happy he was to see her and how eagerly he had awaited their reunion, but his mouth had other plans. When he leaned in to kiss her, she sidestepped him, luring him toward the stairs. "I hope you're hungry," she said. She struggled to sound matter-of-fact and kept her gaze on his lips. "I sweated over a hot stove all afternoon."

"You cooked?" His voice was gravelly. He followed her, his eyes devouring the sexy grace of her body as it climbed the first wide stair. He placed his hand low on her hip, stopping her. He liked the way her skin jumped at his touch. He was glad to know that she wasn't the only one struggling.

"I almost burned the place down." She turned. From her perch, she was able to face him eye to eye. She set her elbows on his shoulders and nipped at his lower lip, drawing out of reach when he tried to capture her mouth in a kiss. "I ordered in." She gave him the full effect of her emerald and topaz gaze. "We could eat now, or—"

He tugged her roughly to him, clasping her buttock in one hand and gripping the back of her head in the other. He kissed her as though his life depended on the quality of the kiss, and she frantically peeled his coat from his body. She struggled backwards up the stairs. Her hair spilled from Lucas's grip as he held her head to his, devouring her mouth in a kiss meant to show her exactly how much he had longed for her.

Lost to his kiss, Miranda stumbled. Lucas caught her, easing her onto her back at the top of the stairs. She shoved her hand under his sweater and down past his waistband. The hard, straining length of him overfilled her hand as he pressed his hips into her. She broke the kiss so she could look at him as she unfastened his jeans and lowered them. Lucas kicked off his boots and climbed out of his pants as they maneuvered into her bedroom in a wriggling knot of limbs and libidos.

Lucas yanked off his sweater and T-shirt while Miranda stretched an arm out for the box under her bed. She had it in her grasp when Lucas pinned her wrist to the floor and began kissing her from her elbow down to her breast. He used his tongue and teeth and lips to work her into a gasping, whimpering creature of carnal need before he moved to her other breast, and delighted it in kind. He was working his way downward, blissfully torturing her further, when she cupped his face and stopped him at her belly button.

She sat up, effectively rolling him onto his back with the motion. Wearing only her boots and a dazzling smile, she straddled his thighs and leaned over him. She guided her hair to fall over her left shoulder, and it tickled and caressed him as she moved lower down, removing his red silk boxers as she went. She took control, slowing the pace of their reunion and in so doing, making his want of her that much more demanding. His hands clenched into fists and he squinted his eyes shut to stop himself from taking her by the waist and burrowing into her.

"I'm glad you wore red." Her words whispered against his aching flesh as her hair tickled over his lower abdomen.

"I didn't want to get *pinched*." He sang the last word as her mouth closed over his velvet tumescence.

She subjected him to erotic torments that made him howl one moment and curse her the next. She used her hands and mouth and even her hair with maddening skill, and she ignored his pleas to stop before he reached his boiling point.

He took matters into his own hands by taking her under her arms and hauling her up the length of his body. With his last particle of restraint, he got her on the bed and himself into a condom before he drove home his mindless need of her. The buttery softness of her boots stroked his skin as her legs fastened around his middle, drawing him deeper. Her hands clasped his buttocks and her muscular control gave him no chance of prolonging their mating. He exploded with a grimace and a roar. He stilled, paralyzed by the riotous rapture spearing through him. He panted through gritted teeth, his arms rigid as Miranda clutched handfuls of her bed covers and arched beneath him. Lucas shifted his hips a bit and rested his weight on his forearms. He caught Miranda's satisfied moan on his lips as he kissed her and tasted the perspiration beading above her upper lip. His strokes became deeper, longer, and he brought his seeking lips to her neck. When the pad of his thumb brushed the tight peak of her right breast, it was like putting a spark to dry kindling.

Miranda's fingernails dug crescents into his skin as her body locked around him. Low, unintelligible syllables issued from her with each muscular flex within her. Lucas, transfixed by the glowing beauty of her face, eased her back from the summit of her pleasure by catching his name on her lips as it left hers. The rest of her went limp even though her hips continued to buck against him. He kissed her shoulders and upper arms, dampening his lips with her perspiration.

She took his face in her hands and kissed his chin before smoothing a sweat-soaked lock of hair from his face. "Thank you for the big rock," she said. "I'm embarrassed that I didn't get you anything."

"You gave the rock its meaning," he said. "That was the best gift anyone's ever given me." He took her hand and kissed it. The sweetness of the gesture deepened the intimacy of the moment.

"When I saw that box, I thought . . . for a second or two . . . that you had some other surprise planned." Her mouth smiled, but her eyes didn't. Lucas eased off of her, and they lay on their sides, facing each other.

"I did." He placed a hand behind her knee and tugged her leg over his. He unzipped her boot and tossed it to the floor. "My original plan was to cart you off to Las Vegas and marry you this very night." At her look of horror, he laughed and kissed her cheeks. "I'm kidding. That would have created the very sort of media circus that you and I both detest."

"And a giant piece of Wales on my street won't?" Miranda sat up and removed her other boot. Lucas played with the ends of her hair, which tickled along her spine.

"It'll be gone soon, love," he said. "My permit to transport it expires at midnight."

"Where will it go?"

"Back to the ship at the harbor, where it will wait."

"Until what?" Miranda asked warily.

"Until all my surprises have been spent this evening." Grinning, he turned onto his back and rested his head on his hand.

"What kind of surprises?" Miranda demanded.

Looking like one of Shakespeare's merry heroes, he refused to divulge anything further. She touched a fingertip to his chest. He watched that soft, delicate fingertip stroke a feathery path down to the crisp whorls of dark hair at the place where his thighs met. "I'll get it out of you," she said. "One way or another."

"You'll find my will is as hard as iron."

Miranda took him in her hand, and she smiled when that part of him became as hard as iron. Torture meant to make him spill his secrets backfired when she let him assert his mastery of her. He primed her, kissing, stroking, and caressing her until her insides liquefied. He turned her onto her stomach and propped a pillow beneath her abdomen before he lovingly invaded the last unexplored territory of her body, bringing her to a climax so keen and powerful that she nearly wept as she bit into her mattress.

"How was St. Louis?" Miranda used a crust of warm garlic parmesan bread to dab up some of the De Viseu red wine mushroom sauce dotting her dinner plate. She stared at the remains of her beef tenderloin as she awaited Lucas's answer.

"I didn't go," he said around the last bite of his own tenderloin.

Miranda stopped chewing and looked up at him.

"It took time and planning to have a five-ton Valentine's Day present shipped and delivered from Conwy to Boston," he said. "I had to be there to coordinate the process. And sign various forms and documents and to bribe the proper barge captains and government officials."

Miranda's mouth curved in a reluctant grin. She didn't want to think that Lucas had changed his plans because of her shrewish response to his interest in Tess Cullor . . . but she was glad that he had. "Calista called this afternoon to tell me that Alec gave her two dozen red roses and a diamond pendant for Valentine's Day," Miranda said. "I can't wait to tell her that you gave me a five-ton rock. She's the only one who'll understand how much I appreciate that gift."

Lucas grinned and shook his head, wondering how she could be so playfully sexy and wholesome at the same time. She was wearing a plain white cotton camisole and a pair of white, man's-style knit sports briefs. The outfit covered her, yet still revealed the feminine shadows of her body. She had pulled her shower-damp hair back into a loose ponytail secured by a black elastic band. Sitting across from him over a pair of burnt-down candles, one foot flat on the seat of the chair and her other leg folded beneath her, she had the rosy sweetness of a forest nymph perched on a sugary toadstool. But as she licked the sweetly spicy De Viseu sauce from the tips of her index and middle fingers, she stirred the animal resting within his boxers.

Her middle fingertip popped from her lips. "Why are you staring at me like that?"

"Like what?" He took a sip of red wine, then licked his lower lip. The subtle movement turned her nipples to pearls against the thin fabric of her top.

"Like you have tonight's winning Powerball number."

"I care little enough about that," he said. He crossed his arms and leaned on the table. "What I do know is that a five-ton rock isn't all I gave to you tonight."

"I'll say." She smiled, comically bouncing her eyebrows. "Four times is a personal best."

"You had five by my count, thank you, and look at your fire escape."

She gave him a quizzical stare before turning toward her living room window. She uttered a small squeak of surprise as she set both feet on the floor and stood, one hand hovering over her heart. A bright star of moonlight glinted off the shining dome of a dark red barbeque grill. The long tails of the silver foil bow tied around the lid floated on the light crosswind between buildings. She didn't hear Lucas leave his side of the table and come to kneel before her. She flinched and dropped heavily into her chair when he took her hand.

"I love you," he said.

She tore her eyes from the grill and stared at him. The simple truth of his statement shimmered in his clear, beautiful eyes.

"Marry me."

It was question, wish, plea and prayer. Most women would have imploded with joy at a proposal from Lucas Fletcher. But Miranda wasn't most women.

"Your lips are moving but no sound is coming out." Lucas gave her a hopeful smile.

"I don't know what to say."

"May I make a suggestion?" he chuckled. He ran his hands along the outsides of her thighs.

Miranda picked up her wine glass and gulped the contents down. She pressed the back of her trembling hand to her moist lips. "I want to say the right thing."

"Do you need some time to think about it? I know this is a big decision."

Miranda nodded and reached for the wine bottle. She took a swig directly from it, and then pressed it to her forehead to cool her suddenly sweaty brow. "That would be good," she said. "A little time. You don't mind?"

Faint lines formed at the corners of his smiling eyes as he took her hands. "I've told you, Miranda. You're worth waiting for."

They had dessert, a delicious coconut cheesecake, in front of the television. Lucas delighted in each squirm of Miranda's supple body against his as she fed him bites of the sweet dessert from the plate propped upon his hard belly. She was cuddled into his side, her head resting on his shoulder as they watched a worn videotape of one of Miranda's favorite movies: *Slap Shot.*

The movie was much better than Lucas had expected it to be, and every time he laughed, he threatened to overturn the cheesecake plate. Miranda's quick reflexes saved it again and again, but she lost it when she applauded the arrival of the Hanson brothers. Lucas adored her enthusiasm for the movie. He shared it, but not because of the great performances. Lounging on a sofa, watching a movie with Miranda was the most sublime pleasure he could imagine. It was such a simple thing, yet something he had never been able to experience honestly.

He'd spent evenings watching movies with women before, certainly, but the women had generally spent more time watching him. They saw what he wanted to see, insisting they had no opinion on the matter. They laughed when he laughed, or they clutched at him at all the appropriate horror bits. They even sobbed, on occasion, and attempted intellectual discourse of the film if it merited such. But at no point had Lucas ever felt that a woman was watching a movie with him because that was what she truly wanted to do. The movie had seemed a chore to be endured until they got what they really wanted. Him. He inwardly acknowledged his hypocrisy. He had wanted the physical, too, there was no denying that.

But he had wanted more to go along with it. Miranda gave it to him. She had chosen *Slap Shot* because it was something special to her, something that she wanted to share with him, and not because it was what she thought he wanted. Piece by piece and moment by moment, she was inviting him into her life. Never had she tried to conform her personality or behavior merely to fit her life into his.

Miranda recited dialogue along with the characters, and Lucas complimented her delivery. She rewarded him with a tender kiss before turning her attention back to the movie.

Lucas watched her, convinced that the proposal had been the right thing to do. She had been shocked, for sure, but at least she hadn't run screaming in the other direction. She was in good spirits, and that in turn brightened his. He had been nervous about proposing to her. It was the hardest thing he'd ever had to do but only because it was the most important thing.

He knew that she was squirrelly about the prospect of marriage, which was understandable. But she hadn't said no. If all that stood between him and yes was time, then she could have all that she needed.

There was nothing he wanted more than to be with her permanently. No more luxurious pit stops in ritzy hotels in foreign cities. No more four-figure long distance phone bills. No more e-mail interludes that left him and his velvet tumescence aching to experience the acts she described, things that put Kitty Kincaid to shame. And once Miranda was entrenched at Conwy, they could say goodbye to swollen crowds of paparazzi and fans stalking them at every turn.

But will she want to live at Conwy? Lucas pondered that as Miranda cheered Michael Ontkean's on-screen striptease on the ice. Her family was in America, but they would only be a plane ride away. And what of her job? Would she be willing to give it up, to live with him at Conwy?

It was hard for him to imagine that she wouldn't love Conwy as he did. She had seemed truly happy there during her short visit. Lucas wrapped both arms around her as he watched the movie, and he contemplated the very questions he supposed Miranda would have to before she gave him her answer.

Miranda cherished the sunrise because it was a time of day she rarely got to see. The light of a new day seemed cleaner and clearer than any other, as though it had the power to erase all that had come before it and start everything off anew and unspoiled. Miranda squinted against the bright colors the rising sun filtered through her stained-glass window. Lucas, his back to the colorful window, slept on beside her. She watched him as she traced the lines of his body exposed by the pale sheet covering him. Goosebumps rose on the muscled cap of his shoulder and the round of his biceps as her hand lightly passed over them.

He wants to marry me, she said to herself. The new day hadn't erased his proposal, nor had it vanquished the discomfort she had managed to push aside the night before. Marriage was an enormous step, and certainly not one she could enter easily. If at all. Her thumb moved lightly over his lips, her nerves whistling in remembrance of what his magnificent mouth had done to her the night before. Lucas had done everything a mortal man could be expected to do to show his love for her. So why hadn't she accepted his proposal right then and there?

Because I couldn't, she told herself.

There were too many things to consider before she could give him an honest answer. There was his life on the road, for one. She knew it wasn't for her. Traveling for a story was different. That was part of her job. It had purpose. Following Lucas around the globe would make her little more than luggage with legs. Sure, she could stay home and they could exchange phone calls and e-mails as they did now, but Lucas was a young, virile man with a very healthy sexual appetite. How long would it be before he'd want to sample some of the voluptuous treats the road offered in abundance?

It had been hard enough to deal with it with Jordan, and looking back, she hadn't cared for him nearly as deeply as she cared for Lucas.

Who am I kidding, she asked herself. *I don't just care for Lucas. I love him.*

She sighed and she felt him in her flesh, her hair, her substance and her thoughts. She loved his tastes, his scents, his heat and his presence beside her. She couldn't survive a betrayal from him. And infidelity was a hazard of his occupation.

Lucas deserved a wife who could trust him on the road, not one who would turn shrew the instant he didn't answer his phone, or go insane when she saw a photo of him on the beach with other women. The realization that she wasn't that woman stung Miranda at the center of her heart. She bit back a silent curse, suddenly furious that Lucas had ruined everything with his ill-timed and unnecessary proposal. She felt as though the battle raging between her head and her heart was poisoning her.

But as she gazed upon his sleeping form, a surge of love and tenderness replaced her wrath. She eased closer to him, rubbing his nose with hers and stroking the place where his neck met his shoulder. She pushed one of her legs between his and lightly caressed his back and hip.

Different parts of him awakened at different rates as she touched him in his sleep. That restless creature between his legs rose to greet her first, but it had help from her soft, coaxing fingers. His arms were next as they pulled her in close. His smile was third, adding its light to that of the morning. His kiss, his hands and his legs awakened at the same time, tangling themselves with her counterparts as they greeted the morning and each other.

Every part of her wanted to marry him. Her right ear, which he tickled with his hair, and her neck, which he covered with teasing kisses. Her skin wanted to marry him; she could tell by the way it warmed and responded as his hands glided over it. Her knees and elbows craved him, and her belly seemed to tumble for him. Even her brain could find no fault in marrying a man whose talent and good looks were outmatched only by his intelligence and compassion.

It was her heart that still needed convincing.

She loved him. With every cell and whisper of breath in her body, she loved him. And that love was the very thing she couldn't bear to risk.

She gave herself to Lucas, to fully enjoy his good morning. The urgency of their reunion had been satisfied the night before, but the tempestuousness remained. Lucas's proposal gave it deeper meaning, and it wasn't lost on Miranda. He eased onto her, giving her a passionate and possessive kiss good morning. He moved between her thighs and made himself a part of her with the easy leisure of a man well in love.

I do, Miranda thought. *I do love you, Lucas.* She savored his weight upon her. He laced his fingers through hers, mating their palms. His kisses covered her face and throat. With his body delving deeper and deeper into hers, his perspiration blending with hers with each kiss of their moist bellies, Miranda became greedy, desiring an even deeper union. Her pleasure was heightened by the fact that he wanted her. Forever. Truly and always.

His lips traveled from her mouth to her throat as her head arched back into her pillows. She immersed herself in the blissful friction of his hardness within her. He spoke her name, and it sounded like a blessing.

Miranda gently took the sides of his face and guided it toward hers. She used one hand to stroke the long locks of his hair from his face, and she looked into his eyes. "I love you."

His jaw clamped shut with a tiny snap.

Her words filled him. They filled his lungs, his brain, his blood vessels, his heart. "I love you, Lucas," she said, holding his gaze. Her soft, husky words and her open, vulnerable gaze touched him in the one place that her body couldn't, unleashing a tide of need and emotion so strong it sent a sharp pain through him. Her words joined them more completely than any physical act ever had or could. For that moment, every breath was shared with her and his muscles moved in synchronicity with hers. In her eyes, he saw the sheer beauty of her love for him. Her image blurred, and he buried his face in her hair to hide his tears. She cradled his head, her soft breath at his ear. That tender caress sent him skyrocketing to breathless heights of love. Miranda's breath came in deep, short hitches. Her arms moved over him as she tried to hold him as closely as possible, to join them more fully as his gaze again sought and captured hers. His muscles bunched and released with his powerful, rhythmic motion atop her, and she moaned his name, hoping it was the key to locking this moment in place forever.

"I love you," she managed on a tearful gasp as a fat droplet escaped each of her eyes and headed south, toward her ears.

Her breathy intonation triggered a volcanic explosion within him, and he shuddered upon her. For once he broke their gaze first, when his body surrendered to the irresistible pulse of hers. He flung his head back, exposing the tense column of his neck. His veins stood out from the force of his arrival, and Miranda cried out as the heat of his fullness throbbed within her. She knew that his every breath, every taut muscle, heart and spirit belonged to her. She held her breath, willing that moment of pure oneness to last.

Miranda clung to him, and he trembled in her embrace, softly kissing her as their bodies calmed. She closeted away his proposal as she loved him again and again. The agony of awaiting her answer was blissfully eased each time Lucas entombed himself within her. Her words and her gaze had triggered the most satisfying release of his life while binding them, body and soul, more completely than marriage ever could. They each derived comfort from that fact, knowing that Miranda would soon have to give an answer.

Miranda knew that it wouldn't be easy, but Lucas was making it ever so much harder by being so happy. He behaved like a man drunk on love as he moved about her kitchen, slapping a sort of brunch together from the contents of her under-stocked refrigerator and the leftovers from Café Brasil. Miranda sat on the sofa and sipped the coffee he had brought to her.

When he appeared before her bearing a tray of toasted garlic parmesan bread, scrambled eggs and sliced melon, Miranda's appetite fled. She mustered a smile to answer his. He sat beside her and she took in his face as though she were looking at him for the last time. His hair was dark and damp from their recent shower. He wore a plain white T-shirt and jeans. His eyes crackled with joy, and when his sensuous mouth pulled into a tiny grin, Miranda had to look away or risk losing her nerve.

"Miranda?" He gave her bare knee, which poked from her robe, a loving squeeze. "Tell me what's on your mind."

She rubbed her right temple. She felt the beginnings of a blinding headache behind her right eye. "In baseball, when a pitcher is throwing a no-hitter, the guys in the dugout don't make any reference to it at all during the course of the game," she started. "It's bad luck to mention a perfect game in progress, or to even acknowledge it."

Lucas selected a sliver of cantaloupe and ate half of it in one bite. He stared straight ahead as he chewed it. Miranda watched the tiny muscle in his jaw work. "It sounds like superstitious rubbish to me," he said at last.

"It doesn't matter if it's rubbish, if someone believes that it's true."

He turned to face her and took her shoulders, spinning her so that she faced him. "Talk to me directly, Miranda. Don't use sports metaphors."

She kept her eyes on the pulse point at the base of his throat as she said, "I can't marry you."

Her quiet words struck him like a lead mallet to the head. He grew numb, but that feeling gave way to an unpleasant hypersensitivity. He felt as though a small animal with razor claws had fastened onto his gut to gnaw at his heart with sharp, venomous teeth. "C-Can't . . . or won't?"

"Does it really make a difference?" she asked softly.

"Of course there's a difference!" he spat, his eyes probing hers for some clue to her deliberate, methodical assassination of his heart. "If you *can't* marry me, perhaps it's because there's something wrong with you. If you *won't* marry me, then the problem likely lies with me. Is it because I spend so much time on the road? That'll change, I—"

"It's not the road," she quietly cut in. "It's what happens on the road." Her robe was thick, and the radiant heat of the sun warmed the room, but Miranda shivered from a sudden chill. "Your lifestyle is not conducive to marital stability."

Lucas's irritation showed in the way he ran his hand through his hair and launched himself to his feet. "For God's sake, Miranda, just speak!"

"This is just a fairy tale," she blurted. "It's not real. It's all romantic and exciting now, and we could probably even fake a happy ending. But reality comes after that . . . the reality of all the temptation there is out there for you." She forced her clenched fists into her sofa cushions. "There will come a day when you give in to it. I couldn't survive that. Not from you."

"I've been faithful to you," he said adamantly. "If you didn't believe in fairy tales, you wouldn't closet yourself away with Kitty Kincaid. Even that *Slap Shot* has a bloody romantic ending! Tell me the real reason you won't marry me."

"Maybe you should tell *me*," she said defensively. "You seem to have an unusually perceptive grasp of what I'm thinking."

"You're so certain that I'll tire of you." He spoke the words as though they tasted of curdled milk. "You're afraid that you aren't enough for me, and that I'll cheat on you the moment I'm out of your sight." He met her gaze directly. "Do you have so little faith in me?"

He roughly pushed the cocktail table away so he could kneel before her. "Why can't you believe that you're all the women I could ever want? You're the temptress who meets me wearing only a smile and red boots with heels long enough to spear my heart. You're the girl next door who's just as happy playing catch in the living room as you are following a sports team all over North America. You are the exotic, intelligent succubus of my most secret dreams. I don't deserve you and I know it, but I can't help myself wanting you. I love you, Miranda." He tugged her hand to his chest and splayed her fingers over his heart. "This is yours, and it has been since we met."

She bowed her face and covered her eyes with her free hand. Her headache had worsened, and the pain was making its way down to her chest. It was so easy to love him, yet near impossible to consolidate that with what she knew was best for her in the long run. And Lucas wasn't making it any easier by being so compassionate.

"You love me, yet you doubt my faithfulness?" he finished.

"What you're offering me is a fairy tale," she said. "It couldn't possibly last, because it isn't real."

"What's more real than ten thousand pounds of Conwy?" he asked. "Or that grill out there? Or me! I can abide your lying to yourself, but don't lie to me, Miranda. You believe in fairy tales and love *and* happy endings."

His beautiful eyes were dark with pain, a deep, soul-bruising pain that she had put there. Her only consolation was that she knew she was sparing both of them worse pain later. "I think . . ." She had to wait for the lump in her throat to shrink before she could move words past it. "I think we shouldn't see each other any more. It's not fair to you, when I know that this is as far as we can go. You want children, and—"

Lucas took both of her hands and held them tightly in her lap. "Are you seriously this short-sighted? Am I the only one of us who's thought of marriage and children and moonlit strolls along the shore at Conwy?"

Staring into his eyes as she was, she couldn't lie and say no. She had thought of all those things, and how behind them she constantly would be waiting for proof that happiness was an illusion.

When she didn't answer, he stood and paced in a small circle. "Clearly some of mad Lady Emberley rubbed off on you at Conwy," he muttered under his breath. He turned back to her, one hand loosely set upon his hip. "If you need an example of a man's fidelity to the woman he loves, look to my side. My father has never strayed. Look at Feast! He lusted after Isabella for two years. They spent a weekend together in Cardiff and they eloped in Australia a few months later. It took Feast only seventy-two hours to know that Isabella was the one woman for him." He took a step and stood right in front of Miranda. He bent at the waist and spoke directly into her face. "I'm smarter than Feast. It took me only two seconds to know that you were the woman for me."

Miranda turned her head in shame.

"I don't have to mention the obvious paternal comparison, Miranda. Nonetheless, I don't appreciate it. I don't deserve it."

"You're right," she choked. "You deserve so much better and so much more. You want a wife and kids and . . . I can't give those to you." With her next words, she shattered her own heart. "I think you should go."

"I promised you time." He latched onto the one shot he had left. "It hasn't been twenty-four hours yet. Forget I proposed. Let's just continue as we have been. You can always change your mind."

"But I won't change my mind." Fine lines of misery sprouted between her eyebrows. "I'm so sorry, Lucas. Please. Go." *While I can still let you go.*

His heart danced erratically as he searched for something else to say, something that would change her mind and take them back to where they had been before his proposal. He wanted to grab her, to swear his eternal devotion to her. But her beautiful eyes were blind to all but the past heartbreaks she had endured. He reluctantly accepted that the harder he tried to convince her, the more willingly she would cast him off.

"As you wish, Miranda."

She sat frozen on the sofa, her stomach twisted into a tight knot. Cold sweat beaded on her forehead. Only after Lucas had dressed, collected his coat and closed the front door behind him did she find the power to speak or move. "What have I done?" she whispered in the otherwise empty apartment. "*Ó Deus,* what have I done?"

A hot wave of nausea washed over her, and she ran for the bathroom. Her torso convulsed from the force of the dry heaves that continued long after she had sicked up the scant contents of her belly. She sat on the bathroom floor for a long time, sure that she had done the right thing, her only comfort coming from the cool porcelain bowl of the toilet.

CHAPTER 11

"What is it with your boyfriends and St. Louis?" Meg asked after slithering alongside Miranda as she made her way to the *Herald-Star* parking lot.

"What the hell are you talking about?" Miranda groaned. She had abandoned her toilet bowl only to come to the office to get her assignments from Hodge and pick up her mail. She had needed to get out of her apartment to escape the Karmic Echo fans who had returned in renewed numbers and chanted, "Will you 'I do?'" beneath her window. She never would have made it out of the building and to her car if her downstairs neighbor hadn't been kind enough to let her climb out of his kitchen window and onto his fire escape, which luckily overlooked the parking lot in the back of the building. Miranda was in her car and speeding down the alley before the crowd noticed her and began to tail her.

For the first time fans were waiting for her at the gates to the *Herald-Star* parking lot. For once, there was actually a security guard manning the attendant's booth. He came to Miranda's assistance when a fan sprinted onto the lot and begged Miranda for her autograph.

A neighbor's photo of Lucas standing on her "engagement" rock had made *Psst!* along with a quote from the double-crossing QWIX courier and a headline that read: *Rock Star's Proposal Rocks* Herald-Star *Reporter.* The courier had vividly described Miranda's Valentine's Day ensemble of Emma Peel boots and soccer sweatshirt, and although he hadn't known for sure what the box contained, he knew that he'd been sent to deliver a ring box. Miranda hadn't been able to mourn in private, thanks to the media storm Lucas's proposal had generated. She'd had to unplug her phone directly from the wall, and for the first time in her entire journalism career, she wasn't carrying a cell phone.

She hadn't logged on to her e-mail account, and she probably wouldn't for the foreseeable future. And now she had Meg tailing her down the urine-colored *Herald-Star* corridor like a pit bull after a wounded duckling.

"I'm talking about Lucas's trip to St. Louis to meet Tess Cullor, that pretty young singer he's supposed to duet with," Meg said. Her heavy thighs hissed in her silk pantsuit as she tried to keep up with Miranda's long strides. "It seems that every time your boyfriends go west, they come back and they aren't your boyfriend any more."

"Drop dead, Meg," Miranda said. "As usual, you don't know what you're talking about."

"Don't I?" Meg said. Her lips made a wet, smacking sound as they thinned into a wide smile. "I know that Lucas didn't go to St. Louis because you threw a jealous tantrum."

Color flared in Miranda's cheeks.

"Don't be so surprised, Miranda," Meg said. "My tipsters come from everywhere, even from airplanes flying over Costa Rica."

Miranda walked a little faster.

"I also know that Lucas asked you to marry him on Valentine's Day, and judging from your miserable face and the fact that you look like you haven't slept in a week, you probably said no. Or was he the one who changed his mind about *you*? Perhaps he's bored of his ethnic experimentation. Did you notice that you were the only . . . how should I put this?" She tapped her chin. "You were the only woman with a *natural tan* in Lucas's top twenty-five. Did you really think that you were the one?"

Miranda broke her stride to step in front of Meg. She backed the wider, older woman into the wall, and stood nose to nose with her as she said, "This stops right now, Meg. This is my life you're messing with. If I see one more tease, headline, or story about me in your column, I will roll the *Herald-Star* into a tight little tube and beat you bloody with it. Do you understand me?"

Meg sidestepped away. "Are you threatening me, you snot-nosed little minx?"

"You bet your fat ass I am," Miranda said grimly as she started back down the corridor.

Miranda spent the next few weeks in hell. A splinter group of Karmic Echo fans, calling themselves the Miranda Penney Fan Club, took turns camping out across the street from her building, hoping to catch a glimpse of Lucas sneaking in to see her. They followed her to the supermarket, the gas station, Mama Brown's, and even attended basketball games so they could cheer *her* rather than the home team.

Her conventional mail and e-mail had quadrupled as Lucas's admirers from all over the world saw fit to write to her, to tell her they were happy that she was marrying Lucas, or to say that they hated her for marrying Lucas. She had her home phone number changed not once, but twice, and even had to get a new cell phone number. Karmic Echo fans were gradually overshadowed by entertainment shows and magazines, all of which were desperate to get to the truth: Did Lucas propose, or didn't he? Did Miranda accept, or didn't she? Most were convinced that Miranda and Lucas were feigning a breakup, so they could sneak off and get married in a private ceremony.

On the first day of spring, Calista arrived in Boston for the second fitting of her wedding gown. The press, particularly the *Herald-Star*, jumped on the visit, speculating that Calista was in town for a wedding, all right, but Miranda's, rather than her own.

Calista and Bernie—who had tagged along for the fitting—giggled like children after fighting through the crowds in front of Miranda's building. They stood at the window, waving at the fans that whistled and called for Miranda. When Miranda stomped over to the window and snatched the curtains shut, her guests decided it was time to get to the bottom of her exceptionally sour mood.

"Miranda," Calista began, "Bernie and I think we need to talk."

"I'm listening." Miranda plopped onto her sofa and turned on *SportsCenter*.

Calista and Bernie sat on either side of her. "I figured you would have spilled the beans by now about what happened between you and Lucas," Bernie said. "You've been holing up in this apartment when you aren't out jumping through b-ball hoops for Rex. You've lost weight, you never smile any more and you're developing unsightly luggage beneath your eyes. I know that Lucas has been overseas for the past two weeks recording at Conwy, but this is more than you just missing him." Bernie threaded his fingers through hers. "What's going on, baby?"

"Did you two have a fight?" Calista asked, placing an arm around her sister's shoulders.

Miranda shook her head. She was afraid that she would burst into tears if she dared speak. She'd had her anger to bolster her when Meg had asked about Lucas, but she had no defense against the united kindness of her sister and her best friend.

"J. Harold Christ," Bernie said suddenly, his eyes wide in shock. "He really did propose, didn't he?"

Miranda nodded, her chin quivering.

"Andy," Calista sighed. She touched her head to Miranda's and hugged her. "I hope you did the right thing."

"I hope so, too," Miranda croaked.

"I don't know how you two have managed to keep it a secret," Bernie said. He took the remote and began flipping through the stations. "I've been getting calls every day from people who want to know if you and Lucas are getting married, if you were already secretly married, or if you killed him and have him stored in your freezer. Rex is being painfully kind to me, hoping that I'll reveal something he can use to sell his dusty old newspa—*The Blue Lagoon*!" Bernie set down the remote. "This is just what you need to feel better. Brooke's eyebrows, Christopher's loincloth . . . Got any microwave popcorn?"

Calista took Miranda by the hand and led her up to her bedroom, leaving Bernie alone with his favorite movie of all time. In the darkened room, Calista kicked an empty shoebox under the bed as she sat on the edge of it. "Why did you say no?" Calista asked.

Miranda leaned against the wall. Her misery seemed to have taken solid form, weighing down her shoulders to the point where the mere act of breathing caused her pain. "I know myself well enough to know that I couldn't survive it if he ever cheated on me," she answered wearily.

"That's not fair," Calista said. "To you or to him. Don't you trust him?"

"Yes."

"I know you love him."

Miranda nodded.

"Is there anything I can do?"

Even in the dim, Calista seemed to glow, like a daffodil against a bed of black soil. She had always been the more easygoing and forthright of the two Penney girls. To Miranda's thinking, Calista was proving to be the most daring, by charging ahead with her plans to marry Alec.

"Don't tell anyone," Miranda said. "My life is hard enough as it is. The last thing I need is for this to get out right now."

Calista went to her sister and gave her a big hug. "You got it, sis. Your secret is safe with me."

Miranda froze, her hand tightening around the paintbrush she was using to cover the wall of her kitchen with pale pink paint. She had thrown herself into the remodeling project to distract her from her desolate feelings about Lucas. Pink was supposed to be a depression-busting color, but the actual physical exertion of painting was doing more for her peace of mind than the color. Calista had stayed a few more days before going back to Maryland, and Bernie had assumed the role of caregiver. He sat in the living room, watching television, while Miranda painted.

But now, Miranda was paralyzed by a voice other than Bernie's.

She knew that Lucas was on the opposite side of the continent, in Los Angeles, yet his voice filled her head. It filled her apartment. And the soulful, melodic words he sang belonged to Al Green.

Miranda's feet spun cartoonishly, her socks unable to gain purchase on her linoleum before she ran into the living room and slid to a stop before the television. Lucas was on the big-screen. He was alone onstage in a soft wash of warm blue light. Blue highlights shimmered in his hair, and a black silk shirt complemented his tanned skin. His head bowed over a slim black microphone stand, he splayed his right hand over his chest. His left hand absently tapped one leather-clad thigh to the beat of "Let's Stay Together."

Miranda swallowed hard.

"It's the Creative Arts Music Council Awards," Bernie said. "According to the press release, Lucas was slated to perform one of his own songs. Guess he changed his mind."

Lucas's voice was enough to make her weep in ecstasy, but the words of the song, and the emotion he put behind them, altered the rhythm of her heartbeat.

"Remote," she gasped, unable to shift her eyes from the television. Lucas, gripping the mike in both hands, subtly shifted his lean hips from side to side in time to the music. "Change it," Miranda demanded anxiously, her hand going to her throat. "I don't want to see this, Bernie."

"Can't find the clicker." Bernie lounged deeper into the sofa.

"Bernie, please," Miranda squeaked. She sidestepped toward him, her gaze on Lucas as she blindly felt for the remote on her cocktail table. "Check the sofa cushions. You have to get rid of him."

The music swelled as Lucas belted out the chorus. His face filled the screen, his plea filling his eyes and his eyes seemed to be right on Miranda. She dropped weakly onto the sofa, tossing pillows left and right, hoping the remote control would appear.

"If you truly don't want to see him," Bernie said flatly, "you could actually walk over there and change the channel the old-fashioned way."

With a groan of frustration, Miranda marched across the room and kneeled before the television. Lucas, his image larger than life, sang the hell out of Al Green's signature song. Her finger on the channel up button, Miranda couldn't bring herself to press it. Her eyes drifted shut, her pulse throbbed in time to Lucas's provocative and soulful performance. "Lucas," she whispered as the song ended and applause rose to drown out the last notes of the music. She opened her eyes and brought her fingers toward Lucas's image. He gave the camera a tiny, brittle smile but his eyes remained somber as he tipped his head toward his appreciative audience.

When her fingertips struck the glass, Miranda found herself touching a deodorant ad. She looked back at Bernie, who held the remote control.

"Found it," he said softly. "Channel's changed."

A production assistant dressed in black muttered into a wireless headset transmitter as she led Lucas through the congested backstage of the Creative Arts Music Council Awards show. She guided him past the "kiss and cry" area, the place where teary-eyed and joyful award recipients clutched their statues and posed for photos while answering questions from a dense crowd of reporters. His role as one of the evening's entertainers completed, Lucas had the option of either taking a seat in the audience at the next commercial break, or going home.

Lucas pulled away from the production assistant's grasp and headed straight for the rear doors. Fellow artists, fans and production staff fawned over him as he pushed his way through the crowd. Women with backstage passes corralled him at every turn, and his bodyguards had to form a wall around him just to get him out of the building in one piece. Once he was safe inside his limo, he directed the driver to take him directly to the airport.

Six months ago, he would have stayed for the rest of the show, quietly basking in the adulation and attention of his fans and peers. He would have been admitted to any after-party he deigned grace with his presence. He would have had his pick of the available women . . . as well as some of the more aggressive and adventurous unavailable ones.

If what he'd wanted was a woman to laugh at his every utterance, who'd welcome him into her body before even telling him her name, and who expected him to wrap her in diamonds and a minute or two of residual fame, then a party would be just the thing.

But Lucas wanted a woman who wouldn't jump at his every desire. He wanted someone who disagreed with him for sport as much as to defend a viewpoint. He wanted a woman who laughed when he passed gas in bed, or punched him in the shoulder when he did it more than once.

He wanted a woman who treated him as though he were an ordinary man, all while making him feel as though he were the only man in the world. He wanted the one woman Fate had ever given him who wasn't like any other woman.

"Damn you, Miranda," he laughed softly.

She was so sure that he would stray, yet in giving him her soul she had ruined him for all other women. If nothing else, the past weeks had taught him that no matter who caught his eye, Miranda had stolen his heart and soul. The irony of the situation wasn't lost on Lucas, and he laughed until he felt tears trickling down his face.

Miranda sat in the third row of folding chairs that had been set up in the Conference Room at the Harborfront Regency. She yawned into her fist as Jordan, accompanied by Alec and a few more of their teammates, stepped onto a dais. Jordan, dressed in a smartly tailored business suit, stood at a podium next to his boss, team owner Buzz Schaefer. Miranda studied her press package while Buzz thanked the media for attending, and then introduced Jordan. Miranda made a point to with-hold her applause as Jordan took the podium.

More and more, Jordan's name—linked to hers—was sneaking into *Psst!* Meg had published Jordan's speculations regarding Lucas's proposal, which gave readers the clear misconception that Miranda had "unresolved issues" with Jordan that kept her from making a decision right away.

The only unresolved issue Miranda had with Jordan was how to get him to stop sending her flowers at work every other week, and to cease his surprise visits to her apartment. Of course, the visits were a surprise only to her. *Herald-Star* photographers seemed to always know when Jordan would be dropping by. The one thing their photos never showed was Jordan's failure to gain entrance to her building every time he showed up.

This press conference was the first time they had been in the same room together since her interview with him, and again, it was work that brought them there. Jordan was launching a new charitable foundation, Bats Not Bullets, which was supposed to encourage inner city youth to take up baseball instead of gang activity. It was a tax write-off for Jordan, but Miranda knew firsthand that his teammates, Alec in partic-ular, genuinely cared about the project and participated for humani-tarian, rather than financial, reasons.

As the largest contributor to the project, Jordan had won naming rights. His partners winced when he repeated the foundation's name. The project's launch had originally been scheduled for mid-April, but for reasons unknown to Alec or Miranda, the date had been suddenly bumped up to April Fool's Day. Miranda had covered a basketball game the night before and hadn't gotten home until two A.M., yet Rex had sent her off to this nine A.M. press conference. If she hadn't been so sleepy and preoccupied, she might have been able to smell an ambush.

When Jordan called for questions, he chose Miranda first of the fifty print and television reporters. "Yes, Miss Penney?" he grinned stu-pidly, rolling his eyes at the absurdity of their formality.

"This foundation is geared toward at-risk inner-city youth, many of whom have been, or are currently, members of gangs," Miranda began. Cameras began flashing at her rather than the men on the dais, and she was embarrassed by the undue attention. "While your motives in forming this foundation may be honorable, the name of your organization has forced community leaders to question whether you really understand or can relate to the very people you hope to accommodate. In fact, local NAACP president—"

Jordan chuckled. "Is there a question in there somewhere, Mrs. Fletch—I mean Miss Penney?"

Miranda ground her teeth. "How do you respond to community leaders who have stated that the name of your foundation is a direct reflection of your ignorance of the people you wish to serve?"

Jordan's grin vanished. He stared blankly into the television cameras trained on him.

"That was a question, Mr. Duquette," Miranda prompted.

Jordan loudly cleared his throat. "Bats Not Bullets isn't a suggestion that kids in gangs pick up bats instead of guns to commit crimes." He laughed nervously. "I just want to stroll down Blue Hill Avenue and see kids walking around with bats and gloves instead of concealed weapons. As for your accusation that I'm not attuned to the needs of my community, let's just say that I'm not the one who's abandoned his brothers of color." He fixed a triumphant stare on Miranda.

Miranda was sorely tempted to publicly remind Jordan of his ménage à blondes in St. Louis. Instead, she silently fumed.

Just as Jordan was fielding a question from a *Boston Sentinel* reporter, a group of about forty young people crashed into the room. A twentysomething man with light brown hair and beady blue eyes scanned the crowd. "There she is!" he shouted, pointing a stiff index finger at Miranda. The group descended, knocking chairs aside as they zoomed in on her.

"You broke his heart!" a woman shrieked.

"If you don't want him, give him to me!" another anonymous female voice cried.

"Lucas is better off without you!" a man shouted.

"You don't deserve him!" the loudest voice declared.

The two *Herald-Star* photographers began snapping photos of the verbal assault, drawing away from Miranda as she made her way to the end of the row of chairs. The angry mob closed around her. Miranda recognized a few of the faces. The stout young man with the green-tipped, spiky hair was partial to sleeping against the mailbox in front of her building. The tall black girl, whose height came from clunky, platform combat boots that laced up to her knees, liked to pace in front of Miranda's building as though she were on a picket line. The other faces crowding and yelling at Miranda blended into one cruelly jeering organism that closed tighter and tighter around her.

Voices assaulted her ears, flashbulbs shocked her eyes and her microcassette recorder clattered to the floor. Her former fans, the "Anti-fans" as they now called themselves, pulled at her satchel and her clothing. She stumbled, but caught the worst of her fall on her hands. From the floor she watched the waffled sole of a combat boot crush her microcassette recorder, and she was helpless as the girl in the boots stumbled backward and stomped on her foot.

The room full of male reporters did nothing to assist Miranda, even as she screamed in pain. Her foot had crunched as though the girl had instead stepped on a bag of corn chips. She tried to stand, but her foot couldn't bear weight. She was going down again, this time from the nauseatingly sharp pain in her foot, when a pair of strong arms caught her up at her shoulders and knees. She instinctively clung to the wide shoulders of the man whisking her through the angry crowd.

He spoke to her, but she couldn't understand a word he said through the continued shouting and the haze of pain clouding her brain. By the tone of his voice, it seemed that he was trying to comfort her. There was no comfort for her, she knew that. Everything her anti-fans had said was true. The misery and melancholy of the past month and a half was no less than what she deserved. Obviously, the truth about the proposal had gotten out, and it didn't matter how. Her foot throbbed with bright, hot pain, but that pain was nothing compared to what she had done to her own heart. Pain was something she had gotten used to, so Miranda did the only thing she could. She closed her eyes and gave in to the sensation of falling.

No-No From Loco Yoko

Far be it for us to say we told you so, but we told you so! Very reliable sources close to *Herald-Star* hottie Miranda Penney have confirmed that our very own sports siren turned down music superstar Lucas Fletcher's oh-so-romantic proposal last month, which involved a very large rock and a very small box.

No reason was given for Penney's thumbs-down, but *Psst!* has learned that it may have to do with some unfinished funny business between Penney and hubba-hubba homerun hunk Jordan Duquette.

Fletcher's camp gave us a ho-hum "No comment" when asked about the proposal. Penney, too, refused comment, but *Psst!* has seen firsthand the ravages the bust-up has taken on Number 25. Let's hope that Luscious Lucas is already finding comfort in the arms of lucky Number 26! *Psst!* has previously revealed that the front-running filly for that spot is fresh young musical wonderbabe, Tess Cullor. After a long visit to parts unknown in Europe, Fabulous Fletcher graced our side of the pond with a three-day stay in St. Louis. Let's hope he and Tess made beautiful music!

Lucas pounded the *Herald-Star* into a ball and pitched it into a tall trashcan as he shook off the rain and entered Boston's Metro Medical Center. He had acquired the April Fool's Day *Herald-Star* at the airport in New York City and had read through it just to pass the time during his short flight to Logan. Gossip reports usually amused rather than angered him, but Meg LaParosa had outdone herself with the Loco Yoko bit. The truth had finally come out, as he'd known it would, but everything else regarding him in the item was grossly false. His worry about Miranda's condition only worsened a mood befouled by Meg's infernal rumor mongering.

He inquired as to what room Miranda was in, and threw a rare celebrity punch when he was told that visiting hours were over and Ms. Penney wasn't receiving visitors. "I'm Lucas Fletcher, damn it, and I will see Ms. Penney," he'd stated, leaving no doubt as to the strength of his determination. "Now what room is she in?"

Deaf to the information officer's request for an autograph, Lucas hopped into the elevator. He took a deep breath through his nose and steeled himself to do battle once more upon encountering a tall, well-built African-American man sitting in a chair outside Miranda's room.

"Mr. Fletcher," the man said, offering his hand as he stood. "This is a surprise."

Lucas narrowed his eyes. The man was pleasant enough, and was dressed in jeans and a T-shirt, rather than a security uniform. He was younger than Lucas, and had an athletic grace about him.

Lucas took the man's hand and gave it a fierce squeeze. "Are you Jordan Duquette?" he demanded.

"Alec Henderson," the man said, his right bicep flexing under his dark skin as he returned Lucas's vicelike grip. "I'm going to be Miranda's brother-in-law."

Lucas let go of his wrath and Alec's hand. "Sorry, mate. It's been a trying day."

"I understand." Alec nodded toward the closed door behind him. "Did she call you?"

Something deep in Lucas's chest tightened painfully. Miranda hadn't called him. He hadn't spoken to her since the day she put him out of her life. "I saw the coverage of the press conference on a cable news channel at a hotel in New York City. I flew here as soon as I could. You were the one who pulled her from that mob?"

Alec nodded. Lucas noticed a faint scratch across Alec's forehead and bruises on his upper arms. He was sure that the mild injuries came from rescuing Miranda.

"How did something like this happen?" Lucas asked. "Are such press conferences typically accessible to the public?"

Alec shook his head. "Jordan was at my place the other day when I was listening to messages on my machine. Calista called, and made a vague reference to Miranda and your proposal. One look at Miranda, and even Jordan could put two and two together and come up with a way to spend Miranda's misery on free publicity for Bats Not Bullets. Jordan and I have been friends for ten years, and he's basically a good guy. I know he feels bad about what happened."

Lucas managed to suppress a skeptical glare. If Jordan was sorry, he'd hidden it well from the cameras that had shown him pointing and snickering as Miranda was being manhandled by her irate anti-fans.

"Her foot is broken," Alec said. "That's the worst of it. She was a little . . . irritable . . . when she was brought here, so the doctor decided to keep her overnight for stress-related anxiety. The doctor figured she could get at least one night of sleep without your fans or the media hounding her. She hasn't been sleeping well."

Neither have I, Lucas thought. Then, as a courtesy to the man who had saved Miranda and continued to protect her, he said, "May I see her?"

Alec stepped aside, and pushed the door open for Lucas.

The room was dim, illuminated only by a wash of brightness from the blinding halogen lamps on the roof of the parking garage in Miranda's view. Half of the room was dark, the other bed unoccupied. Lucas gravitated toward that half as he neared her. The head of her bed was elevated, and her face was toward the rain-streaked windows. Her body looked so thin and rigid clothed in the flimsy hospital gown, while her right foot was immobilized in a cumbersome cast and brace that reached up to her knee.

The room was cool, as though the hospital had a rule that the inside and outside temperatures had to be the same. Lucas's grey ribbed sweater was damp with rain, and the chilly room made him shiver.

It was the scent of rain on the cool air that aroused Miranda. It refreshed and relaxed her after her hellish day. A seam of lightening parted the night sky and brought a shadow into the fringe of her peripheral vision. She turned her head and saw that her sense of comfort and security came not from the spring rain, but from Lucas. She meant to say his name, but managed only a sharp intake of breath.

"I wanted to see for myself that you were all right," he said.

Miranda's eyes closed. Her soul had shattered the last time they had been together, and the pieces hadn't reassembled correctly. Of all the medicines and treatments she had been given at the hospital, Lucas was the cure for what ailed her. She was glad that she was trapped in the bed, because she knew she would have collapsed in relief if she'd been standing. The dark was surely playing tricks on her, though, for his face was hard, despite the care and concern in his voice.

"My foot is broken," she said.

"I know." He stood near the foot of the bed, gripping the side rail. "I heard on the news in New York City. Mr. Henderson told me as well."

"My blood pressure was high, too." To give her hands something to do, she tugged a thin blanket over herself, leaving the bulky cast exposed. "And I was having heart palpitations."

"Alec told me that it was diagnosed as an anxiety attack." Lucas's eyes moved from the tips of her exposed abused toes, up the length of her cast, and along her thigh. It was so hard to be so near her without touching her, holding her, kissing her and loving her. He abruptly stepped back into the darkness. "Well, as long as you'll recover."

"You have to go?" Miranda sat up straighter. A flash of lightening revealed the anguish she'd mistaken for hardness in his face. Misery dulled the brilliance of his deep blue eyes. She clearly saw that she had no right to expect him to stay. But she needed him to.

"I think it's best that I leave, love," he said.

"Are you okay?" She knew the question was pitiful, but it was the only thing she could think of to get him to stay a while longer.

"The days pass." He stared at the floor. "I'm kept so busy, I scarcely have time to think of anything past who I'm talking to or what I'm doing in that moment. But I have to sleep at some point, and that is when I am plagued by you." He raised his head and pinned her with his gaze. "I see your face. I feel your breath on my neck and your legs against mine and I hear the chime of your laugh, and damn if I'm awake just enough to know that it's all just a dream. That none of it is real any more."

The words of her attackers echoed in her head, sickening her with their truth. "I saw the news this afternoon and heard the statement you gave," Miranda said, referring to comments Lucas issued just before he boarded his private jet.

"I'm appalled and disgusted by what happened to Miranda Penney," Lucas had said, the wind whipping through his hair as he addressed the reporters on the tarmac of LaGuardia Airport. "If this is the caliber of fans Karmic Echo attracts, then clearly we're doing something wrong."

She'd watched him board the plane, but she hadn't known that he was bound for Boston. And just as easily, his plane would soon carry him away again.

"The doctor said it was an anxiety attack to throw off the media," she said. She flicked on the light above her headboard.

The tragic beauty of her somber gaze worried Lucas. He went to her side, stopping just short of taking her hand. "Miranda . . . what aren't you telling me?"

"The heart palpitations and the blood pressure had a hormonal cause." Her jittery hands clenched into fists. She clamped her jaw shut to keep her teeth from chattering. The Emergency Room doctor had given her the diagnosis in a calm, matter-of-fact way that contrasted directly with the impact his revelation would have on her life—once the shock wore off and she herself came around to believing it.

"Did the doctors find something wrong?" Lucas finally took her hand.

"Yes." She thrust her fingers through his. "No . . . well . . ."

"Money is no issue." He settled his free hand on the right side of her face, his touch conveying his deep worry, concern and unflagging support. "We'll find the best physicians in the world. Tell me. What did they find?"

"A baby."

Three syllables, two words and one hell of a surprise were like a battering ram against Lucas's chest. He literally staggered back a step. Miranda reached for him, sure that he was actually about to faint. He held onto her hands, reeling from her quiet admission.

"A . . ." *BABY!* he finished in his head. He clapped his arms around her, startling her with his easy acceptance of what she still didn't quite believe herself. She had been late in January, and even then her period had been exceptionally light. She had skipped February entirely, but had chalked it up to the unbelievable stress she had been enduring. She'd called her gynecologist and had scheduled an appointment. But with pregnancy tests being standard for women of childbearing age treated in the Metro Medical Center ER, the news had come to her unexpectedly.

"I came here for a broken foot!" she had hollered upon being told that she was pregnant. "What would you people have told me if I'd broken the whole freakin' leg?"

Lucas—laid back, calm and constant Lucas—practically sang with giddy delight. "I suppose we should have run out for extra caps after all during our stay at Barnsley Gardens," he chuckled. "It's a good thing you became a writer, love, because your math is appalling. Miranda, this is wonderful," he murmured in her ear as he embraced her.

"I didn't know how I was going to tell you," she whispered.

He roughly kissed the side of her head. "A baby," he repeated happily. "For months now I've been watching Isabella grow rounder, and I've been so jealous of Feast that my eyes should be toxic green by now." He drew away and framed her face in his hands. "Are you okay with this?"

"I'm scared out of my head," she admitted. "I never even babysat when I was young. I'm not sure I even like kids. I thought I'd be an aunt before I became a mother." She winced. "*Meu Deus,* I'm going to be someone's *mother.*"

Lucas laughed. "We'll hire as many nannies as you require to handle the nappies and the spills. You'll be a fantastic mum, Miranda.

Can't you just see us domesticated, strolling through Conwy with a baby in a pram?"

"Lucas," she said hesitantly. "This baby changes a lot of things, but I still don't want to get married. It won't change that."

Just as easily as she had given him the greatest joy in his life, she had followed it with a reprisal of the agonizing blow she had delivered after Valentine's Day.

"You can't seriously be considering raising our child alone," Lucas said.

"We can work something out. I wouldn't keep your baby away from you, Lucas. We have seven months to think about it."

He backed away from her, shaking his head. "No matter what issues you have, love, you can't make our child a victim of them. I want my baby to know that I'm her father, and that I love her mother."

"I can't talk about this right now, Lucas," she said, her voice quivery. "The doctor says I've been pregnant for twelve weeks, but in my mind, it's only been four hours." She placed her hands over her abdomen. "I still can't believe it."

"Believe this, Miranda." He covered one of her hands with his, his warmth seeping into her. "Believe that I would never do to this child what your parents did to you. You take your time and properly digest this situation. When you're ready, I'll be waiting for you." He leaned over and kissed her abdomen. "And you, too," he said softly. Without another word or even a look at her, he left the room.

Miranda watched the door a moment longer before she turned off the light and returned her gaze to the window. She hugged her middle, trying to acclimate herself to the life growing within her. The sky cried tears Miranda didn't dare show. She didn't deserve the release, not when her pain was of her own making.

Miranda stared through the thick panel of glass. The room was quieter than she had expected it to be, although she really hadn't known what to expect. Two nurses, both wearing colorful smocks printed with teddy bears dressed as doctors, moved within the room. They recorded information on charts and gave a touch or a caress here and there. The nurses made it look so easy, and when one of them noticed Miranda and looked up, Miranda was struck by her expression. At two A.M., the nurse wore the beatific smile of a sculpted Madonna.

No sane person was ever that happy about his or her job, so Miranda attributed the outward manifestation of the nurse's inner peace to her charges . . . the twelve babies swaddled in pink or blue blankets in the clear bassinets lined up in the room.

"May I help you?" the nurse asked, stepping past the security gate and into the corridor.

Miranda would have made a run for it, if not for her cumbersome cast and the crutches she still couldn't use with any real proficiency. "No, uh, I'm just looking," she said. "I mean, I was looking at the babies." Realizing how insane she sounded, she attempted to clarify. "I'm not shopping or anything, I was just . . ."

"I know," the nurse said with a knowing smile. She joined Miranda at the glass and looked in at the babies. "There's something about them. They're so little and perfect. This bunch is quiet," she chuckled. "These are the kinds of babies that seduce the unsuspecting into wanting babies of their own."

"Uh huh," Miranda said absently. She frowned, trying to see what the nurse was seeing. Where the nurse saw tiny perfection, Miranda saw still lumps of pink and blue cotton weave that looked like giant jelly beans.

"We get lots of visitors here at the nursery," the nurse said. "Doctors who need some sort of emotional relief after difficult surgeries, women who come in for infertility treatments. I think our most frequent visitors are patients who are afraid of babies, for one reason or another."

Miranda looked at the nurse and didn't like the way she was studying her. Miranda leaned a little more forward on her crutches, making sure that her body left no impression against the front of her thin hospital gown. "I'm not afraid of babies," Miranda said. "I don't usually pay any attention to them at all. Even out in the wild I barely notice them."

"The 'wild'?" the nurse giggled.

"Out on the street in strollers and things," Miranda said. "I don't have any friends or siblings that have babies. I wanted to see what one looked like. In real life."

"I can help you with that," the nurse said. She went back into the nursery. She exchanged a word with the other nurse before she went to one of the bassinets near the window, and turned it so that Miranda could look through the clear sides.

As she had when faced with dangerous, carnivorous animals at the zoo when she was young, Miranda cautiously approached the glass. She knew the baby couldn't get at her any more than the tigers and polar bears could have, but she treaded carefully anyway.

The newborn was sleeping. BABY GIRL ENYARD, read the card on the side of her bassinet. The baby wore a pink knit cap that matched her blanket. Only her face and one of her hands were visible. Her face looked like a fist to Miranda's inexperienced eye, but the baby's hand captivated her.

It was so unbelievably small and chubby. The baby splayed her fingers, as though the movement of the air currents in the room had startled her. Miranda marveled at the tiniest fingers she had ever seen, and the way they curled into a tight fist the baby awkwardly worked into her mouth. The longer she stared at the baby, the less she looked like a fist. Her café-au-lait skin looked so soft, and Miranda began to breathe deeply, as if she could smell the child through the bulletproof safety glass. The baby winced, and Miranda's fingertips instinctively went to the glass, as if she could comfort the child. The nurse scooped the baby up and cradled her, swaying gently from side to side. Envy pierced Miranda, shocking her with its intensity.

She passed a hand over her middle. A very pleasant, very unexpected sensation of joy traveled through her, warming her from head to toe. *This is what our love made,* Miranda thought, gazing at the cherub in the nurse's arms. She closed her eyes and her knees weakened in remembrance of the moments she had spent with Lucas, the moments that culminated in the making of a baby. She inhaled a shuddery breath and could almost smell the sage and peppermint soap he favored. She licked her lower lip and could nearly taste the salty warmth of his skin in the throes of their lovemaking, in the very second when he exploded within her to create a new life.

Lucas had touched the very parts of herself she had struggled to keep from him . . . the parts that could never survive a betrayal. And now there would be a baby as beautiful and angelic as the one she now gazed upon.

She caught the nurse's eyes and mouthed, "Thank you," before steadying herself on her crutches and hobbling her way to the elevators.

"Okay," she sighed, once the elevator doors had closed and the car began to slowly drop her down three stories. "I like babies."

She returned to her room and shrugged off her robe, laying it over the foot of her bed. She hopped onto the bed and leaned the crutches within easy reach. After tucking herself in as best she could, she lay in the dark, thinking of the baby three floors above her and the one growing beneath her heart. As she drifted to sleep, the face of the baby in her thoughts began to change. Her skin was cinnamon, rather than café au lait. She was just as lovely and tiny, but her eyes were open, and they were as deep and blue as her father's. And when she cried, she sounded as though she were singing.

When a nurse came in fifteen minutes later to check on her, Miranda was smiling in her sleep.

CHAPTER 12

After fifteen months, the Karmic Velocity Tour was ending where it had begun—at an outdoor concert in Conwy, Wales. The band had taken the stage in the late afternoon with the intention of giving the sea of music fans an experience they would never forget. Lucas had compiled a playlist that would take them well into three hours, but by sundown, he was wondering if he'd last past the first forty minutes.

Whether it was the loyalty of his fans, his skill as an entertainer, or a combination of the two, Lucas didn't know how he'd managed to last as long as he had. His hands and fingers knew what to do with his guitar, and his voice knew the words that accompanied the music that he had written . . . but his mind and heart were not on the stage at Conwy.

They were an ocean away, in Boston.

He had spoken to Miranda several times in the month since he'd last seen her. Their conversations were fine as long as they talked about the weather, the band, how much she was beginning to hate the *Herald-Star*, and Meg's latest falsehoods. Then he would mention the baby, and their communication became awkward and stilted.

He knew that she would rather contract rabies than get married, and he didn't press her. But the issue was always there between them, just under the surface. He'd taken it as a good sign that she had agreed to his help. She had allowed him to hire a security team for her. She had been thankful for the OB/GYN he had hired to make house calls, to protect her privacy for as long as possible before it became obvious that she was pregnant. He had also arranged for a private service to deliver her groceries and prenatal medications. His lawyers had handled the restraining orders for the anti-fans, each of whom had agreed to stay at least 600 yards from Miranda, her domicile, her workplace and her vehicle in exchange for her not pressing assault and harassment charges against them.

He did all the things a concerned husband would have done, save for the one simple thing he truly longed for: to be with her.

Even though she refused to marry him, he had wanted to be there the first time she heard the baby's heartbeat, and the first time she felt the actual stirring of the life within her. He wanted to fall asleep at night with her in his arms, and to awaken each day knowing he was one day closer to meeting the person they had made.

Lucas stood center stage in Conwy, his bass slung over his shoulder, his sweat-streaked face turned up to the rising moon. It was a full moon and it seemed to glow dark orange against the cobalt skin of the early evening sky. A blood Welsh moon it was called, because of its deep, striking color. It was the very same moon he had once shared with Miranda.

Just as it controlled the earth's tides, the blood Welsh moon seemed to govern the course of Lucas's blood, making it fill his heart with all the frustration and despair he had endured in the past two months. He closed his eyes and gripped the microphone stand in his right hand, touching his forehead to his fist. Feast raised a hand to the rest of the band, signaling them to stop playing their cues for the next song. The crowd quieted significantly. There wasn't a man, woman or child among them who didn't know the basic details of Lucas's recent heartbreak.

Lucas stared at the crowd. The bobbing heads and waving arms mesmerized him, the tide of humanity shouting its praise and encouragement. Thousands of people adoring him only made him long for the one woman whose adoration he craved. His playing hand fell from his bass as his eyes slowly closed. As if he didn't feel badly enough, his mind fed him crippling memories. He imagined the fresh, tropical scent of Miranda's bath gel as it had risen around them in clouds of steam in the shower in Washington, D.C. He felt the rapid drumming of her heart as her bare torso adhered to his. He remembered her shivery embrace as she'd hugged his head to hers, and her soft, sweet panting as she regained her breath following their intimate exchange.

Lucas couldn't shake the memory, so he gave in to it. He let his mind go and his body followed. He began picking out notes on his bass, and the simple, hypnotic chords silenced the curious audience. Feast picked up the melody, adding his own improvisation to it. The audience roared back to life when Garrison broke in wildly with drums.

The wail of Feast's guitar gave voice to Lucas's pain; the driving beat of Garrison's drums imitated the rhythm of an angry heart struggling to live without its lost love. Beneath it all was Lucas's plaintive, longing melody, a virtuoso's plea to the woman who walked away with his heart.

The band fed off Lucas's pain, treating their fans to a wholly original composition unlike anything the band had ever played. The crowd raucously shouted its appreciation. Every woman within earshot of the song heard Lucas's heartbreak in every note. At the end of the song, as the last note lingered and died, the sound of weeping almost equaled that of shrieking applause.

Lucas stood on the curtain wall surrounding Conwy. High above the shore, he had a perfect view of the calm sea and the spot where he and Miranda had enjoyed the blood Welsh moon. Their rock, back from its round-trip voyage to New England, had been put back—give or take a foot—in the home it had known for millennia. The rock reminded him alternately of the best and worst moments of his life, and it had become a touchstone. It had been the start and end of everything with Miranda, and Lucas stared at it as he tried to work out a way to get her back.

He was buried in thought, and a full twenty minutes had passed before he noticed that his father had joined him.

"Let her go, son."

Lucas turned to face his father. Vaughan Fletcher knew when to hold back and let a thing run its course, and when to lance a wound before infection set in and killed the patient. When his father spoke, Lucas realized that the lance was particularly sharp. "I can't, Da," Lucas said. He crossed his arms and set them on the top of the wall. He leaned on them and let the cool, sea-scented air sift through his hair.

"You're not yourself, boy," Mr. Fletcher said. "Your mum and I are starting to worry, and your band mates must think you've lost your cabbage altogether after what you did onstage tonight . . . although I hope someone recorded it. It was bloody brilliant. It had something extra."

"Miranda's samba artists are rubbing off on me," Lucas sighed. "Once those rhythms get under your skin, they stay there."

"You were great in L.A., Luke, at the music awards," Mr. Fletcher continued. "R&B suits you, son."

Lucas only nodded.

"Yes, you can't beat the old stuff." Mr. Fletcher uttered a gruff, appreciative sigh. "It gets to the point and comes from the soul. Do you think she heard you?"

"I know she did," Lucas said. He'd felt her. Across the miles and through millions of viewers, he'd felt her. "I'm just wondering if she actually listened."

"If you don't mind me saying so, but why do you want her so much when she clearly doesn't want you?"

Mr. Fletcher's tender inquiry wasn't meant to inflict pain, but Lucas winced nonetheless. "I want her because she wants me, Da. That's the only thing she wants. She doesn't care about my money or fame or my name, or this bloody castle. All she wants is *me*."

"Then what's the problem?"

Lucas turned his head toward his father, and he stared into eyes that were exactly like his own. "When you were still playing, and you were away from mum for weeks at a time, did you ever fancy another woman?"

Mr. Fletcher inhaled, then expelled a long, thoughtful breath through his nose. "So it's the hazards of the job that trouble your Miranda?"

"Something like that," Lucas said.

"A beautiful woman can catch your eye, same as a sudden glimpse of a perfect sunset. She can stir your blood, same as a shot of good Scotch. But a woman can't touch your heart once you've given it to the woman you love. No matter how far the music took me from your mum, she was always right here." Mr. Fletcher patted his heart. "There was no temptation for me on the road, son. No other woman ever looked as good to me as your mum. Even now, the woman's got me heart set right in her pretty palm. And I wouldn't have it any other way."

Just as Miranda dreaded patterning her parents, Lucas feared that he wouldn't get the chance to pattern his. He watched the ocean, how it moved constantly, how even the slightest breeze could change its surface. He would jump into it and swim all the way to Boston if that would prove his worth and fidelity to Miranda once and for all.

"Does she love you, Luke?"

"Aye," he said earnestly, lapsing into his father's pattern of speech. He squeezed his eyes shut against the sting of her absence. The fact of her love had branded him the last time they had been together in her big bed. Even now, the memory of her whispered confession of love was like sunlight upon his skin. "I know she loves me, Da. And she knows it, too."

"Perhaps then, with time, she'll come 'round to seeing things your way." Mr. Fletcher clapped his big hand on his son's shoulder. "In the meantime, you can set to work producing Feast's album and finishing your next. In time—"

"I don't have time, Da." Lucas kept his eyes on the moon-brushed sea. "I only have about four and a half months left."

Mr. Fletcher's brow wrinkled in curiosity. "What happens in four and a half months?"

Lucas grinned. His father smiled in response since it had been so long since he last saw his son smile. "You become a grandfather," Lucas said.

Miranda hurried through the Newsroom, wobbling on her crutches. She paused to brush newspaper ink from the front of her oversized sweatshirt as she went. Security had called up from the lobby to tell her that she had a visitor, "some rock star," and she didn't want to present herself with smudges of black on her clothes. Her heart beat so hard and fast that it hurt as she raced for the lobby. From the top of the stairs leading from the second floor to the front lobby, she could see her visitor. Her heart twisted painfully.

Len Feast, dressed in a black leather overcoat and black jeans, started up the stairs before the security guard could finish writing out his visitor's badge. "This won't take long," Feast called down to the guard, who was pursuing him.

"It's okay," Miranda said to the guard. "He's . . ." She was too shocked to think of what Feast was. He wasn't a friend. So what was he doing at the *Herald-Star?*

"Good afternoon, Miss Penney," Feast said with a bright smile, once he'd reached the top of the stairs. As if he knew the layout of the place, he took Miranda by the elbow and escorted her to the tall, wide window just beyond the stairwell. He sat her, then sat beside her.

"Do you have cable television?" Feast asked. He laced his fingers together in his lap. To Miranda, he looked like the mad scientist he might have become if he hadn't loved music more than chemistry.

"You didn't come all the way from Wales just to ask me that," Miranda said warily.

"If you had cable television," Feast continued, the mad gleam still in his eyes, "you might have seen our closing concert in Conwy last week. You might have seen my best friend," he leaned closer to her, to whisper, "and your baby's father, have a complete breakdown in front of twenty-thousand Welsh fans and half the television viewing audience in the Western world."

"H-How did you . . ." Miranda faltered. "Did Lucas tell you about the . . .?" She couldn't, wouldn't, would never say the actual word within the walls of the *Herald-Star.*

"I've got eyes, Miss Penney," he said, casting their blue light toward her abdomen. "Your Big 'n Tall boy tops don't fool me."

Miranda paled. She had always worn oversized clothing, so her wardrobe hadn't changed as her body had. Only recently had she come to the point where she had to use a ponytail holder looped through the opening of her jeans to fasten them. Her lower belly was definitely more convex than concave, but even Bernie hadn't been able to tell that she was pregnant.

"I'm kidding," Feast said, setting his hand on her wrist. "Lucas told me, of course. And it isn't obvious. Honestly. Well, it is, actually, but only to the practiced eye."

"How so?" Miranda asked.

"Your hair." Feast's tone softened as his eyes moved over her. "And your skin. Dare I even say that I actually see the makings of a bosom there within your sweatshirt?"

Miranda scowled at his last observation. In the past several weeks her hair had seemed thicker and more lustrous, so much so that Bernie had accused her of actually having it treated at a salon. Her skin had become dewier and seemed to glow. And her breasts had a fuller, peppier appearance that she couldn't help but like. Too many times she had wished that Lucas could see them.

But seeing him made it too hard to keep not seeing him, so at her request, they kept in touch by phone and e-mail.

"How is Isabella?" Miranda asked.

A wide smile brightened Feast's face. "Wonderful. Demanding. Irritable. And the size of a classic VW Bug. She looks like a manatee."

"I'm sure she looks beautiful."

"There are times when she's sleeping, and I look at her, and I can't believe that she's *my* wife. That she's carrying *my* baby, a little Feast to turn loose upon the world. I thought making music was the greatest thing I could do with my life, but it's not. Every time I look at my wife, I see what matters to me. What's important."

Feast's impassioned message wasn't lost on Miranda. "I can't be with him anymore."

"That sounds like fear more than anything else, Miss Penney. What did Lucas do to you that you can't forgive?"

Miranda appreciated Feast's lowered tone, but her own voice rose as she said, "He made me fall in love with him."

Feast chuckled. "Is that all? He loves you, too. How is that a problem?"

She gave him the line she kept telling herself over and over. "His lifestyle is not conducive to monogamous relationships."

Feast harrumphed and turned to face the window. "Neither is yours. You run around with male reporters chasing male athletes in their physical prime. A bird like you probably shakes the lads off by the dozens every day."

"It's not the same," Miranda insisted. "If an athlete threw his underwear at me, he'd probably be fined by the league and his team, suspended from a game or two, and spit on by angry fans. Women are expected to throw themselves, and everything else, at Lucas. Temptation is all over the place. He has to have some weakness, and his career lends itself toward the most damaging weakness of all."

"Oh, Lucas has a weakness all right, you lovely idiot. It's you. You're the bird he wants. The rest can go hang."

"Stop calling me 'bird,'" Miranda protested.

"Certainly, duck," Feast said amiably.

"A duck is a bird."

"Perhaps, then, I should call you foolish. Or stubborn. Or misguided. Will stupid do?"

"Perhaps I should put you in another sleeper hold."

"I can see the headline in your favorite gossip column now," Feast said, squinting up at an imaginary banner headline. "'Mum-To-Be Delivers Smackdown to Kind-Hearted Musician.'" He stood and adjusted his coat. "Obviously, it was a mistake for me to come here. I can't begin to imagine what Lucas even sees in you."

"Then leave!" Miranda bit her lip to stave off a sudden rush of tears.

Feast started down the stairs. Miranda swiveled in her seat, bringing her uninjured foot to the windowsill. She hugged her knee to her chest and hid her face in the circle of her arms. She fought back tears, but one or two managed to escape. When she looked up, Feast was sitting at her feet. Without a word, he handed Miranda his handkerchief.

"You're still here?" Miranda said ungratefully as she took the neatly folded black square.

"A woman's tears are magnetic," Feast said. "Especially when they're real. You need to work on your presentation, of course."

Miranda wiped her nose on her sleeve with a loud, braying snort. She swabbed her eyes with the handkerchief before offering it back to Feast. He took it, then used it to gently dab at her moist cheeks. "I've been in Lucas's shadow for twenty years. I've always envied his talent, his ambition, his genuine goodness . . . for once I have something *he* wants. I have a wife, and a child on the way." Feast shoved his handkerchief into his coat pocket. "I can't even gloat about it because I know how much Lucas truly wants you and your child. I think I'm correct in assuming that you've had some bad experiences. But Lucas didn't inflict those wounds. Don't make him suffer for another man's cruelty. He doesn't deserve it. And if you can't see that, you don't deserve him, and he's well rid of you."

Feast took her hands. He held Miranda's troubled gaze, showing her that his concern was for her and her child, as well as for Lucas. "He's a good man, Miranda. You're the only woman he's ever proposed to, and the only woman he's ever professed to love. He won't ever betray you. He's like . . . like . . ." Feast struggled to find an apt comparison.

"What?" Miranda said. "Starts with? Sounds like? Is it bigger than a breadbox?"

"A seahorse."

"Is that a joke?" Miranda reached into Feast's pocket and took out his handkerchief. She noisily blew her nose into it.

"Most certainly not," Feast declared. "Seahorses are noble creatures. They mate for life, and they're particularly choosy about their partners. When a boy seahorse finds the girl seahorse of his dreams, he's ruined. No other female will turn his head. Even if a red snapper devours the girl he's chosen, he will never mate with another female. It's rather sad, actually, to see a male floating alone in the great big ocean, unafraid of red snappers because without the female he wants, his life has lost much of its meaning."

Miranda took comfort in knowing that fidelity existed somewhere on the planet. She wished it were more a part of the nature of her own species. "Did you learn that seahorse crap at Oxford?"

"That, in passing, amid other crap."

"Why are you telling me this?"

"Fletch is my friend. I want him to be happy."

"Thank you," she said, fully meaning it. "But it really won't change anything."

"There's something else about seahorses," Feast said. "The males carry the babies. The girl seahorse comes home from work, she and the male do a wonderful, passionate dance just after dawn, and then she gets him pregnant. Weeks later, he labors for hours to give birth to hundreds of perfect, miniature seahorse babies. And he can't wait to start dancing and get knocked up again."

"Are you telling me that Lucas would make a good mother?"

"Given the chance, he'll make a good husband, too."

Miranda used one of her crutches to batter open the door to Rex's office the day after Feast's surprise visit. His secretary stood to stop her, but an ugly sneer from Miranda glued her in place. Rex was on the phone, but he hastily bid his party goodbye as Miranda thundered up to his desk. She pitched the most recent issue of the *Herald-Star* in front of him. The paper slowly unfurled from the tight baton Miranda had curled it into and came to rest flat on the page featuring *Psst!* Miranda seethed as her gaze was again drawn to the lead item:

Maybe Baby?

Herald-Star scribe Miranda Penney is an ace at keeping secrets but the same can't be said about the company she keeps. *Psst!* has learned that our Miss Penney may be just be in the family way. With Lucas Fletcher seemingly no longer in the picture, we at *Psst!* can only wonder . . . will the new Penney be a singer or a slugger? Your guess is as good as ours!

"This is it, Rex," Miranda growled. "I am totally *Psst!* off! I want you to make those two conniving witches stop printing these rumors about me. I'm not seeing Lucas anymore, and—"

"Did Lucas break it off or did you?" Rex asked greedily.

"You're one of their moles, too?" Miranda almost shouted.

"Proceed with caution, Miranda," Rex warned. "You work for me, not the other way around."

"I want my life back," Miranda demanded. "I'm tired of my business being displayed in your gossip column."

"You can't un-ring a bell, dear. You'll just have to wait until the story dies on its own. As for Meg and Dee, you're a public figure now. You're fair game."

"When Deuce Bagley was dating Laura Vanderpool, you got Meg off his case when he asked you to."

Rex emitted an impatient groan. "A football writer and a local weathergirl don't compare to a female sportswriter who fools around with one of the world's most popular men."

"You could stop them from writing about me!"

"Of course I can." Rex tented his hands on his desktop. "I don't want to. The truth is, Miranda, our circulation has been tops in town every week since you began seeing Lucas Fletcher. I don't think that's coincidence. Boston is a two-paper town, and I'm on top now. I plan to stay there. Whether you like it or not, you're a part of that plan."

Miranda shook with anger. She calmed the instant she said, "I don't like it. I quit."

She turned to leave. Rex sprinted around his desk to bar her way. "Don't be dramatic. I know you're upset and angry, but surely we can talk about this. We can work out a mutually beneficial arrangement."

She stepped around Rex. "You and your gossip hags have put me through hell, but there's an upside to it now. I've been getting offers, Rex. From national sports shows and magazines and other newspapers, including the local rival breathing down your selfish neck. The *Boston Sentinel* offered me my own column, and I've even gotten offers from a couple of news venues in the United Kingdom and Australia." She gave his shoulder a hard pat. "It's time I moved on, Rex. It's time I left the *Herald-Star*, La and Dee, you, and all the rest of my fractured fairy tale behind."

Rex grabbed her by the arm when she turned to leave. "Miranda, don't."

She gave his hand a menacing stare and he released her, patting the sleeve of her sweatshirt in place. "Let's set up a time to talk this over," Rex said.

"I've already given Jed Hodgekins my resignation," Miranda said. "I've kept one in my desk since my second week here. Today, I had a feeling that our meeting would go this way. And if you try to spin this and say that I was fired, I'll sue your gossip trolls, your joke of a paper, and you personally."

His flashed her an icy stare. "Clearly you're distraught over being discarded by Lucas Fletcher."

"*Vai te foder, Rex,*" Miranda said with a curt smile before walking away.

"I came as soon as I heard." Bernie entered Miranda's apartment in a flurry of selfish anxiety. "How could you do this to me, leaving me alone at that wretched paper? The whole place is buzzing with how you walked into Rex's office and beat him unconscious with one of your crutches. Of course, they're also talking about Meg's latest bombshell, that you're pregnant with Lucas's love child . . ." Bernie's words faded as he caught sight of neat stacks of letters on Miranda's dining table. He removed his caramel leather gloves before he picked up a sheaf of the letters and glanced through them. "National Sports Network . . . Universal Sports Channel . . . *U.S. Daily Sports . . . The Sports Roundup . . . Women of Sports America* . . . Miranda? Are all of these job offers?"

"No." She was sitting on her sofa, her broken foot propped upon a fat pillow on her cocktail table. She popped a Cheetos puff into her mouth. "The ones from *SoHot!, NUDZ* and *American Swimsuit* wanted pictorials. They're all frauds. None of those places want me for my writing ability or my body. They want me because they think Lucas comes with me." She leaned forward, trying to reach the drink she had set on the cocktail table. Seeing her struggle, Bernie helped her out.

"Dear God, what is this?" Bernie sniffed at the frightening pink concoction in her glass.

"Strawberry punch and milk. I had a craving."

He covered his mouth with his hand as she drank down half the glass, and then licked the corners of her mouth. "Breaking up with Lucas was the best thing I could have done," she said. She began popping Cheetos, one right after the other. "I don't like having my worth measured by who I'm dating."

"I can understand why you left the paper," he said, "but I'm still not clear on why you shut out poor Lucas. The man loves you."

"To quote one of our favorites, Bernie, what's love got to do with it? And while we're on the subject, why didn't you ever take me to one of Tina's concerts?"

"He's called me, Miranda," Bernie said seriously.

"Who?"

He swatted her thigh with a sheaf of job offers. "The lovelorn Lucas Fletcher."

Miranda finished the last of her snack. She licked her fingertip and used it to retrieve the glowing orange crumbs at the bottom of the bag. "Well, what did he want?"

Bernie shook his head as though he didn't have the strength to respond. "He wants you."

"It's over, Bernie. It was just a matter of time before Number 26 overlapped onto me."

"Is that your way of saying that you knew Lucas would eventually go Jordan on you?"

She balled the Cheetos bag up and pitched it toward the trashcan at the end of the sofa. The ball bounced off the rim and onto the floor. "Let's just say that I didn't want to wait around for it."

"So you threw an amazing man away to circumvent something that may never have happened?" He retrieved the Cheetos ball and gave it to her for a re-shoot.

"I don't want to talk about this anymore. It's done."

"For you, perhaps. But your Lucas can't let go that easily."

"Bernie, stop it."

"He wants to see you. He asked me to intercede on his behalf."

Miranda shot the Cheetos ball and made the basket.

"What did he do wrong?" Bernie asked.

"Nothing!" Miranda insisted. "He did everything right. That's the problem."

"Darling, you're impossible. That makes no sense."

"I can take disappointment from anyone but Lucas."

"You sell yourself miserably short. Lucas was the real thing. He can have any woman on this planet, and he wants you. Doesn't that tell you something?"

"Yes," Miranda said. "It tells me that he won't have any trouble finding Number 26."

"I know that you're only trying to protect your heart, but believe me, Miranda, you're only causing it further damage. Now that you're unemployed, do you plan to sit in this apartment eating junk food and sucking down gruesome pink potions? For three months now, you've been a virtual shut-in when you weren't out on a story."

"What would you have me do, Bernie? I'm not like you. I can't go to every karaoke bar in town and perform 'I Will Survive' to get over this. I'm hoping that the day will come when I don't wake up and wonder if I did the right thing. That I'll be able to get through one damn day without wishing that he would ignore everything I've said over the past few months and just show up."

Miranda's brow creased, and with no sniffling preamble or quiver of her chin, she covered her face with her hands and bawled. Bernie grabbed the tissue box from the end table and placed it on her lap as he sat down beside her. He put an arm around her and let her cry into his shoulder.

"Does it hurt much?" he asked.

"Yes," she whimpered. "All the time. I try so hard not to think about him, that all I do is think about him."

"I meant your foot, sweetie," Bernie said. Miranda looked at him. He winked, and she laughed as tears rolled down her cheeks. "You have a woman's heart after all, Miranda. Perhaps you should listen to it. Tell me, what do you love about Lucas?"

"He eats the fuzzy part of the ice cream, so that I can have the good part underneath." Her voice filled with tears. "He moves over to give me the warm spot when I come to bed. He dances to Tito Puente while he makes coffee for me in the morning. He tans really well. He doesn't get all pink and raw-looking. He reads Kitty Kincaid to me. And he sings my name." She mopped up a fresh fall of tears. "I miss his kisses. He's so good at it. His lips are soft but not mushy, and firm without being stiff. I could live on his kisses alone."

"Those are things you like," Bernie said. "What do you *love* about him?"

"I love how much he needs me and our baby."

"Baby?" Bernie squeaked. "Meg got it right? You're . . . how far along?"

"About five months." She sat up off of Bernie and hiked up her big T-shirt. Bernie's eyes widened at the petite mound of her lower belly. "I haven't told anyone, other than Lucas," she said quickly, to diffuse the indignant rampage she saw brewing in Bernie's eyes. "I haven't even told my parents or Calista."

"No wonder Sir Lucas called me in such desperate straits," Bernie said. "His biological clock is ticking. This changes everything, Miranda. You can't deprive him of his child."

"I don't plan to. But I don't plan to marry him, either."

"Do you really think that's fair to the child?"

"I'm trying to be fair to all of us. This baby will have two parents who love her, Lucas has the freedom to do whatever he wants, and I won't ever find myself in the shoes my mother wore for over thirty years."

"So you'd rather be a baby mama instead of a wife. Well, it sounds like you have it all figured out, then."

"I do," she said. *I hope . . .*

Miranda, now adept with the crutches, hobbled up to the front desk of the Park Plaza Hotel. She watched the clerk's eyes widen as the woman studied the two gargantuan men in black suits who carried Miranda's overnight and garment bags.

"They're my bodyguards," Miranda explained in an embarrassed whisper as she slumped upon her crutches.

"Oh," the clerk muttered. She stood on tiptoe to peek past the guards, to look at the mob of reporters and photographers crowding the front door of the hotel. Then she looked back at Miranda. Her mouth stretched into a wide smile as recognition dawned on her. "Miss Penney," the clerk said. "You're here for the Penney-Henderson wedding."

"Yes," Miranda said. "I have two rooms reserved."

"You're right here," the clerk said, calling the reservation up on the computer. "We have you down for two suites, one for you and one for . . ." She glanced at the bodyguards. "Your entourage."

"Thank you," Miranda snapped. The busy and loud noise of the paparazzi reached her as the hotel's front doors opened. Her bodyguards, Rudolph and Blaze, both former professional wrestlers, grunted as they closed in tighter around her, dwarfing her between their massively wide bodies. Another hotel guest was making his way toward the front desk, with a few photographers following him.

"Could we hurry this up?" Miranda asked.

The clerk understood. She called for the hotel manager as she finished Miranda's check-in and retrieved the keys for her suites.

"Whose wedding are you here for, Mr. Duquette?" Miranda heard an eager voice ask. She turned to look over her shoulder, but all she could see was the black fabric of Rudolph's suit.

"It's *your* wedding, isn't it, Jordan?" another voice suggested.

Jordan answered both questions with a sly laugh. Miranda was tempted to hand Blaze one of her crutches so he could give Jordan a ring-worthy beating.

"Let's just say that Miranda Penney and I will be walking down the aisle together tomorrow," Jordan said, his slick words making Miranda's ears steam.

"Excuse me," came another male voice. "I'm the manager of this establishment, and if you aren't a registered guest or in the company of a registered guest, I'm afraid I must ask you to leave."

While the hotel manager escorted the photographers and reporters from the lobby, Jordan stepped up to the front desk. He flashed a smile at the clerk who was helping him. The woman batted her eyes and bit the outer corner of her lower lip in a coquettish way that made Miranda's stomach turn. When the clerk stepped away to run Jordan's credit card, Miranda stepped around her bodyguards and made her presence known to him.

"Why did you say that?" she demanded under her breath.

"Good afternoon to you, too, Andy. And why did I say what?" Jordan asked innocently. He leaned one elbow on the butterscotch marble counter.

"That crack you just made to the press." She moved closer to Jordan. Rudolph and Blaze, as if Velcroed to her sides, moved with her.

"Who are your friends?" Jordan asked. "Fletcher's watchdogs?"

A low, menacing growl issued from the thick, muscled column of Blaze's throat. Rudolph, his eyes hidden behind dark glasses, cracked his neck, and it sounded like a gunshot.

"Easy boys," Jordan said, his smile wavering a tiny bit.

"Why are you even here now?" Miranda asked Jordan. "It's Friday. The wedding rehearsal isn't until tomorrow night."

"Alec told me that he and Callie and you were checking in a day early, so I figured I would, too. Maybe the four of us can have dinner tonight."

Rudolph, the more judgmental of Miranda's bodyguards, snorted.

"Okay, maybe the six of us can have dinner tonight," Jordan amended.

"You just told those reporters that you and I would be walking the aisle tomorrow," Miranda said. "You deliberately mislead—"

"I told the truth," Jordan cut in. "We will be walking down the aisle tomorrow. Just not the way I would have hoped."

Miranda, her lips pursed in anger, clutched her room key in her hand as she turned and made her way to the elevators. She used the end of her crutch to press the UP button. Ever the professionals, Blaze and Rudolph checked the car before allowing Miranda to enter it. Miranda was safely inside the elevator waiting for the doors to close when she saw another man step up to the front desk. She used her crutch to bar the doors from closing when she realized who he was.

Even from behind she recognized his ramrod-straight posture and wide shoulders. His hair looked a little grayer than when she'd last seen him at Christmas. She even recognized his suitcase. It was the Clava garment bag that she had given him almost a decade ago, for his birthday. The sophisticated yet practical black leather bag had been the perfect gift for the businessman who travels.

She thought of calling out to him, but she couldn't push the word "Daddy" past her lips. She hadn't even spoken to him since the engagement dinner. Since he'd moved out of the house in Silver Spring, her mother had been the one reporting his comings and goings. Miranda lowered her crutch and let the doors close. Now wasn't the time to repair the damage between her and her father. And the lobby of the Plaza certainly wasn't the place.

The next morning, Miranda was having a late breakfast alone in the bridal suite she was sharing with her mother and Calista when her cell phone rang. The phone had come with Rudolph and Blaze, so she knew they were calling from right outside the door.

"Yes?" she answered.

"There's a man here," Rudolph said tonelessly. "About sixty—"

"Fifty-nine, thank you very much," Miranda heard faintly in the background.

"Greenish-brown eyes, graying Afro, and he's tall. About six feet," Rudolph continued. "He says he's your father."

Miranda disconnected the call as she went to the door and opened it. Her father stood there in the Saturday morning costume she knew well: jeans, a plain button-down, a navy cardigan and athletic shoes. He was clean-shaven and bright-eyed. His hair was shorter than she remembered, and the style gave him a youthfulness that contrasted with the gray of his hair. Even in his understated Saturday clothes, he was painfully handsome.

"Hi, Andy," he greeted.

"Come in." Miranda pulled the door wide to accommodate him. He closed it behind him and followed her to the living room area. The remnants of Miranda's French toast and fresh berries were spread out on the low coffee table before the sofa. Clayton waited for his daughter to sit before he joined her. Miranda picked up the remote and turned on the television.

"Mom and Calista are out shopping with Bernie on Newbury Street," she said. "Callie's looking for favors for her bridal party. She wants cinnamon chocolate truffles to match her cake."

"Why didn't you go with them?" Clayton asked.

"Too much hassle. My crutches kill my armpits and the *Herald-Star* dogs me everywhere I go. I need a day off from all the commotion."

"Do you mind if I wait here for your mom and your sister?"

Miranda shook her head. She was grateful for his company and, until now, she hadn't realized how much she'd missed him. She flipped through the stations until she came to the Red Sox game that was just starting. As they had on so many Saturdays throughout her childhood, Miranda and her father lounged on the sofa and watched a baseball game.

"Pitcher's young," Clayton said.

"He was recruited right out of high school. He could give the Sox trouble this afternoon."

"Your mother told me that you quit the paper last week."

"She told me that you bought a condo near D.C."

"It's nice," Clayton said. "There's an on-site laundry service, a pool, a gym. You should come down and see the place."

Miranda toyed with a loose thread dangling from the edge of her denim cutoffs. This was the sort of conversation she never would have imagined herself having with her own father. He was inviting her to his new condo and into a life apart from her mother. "Do you have a roommate?" she asked.

He prefaced his answer with a heavy sigh. "I'm not seeing anyone these days. Anywhere."

They watched the Red Sox first baseman labor along the base path as he bolted from third to home. "This guy gained twenty pounds in the offseason," Miranda said. "He's got to lose it. He did it, supposedly, for more power at bat, but it's slowing him down."

"I'm sorry I lost my temper the last time we saw each other," Clayton said. "And I'm sorry about all the rest of it. I was a selfish bastard, Slugger."

"It's . . . okay, Dad. It's over. I'm glad that you and Mom are still friends."

"Your mother is the best friend I've ever had. She's the best lover I've ever had. And, like a fool, I tossed it all away."

Miranda totally empathized with her father's loss. Lucas had been a wonderful friend and lover. He was one of the best people she had ever known. And she had thrown him away. "I'm a fool, too, Dad. I know where it comes from now."

"Do you? Your mother and your sister have told me all about what's gone on between you and Lucas. What you did isn't about him or me.

It's about you, Slugger. You think you're not enough for him. It's always been that way with you."

Miranda crossed her arms. Her father had plainly stated the one thing she herself had only danced around. Confronted with it, she had no defense for it. "I know what I am, Dad. I'm a flat-chested, sports-loving tomboy. If mom wasn't enough for you, how could I possibly be enough for Lucas Fletcher?"

"You and I might be fools, but Lucas Fletcher doesn't strike me as one. The man wouldn't have hired a pair of gladiators to protect you if he didn't love and care about you."

"He loves and cares about our baby." Miranda knew she was being unfair. "The gladiators are for her. Or him."

Clayton bolted upright, staring at Miranda's midsection. "You're pregnant? He got you pregnant?"

"Don't blame Lucas. I was there, too, Dad. And I haven't told Mom and Calista yet, so try not to bug out."

Clayton sat quietly, color flaring in his face then fading away as he struggled to accept his oldest daughter's bombshell. "Does Lucas know that you're carrying my grandchild?"

"Yes."

"Did he propose to you before or after he knew about the baby?"

"He proposed before either of us knew."

"He wants you, Miranda," Clayton said as if that fact gave him the fatherly solace he required. "Give him a chance. You and my grandchild deserve that."

"I can't risk it, Dad. You, of all people, should know that."

Mr. Penney took his daughter's hand and gave it a firm squeeze before kissing it. "Your mother left me, and I've never seen her happier. You broke up with Lucas, and you're miserable. If you're so sure you're doing the right thing, then why are you so unhappy? Why do I see such pain in your eyes?"

Miranda tried to work out a denial, but her brain wouldn't feed the lie to her mouth. Tension seeped from her as she forced herself to face the truth of her father's argument. "I made a mistake," she said simply.

She had never been happier to be wrong, but accepting her mistake opened a whole new set of problems. Could she get Lucas back? Would he even want her after all she had put him through? He was determined to be a proper father, but was he still interested in being her husband?

The easiest way to find out would be to pick up the phone and call him. It could also be the worst thing for her to do, particularly on the eve of Calista's wedding. How could she stand at the altar tomorrow, watching another couple join their lives, if Lucas were to shut her out of his? And likewise, how could she stand at the altar instead of running to find Lucas, if he wanted her back?

She could wait until after the wedding to call him. It would give her time to think of something to say to him, the right thing to say. And then, for better or worse, she would swallow her fears and take a leap of faith in Lucas. *And myself,* she thought.

Miranda went into her father's embrace as easily as she had as a youngster, long before she knew the truth about him. As he held her and comforted her, she admitted that despite what kind of man and husband Clayton Penney had been, he had always been a good father.

Lucas stabbed the redial button on his phone as he paced the wide space of the solar at Castle Conwy. The computer screen at his oak desk cast the colorful image of page five of the *Herald-Star Online* into the muted light of the room. The page featured a photo of Jordan Duquette taken in the lobby of the Boston Park Plaza Hotel. Jordan's too-handsome, grinning face had been enough to inspire Lucas to put a fist through the monitor, but it was Jordan's quote that had made tiny blood vessels behind Lucas's eyes pop.

"Answer, Miranda!" Lucas demanded between gritted teeth. The phone rang twice more before an automated answering system picked up. Lucas, in a rare burst of uncontrollable temper, hurled the tiny cell phone. No match for the centuries-old stone, the high-tech phone exploded into glittering bits of microchips and plastic.

Lucas growled his frustration. He had called Miranda's home number three times before trying her at the Park Plaza. As he'd expected, the hotel operator had claimed to have no such guest registered, so he'd tried her once more at home. Morgan had tracked down the phone numbers for Calista, Mr. and Mrs. Penney and Alec Henderson, but none of them were at their residences. Lucas was struggling to contain his annoyance and resentment—and jealousy—to work up enough gall to call Jordan Duquette when another option came to mind. He sat at his desk, put his table phone on speaker and dialed.

"What area code is 44?" Bernie greeted upon answering his phone.

"It's the international calling code for Wales," Lucas impatiently explained.

"Sir Lucas!" Bernie's voice hid none of his excitement. "So good to hear from you."

Lucas leaned one elbow on his desk and propped his other hand on his thigh. "Is she marrying that idiot?"

"I'm sorry," Bernie said. "I'm accustomed to beginning a conversation at the beginning."

"I was reading Saturday's *Herald-Star* online and I saw a story about Jordan Duquette," Lucas said. "He claims that he and Miranda are to 'walk down the aisle together' tomorrow at six. Is this another of your paper's falsehoods?"

Bernie's long silence seemed to lengthen the distance between Conwy and Boston.

Dread gripped Lucas's heart. Feast had told him that pregnant women were capable of almost anything under the influence of their fluctuating hormones, but never had Lucas considered the possibility that Miranda would go utterly insane. "Mr. Reilly, I would appreciate an answer."

"I don't know what to say," Bernie faltered. "I would have thought that Miranda would have explained what was going on. I'd like to tell you the truth, but on the other hand, a lie would make this situation much easier for everyone involved."

"Mr. Reilly!" Lucas shouted.

"It's true!" Bernie blurted. "Tomorrow at six, at the Park Plaza Castle in Boston, Miranda and Jordan will stand before God and family . . . and . . . well, you can fill in the rest."

The pops behind Lucas's eye became louder and stronger. "Miranda can't be marrying Duquette. He's the very thing she's convinced herself that I am!"

"Well, she knows what she's getting with Jordan." Bernie seemed to be enjoying his role as beacon of bad news. "She's been such an emotional wreck these last weeks. I said to her myself, I said, 'Miranda, don't go making any hasty decisions that you'll regret,' but you know how headstrong and stubborn she is. With Jordan constantly pressuring her and the hormones making her crazy, I guess she just gave in. Pity. I tried to stop her from making the second biggest mistake of her life . . . the first, of course, being her decision to let you go. I suppose she and Jordan make sense in a wholly nonsensical way. You know what they say . . . uh, women marry men like their fathers."

"Over my bloody dead carcass!" Lucas spat. "Thank you, Mr. Reilly." He hung up the phone and pressed a different button. "Morgan," he directed into the intercom, "call the airport and tell them that I wish to have the plane readied to fly to Boston. I'll be leaving immediately."

He gave Jordan's photo one last look of disgust as he sped past the computer and out of the solar, slowing only when he reached the garage, the stone building housing his collection of motor vehicles. Cars had been his indulgence in his youth, and the colorful array of driving machines lined the stone floor, each snuggled in its own assigned spot. Until he had turned his affections to his pups, creatures he loved that could love him right back, his cars had been his companions. He felt a twitch of guilt as he stared at them after not having driven them in so long, but it quickly passed. He glanced at each of them, trying to decide which would best deliver him to the airstrip.

The silver Lamborghini Murciélago could go from 0 to 60 mph in 3.5 seconds and had a top speed of 205 mph. The cherry red Porsche and the hunter green Aston Martin Vanquish would do just as well for speed, too. The sleek black Italian bike at the end of the first row made his mind up for him. Within eight seconds of straddling the Ducati 999R, and with nothing but the clothes on his back, Lucas was a black blur hugging the winding roads of Northern Wales as he sped closer to Miranda.

CHAPTER 13

"I'm supposed to be the best-looking woman in the world tonight," Calista said after Miranda emerged from her bedroom. The hotel had delivered a full-length, tri-fold mirror to the bridal suite, and Miranda stood in the center of it, scared to look at her reflection. "You look amazing, Andy," Calista said. "That dress looks better now than it did at your last fitting."

"Thanks for saying that, Callie," Miranda said, "but I've never seen you look more beautiful." Calista, the full skirt of her ivory silk taffeta wedding gown spread carefully around her to avoid wrinkles, sat on the velvet-covered stool at the vanity table. Aña Penney fastened a string of heirloom pearls, Calista's something borrowed, around her daughter's neck. The princess-seamed bodice of Calista's dress had a low-cut, straight neckline, and the pearls gave the dress the perfect finishing touch. Aña spent a moment more hovering over Calista before she turned toward Miranda.

Aña wore a pale peach suit dress that complemented her dark eyes and virtually unlined skin. Her black hair was swept into a snazzy chignon, and Aña had refused to let a stylist color the scant streaks of silver.

Miranda sighed as she stared at her sister and her mother. It hadn't been easy growing up in the same house with two of the most beautiful women in Silver Spring, but now, it wasn't envy that colored her perception of them. It was love, pride and gratitude for what a wonderful family she had. She turned away from them before the tears building behind her eyes found their way out.

Miranda finally caught her reflection and was startled by what she saw. The pregnancy that she had worried the dress would reveal actually complemented the garment. Her fuller breasts nicely filled the

Empire bodice, balancing the slender lengths of her crinkled French silk chiffon sleeves. Layers of sheer silk fell to her ankles, beautifully camouflaging the swell of her growing abdomen as well as her cast. The pale apricot silk heightened the rosy undertones of her complexion, giving her a natural, healthy glow that cosmetics couldn't duplicate. At Calista's insistence, she wore a swipe of mascara and a bit of neutral lip gloss for the photos to come later.

Her hair had been done by Marc Antonio, Boston's most sought-after stylist and one of Bernie's close friends. Marc Antonio had trimmed Miranda's "dead ends" before setting her hair with large plastic rollers. He'd used a blow dryer on a cool setting to give her loose, curling waves with maximum volume and shine. He had then styled her hair similarly to Calista's, stacking the curls elegantly at the crown and back of Miranda's head, leaving a few spiraling tendrils to caress her neck and shoulders. A pair of antique drop pearl and topaz earrings, Calista's gift to her maid of honor, completed Miranda's outfit.

Bernie joined Miranda in the mirror. He lightly gripped her shoulders as he set a delicate kiss on each of her cheeks. "You look like royalty."

"Miranda, I can't remember ever seeing you all dressed up." Aña clasped her hands under her chin. "Look at you!" She held out a hand, drawing Miranda to her. She put an arm around each of her daughters. "My precious babies," she nearly wept with happiness.

"Funny you should use that word, Mrs. Penney," Bernie said. He looked at his wrist, which bore no watch. "Goodness, look at the time. I'm late for my very important ushering duties."

"What word?" Aña wondered aloud.

"Baby," Miranda muttered.

Aña waved the absent Bernie's comment off. She helped Calista search through a velvet jewelry pouch. "I can't help it. No matter how old you girls get, I still think of you as my babies . . ." Her words faded as she withdrew a triple-strand pearl bracelet. She took a hard, motherly look at Miranda, and then her eyes went wide. "Baby?"

Valiantly fighting back tears, the tip of Miranda's nose pinked as she nodded.

"Oh my baby," Aña gasped. "My little girl!" She took Miranda in her arms.

"Don't be disappointed in me, Mama," Miranda managed.

Aña drew away enough to cup Miranda's face in both of her hands. "Never. Honey, I'm surprised, but it's a good surprise. Isn't it?"

"Hello?" Calista sang. "Remember me? The bride? What's going on?"

"You're going to be an aunt," Miranda said. "And a godmother."

Calista grinned as she clasped the pearl bracelet onto her left wrist. "I was wondering when you'd finally get around to telling us."

"Did Dad tell you?" Miranda asked. "Or was it Bernie?"

Calista neatly folded her hands over her knee. "You're lucky I'm getting married today, or I'd be pissed that you told Bernie and Dad before you told me. I figured it out on my own, actually. I suspected it at the final dress fitting. You looked like you'd gained at least one cup size. Plus, you had to lie on the floor to zip your jeans up."

Miranda sat down on the chaise near the vanity table. "I'm sorry I didn't tell you, Callie. I didn't want this whole baby thing to steal any thunder from your wedding. If it had gotten out any sooner, the media would have turned this place upside down and inside out."

Calista took her sister's hand. "I checked my messages this morning and Lucas called me from Conwy. He said he's been trying to reach you. He knows about the pregnancy, doesn't he?"

Miranda nodded. She brought her thumb to her lips, to gnaw on her cuticle, but Calista grabbed her hand and held it in her lap. "You just had a one-hundred dollar manicure," Calista said. "If you're hungry, have a cracker."

"How do you and Lucas plan to handle this, Miranda?" Aña asked.

"I'm not sure what's going to happen, Mom. I'm going to call him after the wedding."

None of the Penney women knew that Bernie had returned until he cleared his throat from the archway adjoining the dressing room to the living room. "About the wedding, kitten," he began. "We need to talk about Lucas and that remark Jordan made in yesterday's paper. Did you see it, or hear about it on television?"

Miranda rolled her eyes. "I was right there when he said it."

Clayton, dressed in a black tuxedo with a white vest and cravat, poked his head into the room. "My lovely ladies, it's time."

Miranda went to a small side table and picked up her sister's bouquet. The scent of gardenias, ranunculus and stephanotis trailed Miranda as she crossed the room to Bernie. "I haven't picked up a *Herald-Star* since I quit the place. You'd better go sit. We can talk later."

"Miranda, honey," Bernie started anxiously, "I don't have proof to the contrary, but I have a sneaking suspicion that an unexpected guest might crash this wedding."

"That's why the Boston Police are patrolling the entrance and exits." Miranda shooed Bernie toward the door while Aña gathered the train of Calista's gown. "Thanks to Jordan, all of New England knows about Calista's wedding."

"But sweetie, Lucas thinks that you and Jordan—"

"If you say that name one more time, I'll beat you with my ranunculus," Miranda threatened.

"Which name?" Bernie asked.

"Either of them. Now go. I have a wedding to get through, then I can think about sorting out the rest of my life." She patted her belly. "The rest of *our* lives."

"That's just it," Bernie persisted. "I'm worried about what a sudden shock might do to you or your baby. If you'd only listen for one second, I—"

"Bernie!" Miranda snapped. "Nothing will go wrong today. This will be a gorgeous ceremony. It'll be a wedding to remember."

Bernie's face suddenly relaxed and the tension left his shoulders as he accepted Miranda's final edict. "That's exactly what I'm hoping for." He gave her cheek a tender caress before he turned and left the room.

"Are you ready, soon-to-be Mrs. Alec Henderson?" Miranda asked her sister.

Calista's smile was affirmation enough, but she said, "I'm ready, Mama!" as she slapped her big sister a hearty high-five.

Security problems at Boston's Logan Airport kept Lucas's plane circling New England for two hours before the pilot finally got clearance to land at Manchester International in New Hampshire. A flight steward had radioed ahead to arrange ground transportation to Boston, and by five P.M., Lucas was ordering his driver to break as many driving laws as possible to get to the Park Plaza on time.

Lucas had been traveling for the better part of a day. He drummed his thumb against his thigh and nervously tapped his foot, mentally willing something to happen to delay the wedding. He prayed for something small—an unstitched hem, a tardy clergyman, a squirrel loose in the pews—that would buy him more time. Karmic velocity doubled back on him when his limousine abruptly slowed as they crossed the boundary line into Suffolk County.

"What the devil is the problem?" Lucas demanded. "Whatever it is, can't you drive around it?"

"The Red Sox have a doubleheader at Fenway, and this is a really nice June day," the driver said apologetically. "Everybody's heading for the ballpark, the Public Gardens, the Common and the Esplanade. This is I-93 in Boston. There's always been traffic, there'll always be traffic."

"Tell me, how far are we from the Park Plaza Castle?"

The driver, more familiar with New Hampshire's sites, checked his Global Positioning System for the castle's proximity. "About two miles, as the crow flies." He shook his head as he looked at the five-lane river of bumper-to-bumper traffic ahead of him on I-93. "In this traffic, about forty-five minutes."

Lucas sneered at the digital clock built into the limo's wet bar. "How would I get to the castle from here? On foot?"

The driver told him. Lucas closed his eyes to better visualize the driver's directions, then he bolted from the back of the car. "Good luck!" he heard the driver call after him as he wove his way through the sea of motionless automobiles.

A few drivers recognized him and honked their horns as he hopped over their bumpers. Lucas ran along the shoulder of the off-ramp leading to the Museum of Science and the Arena where he had first met Miranda during his ill-fated opening night show in Boston. Traffic was even more snarled at the five-way intersection at the bottom of the off-ramp, but Lucas managed to safely jaywalk to the Charles River side of Storrow Drive.

"You!" shouted a mounted Boston Police officer who trotted up to Lucas from the river walk. "Don't you know that jaywalking is a citable offense?"

"No, officer, I didn't," Lucas said breathlessly. The driver hadn't exaggerated about the nice weather. Cold pellets of sweat ran down Lucas's back within the lightweight leather jacket he wore. He stripped the thing off and cast it aside as he spoke to the police officer. "Perhaps you can help me, Officer. My girlfriend is getting married as we speak, and—"

The policeman tipped his round white helmet from his forehead, revealing a dark-brown bald head dotted with sweat. "Hold on, Romeo. Seems to me that if she's off somewhere getting married and you're here impeding the flow of traffic on Storrow Drive, she's not your girlfriend."

"I don't have time to explain." Lucas forced himself to stay calm. He would never be able to stop the wedding from a jail cell. "My name is Lucas Fletcher. The woman who's getting married is Miranda Penney. She's . . ."

"Loco Yoko!" the officer yelled, snapping his thick fingers. "I thought you looked familiar! My wife's been following you and the Penney woman in the *Star*." The officer dismounted and withdrew a notepad from his breast pocket. "Could I get your autograph for my wife? Her name is Delores. We just had a baby and she's been a little down in the dumps, with all the night feedings and the crying. She's crazy about you, and an autograph would be just the thing to put a smile on her face."

As slow as traffic had been before Lucas was stopped, it was now at a standstill as drivers and passengers alike recognized Lucas. One enterprising tourist hung halfway out of the passenger side window, snapping photos of Lucas as his car crept past. Another young man, at his female driver's insistence, hopped out of his car, grabbed Lucas's leather coat, and then got back into the car, which kept on rolling. Lucas was deaf to the driver's delighted screams.

"Officer," Lucas said gravely, glancing furtively at a car that appeared to be parking right in the middle of the road, "if you get me to the Park Plaza Castle in the next five minutes, I swear to you on my own life that I will come to your house and not only personally give your Delores my autograph, I will vacuum, mop, polish, launder nappies, prepare supper and sing your new sprog to sleep before I leave." Lucas eyed the officer's disinterested, though fit-looking, horse. "Can you help me?"

The policeman's hands tightened around his horse's reins. His sweaty, sun-blackened face split in a huge grin as he held his other hand out to Lucas. "Officer Brian Petrie, Boston Mounted Police at your service, Mr. Fletcher." The two men shook. "Let's get you to that wedding."

Miranda barely heard the clergyman's words as she stood with Calista before two hundred and fifty friends and members of the Penney and Henderson families. In one hand she clutched a small bouquet of peach and white ranunculus, the moisture from her palm dampening the wide satin band binding their stems. In the other, she held onto a cane, which helped her stand on her broken foot. To spare Miranda the awkwardness of hobbling down the aisle at the end of the ceremony, Calista had decided that the wedding party would disperse with the guests, rather than pairing up and trodding after the newlyweds. Miranda was glad that she wouldn't have to walk with Jordan. The last thing she wanted to see was a photograph of herself paired with Jordan, forever mounted in Calista's wedding album.

She stole a peek over her shoulder. The inside of the castle was predominantly empty space. The walls had been hung with thick garlands of ivy, roses and gardenias that nicely concealed the heraldic banners and flags painted on the walls. Two sections of folding chairs covered in pale peach chintz lined the cement floor. High above them, wooden beams supported a giant chandelier comprised of hundreds of tiny light bulbs.

Miranda swallowed a longing sigh. The Park Plaza Castle was a lovely, romantic place to hold a fairy tale wedding . . . but it looked like it was made of Lego and cardboard compared to Conwy.

Miranda tried to focus on the cleric's words of love, devotion and fidelity rather than on her intense desire to be elsewhere. Her whole body ached with the urge to take off right now, to toss her bouquet aside, scuttle down the aisle, and hail a taxi to take her to Logan Airport. Calista's reception would be glorious, but what was a three-tiered cinnamon chocolate cake and artsy scallop seviche hors d'oeuvres compared to Fenway Franks with Lucas at Conwy?

I have to go to him, Miranda thought. *I had the fairy tale. I had what my sister has, what my mother thought she had, what every woman in this world wants. I had someone who loved me, truly.*

She closed her eyes and bit back tears, hoping Lucas loved her still. *I'll find out, soon enough,* she supposed, deciding right then and there that she would be heading for Logan just as soon as Calista and Alec returned down the aisle as man and wife.

Wizard's mighty flanks rippled with muscle as he galloped down Arlington Street, easily parting traffic. The police horse's ears laid almost flat as he navigated his way past SUVs and compact cars that pulled to the left and right to avoid his massive hooves. When the Park Plaza Castle came in view, Lucas allowed himself a welcome rush of relief.

"I hope we got you here in time," Officer Petrie called to Lucas, who was climbing out of the passenger side of a candy-apple red, late-model Buick before it had even come to a complete stop.

"Thank you," Lucas said warmly to the blue-haired driver. She had been on her way to her granddaughter's apartment on Huntington Ave. when Officer Petrie had walked onto Storrow Drive and enlisted her aid in getting Lucas to the castle. The old woman had been startled and disbelieving, at first, but like most women, she fell victim to Lucas's heartfelt charm and good looks. The woman's sweet, genteel demeanor hid a lead foot that easily kept up with Officers Petrie and Wizard, who had blazed a clear trail to the castle.

"Remember what you promised my Delores," Officer Petrie called after Lucas, who leaped the police sawhorses that had been set up in anticipation of a rowdy crowd. "And good luck!"

Lucas rounded the front of the building. Two policemen at the door tried to bar his entry, but Officer Petrie rode up to explain everything. Lucas shoved open the doors and, like a force of nature, he marched down the long, petal-strewn aisle. He saw the bride's white dress and gossamer veil; he saw the broad back of the groom in a tuxedo. Faintly, he heard a male voice state, "With the power vested in me by the Commonwealth of Massachusetts, it is my happy honor to pronounce—"

"No!" Lucas hollered, gaining speed as his voice gathered force. "I won't allow this wedding to continue!"

Every head in the place turned to look at him. Lucas took special note of the bride's. For the first time in his life, he blushed before a full house.

"Mr. Fletcher, I presume?" Calista's casual inquiry carried through the profound silence of the room.

"Y-You . . ." Lucas stammered. "But I understood that Miranda . . . I saw it in the newspaper." He ran his fingers through his sweat-dampened hair as he approached the altar. He was blind to the doe-eyed looks women threw him as he passed each row of seats. "Jordan Duquette said that he was walking down the aisle with Miranda tonight."

Alec whipped around and glared at Jordan.

"I was misquoted, man," Jordan said, his hands up in surrender.

"I'm glad to finally meet you, Mr. Fletcher," Calista said.

"Calista," Lucas whispered, squinting his eyes in embarrassment. "It's *your* wedding. I should have remembered."

"Lucas."

He drew up short when Miranda spoke his name and his eyes met hers. Completely gobstruck by the sight of her, his feet were the only part of him capable of movement. They carried him to her, where she stood with her eyes perfectly round in surprise. Her hand trembled as she brought it to his brow and touched him, making sure that he was real and not some gorgeous phantom she had conjured to amuse herself during the clergyman's long-winded sermon. His hair and his white shirt were windblown and his cheeks were ruddy, as though he had run to her all the way from Wales.

Lucas put one hand on her waist and lay the other against her jawline. "I always suspected that you were a goddess. Tonight, you well look the part."

She leaned her head in close to him, aware that the entire congregation was listening to her every word. "I was going to fly to Wales right after the wedding." She threw her arms around him, crushing her bouquet against his back. "I wanted to apologize and to tell you that I was wrong. I was so wrong about us and about you."

"You're sure?" he asked, afraid to believe that she meant what she'd just said.

"Yes," she nodded.

"Absolutely?" He searched her eyes for any sign of doubt.

"Absolu—" was all she got out before Lucas caught her up in a kiss that obliterated the anguish and uncertainty of the past months.

"I'm so happy for the two of you," Calista said, her eyes tearing. "But do you suppose you could finish this quickly? I'm getting a little married here."

"I humbly beg your forgiveness, Calista, Alec, for my untimely interruption," Lucas said, "but the future of this ceremony is entirely up to Miranda. I won't leave until she answers one question."

Miranda's heart hammered against her ribs when Lucas turned back to her, his love and desire shining in his heavenly eyes.

"Marry me," he said.

"That's not a question," she whispered.

"I know. It's a choice."

"Then I accept," she smiled.

Fine worry lines in his forehead melted in the light of his exultant smile. "You'll marry me?"

"Yes," Miranda laughed softly. "Yes!" she said, and it echoed through the castle.

Lucas folded her into his arms and kissed her, their hands moving over each other's faces as though hundreds of people weren't watching them. "You won't be sorry," Lucas told her.

"Neither will you," Miranda said.

"So is this to be a double ceremony?" the cleric asked.

"No," Miranda said. "My, uh, fiancé was just taking a seat."

"Sorry," Lucas said sheepishly. "If I'm not terribly mistaken, the conniving Mr. Reilly has likely saved a place for me. But I'll, uh, just park it right here." He backed his way toward the first pew and squeezed in between the two flower girls, Alec's nine- and ten-year-old nieces, who smiled up at him as though he were one of Disney's charming princes. "Carry on, please," Lucas nodded toward the cleric.

"Where was I?" the amused clergyman said.

"You were at the finale," Calista reminded him.

"Ah, yes." He cleared his throat with a little laugh. "By the power vested in me by the Commonwealth of Massachusetts—and with the gracious blessing of Mr. Lucas Fletcher—I now pronounce you husband and wife. Mr. Henderson, you may kiss your bride."

With the exception of Lucas and Miranda, everyone applauded as Alec turned Calista in his arms, executed a showy dip, and kissed her. Lucas and Miranda missed it all, having eyes only for each other.

EPILOGUE

Miranda gripped the small of her back with both hands as she paced the solar. Her shoulders thrust back, she led with her belly, which for weeks now totally obscured her view of her feet. She glanced at Lucas's desk, the top of which was papered with drawings of the cover art for Karmic Echo's latest album, *Blood Welsh Moon*. The artist—the same Italian painter who had done many of Kitty Kincaid's lush and elegant book covers—had perfectly rendered a moonlit Welsh beach with two lovers silhouetted against the night vista. And like most of her favorite romance novels, the album's title would be embossed in gold or silver.

Miranda looked at her husband, who sat reading on the deep, wide leather sofa. His expression was intense and serious, unreadable. Miranda's anxiety swelled a bit and the tightness in her lower back increased.

She went to the tall, broad windows of the solar and gazed upon the sunlit waters of Conwy Bay. Almost five months ago, fireworks celebrating her marriage to Lucas had illuminated the sky over the bay. Lucas had cast all reason and practicality aside in "throwing together" their wedding. The small, intimate ceremony Miranda had hoped for had become a weekend-long affair with a reception featuring performances by Karmic Echo and other Bilious recording artists—including the talented Tess Cullor. The town of Conwy had been invited to the reception, but to Miranda, it looked as though the entire population of Wales had turned out for the occasion. The wedding had been held in Conwy's chapel. The small chamber was only large enough to accommodate their families and closest friends, but an anteroom held a hundred or so more guests.

Never a big fan of white to begin with, Miranda wore a gown of ecru silk, an Abu Ngatanze original. Lucas, who never imagined that

Miranda could ever have been more beautiful than she was on the day of Calista's wedding, wept at the sight of his bride on his wedding day.

Miranda turned from the window to again study her husband. He looked up at her and smiled as he closed the thick manuscript balanced across his knee. "This is the first book I've read that fictionalizes the story of Laith al Kadin and mad Lady Emberley."

Miranda tucked her right thumbnail between her teeth as she ambled over to him, still massaging her lower back with her left hand. "What do you think of it?"

"It's bloody brilliant. The author tells the tale wonderfully with warmth, humor and cleverness. It's not the typical romance novel. I've never read an interracial historical romance. It has the scorching sex I generally search for, but it's also quite literary." Lucas opened his arms and guided Miranda onto his lap.

"Bernie said he liked 'the lyrical turn of phrase.'"

Lucas held up the manuscript and read the author's name. "Is Victoria Ronaldinho a friend of yours?"

"She's me." Miranda grinned and locked her fingers around Lucas's neck.

"I thought some of those love scenes were familiar." Lucas ran his hand along the soft denim covering her outer thigh. "Victoria Ronaldinho," he said grandly. "Why that name?"

"Victoria Holt was one of the first novelists I really liked when I was a kid, and Ronaldinho is my favorite Brazilian soccer player. I figured that if I was going to try to get this thing published, I should do it on the book's merit, using a pseudonym. I don't want your name to be considered one of its selling points." She shifted her eyes from his. "When I left the *Herald-Star*, I wanted to take one of the other job offers that came my way. But I know those companies only wanted me because of you. I want to succeed on my own merits, not because of who I'm married to."

"I understand completely." He gently grasped her chin and turned her face back to his. "I'll have my agent set up a meeting with one of the literary agents at his firm."

"No, Lucas. I want to do this on my own. I know it'll be hard to get this book published, but if it comes too easy, I won't appreciate it."

"That, love, is a lesson I know only too well." He eased his fingers into the hair at the back of her head and brought her mouth to his for a kiss. Miranda slid her hand under his sweater, and smiled at the way his flat belly jumped at her touch as her fingers moved to the zipper of his jeans. The pain in Miranda's lower back seemed to lessen as Lucas nuzzled her breasts through the soft fabric of her white maternity shirt. She was at thirty-nine weeks and she had Alfred Hitchcock's profile, yet Lucas made her feel as though she were the sexiest, most desirable woman in the world.

Which, to him, she was.

She moaned when he began to delicately use his teeth through the fabric, deliciously tormenting the most sensitive parts of her breasts. She held his head in her hands, reveling in the sensations he sent shooting through her.

"Miranda?" He opened her shirt and set precious kisses on the rounds of her breasts.

"Yes?" she panted.

"You've sprung a leak."

It took her a moment to notice the wetness on Lucas's lap.

"I believe your water's broken," he told her.

Miranda felt the strain of her eyes bulging from their sockets. "This is one of the signs!" Her voice seemed to shrink in her sudden panic. "We have to do something!" She lumbered off of Lucas. "Damn, these were my favorite jeans. We're having a baby now, right? It's now?" Tears rushed to her eyes. "Lucas, I'm having the baby!"

"Really?" he said, feigning surprise.

Miranda began to bawl.

Lucas took her in his arms. He soothed her and began walking her out of the solar. "Your mum and your sister are in the village and Bernie is somewhere here on the grounds. I'll call them and have them meet us at the birthing center. Dr. Larch has been on call here at Conwy for the past three days, and I'll send for her right now. First babies are typically long deliveries, at least that's what Feast and Izzy were told. Izzy was in labor for thirty-one hours with Archibald Leonard Lucas Feast, remember?"

"The kid's name is as long as his delivery was," Miranda cracked.

"Are you having contractions?" Lucas asked.

"I felt something odd a few minutes ago, right before the dam burst. I thought it was just a cramp. I've been having Braxton-Hicks's since—" She grabbed the stone wall with one hand and pressed the other to her belly. "*Mãe do Deus*!" she cried as a pain like none she had ever known seemed to radiate from the middle of her body all the way down to her toes. Her knees buckled and Lucas caught her up in his arms.

"Did that one feel like a Braxton-Hicks?" Lucas asked as he hurried with her down the corridor.

"That one felt like the baby's trying to pry her way out," Miranda gasped.

"Your ultrasounds were inconclusive, yet you're still so certain that the baby is a girl," Lucas said.

"She'd better be a girl," Miranda winced. "I have this baby down as a girl in the pool."

"What pool?"

"The baby pool here at Conwy."

"You've set odds on our baby?"

"So far, Morgan looks good for the win. He picked a girl to be born in early October. If the baby weighs eight pounds or more, he'll . . . *Meu Deus*, this is starting to hurt!" She forced her mouth to relax as she began the breathing techniques she'd learned to help manage the pain. "I want to take a shower," she pleaded. "I really hurt now, and Dr. Larch said the shower helps."

"You can take a shower at the birthing center." Lucas leaned against the wall to keep his balance as he navigated his way down the stairs while carrying Miranda. "A pool on our baby . . . honestly, Miranda. I suppose it's too late for me to get in on it?"

Her hold on him tightened as another contraction gripped her.

"There can't have been more than a minute between those," he said, more to himself than for Miranda's benefit. "Morgan!" he hollered once they had reached the Great Hall.

"Sir?" Morgan rushed into the space that still echoed with his name.

"Page Dr. Larch and tell her that Miranda's contractions are a minute apart, and get Mrs. Penney, Mr. Penney, Calista, Alec and Bernard Reilly to the birthing center," Lucas directed.

Morgan rushed off while Lucas trotted through the Great Hall and into a much more cozy chamber. The room had all the equipment that a hospital delivery room would have as well as all the comforts of home that Miranda wanted. Lucas set her on the birthing bed and held her hand as another contraction ripped through her, making her teeth chatter.

"Will Dr. Larch be here soon?" she asked.

Lucas helped her undress and to slip on the Canarinho T-shirt she had chosen to labor in. "She'll be here, love." He kissed her sweaty brow and smoothed damp strands of hair from her face.

Miranda's contractions were stacking by the time Dr. Larch, her nurses and a neonatalist arrived within minutes of Morgan's page. By the time Aña and Calista were slipping on sterile robes, Miranda was in the throes of pushing her first child into the world. Thirty-five minutes after Lucas brought her to the birthing room, Miranda gave him an eight-pound baby girl.

The baby had her father's lungs. Her newborn cries seemed to carry through the Great Hall and throughout the town of Conwy, which raised a collective cheer and rang the chapel bells upon the birth of Lucas and Miranda's child. Cleaned, weighed, examined and dressed, the baby was set in Lucas's arms. His calm joy overlapped onto her, and she quieted.

"Would you like to hold your daughter?" Lucas asked Miranda, who was being tidied by her doctor and nurse.

"You're so much better at that than I am," Miranda whispered, recalling the way Archie Feast had wailed his eyes out the one and only time she had held him.

"I had lots of practice recently, thanks to Officer Brian Petrie and his wife Delores." Lucas sat on the edge of Miranda's bed. "Little Brian Jr. wouldn't let me get the polishing done for wanting me to hold him all the time."

Miranda raised her arms to her child, hoping and praying that the babe would be as agreeable for her as she had been for her father. Lucas set her in Miranda's arms.

"She's so little." Miranda couldn't stop looking at her daughter. Her eyes were closed, her long dark lashes fanned upon her plump, cinnamon cheeks. Her nose was a sweet little button, and the perfect strawberry bud of her mouth suggested the shape of her father's. Silky black curls peeked from beneath the white knit cap the nurse had placed on her head. Lucas eased closer to his wife and daughter, slipping his arm under Miranda's shoulders.

All at once, Miranda felt all the pieces of her life click solidly into place. "We made her. *Meu Deus*, Lucas, we made this beautiful little person."

Lucas nodded. He gazed at his wife and daughter with more love than Miranda thought a man capable.

"You would have made a great seahorse," she told him.

"What?"

"Never mind," she smiled. "What should we name her?"

"I figured we wouldn't know what to call her until we met her, but in keeping with Penney tradition, one possibility occurred to me. Calista means 'most beautiful' and Miranda means 'much admired.' How do you feel about the name Alysia?"

Miranda brushed the baby's hand with her smallest finger. Her daughter's hand opened and closed around it, and Miranda kissed the tiny fingers. "What does it mean?"

"Captivating."

"I like it." Miranda's words broke. Tears dotted her lower lashes, blurring her daughter's image.

"Can I get you anything, love?" Lucas asked. "Before I call everyone in to meet our little Alysia?"

Miranda wiped her tears and grinned at her husband. "Do we have any Fenway Franks?"

The End

ABOUT THE AUTHOR

Crush is the newest contemporary romance by Missouri native, **Crystal Hubbard**, who lives there with her husband and their children. When she isn't busy writing, caring for her children, maintaining her household or hiding out from door-to-door magazine salesmen, Crystal enjoys paintball, bowling, and Po-Ke-No.

CRUSH

2007 Publication Schedule

January

Corporate Seduction
A.C. Arthur
ISBN-13: 978-1-58571-238-0
ISBN-10: 1-58571-238-8
$9.95

A Taste of Temptation
Reneé Alexis
ISBN-13: 978-1-58571-207-6
ISBN-10: 1-58571-207-8
$9.95

February

The Perfect Frame
Beverly Clark
ISBN-13: 978-1-58571-240-3
ISBN-10: 1-58571-240-X
$9.95

Ebony Angel
Deatri King-Bey
ISBN-13: 978-1-58571-239-7
ISBN-10: 1-58571-239-6
$9.95

March

Sweet Sensations
Gwendolyn Bolton
ISBN-13: 978-1-58571-206-9
ISBN-10: 1-58571-206-X
$9.95

Crush
Crystal Hubbard
ISBN-13: 978-1-58571-243-4
ISBN-10: 1-58571-243-4
$9.95

April

Secret Thunder
Annetta P. Lee
ISBN-13: 978-1-58571-204-5
ISBN-10: 1-58571-204-3
$9.95

Blood Seduction
J.M. Jeffries
ISBN-13: 978-1-58571-237-3
ISBN-10: 1-58571-237-X
$9.95

May

Lies Too Long
Pamela Ridley
ISBN-13: 978-1-58571-246-5
ISBN-10: 1-58571-246-9
$13.95

Two Sides to Every Story
Dyanne Davis
ISBN-13: 978-1-58571-248-9
ISBN-10: 1-58571-248-5
$9.95

June

One of These Days
Michele Sudler
ISBN-13: 978-1-58571-249-6
ISBN-10: 1-58571-249-3
$9.95

Who's That Lady
Andrea Jackson
ISBN-13: 978-1-58571-190-1
ISBN-10: 1-58571-190-X
$9.95

2007 Publication Schedule (continued)

July

Heart of the Phoenix
A.C. Arthur
ISBN-13: 978-1-58571-242-7
ISBN-10: 1-58571-242-6
$9.95

Do Over
Jaci Kenney
ISBN-13: 978-1-58571-241-0
ISBN-10: 1-58571-241-8
$9.95

It's Not Over Yet
J.J. Michael
ISBN-13: 978-1-58571-245-8
ISBN-10: 1-58571-245-0
$9.95

August

The Fires Within
Beverly Clark
ISBN-13: 978-1-58571-244-1
ISBN-10: 1-58571-244-2
$9.95

Stolen Kisses
Dominiqua Douglas
ISBN-13: 978-1-58571-247-2
ISBN-10: 1-58571-247-7
$9.95

September

Small Whispers
Annetta P. Lee
ISBN-13: 978-158571-251-9
ISBN-10: 1-58571-251-5
$6.99

Always You
Crystal Hubbard
ISBN-13: 978-158571-252-6
ISBN-10: 1-58571-252-3
$6.99

October

Not His Type
Chamein Canton
ISBN-13: 978-158571-253-3
ISBN-10: 1-58571-253-1
$6.99

Many Shades of Gray
Dyanne Davis
ISBN-13: 978-158571-254-0
ISBN-10: 1-58571-254-X
$6.99

November

When I'm With You
LaConnie Taylor-Jones
ISBN-13: 978-158571-250-2
ISBN-10: 1-58571-250-7
$6.99

The Mission
Pamela Leigh Starr
ISBN-13: 978-158571-255-7
ISBN-10: 1-58571-255-8
$6.99

December

One in A Million
Barbara Keaton
ISBN-13: 978-158571-257-1
ISBN-10: 1-58571-257-4
$6.99

The Foursome
Celya Bowers
ISBN-13: 978-158571-256-4
ISBN-10: 1-58571-256-6
$6.99

Other Genesis Press, Inc. Titles

A Dangerous Deception	J.M. Jeffries	$8.95
A Dangerous Love	J.M. Jeffries	$8.95
A Dangerous Obsession	J.M. Jeffries	$8.95
A Dangerous Woman	J.M. Jeffries	$9.95
A Dead Man Speaks	Lisa Jones Johnson	$12.95
A Drummer's Beat to Mend	Kei Swanson	$9.95
A Happy Life	Charlotte Harris	$9.95
A Heart's Awakening	Veronica Parker	$9.95
A Lark on the Wing	Phyliss Hamilton	$9.95
A Love of Her Own	Cheris F. Hodges	$9.95
A Love to Cherish	Beverly Clark	$8.95
A Lover's Legacy	Veronica Parker	$9.95
A Pefect Place to Pray	I.L. Goodwin	$12.95
A Risk of Rain	Dar Tomlinson	$8.95
A Twist of Fate	Beverly Clark	$8.95
A Will to Love	Angie Daniels	$9.95
Acquisitions	Kimberley White	$8.95
Across	Carol Payne	$12.95
After the Vows	Leslie Esdaile	$10.95
(Summer Anthology)	T.T. Henderson	
	Jacqueline Thomas	
Again My Love	Kayla Perrin	$10.95
Against the Wind	Gwynne Forster	$8.95
All I Ask	Barbara Keaton	$8.95
Ambrosia	T.T. Henderson	$8.95
An Unfinished Love Affair	Barbara Keaton	$8.95
And Then Came You	Dorothy Elizabeth Love	$8.95
Angel's Paradise	Janice Angelique	$9.95
At Last	Lisa G. Riley	$8.95
Best of Friends	Natalie Dunbar	$8.95
Between Tears	Pamela Ridley	$12.95
Beyond the Rapture	Beverly Clark	$9.95
Blaze	Barbara Keaton	$9.95

Other Genesis Press, Inc. Titles (continued)

Blood Lust	J. M. Jeffries	$9.95
Bodyguard	Andrea Jackson	$9.95
Boss of Me	Diana Nyad	$8.95
Bound by Love	Beverly Clark	$8.95
Breeze	Robin Hampton Allen	$10.95
Broken	Dar Tomlinson	$24.95
The Business of Love	Cheris Hodges	$9.95
By Design	Barbara Keaton	$8.95
Cajun Heat	Charlene Berry	$8.95
Careless Whispers	Rochelle Alers	$8.95
Cats & Other Tales	Marilyn Wagner	$8.95
Caught in a Trap	Andre Michelle	$8.95
Caught Up In the Rapture	Lisa G. Riley	$9.95
Cautious Heart	Cheris F Hodges	$8.95
Caught Up	Deatri King Bey	$12.95
Chances	Pamela Leigh Starr	$8.95
Cherish the Flame	Beverly Clark	$8.95
Class Reunion	Irma Jenkins/John Brown	$12.95
Code Name: Diva	J.M. Jeffries	$9.95
Conquering Dr. Wexler's Heart	Kimberley White	$9.95
Cricket's Serenade	Carolita Blythe	$12.95
Crossing Paths, Tempting Memories	Dorothy Elizabeth Love	$9.95
Cupid	Barbara Keaton	$9.95
Cypress Whisperings	Phyllis Hamilton	$8.95
Dark Embrace	Crystal Wilson Harris	$8.95
Dark Storm Rising	Chinelu Moore	$10.95
Daughter of the Wind	Joan Xian	$8.95
Deadly Sacrifice	Jack Kean	$22.95
Designer Passion	Dar Tomlinson	$8.95
Dreamtective	Liz Swados	$5.95
Ebony Butterfly II	Delilah Dawson	$14.95
Ebony Eyes	Kei Swanson	$9.95

CRUSH

Other Genesis Press, Inc. Titles (continued)

Echoes of Yesterday	Beverly Clark	$9.95
Eden's Garden	Elizabeth Rose	$8.95
Enchanted Desire	Wanda Y. Thomas	$9.95
Everlastin' Love	Gay G. Gunn	$8.95
Everlasting Moments	Dorothy Elizabeth Love	$8.95
Everything and More	Sinclair Lebeau	$8.95
Everything but Love	Natalie Dunbar	$8.95
Eve's Prescription	Edwina Martin Arnold	$8.95
Falling	Natalie Dunbar	$9.95
Fate	Pamela Leigh Starr	$8.95
Finding Isabella	A.J. Garrotto	$8.95
Forbidden Quest	Dar Tomlinson	$10.95
Forever Love	Wanda Thomas	$8.95
From the Ashes	Kathleen Suzanne	$8.95
	Jeanne Sumerix	
Gentle Yearning	Rochelle Alers	$10.95
Glory of Love	Sinclair LeBeau	$10.95
Go Gentle into that Good Night	Malcom Boyd	$12.95
Goldengroove	Mary Beth Craft	$16.95
Groove, Bang, and Jive	Steve Cannon	$8.99
Hand in Glove	Andrea Jackson	$9.95
Hard to Love	Kimberley White	$9.95
Hart & Soul	Angie Daniels	$8.95
Havana Sunrise	Kymberly Hunt	$9.95
Heartbeat	Stephanie Bedwell-Grime	$8.95
Hearts Remember	M. Loui Quezada	$8.95
Hidden Memories	Robin Allen	$10.95
Higher Ground	Leah Latimer	$19.95
Hitler, the War, and the Pope	Ronald Rychiak	$26.95
How to Write a Romance	Kathryn Falk	$18.95
I Married a Reclining Chair	Lisa M. Fuhs	$8.95
I'm Gonna Make You Love Me	Gwyneth Bolton	$9.95
Indigo After Dark Vol. I	Nia Dixon/Angelique	$10.95

Other Genesis Press, Inc. Titles (continued)

Title	Author	Price
Indigo After Dark Vol. II	Dolores Bundy/Cole Riley	$10.95
Indigo After Dark Vol. III	Montana Blue/Coco Morena	$10.95
Indigo After Dark Vol. IV	Cassandra Colt/ Diana Richeaux	$14.95
Indigo After Dark Vol. V	Delilah Dawson	$14.95
Icie	Pamela Leigh Starr	$8.95
I'll Be Your Shelter	Giselle Carmichael	$8.95
I'll Paint a Sun	A.J. Garrotto	$9.95
Illusions	Pamela Leigh Starr	$8.95
Indiscretions	Donna Hill	$8.95
Intentional Mistakes	Michele Sudler	$9.95
Interlude	Donna Hill	$8.95
Intimate Intentions	Angie Daniels	$8.95
Ironic	Pamela Leigh Starr	$9.95
Jolie's Surrender	Edwina Martin-Arnold	$8.95
Kiss or Keep	Debra Phillips	$8.95
Lace	Giselle Carmichael	$9.95
Last Train to Memphis	Elsa Cook	$12.95
Lasting Valor	Ken Olsen	$24.95
Let's Get It On	Dyanne Davis	$9.95
Let Us Prey	Hunter Lundy	$25.95
Life Is Never As It Seems	J.J. Michael	$12.95
Lighter Shade of Brown	Vicki Andrews	$8.95
Love Always	Mildred E. Riley	$10.95
Love Doesn't Come Easy	Charlyne Dickerson	$8.95
Love in High Gear	Charlotte Roy	$9.95
Love Lasts Forever	Dominiqua Douglas	$9.95
Love Me Carefully	A.C. Arthur	$9.95
Love Unveiled	Gloria Greene	$10.95
Love's Deception	Charlene Berry	$10.95
Love's Destiny	M. Loui Quezada	$8.95
Mae's Promise	Melody Walcott	$8.95
Magnolia Sunset	Giselle Carmichael	$8.95

CRUSH

Other Genesis Press, Inc. Titles (continued)

Matters of Life and Death	Lesego Malepe, Ph.D.	$15.95
Meant to Be	Jeanne Sumerix	$8.95
Midnight Clear (Anthology)	Leslie Esdaile	$10.95
	Gwynne Forster	
	Carmen Green	
	Monica Jackson	
Midnight Magic	Gwynne Forster	$8.95
Midnight Peril	Vicki Andrews	$10.95
Misconceptions	Pamela Leigh Starr	$9.95
Misty Blue	Dyanne Davis	$9.95
Montgomery's Children	Richard Perry	$14.95
My Buffalo Soldier	Barbara B. K. Reeves	$8.95
Naked Soul	Gwynne Forster	$8.95
Next to Last Chance	Louisa Dixon	$24.95
Nights Over Egypt	Barbara Keaton	$9.95
No Apologies	Seressia Glass	$8.95
No Commitment Required	Seressia Glass	$8.95
No Ordinary Love	Angela Weaver	$9.95
No Regrets	Mildred E. Riley	$8.95
Notes When Summer Ends	Beverly Lauderdale	$12.95
Nowhere to Run	Gay G. Gunn	$10.95
O Bed! O Breakfast!	Rob Kuehnle	$14.95
Object of His Desire	A. C. Arthur	$8.95
Office Policy	A. C. Arthur	$9.95
Once in a Blue Moon	Dorianne Cole	$9.95
One Day at a Time	Bella McFarland	$8.95
Only You	Crystal Hubbard	$9.95
Outside Chance	Louisa Dixon	$24.95
Passion	T.T. Henderson	$10.95
Passion's Blood	Cherif Fortin	$22.95
Passion's Journey	Wanda Thomas	$8.95
Past Promises	Jahmel West	$8.95
Path of Fire	T.T. Henderson	$8.95

Other Genesis Press, Inc. Titles (continued)

Path of Thorns	Annetta P. Lee	$9.95
Peace Be Still	Colette Haywood	$12.95
Picture Perfect	Reon Carter	$8.95
Playing for Keeps	Stephanie Salinas	$8.95
Pride & Joi	Gay G. Gunn	$8.95
Promises to Keep	Alicia Wiggins	$8.95
Quiet Storm	Donna Hill	$10.95
Reckless Surrender	Rochelle Alers	$6.95
Red Polka Dot in a World of Plaid	Varian Johnson	$12.95
Rehoboth Road	Anita Ballard-Jones	$12.95
Reluctant Captive	Joyce Jackson	$8.95
Rendezvous with Fate	Jeanne Sumerix	$8.95
Revelations	Cheris F. Hodges	$8.95
Rise of the Phoenix	Kenneth Whetstone	$12.95
Rivers of the Soul	Leslie Esdaile	$8.95
Rock Star	Rosyln Hardy Holcomb	$9.95
Rocky Mountain Romance	Kathleen Suzanne	$8.95
Rooms of the Heart	Donna Hill	$8.95
Rough on Rats and Tough on Cats	Chris Parker	$12.95
Scent of Rain	Annetta P. Lee	$9.95
Second Chances at Love	Cheris Hodges	$9.95
Secret Library Vol. 1	Nina Sheridan	$18.95
Secret Library Vol. 2	Cassandra Colt	$8.95
Shades of Brown	Denise Becker	$8.95
Shades of Desire	Monica White	$8.95
Shadows in the Moonlight	Jeanne Sumerix	$8.95
Sin	Crystal Rhodes	$8.95
Sin and Surrender	J.M. Jeffries	$9.95
Sinful Intentions	Crystal Rhodes	$12.95
So Amazing	Sinclair LeBeau	$8.95
Somebody's Someone	Sinclair LeBeau	$8.95

Other Genesis Press, Inc. Titles (continued)

Someone to Love	Alicia Wiggins	$8.95
Song in the Park	Martin Brant	$15.95
Soul Eyes	Wayne L. Wilson	$12.95
Soul to Soul	Donna Hill	$8.95
Southern Comfort	J.M. Jeffries	$8.95
Still the Storm	Sharon Robinson	$8.95
Still Waters Run Deep	Leslie Esdaile	$8.95
Stories to Excite You	Anna Forrest/Divine	$14.95
Subtle Secrets	Wanda Y. Thomas	$8.95
Suddenly You	Crystal Hubbard	$9.95
Sweet Repercussions	Kimberley White	$9.95
Sweet Tomorrows	Kimberly White	$8.95
Taken by You	Dorothy Elizabeth Love	$9.95
Tattooed Tears	T. T. Henderson	$8.95
The Color Line	Lizzette Grayson Carter	$9.95
The Color of Trouble	Dyanne Davis	$8.95
The Disappearance of Allison Jones	Kayla Perrin	$5.95
The Honey Dipper's Legacy	Pannell-Allen	$14.95
The Joker's Love Tune	Sidney Rickman	$15.95
The Little Pretender	Barbara Cartland	$10.95
The Love We Had	Natalie Dunbar	$8.95
The Man Who Could Fly	Bob & Milana Beamon	$18.95
The Missing Link	Charlyne Dickerson	$8.95
The Price of Love	Sinclair LeBeau	$8.95
The Smoking Life	Ilene Barth	$29.95
The Words of the Pitcher	Kei Swanson	$8.95
Three Wishes	Seressia Glass	$8.95
Through the Fire	Seressia Glass	$9.95
Ties That Bind	Kathleen Suzanne	$8.95
Tiger Woods	Libby Hughes	$5.95
Time is of the Essence	Angie Daniels	$9.95
Timeless Devotion	Bella McFarland	$9.95
Tomorrow's Promise	Leslie Esdaile	$8.95

Other Genesis Press, Inc. Titles (continued)

Truly Inseparable	Wanda Y. Thomas	$8.95
Unbreak My Heart	Dar Tomlinson	$8.95
Uncommon Prayer	Kenneth Swanson	$9.95
Unconditional	A.C. Arthur	$9.95
Unconditional Love	Alicia Wiggins	$8.95
Under the Cherry Moon	Christal Jordan-Mims	$12.95
Unearthing Passions	Elaine Sims	$9.95
Until Death Do Us Part	Susan Paul	$8.95
Vows of Passion	Bella McFarland	$9.95
Wedding Gown	Dyanne Davis	$8.95
What's Under Benjamin's Bed	Sandra Schaffer	$8.95
When Dreams Float	Dorothy Elizabeth Love	$8.95
Whispers in the Night	Dorothy Elizabeth Love	$8.95
Whispers in the Sand	LaFlorya Gauthier	$10.95
Wild Ravens	Altonya Washington	$9.95
Yesterday Is Gone	Beverly Clark	$10.95
Yesterday's Dreams, Tomorrow's Promises	Reon Laudat	$8.95
Your Precious Love	Sinclair LeBeau	$8.95

Order Form

Mail to: Genesis Press, Inc.
P.O. Box 101
Columbus, MS 39703

Name _____

Address _____

City/State _____ Zip _____

Telephone _____

Ship to (if different from above)

Name _____

Address _____

City/State _____ Zip _____

Telephone _____

Credit Card Information

Credit Card # _____ ☐ Visa   ☐ Mastercard

Expiration Date (mm/yy) _____ ☐ AmEx   ☐ Discover

Qty.	Author	Title	Price	Total

Use this order

form, or call

1-888-INDIGO-1

Total for books _____

Shipping and handling:
  $5 first two books,
  $1 each additional book _____

Total S & H _____

Total amount enclosed _____

Mississippi residents add 7% sales tax